THE ROCK

Gibraltar: a place, a fortress, an idea, a byword. In this novel, John Masters has sought not only to re-create what it was like to live on The Rock at different periods throughout its turbulent past, but to provide the essential core of its history: why it has always been fought over, coveted, threatened by invaders.

Also by John Masters
THE BREAKING STRAIN
FOURTEEN EIGHTEEN
and published by Corgi Books

John Masters

The Rock

An epic

CORGI BOOKS
TRANSWORLD PUBLISHERS LTD
A National General Company

THE ROCK

A CORGI BOOK 0 552 08832 3

Originally published in Great Britain
by Michael Joseph Ltd.

PRINTING HISTORY

Michael Joseph edition published 1970
Corgi edition published 1971

This book is set in 11/12pt Intertype Baskerville

Corgi Books are published by Transworld Publishers Ltd.,
Cavendish House,
57–59 Uxbridge Road,
Ealing, London W.5.

Made and printed in Great Britain by
Cox & Wyman Ltd., London, Reading and Fakenham

For Barbara

CONTENTS

FOREWORD

Coming in low from due east, looking through the curved perspex, it appears first as a pale cloud on the surface of the sea off the mountains of Africa. The first become more sharply defined, and the whiteness intensifies as the morning sun strikes back from it. Darker areas, but still quite pale, take form to left and right of the central white, and the sky beyond silhouettes the shape of the crest. It is a great wall of rock, over two miles long, fourteen hundred feet high at right and centre. It falls sharply to the left – south – and seems to be a gigantic crouching animal, its head towards Africa, its paws extended. Northward the resemblance ends, for there are no hind quarters or tail: the rock ends sheer.

There is a huge straight-sided patch in the middle of the eastern slope, as pale in itself as the grey of the cliffs, but appearing brighter from its smoothness, which more strongly casts back the sun's light. It is man made, the huge patch, perhaps half a mile long and seven hundred feet high; but who knows what it is? There is nothing else like it on earth.

Closer now: parts of the wall are thinly painted in green – a few broad daubs run down gullies, a fine stippling marks ledges, crevices, gentler slopes where soil can stay and plants take hold. Along the shore line the dark mouths of caverns appear, some small, most large.

The outer arch often shelters a lesser inner arch, and that a lesser again, thus gradually bringing the eye from the colossal to the human scale, in the manner used by the architect of the Buland Darwaza at Fatehpur Sikri.

The upthrust rock is sliding past on the right, and the works of man command the eye. The crest bristles like a threatened porcupine. Guns, masts, directors, radar towers, range finders, antennae, guns ... guns ... guns ... scattered large buildings towards the low point of the rock – not houses, but barracks or hospitals, or prisons perhaps ... on the very point, a white and red lighthouse. Turning north, the barracks give way to houses; the houses close in on each other; trees, gardens, streets cling in parallel rows to this western slope. It is more gentle than the almost sheer eastern wall, but still very steep for a town. Directly below us now a big harbour opens up – long sea walls, grey warships alongside, dry docks: more sea – moles – yachts, oil tankers, cargo ships: the houses condense suddenly, the suburbs become a narrow, huddled town. Momentarily, a foursquare medieval castle appears on a bluff above the town. Below it, half hidden, half ruined, there are the regular zigzags of fortifications, more walls, embrasures for cannons.

The landing pad drifts up to the wheels. On the right the sheer cliff which we had once seen as the back of the crouching lion, begins to take on a familiar shape. Everyone knows it, for everyone has seen it in advertisements, and by now it is not only a place, but a byword. The name evokes a geographical location, a habitation, a fortress, yes – but, equally, an idea, an attitude, an attribute.

It is the Rock: Gibraltar.

Everyone knows it, but only in part, because, although it is small in area, it is big in story. No place in the world has witnessed, and played a part, in so much history. It is not only a history of battles and sieges, of that defiance and resistance for which the name has come to stand, but of mankind's climb from the caves – these very caves – to the technological heights exemplified in the artifacts arrayed along this very crest. It is a story of man exploring the world and himself, of building civilizations and casting them down, of the long, eventful journey to the miracles and malaises of today. The Rock has seen it all.

It is a story of immense length and complexity. One of the first problems I faced when I decided to tell it was the lack of human continuity, for the Rock was uninhabited until medieval times, and since then there have been four complete turnovers of the population. I found, though, that except for a single break, very short in our time scale, one people have always been represented here: the Jews. This is not the story of Gibraltar as seen through Jewish eyes, still less a history of the Jews of Gibraltar; but, as in real life, Jewish characters – and the Jewish character, so aptly similar to the attributes of the Rock – have linked what otherwise had no human link.

My second main problem was whether to deal in fact, that is, in what happened: or in emotion, that is, in what it felt like to have it happen. The first is history, the second must be fiction. There was also the matter of pace. The sum total of knowledge about, say, the Barbarian invasion of Baetica in the fifth century can be written on the head of a pin with a blunt nib; yet, the men and women of those times were as real, as human, as others; they did not suffer less, love less, lead less interesting lives because no long volumes survive to describe all their acts and accidents. I wanted to be able to go at my pace, not a pace dictated by the amount, large or small, of available fact. Yet, of course, I needed facts, or I would be building on sand.

After many experiments I wrote the book in two streams, one factual, one fictional; or, if you wish, I decided to cover the ground in two vehicles – one fast, and one slow. Each Book (there are thirteen) covers a period in the actual history of Gibraltar. Each starts with a factual section which describes only the broad shape of events and notes only the principal characters. Some of these sections cover five hundred years in five pages. Then we reach a point where I feel that we should stop the car, get out, step down, and go on foot among the people, seeing, smelling, touching, hearing. At this point the factual narrative stops and a fictional tale, separately titled, follows. At the end of each tale follows the title page of the next Book, and the rapid historical survey continues from where we left off.

The factual sections are as accurate as I can make them, but you should be warned (1) that about some of the early history there are as many 'facts' as there are historians, and (2) that given a choice of interpretations I will usually choose that which seems most interesting. The background of the fictional tales is also as correct as research and common sense can make it, and the principal event which forms the background of each is always historical, as are some of the characters; nevertheless these tales and the people in them should be treated as wholly imaginary.

My third problem was orientation: how to let the reader know where he is as he moves about the Rock, and giving him the means to know, if he wants to, the geographical relationship of Gibraltar to other places that must be named: in other words, how to frame Gibraltar in space as well as time. It was not easy, because most places have had more than one name, and because events closely affecting Gibraltar had their origins in places as far away as Rumania, Mecca, and Lexington,

Massachusetts. The best solution, though not perfect, seemed to be to put at the beginning of each Book, a sketch map showing the places off the Rock which are mentioned in that Book and its following 'tale'.

So now let us go back, this time not in a helicopter, not to east or west or north or south – but back ... to behind us, to the beginning.

Book One

IN THE BEGINNING

To 33,500 years before the present

FOUR thousand million years or more ago, as the molten ball of this Earth whirled through space, it began to cool. Its surface solidified into a crystalline crust. The rocks forming the crust are called igneous because of their fiery origin. They are all very old and very hard. As atmosphere formed new forces began to act upon the rocky surface. Ice, wind, frost, lightning, rain – storms of unimaginable fury lasting for thousands of years on end – relentlessly broke up and wore away the igneous rock, grinding much of it into sand and silt, and sweeping this debris down to the plains, and to the sea.

The coming of vegetation, and of the first forms of life, increased the amount of water that was deposited. In deeper seas the sediment was mostly the calcareous skeletons of marine life; closer to the land masses, where much of the sediment was brought down by the rivers, it was mostly pebbles, grit, and mud.

In the course of hundreds of millions of years these deposits, cemented together by chemical action and compressed by their own sheer weight, formed a different kind of rock: sedimentary rock. In the Gibraltar area the sedimentary rock being formed, far below the sea, was limestone. It continued to be laid down during the Jurassic period (180 million years ago), and was then covered by a thinner layer of shale and grit.

As the Earth continued to cool, it shrank. The crust had to adjust to the new smaller size, and did so by folding. The folds did not take place evenly, but where the crust was thin, weak, or unusually depressed. The Western

Mediterranean is such an area. It is bounded by a huge circle of solid igneous rock masses – the Spanish tableland, the Massif Central of France, and the main mass of Africa. When the pressure forced the Earth's crust at the Mediterranean geosyncline to fold here, it folded inside this resistant shield, thrusting up an inner chain of steep, high mountains, quite different from the rounded masses behind. The new mountains were the Atlas, the Apennines, the Alps, the Pyrenees, and the Sierra Nevada in southern Spain. Gibraltar is at a bend in this great fold.

Looking roughly from south to north the Rock took its shape in three stages (see page 18).

The process of settling and adjusting took a long time. During these aeons the earth sank and rose and the seas advanced and retreated several times, to immense heights and depths. About twelve million years ago other passages between the Atlantic and the Mediterranean closed, and the land sank along the present line, forming the Straits of Gibraltar.

The Rock guarded the north side of the new channel, looking very much as it does now – its steep white faces, of pure limestone, towards the north and east, its sloping and duller aspects, of shale, towards the south and west. It was two and three-quarter miles long by three-quarters of a mile wide at the widest place, and was joined to the mainland on the north by a sandy isthmus about a mile long and gradually increasing from half to a full mile width where the mainland proper begins. The west side of the isthmus curves gently round in a full semi-circle of diameter four miles. Two rivers flow into this bay from the land behind, which quickly rises and fades to distant mountains. On the east side of the isthmus the shore line continues almost due north, curving only very gradually

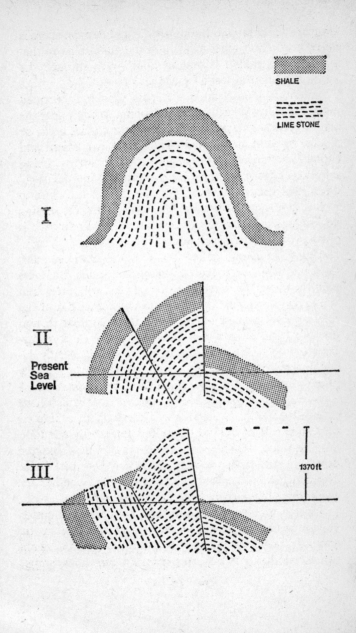

SHALE

LIME STONE

I

II
Present
Sea
Level

III
1370 ft

towards the north-east. South, the jagged African shore is eleven and a half miles away, and the mountains on that side are higher than Gibraltar. South-west, through the Strait, the Atlantic ocean forms the horizon.

Limestone is a clean, hard, pale grey rock, formed mainly of calcium carbonate. It dissolves slowly under the action of water, especially if the water carries acids or alkalis. As soon as the mass of the Rock was raised and exposed, water began to eat into it. Rain water, falling into cracks, enlarged them into clefts, then into 'vertical' caves. Sea water tunnelled into the foot of the cliffs to make 'horizontal' caves at all levels, for during the settling period there were many sea levels (one sea-made cave is 700 feet above the present shore).

The sheer energy of the years created tunnels, halls, passages, rooms, cells, and amphitheatres inside the Rock. And the chemical action of the water not only excavated the caves, it decorated them. As water comes out of the interior of the rock, where it has been under pressure, and enters a cave, it must give up some of the calcium carbonate with which it has been supercharged. A tiny deposit of sinter-limestone is made and, according to the other substances through which the water has flowed – e.g. iron, carbon, shell layers – or the acids which have been added to it, the deposit will have colour, a limitless variety of colours, though all muted in intensity and tone. Limitless, too, are the other forces which will shape and sculpture the accumulating deposits: how the wind blows, whether the roof is flat or sloping, whether the water drips regularly or irregularly, fast or slow . . .

Doubly limitless, then, are these formations of sinter-limestone in the caves – stalagmites rising from the ground, stalactites hanging from the roof, pillars, knobs, warts, candles, palettes, tree trunks, water lilies, straws, frills, flounces, curtains, tracery, leaves, cathedral arches and hammer beams, people, animals ... in white, tan, rust-red, blue, grey. Three of the most extraordinary forms are: helectites (crazy worm casts shaped by wind action, that seem to defy all laws of gravity and reason); cave pearls, or pitholite (formed when the steady dripping of the water keeps rolling the sinter deposit round as it forms); and rimstone (thin ledges round the rim of pools and lakes, or even right over them).

The floor of the caves, if it is not 'live' sinter – that is, still being formed – is an extraordinary dark brown powder, like snuff, of the consistency of fine flour. This is the deposit of millions of years of vegetable mould and, in some cases, of bat guano. It is often many feet thick.

About three quarters of a million years ago the Ice Ages began to modify the Rock into its present exact form. We do not need to know what caused them, or whether they have indeed ended, which is fortunate, as Science has not made up its collective mind on either point. The important facts are that each ice age lasted at least 40,000 years, and that the warmer gaps between them, the interglacial periods, were generally longer, e.g. that between the Mindel and the Riss was about 200,000 years.

In each ice age the north polar icecap spread much farther south than it does now. During one it covered England solid, France was uninhabitable, and Gibraltar very cold. Because so much water was locked up in the ice the sea level fell: at Gibraltar it was some 300 feet below its present level.

During the interglacials the climate was much warmer than it is now. England became tropical and Gibraltar equatorial; the sea level rose up to 300 feet above the present; and the loss of the weight of the ice actually caused those areas that had been under it to rise, while bordering areas, such as Spain, sank in compensation, raising the sea level there still higher.

At each of these levels – and every ice age and every interglacial had different ones – the sea made beaches, sea cliffs and sea caves. Some are now submerged, others are stranded far above the shore, but quite recognizable for what they were.

The ice ages also continued the work of previous aeons in sculpting the Rock. Ice and frost action broke off pieces of sharp-angled limestone, which rolled to the foot of the slope, and were cemented together by the action of the charged water to form the limestone breccia which covers most of the lower part of the Rock. Mixed into it, and also sometimes in considerable depth in and above the shale deposits, is bone breccia, presumably from the victims of carnivorous animals.

Finally, there is sand. A large part of the eastern face of the Rock is covered by a gigantic and very steep slope of aeolian (wind-blown) sand. This sand – some of it cemented by the usual action – was formed in the ice ages, when for thousands of years, without cease, a strong east wind blew sand from the exposed floor of the Mediterranean on to the Rock.

When the last ice age ended the east wind created another special feature of Gibraltar's climate, the *levanter* cloud. Coming across hundreds of miles of Mediterranean, it is always charged with water. When it meets the steep east face it has to rise fourteen hundred feet very rapidly. It cools, and some of its water condenses out to form vaporous cloud, which often hangs oppressively over the top of the Rock, streaming also out to the west, while the sky over mainland, bay, and strait is quite clear. For the rest, the climate is equable, temperately warm, and – except with a *levanter* – pleasant. The rainfall, concentrated mainly between September and March, is adequate.

When the land took its present shape, Gibraltar stood at the gate of the only channel linking the Mediterranean with the Atlantic. The surface current formed: strongly eastward in the centre of the Strait, less so at the sides. For thousands of years no one knew how the Atlantic water pouring into the Mediterranean returned. Then last century British naval surveys found an equally strong underwater current, perpetually westbound, which carried huge amounts of water over the sill of the Strait into the Atlantic. The configuration of the ocean bed causes much of this great river to come to the surface off Cape Trafalgar, increasing the already great danger of that Cape for small vessels, especially in the days of primitive navigation by sail and oar. (These discoveries solved some legendary sea mysteries, notably that of a ship sunk in collision off Tarifa about 1805. She sank in a riproaring eastbound current – and came to the surface the next day off Trafalgar, thirty miles to the west.)

The fish that inhabited these waters were, first, the tunny. The ancients believed that tunny perpetually circled the Mediterranean in an anti-clockwise direction since they had only one good eye, the right. Modern pollution, increase in fishing, and the noise of ships' engines have driven tunny away from the immediate neighbourhood of the Strait. Besides tunny there are or were whale, swordfish, squid, eel, bonito, sardine, sea bream, sea bass, red mullet, perch, pollack and gilthead.

As the land took shape, the vegetation settled on and in it. The Rock is too steep, and the surface soil too shallow or scattered over the limestone, for the vegetation ever to have been lush; but nor was it ever wholly barren. Now, its climate median between the extremes it has known, the pale limestone is overlaid with a thin-woven carpet of scrub, mainly aromatic – heather, rosemary, sage, sodom apple, thyme, lavender, pennyroyal. In the scrub stand steeply tilted thickets, woods, or isolated trees – cork oak, carob bean, holly-oak, wild olive, wild fig.

The flowers do not lie in great banks like cowslips in an English meadow, for there is no rich loam to make the bed for them. Instead they line the edges of runnels, shelter in small crevices, or hang on to tiny patches of earth, exposed to the wind, high on the cliffs. Every month of the year some flowers or other are cautiously displaying their blossoms – clematis, narcissus, mesembreanthemum, stonecrop, ragwort, oxalis, bindweed, mignonette, borage, asphodel, marigold, autumn crocus, periwinkle, bee orchid, snapdragon, rue, mallow, gladiolus, giant-leaved acanthus. In March three score varieties flower, stippling the whole Rock with colour – white and yellow chrysanthemum, jasmine, coronilla, broom, sea aster, giant fennel, freesia, and campion; blue of iris, bugloss, pimpernel, scilla, wild pea; rose and pink of mallow, cistus, snapdragon and a flower that, in Europe, exists only here – the flat white and mauve, many-petalled faces of Gibraltar candytuft.

The birds came, and are as various as the flowers, but in the main not as noticeable – warblers, finches, tits, wrens, orioles; choughs, jays, ravens, kestrels, buzzards, vultures; ospreys, gannets, puffins; and, as with the candytuft, one bird that in Europe is unique to Gibraltar – the Barbary partridge. It is about twelve inches long, so a little smaller than the red-legged partridge. It is studded with small white spots, has a chestnut collar and a metallic blue tinge in the wing coverts, and its legs are red or pale buff. It is a noisy, unsuspecting bird, much hunted by cats, eagles, lizards and snakes.

23

After the vegetation, and the birds, the animals.... They came early and lived through the fluctuations and upheavals of the Rock's formation. Bone breccia of animals was being deposited in some of the rock fissures before the great submergences of more than 30 million years ago. By such traces as this breccia, and the bones under the present cave floors, we know that the wolf came, and the fox, seal, ibex and chamois; all the animals that have since been domesticated – horse, pig, cattle (including the aurochs); rabbit, rat, water rat – and two kinds of rhinoceros; tortoise, bat, gecko and leopard. Most of these lived on the Rock for as long as the species existed in Europe, though there can never have been large herds here, and the bigger, more noticeable animals soon vanished at the arrival of the last comer – Man.

The remotest origins of man do not concern us here, except to note that during the earth's upheaval, land bridges often existed, for millions of years, between Europe and Africa, and probably also between other continents now separated. Over these bridges the various ancestors of modern man passed in both directions, so that 'African' types came to Europe and 'European' types to Africa. One land bridge was certainly at Gibraltar, for the Atlantic-Mediterranean sea passage was at one period farther north, and at another farther south.

At some time more – perhaps much more – than 50,000 years ago, a type of man flourished in Europe, including the Rock, who represented the biggest advance in evolution thus far. He was big and burly, and stood upright, with his heavy head thrust a little forward. His face had a marked frontal bone, eyes deep sunk under it, and wide flat nose, but he was definitely a human, not an ape. He had eveloped only the simplest tools, and lived by hunting deer, ibex, rabbits, and water birds, and by gathering shellfish, nuts, and fruit. He may also, from need or for ritual reasons, have been a cannibal, but probably seldom inside his own family group.

As he had no pots, he could neither store food nor cook it, except by grilling over an open flame. The climate was colder than ours during most of his stay, but not greatly so. With the sea bed lower all round the Rock, those who lived there had a wider terrain in which to hunt, and the sea shore was more easy to get at, for shells and fishing in the rock pools. Two or three hundred feet above the sea, and about a mile back from it, there were many high-arched, deep caves at the foot of the huge cliffs. The cliffs gave good protection, and in these caves the people lived. In the same cave, or a neighbouring one, they buried their dead with ceremonies and artifacts, proving that they had some non-instinctive beliefs about the nature of death, and hence of life.

Not long afterwards another type of man appeared. He may have been a parallel development of the first, or he may have been quite separate. He was not so powerful, but taller, and he had a larger brain. He was more agile, both mentally and physically.

The temperate interlude began to end. The ice again crept southward across Europe. Every living thing which could move fled in front of it, trying to adapt to new conditions as they went, for the 'flight' was spread over thousands of years.

The old man and this new man found themselves in competition for the available game, shelter, and food. The conflict was long-drawn and wide-spread, and took many forms. Here it went one way, there another. In some places, perhaps common sense won and the two types united and interbred. In others it was not the human enemy but the changing circumstances that conquered.

No one knew the details, only the result: by about 33,500 years ago, the old men had gone – vanished – become extinct.

One of their last stands must have been at Gibraltar, for the strait, perhaps six miles wide then, barred all further southward flight. It was the Rock's first human war, its first siege, its first fall. No one knows what exactly happened, but we can imagine . . .

THE WOMAN

THE Woman moved along the shore in a group of women and children, her baby in the crook of her arm. A snow flurry momentarily whitened the reddish hair hanging to her waist, and speckled her naked body with large white splashes. She did not notice, but went on turning over rocks, feeling under ledges and in crevices. When she found a shell, she cracked it carefully between two stones, poured the juice down her throat, and tore out the flesh with her teeth and strong nails. When she threw a shell down, the children pounced on it, snarling and snatching, until the winner ran a little way up the sandy slope to eat by himself.

The Woman hitched her baby round and pushed her nipple into its sucking mouth. Her body ached from hunger and her throat hurt. Straightening her back she glanced up the slope to the cave at the foot of the cliffs. She saw movement there, recognized the Old Woman, and growled 'It is well.' The baby spat out her nipple and began to cry.

As the sun, in front of them, sank towards the crest of the Rock, they turned away from the water. The wind blew colder, driving sand stung her eyes, and the baby howled more loudly.

A half-formed girl, trudging in the lead, stopped suddenly with a low word – 'Deer'. The tracks were clear in the sand coming from the sun, moving diagonally across the slope and disappearing into the scrub on the flat land north of the Rock. The Woman saw from the size and spacing of the slots that it was a stag. It was the rutting season and she could also detect the male rankness clinging to the sand.

They all stared a long time in the direction the deer had gone, then continued up the slope and on to a shoulder of the Rock, above the last low cliffs. Here the Woman just caught sight of a big bird's wing, flapping close to the ground on her right. A vulture. Vultures meant food . . . a sharp pain twisted her belly. She stopped, as though to pluck some of the weeds growing between the stones. A pair of children paused by her, and groped where she groped, pulling up the weeds, sniffing them, looking at her. One said 'Nothing', and they ran on. The Woman slunk away alone towards the three trees where she had seen the vulture. None of the others noticed for a time, then the Big Woman cried 'What?', and the Woman with the baby broke into a run, the baby pounding on her hip. Three vultures took off heavily from under the trees, two remained on the prey. The woman picked up a stone and hurled it as she ran. The last vultures rose, hissing, and she fell on the dead lynx, grabbed the red hole the vultures' beaks had opened into the stomach, tore out a piece of flesh, and crammed it into her mouth. She had her hand on another when the rest arrived. The other women grabbed and snarled, and the children reached between and under them.

When they had torn out what they could, the Big Woman took the bloody carcass and slung it round her neck. They went on down to the lake in the gully. The Woman with the baby felt good, and her belly had stopped aching. In the gully there were trees, and another cave. No one lived in it, but there was a trickle of water, and shelter from the wind. The Woman knelt, cupped her hands in the lake, drank, and then held water for her baby, but it would not drink. The low sun shone full on her, and she pushed back her hair to let the warmth touch her body. Yawning, she reached slowly out towards one of the little green cucumbers that grew among the rocks. The children leaned close, expectant. As her fingers touched the outermost of the cucumber's thousand tiny hairs, it sprang free from its stalk with a sudden pop, and jumped into the air, squirting her finger and face with liquid white seed. The Woman laughed, the children laughed. A small boy ran round screeching with laughter, found another cucumber, and reached cautiously out to touch it. But it was not ripe and did not explode.

The Woman reached over a rock where rain water lay in a flat shallow pool. She saw her face there, and moved her head, and the face moved. She touched the water with her finger and the face broke up, crushed, but slowly came back again. It was her, and it was not her. She scratched herself, and soon they all started back for their own cave, looking for nuts as they went.

It was good also in the cave, the low fire red and hot. The Old Woman had scraped the last of the rotting flesh off the ibex skin the men had killed many days ago. Bent Brother was striking a flint with a stone. Big Woman began to skin the lynx with a sharp flint burin. Soon she had worked one thigh bone free, and thrust it into the fire. Now Small Woman came to the Woman and they squatted face to face near the cave mouth, searching for fleas and lice in each other's hair. When they found one they squashed it between their nails, and licked off the remnants.

Later the Old Woman in the cave mouth muttered – 'The men. They have nothing.'

The Father came in first, the two young men behind. Their hands were empty and clean and they had nothing on their backs. The Father threw down his spear and seized a lynx bone from Big Woman. She growled and for a moment held to it, and he jerked it free and sent her flying across the sand with a blow of his arm. He cracked the bone, sucked out the marrow, then threw it down. One of the young men picked it up.

It was almost dark, and the Old Woman lay down in the mouth of the cave. She wore a long tooth on a thong round her neck. The tooth came from a great magic animal killed long ago and far away, and it belonged to them all, but the oldest woman wore it. Big Woman came back to the fire and warmed her feet. She told the Father of the deer tracks they had seen. The Father grunted, and told how the men had seen a female bear and wounded it, but before they could kill it Others had come and frightened it away.

A shiver crept across the Woman's skin at the mention of Others. She had never seen one but she knew they were not animals, yet they were not US. They were Other. Her baby was sucking, half asleep, at her nipple. She put her arm round it and a low purring growl throbbed in her chest.

One of the young men held his spear point in the fire,

and began to sharpen it with a flint blade. The Father's spear point was a sharp flint, tied on with sinew, and he took Bent Brother's round stone, and struck the flint to make a better edge to the point. Snow flurries whirled past the cave mouth, and a cold wind blew sparks from the fire. The Woman went towards a far corner, past the pile of chips where Bent Brother worked. He was there, squatting, and grabbed her, and put his hand between her legs. She knelt, waiting. He felt her, and licked his fingers, and in a moment mounted her and thrust into her. Her loins throbbed, her knees weakened. She moaned aloud, and jerked so that her baby rolled free in the sand under her breasts. When Bent Brother had ended he pushed her over so that she lay on her side, and he behind her, huddled together. She took her baby to her breast again. Big Woman curled up with the Father. The children huddled together in groups, and the two young men with Small Woman. The Old Woman crept in from the cave mouth, snow on her shrivelled breasts, and put more wood on the fire.

In the first dawn the Woman awoke, stretched, and went out on to fresh snow. The young men were at the place, and as she squatted beside them she watched them pick up snow, and one suddenly threw it at the other, then they both laughed and threw snow at each other. When the sun rose out of the sea, far away, the Father went to the cave mouth, stretched and scratched, and said 'Come'. They all went with him except the Old Woman, who kept the fire. The Father led down the slope to the beach. The sky was a pale blue and the wind had sunk, but the snow and the wind of the night had destroyed the marks of the stag, nor could the Woman smell any trace of it.

They all worked north along the beach. At a big pool

they surrounded it, then all ran in together, and caught six little fishes, which the men ate. Later the Woman found a few limpets and ate them quickly. Later, after the sun had passed its height, one of the young men in front crouched, his spear raised. Everyone stopped. The Woman put her hand over her baby's mouth, listening, but heard only the splash of the waves. The men ran forward and crouched behind a point of rocks.

Three upright animals came round the corner of rock, and Big Woman muttered. 'Others!' There were two males, and a female cub. They were all tall and stood upright. The bigger male carried a spear and the other a heavy flint set sideways on a short stick.

The Other cub, picking up an empty shell, saw them first. It screamed, and at once Father, Bent Brother, and the two young men rushed out at them. The Others turned and ran, but Bent Brother threw a big stone which hit the cub on the head, so that she fell. The young men leaped on to her and she snarled and bit one's hand but the other pushed his spear point into her throat, then quickly held her up and drank the blood while it was still running.

The Woman looked along the beach at the male Others. They ran fast, none could catch them. The children were pulling the Other cub about, turning her over, and sniffing at her. The Woman saw that she looked like a woman of their own, but she was not, she was Other — thin, the teeth far back in her mouth, and smelling dangerous. The Father threw her over his shoulder and started back towards the cave, shouting 'Food, food, food!' and everyone shouted regularly with him.

In the cave Bent Brother hacked with the flint edge, and the men broke her bones and twisted them apart. Some ate her flesh raw and some put chunks on to the red

31

hot wood, and the little children pulled out the entrails, and searched in the carcass for pieces the rest had overlooked. The Woman sank her teeth into a roasted piece of flesh. The juice ran down her chin and her baby sucked contentedly at her nipple.

The Man and his young companion, Feetborn's son, saw their fire from a long way off through the trees, and moved a little faster, for the wind blew colder as the sun sank, and the winter time was coming. The woman Feetborn was tending the fire, and the Man went directly to her and said, 'We met Others by the sea. They killed Red Girl.'

Feetborn was Red Girl's mother, too, and she raised her face to the sky and began to howl. Tears ran down her cheek. When the Man stroked her arm, she turned and hid her head in his shoulder. He touched her back and stroked her long hair and then left her. Feetborn's Son was telling the other women, Cryer and Snowborn, and the children, about their meeting with the Others. He told how the Others had been lying in wait behind rocks on the shore, how they rushed out screaming: many, many Others, one with a twisted hip. He imitated the way the Others stood, his head sunk into his shoulders and stuck forward, his mouth pushed forward and all his teeth showing and sticking out forward, and his hand over his eyes where the Others had a big bone and the eyes deep sunk under it. Then he walked like the Others did, shambling, his knees always a little bent. The women and children listened eagerly, with low cries. They were all huddled together round the fire, against the cold. Snowborn had sharpened a small deer bone and was putting it into her hair and twisting her hair round it, her arms raised above her head and her breasts raised and rounded.

The Man's loins thickened as he looked at her. But Cryer's baby was very silent and blue in her arms. And he kept thinking of the Others. When he first saw one, years ago, he had called 'Friend', mistaking it for a man. For a moment he thought it had understood, but then it snarled and ran way. So they were not men. But they were not animals.

He shook his head, unsure, and growled at the children to get more wood for the fire. Lefthand, the tall young man whose mother was dead two snows past, sat beside him. They talked about the bear the Others had frightened away the day before, but decided not to hunt her again. Lefthand told the Man about a stag that had passed, and they decided to hunt that, the next day.

The children came back with wood, and set it by the fire. Feetborn laid a long bough on a long bough and the flames blew higher. Even close to the fire it was cold, though, and sleet began to fall, slanting down so that for a time the Man could not see the trees across the river. Cryer began to whimper over her baby.

Snowborn came to the Man and sat by him. Gently she bit his ear. He held her breasts and she lay back, singing, and pulled him down into her arms.

When he rolled away he saw Lefthand by the fire, curled up in a ball, no one by him. The Man lay down in the thin shelter of a tree, women and children around him, and slept.

In the first light he went carefully to the running water, watched the forest on the other side, felt the wind – it was less now, but touched with cold rain – drank, and rubbed water on his face and body. Cryer was moaning quietly, her head bent. Feetborn and Lefthand were by her but she cried, 'No. No. No.' The Man went close and thought that Cryer's baby was dead. He touched it and found it

33

was cold and stiff. Cryer bent her head and took his wrist in her teeth, but gently. He stroked her shoulder with the other hand, kneeling beside her, and slowly she opened her mouth and let go of his wrist. He took the baby from her and Cryer let it go. Red Boy took its foot and pulled, as though to play, but the baby did not move and the little leg stuck out stiff.

The Man looked down at the baby in his arm. He felt again the hurt in his chest and behind his eyes that was common, but strange, for it hurt you but you could not hurt it. He set the baby down, straightened its legs and arms, and told them they would put it away the next day. Then he picked up his spear, looked well at the point and the fastening of it, and started out, Lefthand and Feet-born's Son at his heels.

They went through the forest towards the Rock, keeping the running water on their right, until they came to the place where the water was shallow, and animals crossed. There they looked at the marks in the mud, and saw that the stag had crossed the day before. They waded through, shook themselves on the far side, and cast round until they again found the trail of the stag. The Man could not smell most animals, but male ibex and some cats that sprayed the leaves he could smell for hours after they had passed; and the stag in the time of rut, for days.

They loped along all the morning and all the middle of the day, the tracks becoming clearer in the damp ground and half-melted snow. The stag was moving north, and when the sun was high they came out of the forest on to a bare hill, where the snow lay white on the ground. From here they saw the Rock small in the distance. They found the stags' droppings and a yellow stain in the snow. Now the tracks led west along the ridge, but after an hour swung left again, down the hill and back into the forest.

34

All afternoon the three ran with the sun in their right eyes, and every time they came to a break in the trees the Rock was closer. The rank scent grew stronger, and the marks of the stag's passing more recent. They came to mud where the water was still running back into the new-made slots. The Man paused, and turned his head this way and that. The wind was from behind, so the stag would smell them coming. They must get ahead of him.

Lefthand said that the stag was heading for the thick brush under the north of the Rock, to make that his stand for the rutting. The Man thought so too, and the three turned left and ran faster, though they were tired, for they had run from the rising to the setting of the sun, and had eaten no food but a few mussels since the day before yesterday. After half an hour swinging round through the forest, and five minutes crawling through the dense scrub closer under the wall of the Rock, they came to an animal walkway.

The Man was looking for a place to lie in wait when he heard loud calls, and barks. He shrank down and looked, wondering, at Lefthand. Lefthand whispered, 'Others. They are killing the stag.'

The men crept through the tangle towards the sounds. The Man thought furiously, the Others again! There was no respite for them. Invisible in the undergrowth, he watched them. Four males – the same four who'd killed Red Girl yesterday. One big female was with them. The stag was dead at their feet, the body out of sight but the huge antlers towering up above the bushes. They had already drunk blood for their faces were red-splashed.

Beside him Feetborn's Son pointed his spear, and wanted to kill the Others, but the Man knew that he was tired, and they were many, and strong. He shook his head. The big Other female hurried off alone, and a long time later came back with more Others – four more females, one with a cub at her breast, and many bigger cubs. They gathered round the dead stag and instead of tying it to a pole as the Man did, they all took hold, and like ants with a fly pulled it through the bushes and on to the slope below the cliffs. When they were well out of sight the Man said, 'Go to the women. I will come later.'

Lefthand hesitated, questioning, but Feetborn's son feared the dark and was already running back through the forest. 'Go,' the Man said to Lefthand – 'Go, and see that all the spears are sharp.'

When Lefthand had disappeared in the trees the Man went cautiously after the Others. The wind still blew gently from behind, but he did not think they would detect his scent while they were all so close to the dead stag. They were dragging it slowly along at the foot of the cliff, and he could hear them calling and grunting together as they moved. He stole behind in silence.

When they reached their cave it was quite dark. The Man made a wide loop and came up to the cliff again the other side of it. There he was safely downwind; but he smelled ordure and thought he must be in the place where they dropped their dung. He moved cautiously closer to the cave, and up the rocky slope. He could see a little way into the cave. There he stopped.

The Others were cutting up the stag, but their flints were not sharp. The big male was strong, with powerful teeth and neck, for he ripped at the meat like a leopard or bear. They had built a great fire, and watching it made the Man feel colder, for it had begun to snow. There was no snow in the Others' cave. Soon they would be heavy with eating. Tomorrow they would be stronger from the food, but for tonight they would be heavy. His jaws were

36

clamped tight against cold and hunger, but slowly he managed to open them, and put out his tongue and let the snow melt on it. Then, moving stiffly at first, he crept back and down, circled round well below the cave, and headed for his own fire, in the forest.

Cryer heard him first and called, warning, but Lefthand was up at once, saying 'It is the Father. Hold, hold!'

He came in and they were all on their feet, yawning and stretching. He told them how the Others were eating the stag, how heavy they would be, how warm and dry was their cave. Then he told them they would all go now, to kill the Others.

Feetborn's Son growled, 'Food!'

But Lefthand's brow wrinkled and he said, 'For tomorrow?'

The Man nodded. They would eat the Others, yes, but it was not for food that he meant to kill them, but because they *were*, where he wanted to be, where the mussels were, where the water was, where the warm was.

He told them there were four male Others. Someone had to bring them out of the cave so that he and Lefthand and Feetborn's Son could kill them. He looked at the women. Cryer was the fastest runner of them. He motioned to her and Snowborn to come, and Red Boy as well. Then he looked to the spears, and felt that they were sharp. He wound a length of twined hide thong round his waist, and was ready.

They left the fire, the three men with spears in front, then Cryer, Red Boy, and Snowborn last with a flint axe. They heard sounds of animals in the forest, and Feetborn's Son whimpered until the Man hit him; for they all knew, Feetborn's Son too, that no animal would attack them when they were so many, unless it could not run away.

They stopped by a bush near the Others' cave. They saw a small glow of fire on the roof of the cave, but heard nothing. The Man muttered, 'Some sleep.' They went on towards the cave, but lower down the slope. When they were directly below the cave the Man stopped. He told Cryer and Red Boy to stay there until they heard an owl call. Then they must walk up towards the cave until the Others ran out at them. Cryer whispered, 'Yes,' and Red Boy's eyes glowed in the hazy dark.

The Man led the rest – Lefthand, Feetborn's Son, and Snowborn – very carefully up the slope. The moon was making a little, soft, blurred light, and snow and sand and bush and rock all looked alike. He judged the distance as he climbed. When the Others saw or heard Cryer and Red Boy, some would run out at them, and some would not. He must trap those who ran out far enough from the cave so that those who stayed inside could not help them until too late. But he must not be too far. Above all, he must not be heard.

He came to a place he had noticed earlier, a stone's throw below the cave. There was a little cliff, too high to jump down. The Others would run down the gully the far side of it. He went in under the little cliff and looked up. He could not see the mouth of the cave, so a watcher there could not see him.

He brought the rest close, unwound the long thong from his waist, and gave it to the young men. He showed them where to crouch, the thong lying along the ground between them. He did not have to tell Snowborn where to go, for she knew that the woman's task was to kill any wounded or fallen animal.

Now he was ready. He put his cupped hands over his nose and mouth and made the owl's call, quavering slow, twice. Then he picked up his spear and stood, tautly strung, pressed against the rock.

Cryer and Red Boy would be starting up the slope. When the Others heard them, would they ask themselves why they were coming? They would be too heavy and sleepy to wonder. Small stones rolled away under someone's feet, and then he heard Red Boy's breathing. A moment later there was a tiny movement above. An Other had heard it, too.

And in that instant the Man saw, six inches from his right foot, a crouched bird. His heart nearly stopped, for if it flew up now . . . The Others would be creeping to the cave mouth . . . the bird did not move . . . they would be looking down, gathering . . . the bird moved its head, no more: another five steps and it would not matter: four, three, two . . . Cryer and Red Boy were level. The Others meant to let them reach the cave itself, and kill them there.

He muttered. 'Look up. See. Scream. Run.'

As he spoke, Cryer obeyed – stopped – looked up – then she really saw them crouched in the cave mouth above, for her mouth opened in a rising shriek and she turned and hurtled down the slope, Red Boy beside her. The bird shot up drumming from the Man's foot with a loud squawk. Above, there was a bellow, and the pad of running feet. Two young males crashed past down the gully, and the Man let them go. A moment later the big male came, running at full speed, and the Man cried 'Now!' His young men jerked up the thong, the Other tripped over it and went flying head first far down the slope. As he landed, Snowborn crashed her axe into his head. By then the three men were racing after the young Others. Below,

Cryer and Red Boy turned, snarling in the moonglow. The Others slowed, and drew back their spear arms. Neither looked round as Feetborn's Son and Lefthand struck, hurling their spears between their shoulder blades from a few feet away. The Others fell, coughing, and the men pounced. 'Kill, kill, quick!' the Man cried. He stabbed once, pulled his spear free, and stared back up the slope, all the rest with him. There was only one more male Other, the twisted one.

The six of them reached the cave mouth together, all armed now. The old female was there, keening and screaming, the big female behind, and many cubs, all staring, snarling, backing up into the darkness. Where was the bent one, the last male?

The Man saw him, on the left. He pushed Snowborn and said, 'Kill the big female!' Snowborn grunted and ran forward, her axe held high, the Man close behind her. The big female stabbed out at her, piercing her shoulder, but the Man leaning over Snowborn's bent body, passed his spear through the female's throat. Then he turned and ran at the twisted male. He was waiting, crouched, bent. As the Man feinted a thrust he too feinted, and as the Man struck he stabbed upward with his short spear at the Man's belly. The Man felt a burning pain under the ribs, but laughed aloud, for the spear was blunt, and it had not entered his bowels. As he stabbed down at the exposed back, Snowborn hit the Other on the ear with her axe, and he fell. The Man thrust his spear into his throat, waited while the jerking stopped then turned round.

Now all were running about, screaming. In the cave mouth Lefthand and Feetborn's Son struck regularly so that none passed, and beside them Cryer and Red Boy stabbed those who fell. The female with a cub at breast rushed suddenly out of the depths of the cave and brushed past the Man, taking him by surprise. He grabbed at her but missed. The men at the cave mouth were both engaged, and the screaming female ran past them and out into the snow.

Now they searched the cave, and found a female hiding behind a pillar, and several cubs, and killed them all. The saliva began to pour from the Man's mouth, for it was almost done now. There was only the old female left, crawling by the entrance, and her Cryer killed, and took a big tooth that was hung round her neck, and put it round her own.

The Man looked at the bodies and the blood and brains and scattered ordure, and he smelled the pieces of the stag that were still roasting by the fire, and raised his face and cried out in triumph, again and again. Feetborn's Son and Red Boy sang with him; of the males only Lefthand did not sing but knelt looking wonderingly into the open eyes of a dead female cub.

The Man told Left hand and Cryer to go and bring the rest to the cave at once. Then he walked slowly about, chewing a piece of deer flesh. Feetborn's Son began to saw off the head of the big female. Red Boy was stuffing deer meat into his mouth with both hands. Snowborn's shoulder had nearly stopped bleeding. The Man looked curiously at the chips of flint in one corner. The twisted male had had a flint-head spear, but it was blunt. The young males only had hardened wood spears. These flints were not sharp. He picked one up, and made a scratch on the cave wall, then another and another. Now he had made the mark of a bird, like the red-legged bird that had stayed silently by his feet, even at the owl call. They were fat, and good to eat, and easy to kill, those birds, but none of his should ever eat one again, except as a blessing, for now it was his brother.

41

Snowborn had set the big female's head in the coals, and the smell of roasting brains rekindled his hunger. Soon Lefthand and Cryer came back with the rest, Cryer carrying her dead baby. They all stood close, and the Man put a piece of flesh into the baby's mouth, then carried it back far into the cave and pushed it into a high crevice, where no animal could reach it. Cryer wept a little, for her breasts still hurt, but one of the boys drank milk from her, and then the Man told them of the bird, his brother, and all began to talk excitedly.

The Man looked about him, and began to smile. He jumped up and down, and grabbed Snowborn and Feetborn together, one arm about each, and danced with them, twirling round and round the fire, shouting at the top of his voice.

The Woman crouched by a bush far from the cave, under the steepest cliff of the Rock, where the sun never shone. It had begun to snow and her baby was cold. She had fallen in her flight, landing on top of it, and it had not cried or moved or sucked since. Her throat itched to wail, but she dared not. Bent Brother she had seen killed, but where was the Father? The young men? Was there no one? She began to whimper softly, uncontrollably.

Late in the morning two young male Others came, with their tall, straight-up walk. They would have passed below, but her skin prickled and before she could stop herself she jumped up and ran away. Then they saw her, and she heard their shouts, behind her. She ran with all her strength, but they closed fast. She threw her baby away and dived into the thick brush at the foot of the cliff. She ducked and twisted through thorn and creeper, but they were very close. A cleft in the rock, narrow and low, showed black before her and she slipped in, dropped to her

42

knees, to her belly, wriggling frantically forward. Soon the cleft widened. She turned and waited, her hands like claws and her lips drawn back from her teeth.

She heard the Others at the cave mouth, and the thin light was blocked. They growled and hissed for a time and then they too waited. They made no sound but the Woman smelled them. When the sun set, they went. The Woman lay without movement of hair or muscle, until no light at all came down the narrow slit. Then she began to unwind and wriggle towards the entrance. As she moved her left knee against the side of the cave a mass of rock broke free, fell, and crushed her leg. It was a big black block, sharp edged, and however hard she tried, she could not move.

Book Two

OUT OF THE CAVES

To the Jewish year 3188, which was
− 180 A.U.C. (180 years from the founding of the city of
Rome)
− 573 B.C.

THE loser in the encounter just described, and in the general struggle for existence, was Neanderthal Man; the winner was Cro-Magnon man (both named after the places where their remains were first identified). Europeans of today, however, are not direct descendants of Cro-Magnon, but rather the result of a further 30,000 years of inter-breeding, movement, and evolution in particular environments. These movements were accelerated and extended by each advance in human technology, but until food growing took the place of food gathering and hunting (an advance which had to await the passing of the Würm) the caves of Gibraltar were as good a place as any to live, and better than most. Most of the big horizontal caves, such as that described in *The Woman*, were again at sea level, and in the floury earth of their floors man began to leave the pottery, basketwork, stone tools, shell amulets, ornaments, metal weapons, and coins which trace his progress.

When we reach the dawn of history, about 5,000 years ago, Spain was occupied by tribes of people since called Iberians. They came from the northern flanks of the Caucasus, but before that from the Middle East. Their language was of Hebraic origin. The word *iber* itself derives from *eber*, meaning 'ultimate, beyond', in Hebrew; *Iberia* is thus, the last land. The *Iberian* tribe which lived on the mainland opposite Gibraltar was called *Turdetani*; and some Spanish scholars claim that this is from an old Hebrew word meaning 'region, country'.

Southern Spain was known to the ancients as Tarsish; and in it there may or may not have been a great capital called Tartessos, and a great king called Argantonio. If it did exist, no one has yet found a trace: if it did not, the 'city' was probably a symbol used by Greek and Phoenician poets to personify all the wonders and marvels of the far west.

Tarsish is mentioned several times in the Bible. Jonah met his misadventure with the great fish while on his way there:

> But Jonah rose up to flee unto Tarshish from the presence of the LORD, and went down to Joppa; and he found a ship going to Tarshish: so he paid the fare thereof and went down into it, to go with them unto Tarshish from the presence of the LORD (Jonah 1:3)

and, as we know, there were whales in the Straits.

Solomon had commercial dealings with it:

> For the king had at sea a navy of Tarshish with the navy of Hiram: once in three years came the navy of Tarshish, bringing gold, and silver, ivory, and apes, and peacocks. (1 Kings 10:2)
> The Kings of Tarshish and of the isles shall bring presents ... (Psalms 72:10)

The reference to peacocks and ivory shows that there was a trading link between Tarsish and Africa, and this is not strange when it is realized that the Egyptians later sailed right round Africa (it took them three years). The truly revealing reference is the mention of gold and silver, and again *Silver spread into plates is brought from Tarshish ...* (Jeremiah 10:9), for these coasts had long before

Solomon felt the first thrust of the civilizations beginning to flower in the Near and Middle East. The Egyptians started to use gold, silver and copper very early, and soon after 3000 B.C. they were getting some of it from Tarsish – specifically, from near Almeria, and from the Rio Tinto region, which is west of Gibraltar. An Iberian on the Rock, then, tending goats perhaps, must have seen vessels of the most ancient design creeping past, westbound with oil and cotton and blue beads for the natives, eastbound with the sheets of copper and silver.

The Greeks came to share in the trade; and about 280 B.C. the Minoans, who brought with them, and left in Spain, a deep-rooted belief of their religion: bull worship. The trade went beyond Spain to England, and beyond copper to tin, and soon copper and tin were being melted together to make a new harder and tougher metal – bronze. The Age of Bronze was born close to the Rock, and soon the Iron Age would follow from the same womb, for large iron deposits, too, were in Tarsish.

Several peoples traded past the Rock, but it was the Phoenicians who dominated these western waters for over five centuries, and, through the colonies they planted, for another three after their own decline. They were the Canaanites of the Bible, who occupied the coastal strip of Palestine north of Carmel – the land allotted to the tribes of Asher and Zebulon at the Exodus, though the Jews were unable to turn the Canaanites out. They were a Semitic people as old as the Jews, and closely linked with them by many ties. The Hiram of my quote from 1 Kings was king of Phoenicia, and a close friend of David and Solomon. When, after the death of Solomon, the ten northern tribes broke off to form the Kingdom of Israel in 975 B.C., Phoenician friendship with the southern kingdom of Judah cooled, but with Israel increased; for the people of the north, largely renouncing the Jewish God, took to sharing the worship of the Phoenician gods, Baal, Adon, Moloch and, the chief ones, Melkarte and Astarte, and in many ways began to blend with the Phoenicians.

The ancient world held the Phoenicians in awe for their industry and intelligence – they invented the alphabet – and at the same time, in aversion, for their custom of burning small children as sacrifices to Moloch. Their temples enjoyed the services of religious prostitutes of both sexes, but this was not uncommon in other religions.

They are remembered now not for their vices or virtues, but for their skills as sailors and merchants. Their own capitals were Tyre and Sidon, but in 1100 B.C. they founded Gadir (Cadiz) and in 814 B.C., Carthage (near modern Tunis, on the north African coast). They also founded in 940 B.C., a town on Gibraltar bay.

Or did they? There are doubts.

Walking north and west from the Rock round the head of the bay, you come after a mile and a half to a river often appropriately called First River, the modern Guadarranque. On the left bank there are the ruins of an ancient town. Everyone agrees that the town was called Carteia; the doubt is, when was it founded? Some modern scholars tend to believe there was no town here before Roman times or perhaps only an Iberian village; but the Greeks had a word for it – Heraclea; and if the river and beach were properly shaped for a port, as everyone agrees they were, it is a perfect site, with better natural shelter than any other in southern Spain (except Gadir). I choose to believe therefore that Carteia was founded by the Phoenicians in 940 B.C. to exploit the tunny fishing and the beds of murex, the shellfish from which they extracted the famous 'Tyrian purple', the colour which later became the fiercely guarded prerogative of Roman nobles and emperors. It was never in fact a true purple, but something between rose and dark violet. The dye was made by extracting the shellfish and dropping them into large vats or tanks, often of stone. When they rotted they secreted a yellow liquid, which was the dye. The vats were always placed downwind for obvious reasons.

The colony's real name was Melkarteia, after the god, but that soon became abbreviated. A thousand years before Christ, therefore, the Rock looked down upon, and was surely regarded as the sacred mountain of, its first real town.

These are all facts, as best we can trace them through the deceptive and ever shifting curtains of the years. The ancients, with ancestral memories sharpened by tens of thousands of years when all knowledge, experience, and wisdom had to be passed on by word of mouth, recorded them differently. They did not have our tools of discovery and analysis, and having been actors rather than spectators, were more interested in transmitting emotion than fact. History was recorded and passed on in myth and fable. One that concerns this epic more closely is the story of the opening of the Straits of Gibraltar. Although it is inconceivable that thinking Man could have been present on Earth when it actually happened (at least 30 million years ago) yet the most ancient voices of the past seemed to find it necessary to explain that it had happened, within human ken. The act is attributed to a god or demi-god, in the Greek version called Heracles and in the Latin Hercules (this figure was probably the same as Tubal), who tore the mountains apart and set up pillars inscribed *Non Plus Ultra* (Nothing beyond) to mark the end of the earth. From the very beginning it was known that these Pillars were the mountains called Abyla on the African shore and, on the European side, the limestone block which the Phoenicians called Alube and the Greeks Calpe, meaning *urn, hollowed out*. This was the Rock, Gibraltar, and it was *hollowed out* because of its innumerable caves, especially one very large one high on the west face, the Great Cave.

About 1100 B.C. one or several Greek poets called Homer began to compose the *Iliad* and the *Odyssey*, which are, in fact, history and geography books, respectively. In them the bards set out in metrical form (so that it could more easily be memorized) all that was known of their own past, and of the outside world.

In the *Odyssey* Homer's archetypal wanderer, Ulysses or Odysseus, passes through a narrow strait. Here is the relevant passage in the lucid translation of S. O. Andrew:

> *Of the two other rocks, the one reaches up to the sky*
> *With sharp-pointed peak, and a cloud encompasses it*
> *That never disperses, nor clear air ever reveals*
> *Even in summer or autumn its heav'n-soaring crest.*
> *No mortal that perilous summit could scale or descend*
> *Though with twenty hands and with twenty feet he*
> *   were born,*
> *For its surface is smooth, like polish'd marble, and*
> *   sheer.*
> *Midmost the rock is a cavern, misty and dim,*
> *Turn'd toward the region of darkness where Erebus*
> *   lies,*
> *And beneath it, O noble Odysseus, your bark ye must*
> *   steer.*
> *Not even an archer of power with a shaft from his bow*
> *Could shoot from a hollow ship to the depth of that*
> *   cave;*
> *Therein has yelping Scylla her secret abode,*

Her voice like a newborn whelp's no greater yet she
Is an evil monster indeed, nor would any that pass'd
Rejoice to behold her, not though an Immortal he were.
She has twelve feet, which she dangles down in the air,
And above, six necks, very long, and on each of the six
A hideous head which is arm'd with a triple array
Of teeth set thickly teeming with black-venom'd death.

and, nine lines later:

But mark thou, Odysseus, that other rock which is low,
Quite near to the first (thou could'st shoot with an
    arrow across),
And on it, in full leafage, a fig-tree there is,
Whereunder the mighty Charybdis sucks down the tide.
Thrice in the day she disgorges and thrice in the day
She sucks it again; mayst thou never be near when she
    sucks. . . .

These passages have sometimes been taken to refer to
the Strait of Messina between Sicily and the Italian mainland, but the description fits the Strait of Gibraltar much
more closely. Gibraltar was also very far off, and its links
with the fabulous Hercules and the hardly less mysterious
Tarsish would make it a more attractive location for
marvels. The cloud hiding the Rock's head is the most
telling evidence, for the *levanter* cloud is unique in the
Mediterranean; and one can easily trace, in this poetic
version of returned seamen's tall tales, the great cave, the
sheer eastern and northern cliffs, the giant squid with its
black ink 'venom,' and the dangerous race which forms off
the point of Septa on the African shore. The only factors
against this identification are that the African pillar
(Charybdis) is in fact not lower than Gibraltar but con-

siderably higher and the distance between the two is a good deal more than bowshot; but the dramatic isolation of the Rock so dominates the strait that several later travellers fell into the first error, and the bow-shot distance is a liberty required by Homer's plot.

To return to the harsher yet still breathtaking light of history . . . Let us look at Gibraltar, about 600 B.C. The trees grow thick on the lesser slopes, and sailors often go ashore but do not tarry unless they mean to worship at a shrine of Hercules, for the demi-god inhabits the place, and is not mocked. Above all none but the very devout, or the very blasphemous, enter the Great Cave, though it is known to the whole civilized world – it goes into the womb of earth; it holds armies and is not filled; it is dark, but a torch held high shows pillars and walls and steps wrought and decorated and coloured beyond the power of mortals to describe . . .

The small town by the First River flourishes. They have increasingly close relations with the hinterland, where the Iberians are being diluted by successive waves of another people from the Syrio-Turanian region – the Celts – to form the Celtiberians (this particular influx goes on, in dribs and drabs, for about 800 years, for Julius Caesar records some 6,000 Celts, with women and children, entering Spain in 49 B.C.).

In the basin of the Mediterranean the peoples, having developed and spread, begin to fight for empire. Phoenicia is attacked by the Assyrian Shalmaneser V in 721 B.C., and much weakened:

The burden of Tyre. Howl, ye ships of Tarshish; for it is laid waste, so that there is no house, no entering in . . .

(Isaiah 23:1)

Carthage breaks free of the mother country, as colonies will, and from now on it is Carthage, not Tyre, which controls the Phoenician settlements in the west.

The Babylonian Nebuchadnezzar besieges Tyre in 587 B.C. The following year he destroys Jerusalem, sacks the First Temple, and takes some of its people captive. From both the Assyrian and Babylonian invasions many inhabitants of Phoenicia and neighbouring countries, including Judaea, escaped for refuge to Gadir, Carthage, and Sexi (modern Almuñecar), Carteia, and a dozen other settlements at the far end of the Mediterranean.

It is nearly 3,000 years since men first deliberately sailed past the Rock, seeking the wider world, the richer life that their intelligence told them could be found. The Phoenicians and Carthaginians, however, are still doing their best to perpetuate the legend that beyond Calpe and Abyla, *non plus ultra* – nothing, the end! – it keeps out the competition. But these men are real sailors, real explorers. Whatever they tell the rest of the world they themselves know that Calpe is not really the end, but the beginning. *The kings ... of the isles shall bring presents.* Britain (the Tin Islands) they have known for a thousand years, but there must be other islands, other lands beyond. Atlantis? The Isles of the Blest? A new continent? ...

BEYOND THE PILLARS

THE girl stood in the stern of the long galley *Kedesha*, holding with one hand to the gunwale beside her. The

54

wind moulded her cotton dress against her thighs and breasts, and whipped tendrils of her black hair about her ears. Beside her, two bare-chested sailors held the steering oar, their feet braced strongly against the slats in the deck.

The great grey mountain in the sea towered close now. They had been rowing towards it all day, and in the morning, from afar, it had looked like a crouching beast, but for an hour now its cliffs had cut off the sun from them. The wind, which had blown in their faces all day, was beginning to slacken, and the sea was calm, although still, at every wave, the bow rose, hesitated, and plunged down, sending out huge bursts of green water on both sides, and the mast weaved and jerked against the background of the cliffs.

Daniel, her husband, came up from the rowers' deck and stretched and yawned. He looked over the side, and called, 'Pendril! It's getting calmer. We can go round the point.'

She heard the boatswain's strangely accented Phoenician calling up from the rowers' deck below her feet – 'That's because we're in the lee of Alube, Daniel.'

'I don't think so,' her husband called peevishly. 'It's calm. Keep them rowing.'

Tamar nodded approvingly. The new boatswain was a rough, rude man, square built and strong, with extraordinary deep blue eyes, reddish hair, and bronze skin – an old man, at least thirty. Daniel was too gentle with him.

The boatswain's head appeared in the hatch. 'Look at the point, Daniel,' he said. 'You can see the waves from here. There's a very dangerous race off there, in this wind.'

Daniel stamped his foot, 'I am the owner and captain! We will not anchor! We will go round the point and into

Carteia.' Tamar nodded again. She caught the boatswain's quizzical blue eyes on her, and scowled at him.

The boatswain said, 'You're the captain, but you're not the god Melkarte. The rowers are exhausted. The race prevents the oars getting a good bite. We will not get round the point, however long we try.'

'Go farther out into the strait,' Daniel said, 'there is no race there.'

'No,' Pendril answered, 'but the current against us is over a knot faster than we can row.'

'Oh, anchor then,' Daniel yelled, and flounced up to the bow, and stood there with arms folded.

Pendril shouted below, 'Stand by to anchor,' then ran up on deck and stood at Tamar's side, but ignored her. The rowmaster stuck his head through the hatch, where he could hear the deck commands and bob down to give the necessary orders to the rowers below. One sailor stayed at the steering oar, the other four went to the bows, pushing Daniel out of the way with little ceremony. He came after, and she went to him.

'The gods have turned the wind against us,' he said gloomily.

'Or perhaps it is Pendril who makes us go so slowly. I wish you hadn't hired him.'

Her husband shrugged. She knew he had no choice, for the real boatswain had deserted at the last port, Sexi. It had been a stroke of good fortune to find a qualified man ready and willing to take the long journey to the Tin Islands, and without one they could not go, for Daniel had so far never sailed beyond beyond Gadir.

'Come,' she said, 'the cook's making a savoury smell . . .' He brightened, and rubbed his hands together gleefully, for his moods were never deep or long held, but like a child's.

She slept badly that night, partly because the motion of the ship was different from when it lay in harbour, partly because dreams disturbed her. She had hoped, after supper, that Daniel would take her as a man had a right to take his wife, though he so seldom did. She had yearned towards him, caressed him while they ate, pressed her body against him when they lay down, sent him messages of love and desire from her eyes. But he was tired and did not answer, but slept.

Sleep did not come to her for two hours, and when it did images of lust filled it. Unknown men came upthrust and hard upon her and into her and she welcomed them, one after another. Daniel shook her at last, where she lay beside him, on the wolf skins, and said she would waken the whole ship, she was making so much noise. But though she put her hand upon the trembling void of her womanhood, and tried to soothe it, she could not sleep.

In the morning the wind still blew strong from the west, and broken white water extended far out from the point of the Rock. She was pacing the deck by dawn, tired but unable to rest, biting her nails, patting her hair, looking at the sailors asleep by the mast. Daniel came up, followed by Pendril.

'This wind will hold all day,' Pendril said.

'We'll stay here till tomorrow then,' Daniel said at once, as though to forestall the boatswain suggesting the same thing.

'Aye, captain,' Pendril said. 'Then I'll go ashore to Carteia. It's Midsummer's Eve.'

'Very well,' Daniel said.

'I'll be back before dawn tomorrow ... I suggest that half the sailors and rowers be let ashore, too. They will ...'

'No.' Daniel snapped, and turned his back.

57

'I want to go,' Tamar said suddenly, astonished to hear herself saying the words. 'Take me, Daniel.'

'But, dearest, we'll be there tomorrow, or as soon as the wind drops.'

'I want to go today, now,' she cried, 'I'm tired of being shut up in this ship.'

Daniel said, 'I don't want to go, Tamar. I don't feel very well . . . Why don't you go with Pendril, if you must go?'

She hesitated. Pendril was launching the little round horse-prowed dinghy over the side. He and a sailor dropped lightly into it. He called up roughly, 'If you're coming, come.'

'Wait,' she commanded, and rushed to her cabin, tidied her hair, put it up with her silver pins and comb, donned her best robe, fastened it with a little bronze scarab-brooch, and made up her eyes with antimony. Then she returned to the upper deck. Pendril's eyes, staring up from the bobbing *hippos*, widened when he saw her, but he only snapped, 'At last.' Then a sailor took her hands and lowered her into the *hippos*, where Pendril caught her, his hands under her breasts. She scowled at him and sat down. 'Enjoy yourself,' Daniel called down, smiling, 'Pendril will protect you.'

Then the sailor started paddling towards the cliffs, and in a few moments they reached the small waves in the shallows. Pendril jumped into the water and held out his arms. She ignored him, lifted her robe above her knees, stepped over the side, and waded ashore. The sailor paddled the *hippos* back to the *Kedesha*.

Ahead, a great cave opened at the foot of the cliff, a steep slope of sand and earth leading up into it. Pendril started up into the cave, and Tamar followed. Perhaps the cave was a tunnel, she thought, and led out on to the flat land above. Deep in under the overhang of the arch she found Pendril on his knees, digging with his hands in the powdery earth. He looked up – 'You here?'

'What are you looking for?' she asked.

'*Could* be anything,' he said, 'I've found bones, pots, baskets, old bronze knives, everything. Sailors have been sheltering in this cave for a long time, if you ask me ... But what I *am* looking for ...': his hands touched something, he scrabbled about a little more and pulled out a stoppered jar – 'is this. Strong wine. I buried it a year ago.' He broke the seal, poured some of the almost colourless liquor down his throat, gasped, and handed her the jar. 'Try it,' he said. 'It'll enable you to suffer my presence. And me yours.' She drank a little, and almost choked, it was so fiery.

Pendril drank again, and started back down the slope, the jar swinging in his hand. The blue and yellow *Kedesha* rocked gently in the swell, two hundred feet from shore. Everyone on board seemed to have gone back to sleep. The figurehead glowed like a woman of burnished gold in the low sun. It was a *kedesha*, a temple-priestess of Astarte, those mistresses of every vice. Her face was turned up to the sky, her pointed breasts jutting, her hands cupping them, her legs spread and bent back so that the rounded column of the ship's stem entered her body. Whenever Tamar saw the figurehead from ashore, with its swollen sexual lips so greedily taking the column in, she found herself deeply troubled.

'Are you coming, or are you going to stay here and hope Daniel will join you after all?' the boatswain said. 'Because you'll wait a long time.'

'Hold your tongue,' she snapped. 'Lead me to Carteia.'

'This way, princess, this way,' he said with mock obsequiousness. She followed him a little along the beach and then on to a narrow track up the cliff. It was steep, but they climbed steadily and soon stepped out on to rough but flat ground. The west wind blew hard, shaking the grass and wild flowers about her feet. The sea was grey-green, shimmering under wind driven spume. Over there the African Pillar towered out of a glittering sea haze about its feet.

Pendril was striding away from her across the flat, and she hurried to catch up with him. As she came close a red-legged partridge ran out from a bush. Pendril picked up a stone, but she struck down his arm as he threw. The bird rocketed away with a hard clatter of wings.

'Why did you do that?' he said, aggrieved. 'They're good eating.'

'Because . . .' she said, and stopped. Because she felt like annoying him: because the bird was beautiful: because the sun shone: any of those answers would have been right, but why should she answer at all? He was a boorish half-Iberian, half-Phoenician sailor, beneath her notice.

They came to a patch of thick forest, and Pendril said, 'There's a mighty cave up in there, and a shrine to Hercules, they say. I've never been in.'

'What are you afraid of?' she said. 'There is but one God, Jehovah . . . Shall I escort you in?' she mocked.

'No, no,' he said sullenly. 'The gods of this Rock are not to be blasphemed.' He led downhill past the forest, and later on to a sandy beach by a sheltered bay, and soon she saw houses, and a river, and warehouses, and smelled many smells, of fresh fish and rotting oysters, and savours of cooking spice and oil.

'Carteia,' Pendril said. 'A small place, but some prefer it to Carthage . . . I have business to attend to in my village. It is over that hill, six miles away. I will be back before dusk, when the festivities begin. The people in this little house here are relatives of mine. They will give you something to eat, and you can rest with them when you wish. I will introduce you . . .'

After Pendril had gone Tamar talked a little with the people of the house, then set out to explore the town. The fine river slid by blue-green and fresh, and she saw many fish in it. The air was clean, and birds sang in the woods at the edge of the crop land. Fishing boats big and small passed in from the sea, past the Rock which stood like a sentinel over their comings and goings. Along the docks she saw the great blue-backed tunny fish, strung on hooks, and men cutting them up, and women rubbing salt into the flesh. One of the women wore a silver brooch with the open Torah represented upon it, so Tamar said, 'Are you from Judaea?'

The woman rested, her hands on her hips. 'Yes. From Jerusalem.'

'I too,' she said eagerly. 'My father was a priest. He was killed, with all my family, except an uncle who took me to Carthage.'

'You were lucky,' the woman said. 'You must have been only a child. You had nothing to lose. Some of us . . . everything.'

'There are more here?'

'About twenty,' the woman said. 'We are all working today, because most of the heathen do not . . .' She nodded and stooped again to her work.

Early in the afternoon Pendril's relatives stewed a fat dog with herbs, olives, onion and wine, and then Tamar rested, and waited for Pendril to return.

Towards dusk as she sat outside the little house, the people seemed to be wearing finer clothes, and there was

61

an air of importance to their movements. She heard distant shouts and orders, and the tuning of stringed instruments. Men carried great wine vessels to and fro, and women set earthenware pots around the houses and lit the rope wicks in them and they gave out a smoky reddish light. At the ege of the river and in the open place outside the little wooden temple to Astarte, boys lit fires. The fires grew larger, the dark beyond more dense and impenetrable. Shapes passed, embracing, and still Pendril did not come.

When at last he came she saw that he had been drinking. He had a small wine skin now, which he held up at arm's length, and squeezed a jet of wine into his mouth, then, although she protested, into hers.

'Come,' he said thickly, 'come to the feast, the dance . . . This religion's not yours, but come!' His gold earrings shook, glinting in the red light.

She went with him then, into the celebration of Midsummer's Eve. The time, like the people, passed with gradually increasing pace and passion. For the first hour she felt like a sleepwalker, gliding very slow, one of the race of sleepwalkers. Then she moved more briskly, and they too, and the songs grew louder, and louder, and faster and the twanging of the plucked strings from the temple, and taller the fires, tall as men, and the young men began to jump over them at the sides, running, calling to each other, then leaping, and afterwards shouting again in triumph. The wine splashed in her face, and a string snapped in her head, her feet moved, faster faster the drummer pounded, sweating, and suddenly there were women in serpent headdresses of gold and silver, necklaces between their breasts, dancing in front of the temple. They were naked from the waist down, silver belling on their ankles, breasts jerking, their flat, oiled bellies pulled in, their smooth-shaved sexual mounds thrust forward. They sang, the fires roared higher, and suddenly with a great shriek a man passed her, naked, and leaped like an antelope through the top of the fire. The people gasped, a dancer wrapped herself around him and in a moment Tamar saw as the dancer slowly swung, her feet spread wide, her body arched far back, that the man had entered her, and they danced thus, locked, the man's face straining.

The priests were out, chanting. She heard snatches of Hebrew, the sacred names of Jehovah, then other languages, other names, other gods. There was kneeling and bowing before images of Sun, Moon, Stars, Winds, Clouds. The Golden Calf gleamed inside the temple, its doors now flung wide. The child that would be sacrificed at dawn sat enthroned in gold and silver finery, its eyes feverish and bright, its lips parted in excitement. All around her there was dancing and making love. She stood pressed against a house, facing the temple, Pendril beside her.

The fire burned her face and the sweat poured down her body. She trembled with the sounds about her – the sharp cries of women groaning under men at her feet, the regular chant of the dancers, the shrieks of a boy missing his leap and fallen into the fire, the smells of flesh, wine, lust.

A *kedesha* stopped before them, thighs wide, knees bent, the painted tips of her fingers thrusting a large artificial penis, with two huge golden balls, in and out of her sex. Her lips were bright red, her eyelids painted dark green. Her eyes shone into Tamar's, worming down into the secret parts of her body. 'Take her' the dancer commanded Pendril.

Pendril's voice was thick and deep – 'Lie, Tamar!' His

hand caressed her breast. She jerked away – 'Don't touch me!'

'You need him,' the dancer exulted, 'Take him in, all of him.'

'No!' Tamar cried. 'I have a husband . . .'

Pendril laughed loudly. 'That groaning and moaning last night didn't fool me,' he said. 'I'm too close, and only the canvas curtain between us. Daniel never touched you. He never does, does he? Twice a year, perhaps?'

'Take him,' the *kedesha* said. 'He is a good, strong man.'

'And you passionate and dark and beautiful as a deer.' Pendril said. His hand was back on her breast. 'Why do you think he let you come with me to the feast here, alone?'

'Because he's ill,' she cried. 'Because you're just an animal to us. No more than a dog.'

'No! Because he wants me to keep you quiet!' Pendril shouted.

She turned, and stumbled away. It was dark by the river now, and she heard him running behind her. She slowed, and at the edge of the forest, turned, her back to a tree, her arms spread. She waited, her heart pounding.

He came slowly to her, and she closed her eyes. Her body ached and trembled, and there was a sudden warm wet release at her loins.

He said, 'I spoke ill. I am sorry. Come. Let us go back to the ship.'

Gradually her heart stilled, the trembling stopped and she felt unutterably cold and alone. She began to cry. He said gently, 'Walk. You'll feel better.'

Now clouds obscured the moon, but a faint light filtered through and she walked at his side in a gusty wind along the sand towards the milky loom of the Rock.

'Where did you meet your husband?' Pendril asked.

'In Carthage,' she said, sniffling. 'I was seven when Jerusalem was sacked. His father Eliab lived close to my uncle, and they were rich. They are of the tribe of Zebulon, but do not keep the Law. We grew up together . . .'

'And married – how long?' he asked.

'Three years.'

'And you are – twenty-one?'

'Twenty.'

He seemed about to say something but a flash of lightning lit up the Rock, and thunder boomed around the bay, and he broke into a trot. The lightning grew more frequent, the thunder rolled up from the south. Pendril gabbled prayers under his breath as they passed under the sacred grove and the magic cavern of Hercules, and Tamar felt better, even smiling to herself at his superstition. As the first huge drops of rain began to fall they reached the western beach.

'Up into the cave,' Pendril said. 'They'll never hear me calling in this.'

They sat down deep in the cave, while the rain poured down outside and the lightning flashes momentarily painted the *Kedesha* a more livid blue against the greenish sea.

Pendril said, 'I was going to say, before the thunder began – stay in Carteia, Tamar. Tell Daniel you don't want to go to the Tin Islands. He'll be pleased, and relieved. I know it.'

'But I *do* want to go,' she said. 'I became sick and weary of staying at home, caged like a pet bird, alone. We have no child . . . So I insisted that I come.'

'There's nothing to see in the Tin Islands,' he said. 'Savages. They eat pigs! A few big stones. The tin mines. Fog. Rain. Rough seas on the way.'

'I go!' she said.

'Very well,' he said. 'Don't say I didn't try to dissuade you . . . This rain's settled in for a few hours. Everyone on the *Kedesha*'s below and wrapped in his blanket. Take this—' he gave her his cloak – 'Sleep there. Have no fear of me.'

She thought she would lie awake all night again, with the thunder and lightning, and the presence of the strange man, brutal but sometimes gentle, brave but superstitious, ignorant but skilful, so close to her. But after she lay down, wrapped in his cloak, the next thing she knew was his hand on her shoulder, and his voice 'Wake up. They've seen me. The sun is rising, it's stopped raining, and the wind is in the east.'

She stood up, yawning, and stretching and put her hands to her hair. Then she straightened her robe, but when she wanted to refasten it she found that the little bronze brooch was gone.

'I've lost my brooch,' she said. 'It must be here though, because I remember feeling it when we reached the foot of the path last night.'

'Look quickly, then,' Pendril said. 'They're launching the *hippos* and making ready to hoist the sail. We can't afford to lose any wind.'

She hurried all over the cave, down to the beach, back up, but saw nothing. She began to dig with her hands where she had slept, close by the hole where Pendril had dug up his strong wine. She put her hand into the earth, dug down with her fingers.

He said, 'The *hippos* is here. And they're hoisting the sail. Idiots!'

She touched something hard and cried. 'I have it! . . . No, this isn't it.'

'Come,' he said, this time as a command. She pulled the hard thing out of the earth and followed. She held in her

66

hand a great fang, six inches long, with a hole bored through the thick end. She held it out to Pendril. 'What animal is this from?'

He turned it over curiously. 'H'm. I don't know.'

'Could it be a tiger?' she asked eagerly. He shook his head, and said. 'No. But it's ivory. All ivory on a ship belongs to the boatswain.' He tucked the fang away into the breast of his short robe.

She cried, 'It's mine! I found it!'

'It's mine now,' he said, and stepped into the coracle. She followed, tight-lipped. As soon as Pendril's foot touched the deck of the *Kedesha* he shouted, 'Down sail! We can't put it up till we're clear of the point, Daniel, or we will be blown on to the cliffs . . . Rowmaster, make ready. Stand by the steering oar. Up anchor. Row, starboard side . . . Row all.'

Two days later, heavily loaded with amphorae of water and barrels of flour, dried fruit, salt meat, and pickled fish the *Kedesha* swam past the Rock, its top crowned now with a grey cloud, and out into the gut of the Strait. The great pillars passed slowly astern and at last the curve of the brown and green land hid them, closing the Strait. They were on the Ocean.

Later in the afternoon they came to a low sandy cape, a hill covered with trees set back behind it. The waters ran very troubled off the cape, and Pendril, beside her, pointed to a little stone building on it and said, 'That is Cape Astarte, and that is her temple. Here great currents come to the surface, bringing up strange fish. It is a dangerous place.' He threw a little bread upon the water, and said a prayer to the goddess.

Daniel was there, too, and Pendril turned to him with a peculiar smile. 'We change course now, master.'

67

Daniel was looking at her and smiling, too. 'Very well,' he said.

Pendril said, 'Steer to port. More. There. Just left of the sun.'

The red sun was sinking towards the ocean. The sailor at the steering oar said, 'Where is this course for, boatswain? At Cape Astarte it's starboard a hand for Gadir.'

No one answered. Tamar looked from Daniel to Pendril. 'Are we not going to Gadir and then the Tin Islands?' she said.

Pendril said, 'No. We are going to the Isles of the Blest.'

A strange moaning rose from below deck, where the unseen rowers had heard him. He raised his voice – 'Islands where ripe fruit falls into your mouths from the trees, and women, more beautiful than goddesses, more lustful than the *kedeshot*, crowd to serve you.'

The moaning changed to a ragged cheer. Pendril cried, 'And, you sailors and rowers, there is a marvel there above anything else on earth. The women are slit across, not up and down.'

The rowers below roared with laughter and rattled their oars like thunder in the tholes. Pendril said, 'Rowmaster, let them all rest while the wind holds fair. And an extra ration of meat and wine tonight.'

Tamar turned to her husband. 'You didn't tell me about these islands! How far are they?'

'No one knows,' the sailor at the steering oar cut in. 'No one's ever been more than two days west of land and then only when they were blown out. *And* they had a hard time getting back.'

'Hold your tongue, or I'll cut it out,' Pendril snapped viciously.

68

Tamar ran down the ladder into the cabin and threw herself on to the wolfskin. Daniel came a moment later and knelt beside her. 'Don't be afraid,' he said. 'We'll turn back if it gets rough, or if we don't come to the islands in say, ten days.'

'I'm not afraid,' she said between sobs, 'but why didn't you trust me? That Pendril knew ... but *I* didn't! He's been laughing at me.'

'I tried to stop you coming,' he said, 'I tried to put you off to another voyage.'

'Is this why the first boatswain deserted in Sexi? Did he know?'

Daniel said, 'Yes.'

'How far are the islands? Where are they?'

'Due west from Cape Astarte, four hundred miles. I bought the secret from an old wizard in Minos, on a voyage a year ago. There's gold lying about on the ground, Tamar ...'

She sat up, drying her eyes. From the deck above she could hear the sailors arguing with Pendril. 'We have food and water for three months,' he was saying. 'The ship's sound. There's nothing to fear.'

'We'll go over the edge,' one of the sailors said.

'There is no edge,' Pendril cried. 'There can not be! Think! How could the water stay in the Ocean unless there is a rim to keep it in? Besides, I don't think the sea is flat. The land may be, but not the sea. You have seen ships coming over the horizon, haven't you? From all directions, as though we are always on top of a round ball, wherever we are?'

A sailor said, 'The sea can't be round. The water would all roll down.'

'I don't know why it does not fall,' Pendril said, 'but it does not, and it will not ... We sail west, and he who

69

questions that order, or spreads despond, will go over the side.' A moment later she heard him enter his cabin, next to theirs and only separated by a hanging partition of heavy sailcloth. Then a steady scraping sound began. She did not know what it was, and did not care. She reached out her hand to Daniel, and said, 'I'm sorry I became angry, husband.' He slipped free, saying, 'It is nothing . . . I think I'll go on deck.'

On the third night the wind dropped, and on the fifth turned contrary. The sailors took down the sail and from that moment the sea began to rise, slowly but inexorably, more each day. At first Tamar crouched in the cabin, feeling the ship rise giddily, then drop, leaving her stomach behind. Later she spent her days on the poop, clinging to the gunwale, and watching from there. Gradually, as the ship kept rising to the endless waves, a sort of exhilaration began to mingle with the anxious fear in the pit of her belly. Half the oars were unshipped now, and lashed under the benches. That gave four men to each of the remaining oars, three always at work and one resting. The white foam rose higher on the waves and every now and then she felt a sense of miracle as a mountain slope of blue-black water marched by, lifting them to its summit, and for a moment the wind blew salt into her face and the horizon was the end of the world and all between a continent of waves, water, tossing spume, no living thing on it but themselves and the grey and white seabirds.

But Daniel had begun to bite his lip, and he did not eat well, nor slept, and seldom went on deck. She was on the poop, on the twentieth day, when he came suddenly up the ladder, and said abruptly, 'Turn back, Pendril. There are no islands. I've been cheated.'

'Not so, Daniel,' Pendril said. 'The islands may not be

exactly four hundred miles from the cape. And who knows where the currents have set us? But we have come to no harm . . .'

'I want to turn back,' Daniel said fretfully. They faced each other, the thick, square red man and the tall, willowy dark man: deep blue eyes and liquid brown eyes. Tamar saw Daniel bending under the other's blunt obstinacy, and cried 'My husband is the captain. Obey him!'

'Him, perhaps. Not you,' the boatswain said . . . 'Think of the gold, Daniel. You'll be rich.'

'We're rich already,' she cried. 'Turn back, Daniel.'

'Gold,' Pendril said again; Daniel muttered, 'Keep on another week then. Seven days. No more.' He turned and went below.

She stood face to face with the boatswain, her hands clenched. Anger and hate were tensing her like two powerful arms bending a bow. Pendril smiled grimly and she lashed out with all her strength, and his hand went to the knife at the back of his belt. Then he turned his back on her. In that instant something fluttered out of the sky and landed between them, at her feet. She stopped, wondering – it was a little bird with a short, thick beak and yellow and green plumage. It lay trembling in her hand, its heart pounding.

She said 'It's a land bird. Come from the west.' Pendril's eyes were steady on her, and a redder mark was spreading on his ruddy cheek. 'It's from the islands,' she said. 'You were right . . . I . . . I apologize. I'll show the bird to Daniel. Then he'll know you – he – both of you, were right to go on.'

Pendril stalked forward before she had finished. She took the bird down to her husband, but he refused to be cheered, only crouched, his back against the stern port, brooding.

71

Three more days passed. She fed the little bird, and it lived in a nest she made for it out of some wool. Daniel brooded, and saw no one until the twenty-fourth day. Then, the wind blowing stronger, a slanting rain driving down from low clouds, and Pendril at the steering oar, he beckoned one of the sailors into the cabin and told Tamar to go on deck.

Next day the wind dropped a little, and the white water tossed less violently on top of the waves, though the waves themselves grew larger. Daniel spoke, one by one, with three more sailors. On the twenty-sixth day the clouds built up again soon after noon, and the light began to fail. Towards mid-afternoon the sun slid behind dark clouds. Here and there a thin ray stabbed down on to the mountainous waste of the ocean, the water slate blue and the clouds the same colour. To the north-west, deeper grey rain curtains hung from cloud to heaving sea.

Pendril was on the poop. She felt deeply uneasy, for she had never seen such a sky, or such a sea. She spoke low to him, 'Should we not turn back? This frightens me.'

For a moment she thought he was going to curse her, but he said, 'It does look frightening, and we will be shaken about. These are big waves. But the ship is good. We have only to keep her head to the waves, and not lose our nerve. Go below, to your husband.'

She shook her head – 'I'd rather stay here, where I can see.'

The wind note rose like a keening bird, the bow gave a sudden violent lurch, a sheet of water surged out to either side, and the figurehead plunged in to her neck. The sailors had often told Tamar there was no danger until the *Kedesha* wet her breasts: now she was going deeper at every wave.

The black storm raced across the sea and struck. Tamar

crouched gasping under the gunwale. The wind shrieked, the rain deluged down. Lightning split the sky directly over the mast, thunder cracked round the whole horizon. The sea was lit by shivering curtains of light. Under the thunder she heard the howling of the rowers like doomed animals below. The stern sank and the figurehead's back-thrust shoulders shook against the lightning in that same obscene dance she had witnessed at Carteia. The stern rose, the dancer plunged her breasts into the sea. Sheets of water surged along the deck and poured down the hatches on to the rowers below.

As suddenly as it came, the squall passed, and fled eastward on the wind. Daniel put his head up through the hatch, looked about, and disappeared. A sailor called from below deck, 'Will you come down here a minute, boatswain?'

Pendril shouted, 'I can't. I'm at the steering oar. What is it?'

No one answered for a moment and then a sailor came up out of the hatch, and another, and another . . . 'What's this?' Pendril's voice was sharp. 'No more on deck!' But they kept coming.

Pendril threw his weight on the steering oar, the bow swung to starboard, and the ship keeled far over. Half a ton of water crashed on the deck, forward, as she rolled diagonally across the seas. All six sailors were on deck now, and Daniel too, all hanging to the port gunwale.

'Put the oar down, Pendril, or you'll have us all over!' a sailor screamed.

'What have you come for?' Pendril said. 'Ah, I see it in your faces. To kill me! Because our captain's lost his nerve. How much has he promised to pay you?' He glared at Daniel. 'We all go together. A move, and I'll put her over.'

Daniel muttered something that Tamar could not hear, and two sailors dropped out of sight down the hatch. Daniel said, 'We don't mean any harm, Pendril . . . Only, you have disobeyed my orders . . . I told the sailors . . . we think you should . . . just be reasonable . . .'

'They're getting a bow,' Pendril said suddenly. 'I'll put her over now.' He looked at Tamar. 'For your sake, I'm sorry.' She was standing very close to him and he muttered. 'Will you take the oar? Lean on it, as I do . . . but the other way. Will you?'

'What's he saying?' Daniel called. 'Do nothing, Tamar. Stand back . . .'

She hesitated. Her husband . . . the great waves, terrifying her, loosening her springs of action . . . the sailor coming up through the hatch, the bow in his hand, the arrow already notched . . . Pendril's deep blue eyes, and a word half formed on his lips . . . the little bird . . . She lunged forward and threw her weight against the steering oar, the bow heaved slowly round. Pendril stepped back, whipped his knife from its sheath, and flung it. The man with the bow and arrow dropped back down the hatch, and it was in her husband Daniel's throat that the knife quivered, only the handle showing. Daniel plucked at it, a terrible gurgling in his throat. He stumbled to the side, and Tamar let go of the oar and ran towards him. The ship lurched and Daniel fell over the gunwale. She looked over the side, but could see nothing, only the sea.

'Back to your posts, all,' Pendril said quietly from the steering oar. 'The storm is coming back. We must pull together or we will . . .'

A bolt of lightning and a close chord of thunder drowned the rest of his sentence, and a savage jerk of the vessel flung Tamar to her knees. 'Hold *hard* now,' Pendril said.

Night fell.

Daniel was dead. Her husband. Or her child? Why did he marry her? Had he expected to go on playing children's games all their lives? Even this searching for gold was a game, a treasure hunt, to him.

Pendril shouted, 'I am sorry, Tamar.'

She went below, and tried to think of Daniel-ben-Eliab, because she thought she ought to; but she could not. After an hour she got up, and went about the ship, giving the rowers water, and the sailors wine.

It was the opposite of the night of the orgy at Carteia. Then the hours started slowly and gradually moved faster; now they went fast, and gradually slowed, though there was no minute, no second free. The roaring and groaning of creaking and crying were continuous. There were always three sailors at the steering oar. Pendril was always moving, from bow to stern, from upper deck to lower, exhorting, cursing, encouraging. In the reflected lightning she saw oars smashed and new ones put in the rowers' hands. She saw three rowers rise together from their bench and stumble like blind men towards the ladder to the deck, and Pendril run at them, his knife drawn. One man fell in the gangway, another was flung like a stone against the bulkhead by a lurch of the ship, and the third, when he stumbled back to his oar, could not control it and the end kicked up under his chin, breaking his neck. Pendril pulled in the oar and lashed it down.

As time slowed her bones ached, her head throbbed, and she did not know where she was or what she was doing. Once lightning fell slowly from the sky and in it, like a held lantern, she saw Pendril's face, the teeth bared, the water held on his skin, not falling down. Then again darkness. Out of the darkness he spoke – 'I love you.'

Light spread, and all was grey where before it had been black or violet or slate. Low clouds raced across the sea, but the waves were becoming less. After two hours a yellow tinge came to the day, and watery rays of sunshine began to lighten the colour of the waves. By noon, the storm was past.

'Take in four more oars a side,' Pendril said wearily to the rowmaster. 'Just keep her head to the sea until dark, Let the rest sleep.'

Then he looked at Tamar and said quietly, 'Will you go to my cabin?'

She went down the ladder and into his cabin, and pulled the canvas curtain closed across the front, towards the rowers. She knelt on the sheepskin which was his bed, took the silver pins from her hair and shook it down. Something white swayed on the wooden side of the ship beside the sheepskin. She leaned forward, peering in the dim grey light, and saw that it was the fang she had found in the cave on the Rock, but carved now into the shape of a naked woman, the hole in the thick part now made as though a part of an elaborately rolled arrangement of her hair, piled on top of her head. She was lovely, a small smile on her face, the breasts pointed, the sexual slit clear. So this was the meaning of the scraping she had heard so often, so long, since they left the Rock . . .

Arms slipped round her from behind, and his voice whispered in her ear. 'It is for you, Tamar. It is of you, also – as I imagine you.'

She turned and lay, eyes closed, feeling him raise her robe, and slide it gently over her shoulders and head. She waited. His face came down on hers, wet and cold from the sea. Her lips parted, her body gave one fierce tremor then all cold was gone, all fear. She was warm, and she heard her own voice murmuring, 'Dearest . . . Pendril!' A

76

luxurious flowering began in her body and she spread herself to enfold him, lying now spreadeagled, all herself exposed and given, her arms round his neck, her eyes wide, smiling up at him. She clasped her legs around him and a long thrusting began, sliding deeper to her heart. Tears flooded her eyes, and she moaned in time with the creak and heave of the ship. The *Kedesha* rose on a mighty wave, slid down, farther, farther, surely she must go under, go under ... rose again, intolerably fast now, dizzy, shaking against the sun, down, faster faster, and this time under, plunged into swirling green-blue-red depths. She heard a long cry, like a seagull whistling down the wind, and was gone.

When she awoke she was alone. She lay back, her arms folded behind her head, and basked in the warmth still glowing inside her. There was no light, so it must be night. She stretched and smiled. He would come back soon.

She heard his step, then the rustle of the canvas, and held out her arms; but he fumbled for her hands, found them, and held them. He said, 'We've sprung a leak on the waterline. It's not serious, but I must lighten the ship to raise the place out of the water ... throw overboard all the cargo. And all the food and water we can spare. They've started doing it already. So we must turn back.'

'There'll be another time, when the wind is fair,' she said.

'Will you come?'

'I shall come.'

'I told you, I was sorry about Daniel. I liked him. He could see farther than I. I have to touch, to feel, smell something before it is real, but he could imagine ...'

'Too much,' she said sadly.

He kissed her hands. 'We're going back. I think I will build a house in Carteia for us.'

'The Rock will be our fortress,' she said. 'Or will you be afraid of the spirits of the great cave?'

'Not if you're with me,' he said seriously. 'I shall go to sea sometimes. And I shall harvest the shells to make the Tyrian purple. I shall grow grapes and olives such as they have never tasted in Carthage. My phallus shall plough my own soil and make it fertile of lusty men and proud women.' He put his hand on her belly, and squeezed gently.

'Our children shall be sons of the Covenant,' she said. 'For they will be born of the womb of a Judaean.'

He said, 'Well, I shall learn to do the correct things and say the proper prayers. Anything for a quiet life in the house. Besides, I like the sound of Hebrew songs.'

'Good. But you have yet to ask me to marry you. I am not a slave, to be disposed of at someone else's will.'

He said, 'Do you say yes, or no?'

She said, '*Verastech li leolam*. I betroth thee unto me for ever.'

Book Three

PHOENICIA, CARTHAGE, ROMAN REPUBLIC

The Jewish years 3188–3831
180 823 A.U.C.
573 B.C. – A.D. 70

THE rulers of the Rock, and the overlords of Carteia, were the Kings of Carthage. In 273 B.C. arrived Hamilcar, King of Carthage, with his son Hannibal, to extend their grip from a few coast towns over most of Spain. This brought Carthage into conflict with the Roman Republic. In 190 B.C. Carthage was finally crushed, and succeeded by Rome. Gadir became Gades, and as the Romans put more men and money into the conquest of Spain, their first real colony, it increased until it became the second city of the later republic.

Carteia fell on bad times. It had been founded by a commercial people to take advantage of the tunny fishing and the supplies of murex to make the purple dye. In times of war and conflict the Rock goes up in importance, but a small port like Carteia goes down. By the end of the Punic Wars (Rome against Carthage) it was perhaps in ruins, perhaps vanished altogether. Its resurrection was close at hand.

In 171 B.C. the consuls for the year being Licinius Crassus and Gaius Gassius Longinus, the Praetor Lucius Canuleius found himself with a problem. His legionaries had fathered some 4,000 children on Celtiberian slave women encountered in the course of the wars in Spain. They were not allowed to marry these women though in many cases they wanted to, as a legionary could not marry a slave. The Praetor solved his problem by founding, on the site of Carteia (if it previously existed!) a Colonia Libertinorum of the same name. It was sufficiently important to be permitted to mint its own coins.

As Spain had been the scene of the first spreading of the wings of the Roman Republic, so in its soil was laid the first foundations of the Roman Empire, when Julius Caesar defeated the sons of his chief rival, Pompey, at Munda (near Coin, province of Malaga) on March 17, 45 B.C. After the battle, while Caesar concentrated on seizing the rest of Andalusia, Gneus Pompey and some of his followers escaped to Carteia. Pompey was carried there in a litter, since he had been wounded in the foot. As soon as he and his party arrived, the town magistrate sent a message to Caesar offering to give him up. Caesar sent a detachment down to take him, but Pompey managed to escape in a boat – past the Rock he must have gone, past the magic forest, the great cave, the secret shrine of Hercules: but Caesar's men pursued, a sea fight followed, and Pompey was driven ashore. He limped away to a last fight on a hill. Defeated again, he took refuge in a cave, and there on April 12, with Caesar's relentless hounds on his heels, he fell on his own sword.

It is a grim tragedy, marching inexorable as the legions to its appointed end. But what hill? Where was the sea fight? Did they never leave the bay? Was that the last scene played out in one of the Rock's uncountable caves, which have given brief refuge, over uncountable years to uncountable other victims?

Caesar is dead. Long live Caesar.

In Judaea a child was born into a time of trouble for the unruly province and its stiff-necked people were beginning to chafe under the yoke of new masters – Rome, again. In A.D. 68, on the death of Nero, a series of civil wars broke out for the possession of the purple. Galba, Otho, Vitellius and, at last, Vespasian, succeeded each other in rapid succession. An uneasy calm returned – a little war here, a little insurrection there, some expansion here, some withdrawal there – which was to be the general condition of the Empire for three centuries.

The *Colonia* of Carteia, near the western limit of the Empire, lived through this time, too . . .

A PRIVATE SACRIFICE

THE twenty men of the Town Watch moved slowly across the side of the Rock, their spear points glistening dully, loose stones rattling under their sandals. Julius, their honorary commander, was in the centre, carrying a sword and wearing his old centurion's helmet with the transverse crest. Fifty paces behind him, the Aedile Octavius led a dozen volunteers of all ages, who had come out to join in the manhunt for the pleasure of it. It was a close and airless day, for the east wind was blowing and its oppressive cloud hung over the Rock.

Julius saw that all his men were sweating heavily, and they looked tired, though they had been on the go barely three hours. Everyone was too young or too old, that was the trouble with watch-and-wards everywhere. In a legion the men would hardly have been damp by now, just smelling a little acid as the wine leached out through their leathery skins. His helmet felt intolerably heavy, and he discovered he was walking like a turtle, his head thrust forward under its weight. He swore and straightened up; but age was one enemy not even a retired centurion of the Twentieth could hold at bay for ever, he reflected gloomily.

He stubbed his toe on a sharp stone and swore again. This was a bad way to be celebrating the first week of a new year – it was the 6th of Tishri – hunting down poor devils of escaped mine slaves. Work in the mines up-country was enough to drive a free man to drink even with the good pay. That's why the only free men were over-seers. The rest were slaves, captives of war, criminals, and such as these Turdetani, local tribesmen rounded up by a pressgang for the mine management. 'Run them down like dogs,' Marcus the Duovir had said before they started out.

From behind, one of the volunteers called, 'Straight ahead. A hundred paces!'

Julius looked up sharply, for it was his son's voice. The young man ran to his side, calling, 'There, father!' Ahead he saw several human shapes flitting in and out of the wild olives. Now they were in the open, running away along the slope towards the south.

'Well done, Fidus. You have sharp eyes.' The Aedile's voice was languid, as always.

Julius plodded on. His eldest son, Barak – or Fidus, as he preferred to call himself – would go a long way. Any father should be proud of such a son. But – Julius frowned – he was a little too eager to please, a little too eager for blood. It was all very well for the Duovir to talk of these Turdetani as dogs, but they weren't, they were peasants of the soil, mountain men, goatherds, players on the oaten pipe and the bagpipe. In their own village they wore roughly worked jewels and coarse-hammered armlets of gold. Their women were beautiful, and for great occasions twined their long hair round long rods set on top of their heads, and then draped a veil over all.

Dogs? If they were dogs, then so were the Judaeans, his own ancestors, whom Rome was chastising at this moment. As a legionary he used to think that all the people he fought were ignorant savages; but the police action in Judea, which seemed to have started last year, made him think again, and deeply. His father used to pray for Jerusalem every day. His mother had wept, on her death bed, because she was going to die without seeing the Temple. If Jerusalem meant so much to him and his people, then all these others, the barbarians, must surely have their own proper loves and prides, which ought to be respected.

A man to his right said, 'Here they come!' It was just below the Great Cave. Perhaps the six Turdetani had thought to shelter in it, but they were out now, running, with a high, trembling scream. They came straight at Julius, and the watch closed in. The Aedile called, 'Try not to kill them, men. They're worth good money!'

But the fellow running bare-handed at Julius seemed determined to be killed, a wild-eyed tall man with reddish hair and eyes as blue as Julius's own, naked but for a rag round his loins. Julius made to lunge with his sword and as the man dodged sideways, snarling, he stepped back, and hit him hard on the temple with the pommel of the sword. The man stumbled and Julius jumped on him, hit him again, and cried, 'Lie still, fool. You want to live, don't you?' For a minute the fighting was general, and Julius saw his son kill a tribesman with a neat spear thrust: but it had been necessary, he gave him that. Then suddenly it was over, and they had five battered prisoners and a corpse.

Julius took off his helmet and mopped his forehead. The Watch began to rope the prisoners together. The Aedile Octavius said, 'For a moment I thought they'd gone round to the Eagle's Nest cave at the Rock. It's a bad place to have to get them out of.'

'Nearly impossible, Aedile, I think,' young Barak said importantly, 'but there's no escape, either. They'd either have to surrender, starve, or jump. Seven hundred feet!'

'There's no escape anywhere on the Rock,' the Aedile said, 'except perhaps in the Great Cave. No one's ever explored that. Some say it goes on for ever.'

'There's no escape from Rome anywhere, now,' Julius said. 'The Rock at least looks like a place where you can die with honour.'

Then they started back for Carteia, the prisoners carrying their dead comrade, and the Watch and the volunteers surrounding them.

'Walk with me, Julius,' the Aedile Octavius said. 'They can look after themselves ... especially with your Fidus among them. A very capable young man. You know, if we spend a little money, I believe we have influence enough between us, with Marcus's help, to get Fidus appointed to the Seventh as a tribune, direct.'

'He would be overjoyed,' Julius said formally.

'I will speak privately to Marcus,' Octavius said.

The two men fell silent, and walked on together without more words. They were both near fifty; both had served over twenty-five years in the Twentieth Legion, *Valeria Victrix*; both had been settled six years in Carteia, which special privileges and exemptions to veterans made a particularly desirable place of retirement; they were friends, liked and admired each other well, and in the years of campaigning had saved each other's lives and got drunk together more times than either could count, and in the long British wars shared several snub-nosed English whores. Both were married – Octavius recently and officially; Julius in Rome 23 years ago to a slim girl of his own faith; but, as private soldiers were forbidden to marry he had to pretend through the rest of his army career that the woman who trailed along behind the legion as and when she could was only a concubine, like the rest of them.

For the rest, they were different as men could be: Octavius – Roman-born, cynical, immoral, brave only when he had to be but then amazingly debonair – the perfect Camp Prefect and politician: Julius – Carteian-born, son of a Judaean ex-legionary, direct, courageous, devout, dutiful above all – the perfect centurion, farmer, and honorary, incorruptible head of the Town Watch.

Striding easily along together, as they had done so often, they turned the last angle of rock and passed from under the cloud into sunlight. The sandy isthmus curved away like a golden finger crooked below them. The sun shone on rippling blue water, and white clouds travelled like lambs across the mountains beyond. They could see the river mouth, a score of jetties thrust out into it, palm trees and the masts of ships; and in the town, houses of white and marble, the green of gardens, and all around golden wheat, rusty vineyards, grey-green olive groves.

The Aedile sighed – 'Peace, plenty, bliss. Or so it appears on the surface . . . What do you hear of Horatius Naso?'

'The man who some of us hoped would succeed Galba?'

'Yes.'

'Nothing. Why?'

'Well, as you know Vespasian succeeded Galba, and is our undoubted Emperor. Nevertheless, it seems that many are still not content, and are working in secret to elevate Horatius Naso to the purple. You know I went to Gades last week . . . it was to learn more of this movement . . . to decide whether it would be wisest to denounce it, or join it. I learned that it is strong, but not strong enough. It is supported by a number of discontented or jealous men, and by the people of this new blood-drinking sect, the Nazarenes ... and by many of your co-religionists.'

'Jews? Why?'

'Because of the severe campaign Vespasian's son is waging in Judaea, I suppose.'

'By God, in that case I could join this Horatius Naso myself,' Julius said.

'And lose your land, and your head! Listen to me, my friend. First, Naso cannot win. Understand that, grasp it! *He cannot win*. Second, the loyalists will use the conspiracy for their own advancement. To be safe, you must act on the winning side, and you must do it publicly. This is doubly important for you, as a Jew ... The conspirators are not quite ready yet and we are going to strike first. In Carteia there are some thirty of us, all men of influence. Marcus is our leader, and though we hope we shall not have to shed blood we are quite prepared to do so. We shall seize the chief places and people of Carteia – as our friends will be doing in Gades and Hispalis and other towns – in order to make sure that no local authority can declare for Naso. At the same time we'll imprison the local conspirators until it is clear that the rising has failed all over Hispania ... or, if it *should* perchance succeed elsewhere, then they will be useful to us as hostages.'

Julius said, 'Why are you telling me this? I don't want to take part.'

'You are the commander of the Watch, are you not?' Octavius said gently. 'Does it not strike you that you would be one of those we would have to seize, unless you were on our side? Besides, your son is leading the assault group. He will be the one to take the other magistrates prisoner.'

'Barak?' Julius cried. 'He didn't tell me.'

'Join us,' Octavius said. 'Marcus detests all Judaeans as insolent rebels. And he's been trying to get your vineyard ever since you planted it.'

Julius strode on along the sand, his head glumly bent. It was like the army again: will you have bread for dinner or bread? He said, 'I'll come. But . . .'

'Midnight then, the third night . . . We meet in your back garden. Fidus suggested it.'

They were at the gate of the town, and soon afterwards parted. When Julius reached his house his son Barak was not yet home. He'd have to talk to him tomorrow about this idea of getting a tribuneship right away. It was a great responsibility for an inexperienced youngster. Besides . . . His wife Gavrielah put her hand on his arm and said, 'You look worried. What is it?'

'I wish I could tell you,' he said. She seemed older than her forty-one years. It had not been an easy life, following the legion and trying to raise a family on soldier's pay. She was almost as tall as he, frail now, some of her teeth gone, her hair grey and her skin wrinkled, but the eyes – deep, large, dark – had never lost their first magic for him. He looked solemnly into them now, and saw that his worry had infected her. 'Is it about Barak?' she asked.

'No,' he said, then – 'Yes. In a way . . . And about Jerusalem.'

'We'll be able to go next year, as we planned, won't we?' she said anxiously. 'Surely the war will be over by then.'

'It'll be over,' Julius said grimly.

'You promised your mother you'd go to Jerusalem, and celebrate Passover in the Temple, and make the sacrifices.'

Julius did not speak. The Temple at Jerusalem was a dream to him, yet as real as the Rock outside there. He was a Roman citizen, but his body and spirit shared two homes, mysteriously unified – the Rock and the Temple.

'I don't know,' he said finally. 'I'll have to do my duty, that's all.'

The Naso conspiracy was not much of an affair, and two hours after the loyalist group had moved out from Julius's back garden the forum, curia, temples, baths, and mint were secured, and a score or so prisoners safe in jail, including two of the other magistrates and the Quaestor. Julius himself had held the jail with six reliable men of the Watch, and received the prisoners as they were brought in. His son Barak came early with the magistrates, went off, and returned half an hour later with half a dozen other dazed and frightened men.

Most of the prisoners started clamouring of their innocence before they were through the gates, but Shmuel Ben Zion, a short fat old lawyer and the head of Carteia's small Jewish community was defiant, 'Stop whining!' he snapped at the others jammed into the little cell with him, as Julius bolted the door – 'We should have struck earlier, that's all.' He glowered at Julius through the bars in the smoky lantern light. 'And may the plagues of Egypt afflict you and your fine son and all your family, for what you have done tonight.'

'I have only done my duty to my acknowledged and lawful Emperor,' Julius said angrily, for he felt guilt over the business. 'He is your Emperor, too.'

'No more,' Ben Zion said. 'He is no Emperor, but abomination.'

'Hush, hush,' the other prisoners hissed nervously.

'Abomination,' Ben Zion repeated. 'Every stone of the ruined Temple cries out, Abomination!'

Julius's head began to ache. 'The Temple?' he said. 'Of Jerusalem? Ruined?'

'Utterly destroyed, razed, not one stone left upon another. The ground ploughed and sown with salt. The Ark of the Covenant taken to Rome for a triumph. All this by your Vespasian's son, Titus, in *his* name and with *his* approval.'

'But, when . . . ?' Julius began.

The lawyer said, 'Go, Julius Cohen-ki. No true Jew has anything more to say to you.'

In the public baths next day, Julius lay naked on the marble slab of the caldarium, his eyes closed. His son Barak occupied the next slab. They were sweating heavily as attendants scraped their skins with strigils.

'The Temple was destroyed, Jerusalem sacked, and all the Zealots killed on the 9th of Ab in your calendar,' Barak said. 'Nearly two months ago. The news was suppressed to give the authorities throughout the empire time to take measures against possible uprisings. Marcus and Octavian knew some time ago . . .'

The heat burned Julius's eyeballs through the closed lids. His hair was scorching, his very fundament burning. What law said a man had to suffer such torture? He sat up to go.

'They told *me* a week ago,' Barak said proudly.

Julius sank back. It was will-power that had to be practised, and maintained. It was man's duty to face the caldarium and the frigidarium. YHWH did not intend life to be one long doze in the baths, under the hands of skilful catamites.

'Barak,' he said. 'Do you feel ashamed that we helped, even so little, to keep Vespasian in power? I do.'

'Finished,' the attendants said. Julius and his son staggered into the next room and stepped down into the huge hot bath.

'I do not,' Barak said. 'And I am going to give up the practice of your religion. I no longer believe in it, and it will be a handicap to me in my career. Please call me Fidus from now on, as my friends have been doing for some time now.'

It was strange, how this very hot water felt quite cool after the caldarium, Julius thought. For a time, that is; soon the effects wore off, and you began to wish they'd pour some cold in.

'Marcus promised me, last night, that he'd get me a tribuneship in the Seventh,' Barak said.

No, it was Fidus now. *Fidus*, faithful. Faithful to whom? to what?

'I had to worship Divine Caesar, of course,' Julius said. 'Everyone does. That's forbidden by our Law, but our priests wink at it. Otherwise I never found being a Jew any hindrance to me. Rather the opposite for people like us, who are not Romans of Rome. Jerusalem and the Temple were strong-holds – places of refuge – home, for the spirit, when it was oppressed.'

'Time,' the attendants said. They moved to the unctorium and lay down on two marble slabs. The perfumed attendants began to rub perfumed oil into their skins.

'*My* spiritual home is Rome,' Fidus said. 'And you were only a centurion. Higher up, I think, to be a Jew would be a severe hindrance, even danger, to me.'

He's twenty-two, Julius thought, and in a few months he'll be higher up in the army than I reached in twenty-five years of service. At the same time he'll gain equestrian rank. Then there'll be no limit to what he might become – tribune, governor, legate. . . . Caesar. Yes: do your duty, guard your back, obey orders, look out for the main chance, kill rivals, and any citizen could become Caesar.

He shook his head and muttered, 'Impossible.'

'What is, sir?' the attendant said.

He said, 'Nothing. I didn't mean, *impossible*. I meant *wrong*.'

He must talk to Gavrielah. He got up and headed for the apodyterium, where his clothes were. 'Sir, you've missed the frigidarium,' the attendant cried reproachfully. Julius swore under his breath, turned, and went to the frigidarium.

When he reached home the younger boys and girls – there were five of them – seemed subdued, and Gavrielah's eyes were damp. He beckoned her to follow him up to the roof. He sat down there under the rush awning, and she stood before him, arms folded. 'Marcus has ordered the execution of four of the chief conspirators tomorrow. Cneus, the Quaestar. Sextus. And two Jews – Jochanan the wine merchant, and Shmuel Ben Zion. The rest he has fined and released.'

Julius nodded. 'Is that all?'

'No. He has taken the *menorah* from Jochanan's house and Ben Zion's *Torah*, and thrown them down before the statue of Vespasian in the Temple, as offerings.'

Julius stared dully at the great Rock face a league away to the south. No refuge there. No refuge anywhere.

'It must not be,' he said.

'No,' his wife said. 'It must not be.'

Refuge was the wrong word now, he thought it was no

longer a matter of refuge, but of duty, or sacrifice. Whose sacrifice?

'I am ready,' Gavrielah said. 'With the Temple gone, that all my life I had dreamed of, I do not feel that I am really alive. Yet I love you.' She put her hand on his head, and stroked his cheek.

'Our people will be dispersed all over the world,' Julius said. 'They will have no home now. Nor will we, for Jerusalem was our home, too.'

'Perhaps we should bow our necks, so that they of the dispersal will have places to come to,' Gavrielah said.

'Perhaps,' Julius said, 'but what if bowing the neck only makes it easier for them to cut off your head? . . . And there are the children to be considered. Ophira's only eleven . . . Leave me, wife, I must think.'

It was the 9th day of Tishri, harvest time. From his roof here near the edge of the town he could see the woods across the river. The hills beyond were full of great bustard and succulent partridge. All around stretched the wheat. On the threshing floors mules trotted out in circles, drawing sledges, and children rode the sledges, threshing the wheat. Men threw up the grain on long shovels, winnowing, and the wind blew the chaff away in a golden haze. He could see the paved road, and the warehouses piled with wool, and the long sheds of the tunny pickling factory. The wind blew from the west, cool with a freshness from the great ocean. There was a smell of autumn flowers and ripe corn in the air, and over all the gold of the threshing. They would have been harvesting in Judaea, too, when the legion went up against the city. He could see the auxiliaries, out in front, making their short rushes, shouting their shrill war cries that made the legionaries laugh and imitate them. Behind, he saw the steady tramp and clink of the legion, the *optios* on the flank measuring the pace for each century, the eagle riding steadily on above the dust . . .

Near the sunset there was a purple light on the bay and he could think that it was not a reflection of the sky but the dye itself, leaking from the vats to the west to stain the sea. It was the colour of the Judaean priests, that purple. Men wore it in stripes on their prayer shawls, and often the wrappings of the Law were dyed the same purple. Two years ago the community here had bought a specially good amphora of the dye and sent it as a gift to the Temple treasury at Jerusalem. It would all have been used up before . . . the end.

The Rock stood up like a strong man, uncapped, bare-headed, neck unbowed, shadowed grey face turned square to the land. It was a strange Rock, joined to the land but not part of it. Many grazed their flock on it, but none owned it, not even the colonia. The idea of owning it seemed sacrilegious, as to say, who owns the TZUR YIS-RAEL, the Rock of Israel? It was a good place to make a sacrifice, even as the pagans and the tribes did.

The sun set. The 10th day of Tishri, the Day of Atonement, had begun. He got up, sighing and shivering. Then he squared his shoulders. It couldn't be any worse than facing the frigidarium.

Two hours after he lay down to sleep he awoke, because he had set himself to do so. The little naked woman of ivory, his family's heirloom and love charm for the marriage bed, gleamed pale where she hung on the wall above his head. He knew that Gavrielah, beside him in the alcove was awake. Probably she had not slept at all. He said, 'I must go now, my love. I may not come back.'

'I know. What do you tell me to do?'

'Know nothing. Rely on Fidus.'

He bent and kissed her long on the mouth, then left her, went to the outer room, and dressed as though for a legion ceremony – tunic, breeches, cuirass, cloak, woollen neck cloth, sword, dagger, boots and his centurion's helmet. He hooked his shield on to his left arm and faced the alcove where the gods would have been kept in a pagan household. He bowed three times to the menorah set up in it, then left the house and marched slowly up the street towards the prison.

He met and saw no one. A cloud passed over the moon as he neared the prison and he approached the sentry's post in almost complete darkness. The man was half asleep, pacing slowly in front of the main gate, his drawn sword rested flat on his shoulder, his head nodding. It was an old ex-soldier of the Seventh. He turned as the cloud passed away from the moon, and saw the centurion striding towards him, the cloak billowing, the great helmet glowing. He straightened, bringing the hilt of his sword to his mouth. Julius raised his own right hand in salute, and stepped straight in behind the short dagger in his left. It struck under the ribs and the sentry toppled silently, blood gushing from his mouth. Julius lowered him to the ground, and quietly opened the main gate. As he thought, the rest of the watch on duty were asleep in the guardroom, and closed the gate, bolting it from inside.

With the dead man's sword in hand he entered the prison building and went to the cell where the five Turdetani were awaiting an escort from the mines to take them back into slavery. They were awake, and he whispered in their tongue, which he knew almost as well as he knew Latin – 'I am going to release you, on one condition. That you take four other prisoners, Romans, with you, and see that they escape to Hispalis, or wherever in Baetica they want to go.'

95

No one spoke. Then a voice from the dark muttered, 'Who is it? Why do you do this?'

Julius said, 'I am a Jew. The Romans have done worse to my people than to you. I do this . . .' he searched for the right words, that these men would understand and appreciate: '. . . to make peace with myself.'

'You are he who saved my life when you could have killed me on the Rock,' the voice said. Julius remembered the man well, for his red hair and blue eyes, though he could not see them now. 'I am called Pendreth,' the man went on 'a leader among my people. We will do as you ask. I give you my word.'

Julius pulled back the double bolts and said, 'Take this sword. Use it if you have to. Come.' At the end of the prison he found the four condemned conspirators in a single cell. One muttered, as he worked the bolt, 'Already?' but Julius answered 'Quiet! I have come to release you. The Turdetani will take you to the hills and hide you until this blows over, as I think it will soon. Or you can start life again in another city, and send secret word for your families to join you . . . Follow me now, all, but make no sound.'

He led the way out of the building. The Watch snored in the guardroom and when he was outside, he bolted them in. Then he pushed the tribesmen and prisoners into a rough file and, at their side as though in charge, sword drawn, he marched them to the wicket gate in the town wall, near his house. It was unguarded except in times of war or tribal unrest. 'Farewell, Ben Zion,' he said in a low voice. 'If I do anything for the Covenant tonight, it is thanks to you . . . Farewell, Pendreth.'

The chieftain clasped his hand – 'Where are you going? Come with us.'

Julius said, 'I have more to do yet. None of you should

know of it, in case, later, you are interrogated.' He raised his hand, closed the gate, and went back into the town.

The Temple of Jupiter and the Temple of the Divine Caesar stood next to each other in the Forum. Votive lamps burned in each, shining on garland-hung busts of gods and emperors. Before the busts there were offerings of food in earthenware bowls, and wine in rare jars.

Julius threw down the images so that they broke. He scattered the flowers, overturned the food and wine, and set fire to the curtains with the votive lamps. It only took two minutes, then he gathered up the *menorah* and the *Torah* that had been cast before the bust of Vespasian, and went quickly towards the house of Marcus, the chief magistrate. Putting down the sacred objects at a little distance, he went on. A servant lay asleep across the threshold, but Julius's dagger quietened him before he could stir. Julius went through the atrium to the side room where he expected that Marcus would be sleeping. He was there, a low oil wick smoking and his wife beside him on the couch. He started up with a cry as Julius entered the room, snatched a torch and dipped it in the flame. He stumbled back, fumbling for the sword on a table behind him, the red flames bursting high, his wife's face frozen.

'Julius, the centurion,' he cried.

'Julius the Jew,' Julius said. 'Come to make amends for what I did . . . or didn't do . . . last night. And to punish a needless sacrilege.'

'You'll never escape alive,' Marcus said. 'And killing me won't help the Jews in Judaea, or anywhere else.'

'There are times when a man can't afford to be reasonable,' Julius said. 'Otherwise he finds himself walking meekly into the slaughterhouse.'

Marcus snatched the sword from the table, but Julius struck first, plunging his sword straight through the other's body and a hand's width out behind, to the left of the spine. The Duovir fell back across the couch. Julius put his foot on his neck and jerked out his sword. To the woman he said, 'I am alone. Tell them, when they come.' He strode out of the house, gathered up the *menorah* and *Torah*, walked to the wicket gate, and left the town. At the beach he turned left and walked along the sand towards the dim bulk of the Rock. When he reached it he found a patch of grass, wrapped his cloak about him, put his shield under his head, and slept. After a time dreams troubled him, but not of his wife or children, whom he could never see again, nor of all the dead in all his battles; but of a naked woman, terrified, running, a low-browed woman, ugly but with deep, lovely eyes, who cried to him for help.

He awoke then, and it was dawn. He continued south, moving diagonally up and across the West face of the Rock, past the Great Cave but lower, until he reached a flat place half a mile from the southernmost point, where the mass of the mountain ended its first severe southward fall. Here he sat down, facing the way he had come. He felt hungry for a time, but that passed.

He waited there on the edge of the escarpment until nearly noon. Then he saw the party working along the edge of the sea below. There were six horsemen including some dignitary in a purple-lined cloak, and twenty men of the Watch, on foot, led by the Aedile – he recognized Octavius's grey stallion. He smiled slightly to think what a compliment they were paying an ageing centurion to bring so many against him.

At last one of the men saw him – the sun may have glittered on his helmet, or touched the red of its horsehair plume – and pointed, and called out. Julius stood up and, without hurrying crossed the escarpment towards the eastern side. A goat track led from the corner along the western cliffs. For a hundred yards it was four or five feet wide, and flat. Then the cliff swept down vertically from above, and dropped again vertically below, and a narrow ledge snaked between, sharply curved round the beak of the mountain. Beyond, the path ended in a big cave – the Eagle's Nest. There was no other approach.

Julius put away his shield – he would not need that there – and, with a brief prayer, threw the *menorah* and *Torah* into the sea seven hundred feet below. Then he waited behind the angle of the path, looking out over the water shimmering far below. The autumn crocus were in bloom, stems sprouting like tall pink girls from the crevices in the limestone. A red-legged partridge saw him and flew out from the cliff, but a falcon stooped, striking it with a great burst of feathers.

Julius was looking towards the east, towards Rome, and, beyond Rome towards Jerusalem, that was no more. The wind was from the west, so he was in shelter here, but eddies sent whorls of dust down the cliff and shook the tiny flowers in the crevices.

He heard the clink of metal on stone, and took up position, pressed into the cliff, sword raised. From round the corner Octavius spoke – 'Are you there, Julius? Alone?'

'Yes.'

'We came here once together, didn't we? The year we settled in Carteia. We were looking for wild pig, and ate bread and onions and wine in the cave. It was the first time I'd ever seen a squirting cucumber. And Fidus talked of the cave the other day. A place of no escape, he said. ... Now that Marcus is dead, and another Duovir fled, our Chief Magistrate is Plinius – a friend of yours. Things might have been arranged, but you chose a bad day. The

Procurator of the Province arrived on a surprise visit, at sunrise. He has come out with us, to see that we do our duty. He has ordered that you be taken at once, at all costs.'

'And then . . .?'

The voice from round the angle of the cliff said, 'Crucifixion, in front of the Temple. But you have a sword. I'll give you five minutes, then we'll have to come.'

'It'll be an expensive business, Octavius.'

'I know. I shall lead. In five minutes.'

Julius waited. Time passed. Another partridge, forgetful of the fate it had just witnessed, whirred out over the gulf. No falcons struck. It was warm, the sun blazing along the cliff, Africa shimmering beyond the sea, the gusty wind laden with the smell of hot stone and lavender.

Octavius came fast, crouched behind his shield, another man on his heels, spear arm drawn back. Julius stooped and stabbed at Octavius's legs below the shield. The spearman thrust, the point entering Julius's left shoulder. He hurled himself bodily against the shield, and Octavius fell. He struck left handed with the dagger. The Aedile rolled over and vanished over the cliff. The second man turned and ran.

Julius waited. He heard murmurings from along the path. Then, after a quarter of an hour, leather creaked close by.

'It is I,' a voice said, and Julius stiffened – 'Fidus.'

'My son.'

'A tribune of the Seventh Legion. The Procurator has confirmed it.'

'Your career may be rather short.'

'I am not afraid.'

He came round the angle of the rock then, spear in one

hand, dagger in the other, and no shield. Julius waited for the spearthrust, then seized the haft, jerked it out of his son's hand, and pushed it between his legs. Fidus stabbed with his dagger as he fell. The blade struck Julius low on the right side, under the ribs, and he knew he was badly wounded. Fidus fell, one leg over the edge. Julius pulled him back, his sword point at his throat.

He was bleeding heavily now. His son stared up, his eyes cold. The Day of Atonement was near its end. Julius said. 'Remember you owe your life to a Jew – twice.'

He stood, and leaped out over the edge, his legionary's sword flashing. As he dived through space he shouted 'Sha-lo-o-om!' The wind began to press against his eye-balls, and the light went out on the sea.

Book Four

ROMAN EMPIRE

The Jewish years 3831–4178
A.U.C. 823–1170
A.D. 70–417

THE sacking of Jerusalem and the destruction of the Second Temple, in A.D. 70, were only single strands in a larger pattern. Although Rome had from early times turned one face east, now it bent its whole attention in that direction. From Spain, the tide receded. Cadiz began to lose its wealth and fame. Instead of prominent Romans making their name in Spain, intelligent Spaniards made their name in Rome – for example, Pomponius Mela the geographer, born in Carteia under the Rock: and two of the greatest emperors, Trajan and Hadrian, both born in Italica, near Seville.

Life continued. At Belo (beyond Traducta) citizens worshipped at a famous temple dedicated to Jupiter, Juno, and Minerva. Trafalgar was called Cape Juno, and on it there was a temple dedicated to the goddess. Calpe-Carteia (so called to distinguish it from another Carteia near Seville) was one of the stages on the official march route between Malaga and Cadiz. The tunny fishing and preserving again flourished, and the Carteians retained their skill in making the necessary pickles and sauces. There was enough prosperity to enable some people to hoard coins in large quantities. (One such hoard was discovered on a farm near Jimena de la Frontera in the 1930s, and there must have been many more). But the hoarding of gold is not a healthy sign in any time or place. The tide of Empire began to ebb, not only in the west, but everywhere. Rome became a bauble, squabbled over by the Praetorian Guards. Justice fled, and respectable citizens, oppressed and insecure, followed the idle and the criminal into outlawry. The Rock itself suffered an extra blow from nature: about the year 300 an earthquake threw up a sandbar which ruined the harbour of Carteia. The town and colony began to decay, though the process took centuries, and even today foundations, lines of walls, and one tall tower, the so-called Tower of Cartagena, still stand from the Phoenician and Roman colony.

For several centuries the Rock had watched over Carteia. They had been years of growth, of increase, of expansion in material achievement and in man's concepts of the universe and of his place in it. There had been violent change – that had come to Neanderthal Man, too – but now, for the first time, the Rock was to witness regression, and rot.

It was not all bad, for as man suffers, the rest of nature rejoices. The carob tree and the wild olive and the wild fig would flourish, and if fewer men enjoyed the windblown scents of the Rock's rosemary and thyme and lavender, nature did not care. There would be more lynx, wildcat, pig: and the Barbary partridge, the Rock's own bird, would learn once more that its chief enemies were snakes and lizards and eagles, not man.

In the empire the milestones began to pass with increasing speed. In 323 Constantine made Christianity the official religion of the Empire. Jews were already specially taxed, but now persecution increased until another emperor, the great Julian the Apostate, restored paganism and abolished the Jews' Tax. Beyond the frontiers – indeed, inside them – the wolves gathered. The Rock was about a thousand miles from the nearest barbarians in Scotland and on the upper Rhine – but the ones who finally reached and passed it did not come from either of these places. They came from much farther away.

Until 376 the Visigoths (Western Goths) lived in what is now Rumania. Then they entered the Empire, and for a few years inhabited Bulgaria. In this period some became converted to Arian Christianity. (The difference between Arianism and Catholicism centred on barely comprehensive metaphysics about the nature of the Trinity, but that did not prevent the sects slaughtering each other in enormous numbers.) Only half pagan now, and all officially labelled as guests and allies of Rome, the Visigoths moved on west across Northern Italy and Gaul.

In 409, three other barbarian groups – the Vandals, Alans and Sueves – crossed the Pyrenees and entered Spain. In 415 the Visigoths followed. Finding the others unwilling to give up or share possession, in 416 they marched south to the Straits, gathered boats, and made to cross over to Africa. Their boats were wrecked, and those in the first wave drowned. The rest decided it would be safer to fight the Vandals than the sea, and (still ostensibly acting on behalf of Rome) set about their new enemies with a will.

While barbarians from the ends of the earth fought and marauded, sacked, pillaged, raped, and murdered, what of the ordinary people, caught in the death convulsions of the huge organism which had formed and sheltered them? How did *they* live, in these times? *Could* one live . . .?

INTO THE DARK

THE goats heard the sound first and stopped, heads
cocked, listening. Then the dog barked, and a man strode
up out of the gully ahead. Rachel saw with surprise that it
was Theophilus. He was totally naked, as always, his
white-streaked grey hair hanging like a mane on his shoulders, but she had never seen him anywhere except squatting in the mouth of his cave, in a gully at the far end of the
Rock, a bowl beside him. Now the bowl was in his left
hand and a new-peeled staff shiny white in his right. She
remembered she had brought a hard boiled egg for him,
as she usually did. She found it in her scrip and held it
out.

He said, 'The wrath of God is at hand. Say the Holy
Creed after me, and though you will die, your soul might
be saved, perchance.'

She said, 'You know we are Jews.'

'Aye, aye, murderers, drinkers of Christian blood . . .'
He passed on, muttering to himself. His body smelled like
the goats, who had fled when he appeared but gathered
again as he talked, some leaning forward to sniff his
knees.

Rachel whistled and called, the dog ran to and fro and
the goats moved on round the side of the Rock. She was
eighteen, slim, full breasted, black haired and blue eyed.
She walked barefoot on rock and thistle, and all her clothing was a black kirtle to the knee, the waist pulled in by
thirty feet of coarse cord, wound round and round into a
sash. Above, the kirtle swelled out to hold her breasts, and

in there she could put a lamb, or take bread to her father, when the scrip was full.

She moved the goats slowly along, watching them pluck sustenance from holes in the rock and climb up thin trees to eat the young shoots. In the gully near Theophilus's Cave a spring of fresh water gushed from the earth. She drank, then shooed the goats on to the flat land by the point. They spread out to graze. It had rained much the past week and the grass was lush. Rachel sprawled on her belly on top of a rock, her chin in her hands. She remained aware of the goats – she had been guarding them for twelve years now, and did what was necessary by instinct – but her thoughts were elsewhere . . . the other Pillar of Hercules, there across the narrow sea, a little cloud upon it: how near to see, how far to attain! The pale scent of a yellow flower growing in a crevice of the rock under her nose. The wind in her hair. Two partridges, red-legged, bright-eyed, oblivious in the act of love, bodies pressed down like her own, against the earth. Warm rock firm against her belly and between her thighs. She was betrothed. The marriage was for next month, when the sowing of the fields would be done. Not long to wait.

She thought again, shall I bring Avram to my cave, or shall I keep it secret, inviolate? He will enter my body, so should he not know the other, too? But, if he had done the one, would it not be all the more important to preserve to myself alone, virgin, the cave?

She got up, stood on a tall rock, and looked all round. No one. The wolves did not come to the Rock by day. The dog knew to stay with the goats, and not follow her. She could safely leave them for a few minutes.

She ran lightly up a runnel in the low cliffs behind her.

On the plateau above there was a tall standing stone – a magic stone, men said – and close to the stone she crawled into a thicket, and out of sight. Then, sliding sideways into a narrow cleft in the ground, she entered a tunnel. After twenty steeply down-tilted paces, she knew she was in the cave, *her* cave, Rachel's Secret. She closed her eyes tight, dropped to her knees, and waited.

After a long time she opened her eyes. Now the thin light streaming in from a crack in the roof of the cave showed the glistening walls, the shallow pond beside her, and, hung directly in front of her – herself, the goddess, a little naked woman of ivory, her hair coiled up on her head to make a loop, and by that loop Rachel had hung her on the wall of the cave.

'Give her love,' she whispered. 'A child of Israel. A man. Peace.' The ivory woman was herself, and so was she, herself. It was for both of them that she prayed. Her father and the Wise One would upbraid her bitterly if they knew, for the Lord YHWH was a jealous god. But they never would know.

'Give her goats, sheep,' she prayed. 'Land. The Rock. This place, Rachel's Secret, for ever.'

She closed her eyes again, and a little later rose, scrambled back up the steep dark tunnel and out into the open. The dog was barking, and after creeping carefully through the trees until she was far from the mouth of the cave, she broke into a run.

The goats had scattered, and the dog was barking at a man throwing stones at them. It was James, the father of the Christian family in the other part of their house. He saw her and called. 'This land is not to be grazed until next week, Rachel. It was agreed between your father and me and the others.'

She said, 'My father sent me this morning.'

'He is wrong!' A flung stone hit one of the goats in the head and Rachel said, 'Stop.'

'Take your goats, then. Go.'

She called the flock, tears in her eyes, and led them back. There was no other free grazing this side of Carteia, so she took the flock back very slowly, letting them search along the shore, and did not reach the town much before the usual time. Her family lived in part of a ruined marble palace. All the livestock shared the great hall, where part of the mosaic floor was still intact; but they had had to block up the spaces between the pillars with brush and thorn, and the grand staircase to the upper storey now ended in mid-air, so there was a ladder instead. Upstairs, there were pictures painted on the walls – black and red women in long pleated robes, gladiators, a woman being covered by a swan. Part of the roof had gone, but it was repaired with straw. Another ladder led up there, and it was a pleasant place to sit in the evening.

Her mother called to her to bring the milk vessels, and she went to help her mother with the cooking. In another room she heard her brother Yakov's wife whining and the baby twins crying.

After they had all eaten, and the dishes were cleaned, and she had gone twice to the river, bringing back jars heavy with water, she told her father how James had turned the goats off the Rock. Yakov's wife cried, 'Shame!' and Yakov, who was twisted and lame from birth, snapped his fingers and said, 'Dogs . . . Christian dogs!' The three men argued – her father, Yakov and Akiba, who was a year younger than she; and the women listened – her mother, Yakov's wife, and herself, with the baby twins and the infant son Isa, whom her mother had borne in her old age.

Yakov said, 'Father, I was there, when we settled this matter. It was *you* who said that none should graze on the Rock until the aedile gave word, and *James* who said, "There is no aedile, nor has been for years, so let us start at the time of the spring festivals" ... Send Rachel back tomorrow, but let us all follow, hidden and armed.'

After a long hesitation her father said, 'Be it so, but we will take no arms. Let us argue, let us persuade them.' There was no grey in his hair, but he looked old, his brow always furrowed and his narrow shoulders bent, like a thin crow.

Akiba said, 'What has come to Theophilus? He walks the town, naked, preaching doom to all.'

Yakov said, 'His name means "Lover of God" in Greek, but he loves no one. The Christian bishop has come from Asido and reasoned with him, but he will not hear. He is mad, madder than our Prophets.'

'Speak not so, son,' her father said. 'Perchance the Lover of God is mad, but as to preaching the end of the world, that he is right. I was born 44 years ago, and all was bad then – our river silted up, the docks of our ancestors sticking out of the sand a hundred yards from the water, fine houses empty and falling into ruin, bribery, oppression. I believed it could not get worse. I was wrong. It has been getting worse all the time ... wolves roaming the town in winter, outlaws infesting forests and mountains ... and they are not escaped slaves, murderers, deserters – as such used to be – but men of substance, family men – all driven to turn outlaw because their land is seized without cause, their business infamously taxed, their rights trampled on by the rich, by every petty official.'

'And, since *I* was a boy,' Yakov said, 'the barbarians ... Alans, Sueves, Vandals, Visigoths. But that one who was washed up on the Rock last year, the day of the storm, said that they were fighting *for* Rome, against the others.'

Her father cried, 'I don't know their tribal names, nor what they claim to be doing. In fact they sack and burn and kill ... It is my turn for guard upon the Praetorian Gate tonight, so I must go. Woman, it is the Haggadah night tomorrow. Do you have all that you need?'

Her mother said, 'All, save the kid. Pick and slaughter one for me before Rachel takes them out in the morning ... And there is no wine.'

'Yes, there is,' her father said. 'There are two small flagons behind our couch hidden from those who might make over free with it. They are properly sealed.' He looked meaningly at Yakov, and went out.

Sighing, Rachel took down the bronze menorah from its niche, began to polish it with the end of her dress, and thought of Avram.

The next morning early, after her father had ritually killed one of the kids, she herded the remaining dozen into the street, out of the eastern gate, and through the fields to the shore. She moved them smartly along, whistling and crying and running to head them off if they tried to break into the fields, for they were mischievous and cunning as devils.

At the place which she called, for herself, the Woman's Stone, for it was here, under the stone, that her dog had turned up the ivory woman, a man now stepped out of hiding, his arms spread. It was a narrow place between the cliff and the sea, and the goats stopped. She saw it was Peter, James's son, a young man little older than herself, but much taller, for all that family were tall, slender, and graceful. 'No farther, Rachel Cohenky,' he said. 'It was agreed ... What is this?' His voice changed as her father and young Akiba and Yakov hirpling on a staff came up from the beach towards them. Then he smiled, 'We seem to have had the same idea.' He put a finger to his mouth and whistled. His father James, and his younger brothers, John and Young James, scrambled down from the rocks higher up the slope. The two families met round Rachel and her flock.

'What are you doing?' Yakov shouted angrily. 'We have the right.'

'Not yet,' Peter said.

A stone whizzed past his ear. Her father shouted, 'Don't do that, Akiba! James . . . boys . . . be still! We want to talk . . .'

But the young men were at each other's throats, snarling like dogs, rolling on the ground. Rachel saw John grab her brother Akiba from behind, and ran to help him. Peter held her with ease as she struggled and spat in his face. Smiling, he drew back his head. She sank her teeth into his arm. He flung her away with a yell. As she lay half stunned, the fighting stopped. The men stood separated, breathing deeply and muttering fiercely at one another. Akiba's nose was bleeding and so, she saw happily, was Peter's arm, and there was a taste of blood in her mouth. Her father turned on his heel and called curtly, 'Come.' He led his family towards the town. James and his sons followed a hundred paces behind.

Yakov was crying with vexation – 'Oh, why did you not bring your spear, father?'

Akiba growled, 'Where is our flock to graze now?'

They tramped back in silence to the town. Outside the gate her father said, 'Take the goats up the river, Rachel. There is some fresh grass on this side, less than a mile up, on land which is fallow since Terence's wife died and he ran away.'

The dog began to herd the goats round the outside of the town, but she heard a startled yell behind her, and looked round. James, the Christian father, was falling backward, an arrow in his throat. Then she saw men coming out of the rank scrub which reached right to the wall. Peter cried, 'Outlaws!' The day watchman at the gate seized his horn and blew until an arrow thumped into his chest, and the note quivered, hiccuped, and died. Rachel ran into the town. Akiba and the goats helter skelter behind her. She saw a ragged outlaw rip his knife across Yakov's throat, then feel in his scrip. As she ran she shrieked, 'Outlaws! Outlaws!' Women rushed into their houses, doors slammed. Most of the men are in the fields, she thought, but they will hear the horn, they will come.

Theophilus stood naked in the middle of the street, his hand raised, his grey hair streaming, 'Die, die! The hour of wrath is come! Slay the Jews, slay the wicked, let evil be wiped from the earth!'

She ran into her house, crying 'Block the door! Mother!'

Yakov's wife screamed, 'Mother is at the river with Hadassah. Where's Yakov?'

'Dead,' she snapped. Yakov's wife sank wailing to the floor. Rachel swept up the baby twins, hurried up the second ladder to the roof, left them, went down, found little Isa playing in the kitchen, and took him up too. Akiba had seized a spear, and Rachel took a short strong knife from her mother's carving board. She went back up to the roof.

The shrieking and shouting that had been so loud by the gate was muted here, and she saw few people – a man running: two outlaws, recognizable by their matted hair and short, filthy kirtles, breaking into a barricaded house across the street; a woman dead in the dust directly below the corner of the house.

The ladder creaked and Peter joined her. 'It's hopeless,' he said, 'there must be a hundred of them, and we are ... a hundred women and children, twenty men. John's dead. Clubbed when we were trying to close the gate. Your father's safe in our part of the house ... Here they come!'

She heard her name called from the street below, and went to the edge of the parapet. Two score outlaws were gathered there, and out in front, by himself, Julius, the pagan who had been a lawyer and had fled to the mountains. She remembered him well.

He called up, 'Let us in, and no harm will come to any of you.'

She said, 'Let them in, Peter. Or they'll break in, and kill us all. I have children to look after.'

A minute later Julius came to her on the rooftop. She heard the sounds of pillaging in the house. Peter stood back, glowering. Julius spoke in a low voice – 'Your mother and little sister are dead. They saw us coming and some of our men held them under water. So is Avram. I had to kill him myself. Were you not to be betrothed to him?'

She wondered whether she would be able to sink her knife in his heart before he could raise his short old-fashioned legionary sword.

He said, 'Come with me to the forest, Rachel. You heard the Lover of God? He's right. There is no law, no government, no god.'

'We trust in the Lord God of Israel,' she said automatically.

He said, 'I love you, Rachel. When I left, you were – what? 13? – and I loved you then.'

She thought of Avram dead. Now she had no man to be her husband. Julius was strong and subtle and clever. He would give her babies and protect them. But where would be her home? What would be her land? She would never return to the Rock, towering there, cloud crested. And what of her Secret, the deep-cleft ivory woman?

She said, 'I must stay.'

Confused shouting and curses rose from below, and Julius swore – 'Those people are hard to control, even for a moment, even in their own interests. Well, we shall be back when you have saved some more food.' He ran quickly down the ladder and out of sight. Soon all the outlaws had gone, staggering back into the woods with their booty, and driving stolen livestock.

A little later Rachel's father came to the rooftop. 'They have taken everything, except my special wine.' He laughed wildly. His eyes glittered, and he moved with a quick nervous energy. 'Your mother and sister are dead. Did you know?' She nodded – 'It will be you next . . . me . . . all of us.'

She said, 'Father,' sorrowfully and suddenly he broke down and wept, wailing brokenly. Her breast ached and her eyes filled. Could this be her father, the lord of the household, now weeping like her child in her arms?

Peter said hesitantly, 'Isaac, we can not stay here. There is nothing, no seed corn, little food, only one or two animals. We must throw ourselves on the mercy of Vitellius at the Villa Flaviana.'

'Why should he take us?' her father said. 'He already has a hundred men, all armed, and most of them ex-legionaries.'

Peter said, 'Because if he does not, then we must join the outlaws. All together, we would be strong enough to take the villa and sack it.'

'Take, sack, burn! Ai, what a world! But I fear you are right. Gather our people. I will speak to a duovir, if I can find one.'

The Villa Flaviana was two miles round the bay to the west. The estate, covering 5,000 acres on the near bank of the next river, was one of the great latifundia where the very rich escaped from the duties of the towns and the supervision of the tax collectors, and lived under the care and protection of a private army of field hands, guards and servants, who were in fact almost slaves, but better off in their semi-servitude than as free men in the decaying towns.

Rachel thought, there would be no place but a barn or empty hay loft for them to sleep, no pots, no utensils. Yakov's wife was less than useless. She was the mother now. She called, 'Akiba, here, fill that sack with . . .'

The doorman at the great house called loudly to the interior when he saw them coming. Other servants came out, swords drawn, but Isaac went forward steadily, bent under a heavy sack, and then Peter, and she after. Soon the major-domo came, and then the lord of the estate, old Vitellius Flavius, fat and small-eyed, and later his son, young Gaius, plump and smooth, estimating her like a piece of choice meat. Isaac began to talk, dignified in his weariness.

She looked back. Ten more families stood behind them, patient in the spring rain. Ten more were on their way, and as many would come tomorrow. The rest had decided to stay in Carteia. Vitellius stared nervously at them from the porch, the twilight fading fast and his servants lighting

117

lamps along the outer arcade. 'They look dangerous to me,' he said to the major-domo.

'We must take them in, master,' the major-domo muttered. 'There's that band of Vandals to the north, and I hear, Visigoths coming down from the east. We may need every man we can muster.'

'Very well,' old Vitellius said. 'Put them in the barns. Give them something to eat. See that they work for their living, and fight, if need be.'

The major-domo motioned them round to the side, to the scattered buildings of the home farm. He showed them into a huge stone-built barn, nearly empty now of the hay which the cattle had been eating all winter. 'Here, and in the next barn,' he said, 'but no fires inside. Food will be distributed in ten minutes.'

Isaac's family settled in a corner of the barn, and Peter's close by. More families moved in, and spread out, until the barn was nearly full, but there was very little noise. Servants brought bowls of pease porridge, but Isaac took cakes of unleavened bread from his sack, and gave a piece to each of his family. Next he opened a flagon of wine, and mixed it with water in his brass cup. He bowed his head over it, and said, *'Baruch atta adonay elohenu melech ha-olam borey peri haggafen* – Blessed art Thou, O Lord our God, King of the Universe, who createst the fruit of the vine.'

Then over unleavened bread, 'Blessed art Thou, O Lord our God, King of the Universe, who bringest forth bread from the earth.'

They drank, and ate. The rain beat louder on the high roof. Isaac turned to Akiba, for his youngest son, Isa, was only two. 'Akiba,' he said, 'do you remember the questions boys asked of their fathers at the Haggadah night?'

Akiba intoned, 'Why is this night different from all other nights? For on all other nights we eat either leavened or unleavened bread, but tonight . . .'

The ritual of the Haggadah continued, with Isa asleep in Rachel's arms and Yakov's fatherless twins sprawled in the hay. When Isaac had finished retelling the Passover story, Peter came over to them, and said, 'We wish you a happier Passover next year than this.'

'And a happier Easter for you,' Isaac answered gravely.

Peter's chest was wide and flat, crossed with smooth bands of muscle. His eyes were wide set and his nose short and straight. He was looking at her now, and she remembered how close he had held her . . . could it have been this same morning? She remembered the taste of his flesh in her teeth, and lowered her eyes.

Soon they settled themselves to sleep.

The next day they sent for her to work in the big house. She protested that she had little Isa to care for, but the servant said Yakov's wife must do that. Peter looked unhappily after her, but she had to go.

At the villa they had a swimming pool and a heated bath house, and tinkling bells, and everywhere a subtle perfume. They gave her clean clothes of fine linen and wool, and told her to wait upon the lord's youngest daughter. She ate their leavings, and even so ate more, and better, than she had ever known. Young Gaius smiled lazily on her and after a week said, 'Come to my couch tonight, Rachel.'

She made to pass by, but he said, 'Otherwise, back to the barn, and work in the fields.'

She hurried on, frowning. But as the hours passed she knew she would go. It was too cold, too wet, out there.

With him she would never feel hungry again. He was not as handsome as Peter, or even her dead Avram, but he was a man. He would give her children – and the Rock was still there, within reach.

In the big house everyone slept for a couple of hours in the middle of the afternoon. She awoke to a scream – 'Up, up! To arms!' She scrambled up, rubbing her eyes. A trumpet began to call. She ran through the villa to the front door. A ragged mob of barbarians were sweeping up from the river, shrieking, screaming, waving spears and clubs. Ahead of them, in the centre, pranced the Lover of God, a flaming brand of wood in his hand. She heard his strangely accented Latin above the din – 'Kill, kill!' Rachel ran to the barn.

The Flavian men-at-arms and the male refugees from Carteia hurried together out of house and stable and granary, short swords drawn, buckling on light armour, helmets awry; but more barbarians came from the river, and they were not such a rabble as they seemed, for groups of them wheeled in blocks, one such taking Vitellius's servants in the flank with a mighty shout.

Yakov's widow had vanished, with the twins. Rachel picked up Isa, grabbed her short knife in the other hand, and went back to the door. More barbarians were coming down through the olive groves, and the women who had fled that way ran straight into them. She saw a sword rise. Yakov's widow fell, cut almost in two. Peter's mother and sister went down under clubs, and a man with a wolf's-head hood picked up the baby twins and swung them by the heels against an old olive tree.

Now they were coming from the big house towards the barn, the Lover of God in the van. Her father and the young men were trying to hold them. Her father drew back his spear arm, and a tall barbarian stepped in under the throw and rammed a knife under his ribs, so that he jerked, coughed, and fell. Peter killed one barbarian and stepped back quickly, his sword flickering out again. At his side his brother Young James died, felled by a spear thrust in the knee, and then clubbed on the ground. Akiba the Jew and Peter the Christian fell back slowly, side by side. Rachel waited, her knife ready.

Now, with no apparent reason, the blocks of barbarians began to eddy, and break up. Some ran this way and some that, until the actual attackers here were reduced to eight men, led by one as tall as Peter, but older, and stronger, with reddish hair. His face was wide, square and flat, his eyes pale grey. This man rested his heavy sword and called in a guttural Latin, 'Hold, Romans! No need to die. We want slaves.'

Rachel saw Peter's back muscles tighten up and called out quickly, 'No, Peter!' and then, in the tongue of Hispania, she added, 'Tomorrow is another day. Put up your swords.' To the barbarian leader she said, 'We have nothing. We are in flight here ourselves from Carteia. The outlaws took all that we had a week ago.'

'All? Priest say all mans rich here,' the leader spoke, glowering.

'He is wrong. There was plenty in the big house, nowhere else.'

The barbarian followed her eye. A group were dragging Vitellius's body out of the front door of the great villa. Another half dozen ran by hurling the head of young Gaius from hand to hand in a boisterous game.

The barbarian slipped his sword back into its hanger and pushed past Akiba and Peter as though they did not exist. To his men he threw a dozen words over his shoulder, and they hurried off towards the big house. He said, 'I am Wildigern, Visigoth. You are surprised I talk

Latin?' He glowered down at her. 'I live near Romans all my life. Romans ... *poof*.' He blew into the air. 'I kill many. Come.' He laughed, and led the way to the barn. Rachel went with him, little Isa holding tight to her hand, and Akiba and Peter followed doubtfully behind. The barbarians were strange, she thought: all the killing seemed no more than a passing storm, and now the sun was out and all was forgotten. This Wildigern was quite without fear, going alone now into the darkened empty barn with Peter and Akiba, armed, at his heels, their kin lying slaughtered under the olives.

Wildigern looked about – 'Rich. Rich land. Farmers?' She nodded. 'Your land, where?'

She pointed over the arm of the cork woods that separated the Villa Flaviana from Carteia. Wildigern gazed, 'H'm ... by the white mountain. What call?'

'Calpé,' she said. 'The Rock.'

Wildigern made up his mind. 'This place here—' he waved to the great estate – 'This for our leader Wallia. For me – your house, land, all. You cook, make babies for me. You' – he jerked his chin at the two young men – 'you work fields, teach me. Together we fight Vandals, kill outlaws. Together – eat, drink! ... Come.'

He strode out of the door and raised his voice in a great bellow. His eight men tumbled out of the villa, staggering under loot. Four Roman servant girls, and a couple of wounded men-at-arms followed, also heavily loaded.

Peter muttered, 'If he touches you, Rachel. I shall kill him. I love you. I learned that while you were away from us in the big house.'

She said, 'See that plenty of wine and brandy are brought to Carteia from the cellars.'

'But ...'

'I can't talk now. Or think. Later.'

Theophilus, the Lover of God, was seated cross-legged outside the gate of the villa, his eyes closed, his hair and beard splashed with blood His begging bowl lay beside him, and, as they passed, the Visigoths threw rings and coins and gold ornaments into it, with a curious defensive gesture, as though they feared the fanatic might turn them to stone. She thought, they may call themselves Christians, but it was the gods of their forests, and magic, and madness, that they really feared. She made sure her knife was in her waistband, and followed the others into the cork forest.

Two hours after dark, the Visigoths lay dead drunk all over the house – upstairs, on the roof, and sprawled in the goats' droppings below. The captive Roman men-at-arms, all Spanish-born, had fallen into the service of the new masters as easily as the old. After the first flagon of wine the servant girls abandoned themselves to the barbarians' lust with no shame or hesitation, so that there had been a singing and coupling and grunting all evening. Once Wildigern dragged Rachel to him, but she held him off, smiling, fearful for Peter's life, for he was close by, white and shaking. Later, another Visigoth tried to rape her, and Wildigern cracked his skull with such a blow from the butt of his sword that the man lay unconscious for an hour.

Now it was quiet save for the snores and drunken mumbles of the sleepers. She went to a dark corner of the first floor, near the head of the ladder to the street, and Peter and Akiba came to her. Peter said, 'We must go – now. But where? To the outlaws?'

'No,' she said automatically. If they went to the outlaws, Peter would not live long; for Julius the Pagan wanted her, and he would not tolerate a rival. But, more important than that, the outlaws promised no home, no children, no peace, only the opposite – a return to the way of the hunter, a descent from house to cave, from tilling fields to gathering nuts . . . and surely, soon, back to holes in the ground.

'Where, then?' Peter said. 'Hispalis? Corduba? But the barbarians must have taken and ruined those cities on their way here.'

Akiba said, 'I know! . . . We will go to Africa. I know where there is a boat hidden in a sea cave of the Rock. It belonged to Simon the merchant and he used it to smuggle salt. No one else knows. I . . . I helped him some-times.'

Rachel did not hesitate. Perhaps they would go to Africa; perhaps they would not; perhaps she could stay here – for Wildigern was no worse than many other men, only less subtle in his cruelties, and as her mother had told her often enough, *what is born of a Jewish womb, is a Jew:* but the plight of the young men tugged at her heart, so she said, 'Very well. Think now what we will need. Pots. Water vessel. Tinder, Knife . . .'

They passed over the isthmus on to the Rock before the middle hour, with Akiba ahead carrying Isa, and Peter behind, and all heavily loaded. By the goat track along the lower western slopes a pack of wolves bayed round, and tried to attack Akiba, but fled before Peter's sword. From the Lover of God's gully they crossed to the east side, going close by Rachel's Secret, and then turned north, as though to continue the circuit of the Rock. Here Akiba led slowly down the steep slope, Isa asleep on his right hip. After a careful, almost vertical descent, they stood on a tiny sandy beach. Starlight gleamed on wet rocks, and small waves regularly washed their feet. 'It's up there,' Akiba muttered, 'pulled up into the cave.'

He gave Isa into her arms and disappeared into the gloom of the overhanging cliff. He was gone a long time, and then suddenly he was back. 'It's broken,' he said. 'Two planks smashed, and the oars gone.' His voice cracked.

Peter said, 'That storm a week ago must have sent the sea up to it. We're lucky it was not swept away altogether, like the oars. Let us see it. Perhaps we can repair it.'

She followed them up the sand slope. She thought that the boat, which she could feel but barely see until her eyes became used to the darkness, would be very small for the three of them and Isa. The holes were not large. A pair of smooth short planks, well nailed down over felt or canvas, and caulked with pitch, would make the boat watertight again.

They stood some time in the end of the rock cave, around the boat, not speaking. Then Peter said, 'We must have oars . . .'

She said quickly, 'They might be in this little cove somewhere. We can look by daylight.' She knew what Peter was going to say next, and he must be stopped. Two or three hours of the night remained, Isa slept, and Akiba was very tired. Tonight, as soon as Akiba slept, Peter would come to her. There might never be a tomorrow.

Peter said, 'Perhaps . . . But we must have planks, nails, canvas or, better still, thick wool, pitch . . .'

'Get it tomorrow night,' she began.

She saw the decisive shake of his head. 'Now no one knows we have left Carteia. I can find what we need and be back here before dawn. Tomorrow there may be a hunt up for us. Tomorrow they will not be drunk. There will be sentries, guards. No, Rachel, I must go now.' He took her quickly in his arms, and kissed her. 'Stay hidden. Look after them, Akiba.'

She did not weep until the same hour the next night, when he had not come. Then she sat by the boat, folded her arms on her knees and wept. Akiba muttered – 'Perhaps he was seen, and driven inland . . .'

She had hoped that, too. That was why she had waited until this later hour to weep. Now she knew he would never come back.

Akiba said, 'I'll go tomorrow night, if he doesn't come. We only need to mend the hole.' She nodded, for they had found both oars as soon as they began to look round the cove by daylight.

They lay down, but Rachel's eyes never closed. In seven days she had lost three men who had wanted to put their seed in her, that children might grow in her womb. She had fled from the Rock, and returned. Now what? Who could tell her what she must do?

At once she knew; and as soon as Akiba slept she climbed the cliff, went to the thicket, and for half an hour knelt in total darkness in her Secret, holding the ivory figurine between her breasts. Then, her questions answered, she returned, and fell asleep.

Next night Akiba left the cave at dusk. Rachel waited till he had gone, then began to gather the collected driftwood close round the fire, and cut herbs into the pot, with salt and water. She sliced some of the tender lamb they had stolen from Wildigern, and he from the Villa Flaviana. She kept Isa awake running about and playing with some bronze baubles she had found. When his eyelids drooped she gave him wine from the flagon, laid him down carefully in the high back of the cave, and covered him with Peter's cloak, that he had left behind.

Akiba returned early, put down his burden, and sat by the fire. His face was taut. 'I knew where Simon kept his materials,' he said . . . Then, suddenly, 'They have flayed Peter and nailed his skin to the house where Theophilus sits.' He shuddered and buried his head in his knees.

She stroked his hair. 'Think not of it, Akiba. It is all done. All gone. Except us.'

Akiba was seventeen, and healthy. He sniffed the air – 'That is savoury stew, sister. But we must not waste food. It will take me two or three days to make all ready. Then we must await calm weather.'

'There is enough,' she said gaily. 'Tonight we eat well, and drink wine.'

'How can you smile?' he said. 'If you had seen him . . . Your eyes glitter like stars, Rachel. Have you taken wine?'

'Not yet. Here. Drink. Again. Forget. But say the blessing, that the Children of Israel may never die from the earth, for surely we are the last.'

He spoke, and drank. She watched, to see that he took enough to wipe what he had seen from his mind, but not too much. Herself, she ate sparingly, and kept the fire burning. As Akiba neared the end of his eating she began to sing love songs, that the young men sang to the girls on summer nights by the sea. Akiba beat time with one hand, holding the wine flagon with the other. 'I wish father were here with his lute,' he said.

His eyes clouded and Rachel jumped to her feet. 'Remember last year's spring festival?' she cried. She danced now as the wild Turdetani of the Ronda hills did, when they came down and danced at the festival. She bent her body back, clapped her hands, thrust out her breasts, and stamped her feet. She saw her brother's eyes on her swelling breasts, on her legs, visible under the thin linen. As she danced she raised her arms, slipped free of the dress, and let it slide down her body to the sand. Akiba licked his lips, and she danced closer to him. He pressed back against the wall of the cave. Little Isa lay asleep above, the firelight playing on his face and his fat, dirt-stained cheeks.

Rachel sank down by Akiba's side, took his arms and whispered, 'Come. Be a man to me!'

'Rachel!' he cried. 'It is a sin, an abomination.'

'We are the only Jews left in the world,' she said. She put her hand to him and found him upthrust and hard, against his will.

'Sister, sister!'

She spread herself, and pulled him down on top of her. As she grasped him with her legs he entered into her for she was slippery to receive him. She cried out at a sudden pain, and held him tight as his body began to move. In a moment it was he who held her, crushed her, rammed into her as though to bury her in the sand. Soon he lay still on her, moaning 'Oh Lord God, what have I done?'

She said, 'You have preserved our race, even as we are *all* children of Lot and his daughters.'

He said, 'There must be other Jews left alive somewhere in the world.'

'Why?' she said.

He got up and went out of the cave. She lay back, as though carefully guarding the seed that he had left in her.

On the evening of the seventh day since her brother first lay with her, he came up from the little beach and said abruptly, 'We are going. Tonight.'

He was always constrained with her now, though he had made love to her every night since the first night, and many times by day also. He took her with ever growing lust and sureness, so that she began to look forward to the act for itself ... yet, when it was done, he was withdrawn and hostile.

He had made the boat ready by the third day. She had forced him to stay four more. Her period would not come for another seven, but she could hold him no longer. The old women said that if a woman's husband came to her in the middle of the month, she was the more likely to conceive. She had done her best.

Now she said, 'I am not going. I will keep Isa. Go alone, if you must.'

Again his voice cracked. 'Not coming?'

She said, 'The boat is very small, Akiba. When you tested it, the water dashed in even from the little waves here. I do not think it can reach Africa. Stay here, brother. It is our home. Under the shadow of this Rock.'

'What?' he said violently. 'As a slave of the Visigoths, who murdered our father? As a louse-ridden outlaw? No, I go to Africa ... I go,' he repeated, almost happily. She saw, what she had not expected, that he wanted to get away from her. 'And you, to Julius the outlaw, I suppose?'

Rachel nodded. There was no purpose in explaining. She watched Akiba put some hard bread into his scrip, and drape a blanket on his shoulders. Turning, he pulled her to him, his face blind with the familiar lust. Her loins ached for him, but she said softly, 'It is enough, brother. I am sure I am with child.'

The desire dissipated slowly from his face. He went to kiss the sleeping Isa, then held her hand and for the first time since he had taken her maidenhead, seemed unconstrained. 'God be with you, sister. If I can ever come back, I shall, to look for you.'

He ran down the slope, and in a moment the little boat

129

set out, dimly seen in the twilight, Akiba rowing and the boat rising valiantly to the waves. She watched until the darkness hid them.

The next morning, when the sun was yet low, Rachel came to the main gate of Carteia, carrying Isa in her arms. A sentry of the Visigoths, lounging against the wall, waved her in before she could speak: no one feared a woman with a child. On the way to her father's house she passed the Lover of God, squatting against a wall, dozing. Peter's skin and mask were pegged out on the wall behind him.

She went into the house and found Wildigern on the roof. His face registered astonishment, pleasure, anger. He seized her arm and shook her – 'You ... where you go? I kill you!'

She said, 'The men forced me.'

His grip softened. 'That one, the dead one, your man? Lover of God saw him, gave alarm. My men made double eagle of him. I said no, but Lover of God said yes ... Where is other man?' he asked, again suspicious.

'My brother? Gone to Africa.'

'And you ... why not you go with?'

Perhaps these barbarians would stay, perhaps they would move on. Other barbarians might come. But the Rock would remain. She watched a pair of partridges, like those she had seen mating, burst up out of the scrub and fly towards the grey cliffs. Her goats would graze there. Her son would explore the Great Cave high on the west face, which was bigger than the Christian basilica in Carteia. Her daughter, when her first blood of woman came, she would take into the Secret, and to her give the ivory woman, the other, eternal Her.

She raised her chin – 'I have come back, to bear your children . . . if I am allowed.'

'Allowed? Who not allow?' He frowned. 'I am Wildigern. This Carteia mine, under Wallia'

She said, 'The Lover of God will have me killed, because I am a Jew. You will not be able to save me. You could not save Peter.'

'No, no,' Wildigern said. 'He do nothing. He priest. I lord.'

Rachel put her hand to her waist and slowly drew the short knife. She held it under her rib cage on the left side, pointing in. She said, 'Wildigern, I want the Lover of God's head, here, now. I will not belong to a man afraid of a priest.'

Wildigern stared at her with the same fearful wonder that she had seen several times in Akiba's face. Then he seized his great two-handed sword and ran down the ladder.

Book Five

VISIGOTHIC KINGDOM

The Jewish years 4178–4471
A.U.C. 1170–1464
A.D. 417–711

RACHEL may not have been allowed a long domesticity with Wildigern, for the following year the Visigoths were summoned by their nominal masters in Rome to leave Spain and settle in Gaul, around Toulouse. Although they were winning their fight against the Vandals, they obeyed, and marched north. (Perhaps Wildigern deserted, to live with Rachel under the shadow of the Rock.)

The Vandals stayed in Southern Spain only long enough to give it the name by which it has ever since been known – Vandalusia. Then, in 429, they succeeded in doing what the Visigoths had failed to: they took ship and crossed to North Africa, where they stayed. The Celtiberian-Romans regained possession of Spain – rather, they shared it with the outlaws and the other barbarians – until 507. In that year the Frankish King Clovis attacked the Visigoths, killed their leader, and expelled them from Gaul. They recrossed the Pyrenees, and set up the Visigothic Kingdom which soon held rule over all the Iberian peninsula. (A century later one of their princesses went back north to become a Frankish queen, and quite famous in song and story: her name was Brunhilde).

Gibraltar remained uninhabited. Carteia's ruin became complete. Over the bay, as over all of Europe, darkness descended ... Yet the Visigoths were not 'barbarous' in the modern sense. They were more dangerous than that, both to the world and to themselves. They were savages, advanced and retarded at the same time. They came to wear long cloaks, robes of fine wool, and richly worked jewels – but they used neither shoes nor stockings; and while the king's head rested in his mistress's lap, she hunted it for lice. Their laws were usually wiser and more humane than the Roman laws they replaced – but they could not prevent the election of their kings developing into anarchy. They had conquered by the sword – and neglected either to keep it sharp, or replace it with some other form of security (if any such existed in that time). At their core was a cult of personality rather than of organization – and then they failed to produce the personalities. Finally, they were disunited. They already distinguished between themselves and their Roman or Celtiberian fellow citizens; and in 589 King Reccared formally changed the 'official' religion from Arian to Roman Christianity, which was, as we have seen, a much less tolerant form. From 617 on king and church waged an ever more frenzied persecution against the Jews.

The State went down hill, not violently, except at the upper levels, and not rapidly, but steadily. For over a century Gibraltar was a dinghy tied to a ship whose sails were rotting, whose captain spent his time with wine, women and worse, and whose multi-racial crew of many faiths and of none, near starvation, had no incentive, no knowledge, and no share in the vessel's fate.

In the normal course of history such a situation worsens until it becomes intolerable; then there is a revolution and a new leader takes hold – as Charles Martel was to do in Frankish Gaul, for instance. But the Visigoths were not to be given the chance to reshape their own history. Three thousand miles to the east, in Arabia, an obscure caravan conductor began to preach a new religion – that there was one God, Allah: and he, Mohammed, was the Prophet of God. In 622 the Prophet was driven from Mecca to Medina and from this flight, *the year of the hegira*, the

Muslims soon dated their events, using a lunar calendar. Mohammed died in A.D. 632 (A.H. 11), but by then the new religion was well on the move, and every day the word of Mohammed's successors, the Caliphs, Commanders of the Faithful, became law over new lands. Very early in the eighth century the Muslims reached Morocco. In Morocco, across the Strait from Gibraltar, lies Ceuta, the Roman Septa (for its situation on seven hills). The Governor of Ceuta at this time was a man called Count Illan, Julian, or perhaps Olban. Some historians think he was holding Ceuta for the Byzantine Empire, which seems very unlikely; some, that he was a Christian – of Vandal descent, perhaps – who was holding it for his own people; and some, that he was Governor on behalf of the Visigothic King Wittica in Spain. His problem, faced with the sudden arrival of the all-conquering Muslims, would not have been much different in any of the three cases, but I am assuming the last theory to be the correct one as upon it has been built a lovely fabric of myth, legend, and history, complete with heroes, villains, high life, sex and debauchery.

In 709 one Roderick murdered Wittica and usurped the kingship of Spain. Wittica was dead, but many bitter supporters still lived, including two sons; a brother, Oppas, who was the powerful Archbishop of Seville; and a daughter, Faldrina ... who was the wife of Count Illan. Their daughter, Florina, was a maid of honour at Roderick's court.

Tales of the richness of the Spanish soil, and the dissensions of its rulers, crossed the narrow strait, and were eagerly heard by the Caliph's ambitious and able Governor of Africa, Musaibn-Nusayr. In 710 he sent a lieutenant, Tarif, over into Spain on a reconnaissance. Tarif landed at Traducta and marched inland. After an extended excursion he returned to Musa with the news that Spain was ripe – overripe, rotten. About the same time Florinda sent a message to her father, Count Illan; King Roderick had foully seduced her.

The scene is set for the first known incursion of Gibraltar, as actor rather than spectator, into history. The year is A.D. 711, the 92nd since the Hegira . . .

BROTHER AETHELRED'S STORY

TRANSLATED FROM THE LATIN

In the name of the Father, the Son, and the Holy Ghost, Amen. Obeying the command of the Holy Abbot, I set down here all that befell me, Brother Aethelred of Glastonbury, on my journey from Isca to Rome in the year of Our Lord 711.

Early in that year the Holy Abbot summoned me, I being then in my twentieth year, and told me that the Bishop of Rome had bidden him send a young man to the city that he might study there for a period of years, and when he had learned all he could, return to Glastonbury. As I was somewhat more intelligent than an ox, the Abbot said, and there was no other young man, he would send me. I set forth at once in a Byzantine vessel, for Gaul was infested with outlaws.

At sea I suffered from a revulsion of my stomach so that I became weak as a child, though I was strong and tall in those days, with a beard and tonsure of gold, and blue eyes. (I write this not to boast, but that all may be made clear.) After many weeks the vessel came to a narrow place, and the master said these were the Pillars of Hercules. Our sail was set, and a strong wind behind blew us speedily on, bearing close to the northern Pillar, when we struck a piece of floating wreckage which ripped a mighty hole in the bow. The master put up the tiller and steered for the point of the headland, but the wind pushed the bow round, a great following wave fell upon us and cast us over, and in a moment we were all in the sea. By the chance of spending my childhood swimming in the river when I should perhaps have been watching my father's swine, I was able to swim out from beneath the sail which threatened to smother me, but I was alone. I swam hard, and crawled ashore near the point of the headland. Arrived with difficulty at the top of the cliff I looked seaward and saw that the vessel was gone, borne to the bottom by the sea and the weight of her cargo. None but I had survived. I wandered and climbed about the rock, and it began to rain. As darkness fell I saw a huge cavern, and hurried into it for shelter. It was a place wrought by God, full of marvels of shaped stone, but I was tired, and soon fell asleep. Next day, I saw a goat girl, who pointed out to me the path off that Rock, and showed me where was the nearest castle and village, which she called Torrox. I walked near three hours to Torrox, passing first, on the bay, the ruins of a city such as we have in Wessex, and the Holy Abbot says are the work of the pagan Romans. As I reached the gate of Torrox a red-faced young nobleman in a white tunic with a gold and green mantle rode out, followed by servants. The nobleman reined in, frowning, and spoke sharply to me in his tongue. I told him in Latin who I was and what had befallen me. He answered in Latin, poor but easily understood – 'God be praised, for

138

my clerk has just been drowned. I am Count Anseric, with my brother lord of all this country. Until all my letters are written and answered, you shall be my clerk . . . You are a well-formed man, Aethelred . . . and if I cannot persuade you to stay, then I shall arrange your onward passage to Rome.' He smiled at me, spoke to a servant, and rode on.

The servant led me into the castle. Torrox was greater than anything I had seen in Britain, though small compared to the mighty works I later saw in Rome. It was of two storeys, all of stone, of which there is an abundance of all kinds in that land, made in the form of a hollow square, with only one gate. The roof was not of straw, as in Britain, but of tiles. Many servants, men-at-arms, and women resided there, perhaps to the number of two hundred souls. The village lay down river and contained about fifty houses. The servant showed me to a small cell on the second floor, facing south-west and furnished with a bench, table, and pallet. Through the arrow slit I could see that great grey Pillar of Hercules which, though three leagues distant, seemed to frown down directly upon all that country. The servant gave me to eat and brought fine robes, which may have belonged to the drowned clerk, then led me to the great hall and introduced me to the nobleman dispensing justice there. I started, for this Count Theodomir was the twin of Count Anseric – they were indeed twins, twenty-five years old and at first glance I thought it was Anseric returned; but this Theodomir was grave and calm, his skin pure and his gaze straight, whereas Anseric's skin was red and mottled, his eyes bloodshot and always moving, his lips loose.

Count Theodomir's Latin was better than mine, and he welcomed me warmly, 'I hear there is much correspondence to be dealt with,' I said.

'Yes,' he said, adding sombrely, 'Though it is the Holy Spirit we need from you, Brother Aethelred, more than we need your learned pen . . . Come to me at any time, ask what you will. You will be heard.'

'Or come to me,' a woman's voice said behind me, 'you will be even better received. Unless you are of brother Anseric's faith.' Count Theodomir's face went cold and tight, and he said, 'My wife, the Lady Hildoara. This is Brother Aethelred, from Wessex.'

'A monk,' she said, eyeing me as though I were an animal at market, 'but more of a man between the legs than you, I'll be bound.'

He snapped at her in their tongue and turned away. She shouted rudely after him. I suspected that all was not well between them.

A month passed. I prepared and answered correspondence for Count Anseric, who was usually drunk, but showed himself most generous towards me, for though I was but a penniless monk, he lavished small gifts upon me, embraced and kissed me, and stroked my beard in wonder at its fairness. Of Count Theodomir I saw little, for he was always out upon the king's business in that province. His wife, the Lady Hindoara, spent many hours each day closeted with servants, captains, knights, and passing travellers, upon her Lord's business, and once even sent for me. When I entered, she was lying naked on her couch, so I knew she had forgotten her summons, and slipped out quietly to save her shame. For the rest, I passed two hours each day with the priest of the church, learning the Visigothic tongue. Of the language I learned something, of the state of the kingdom and country, much more.

All Hispania was rent by fear and hatred. Many believed that King Roderic had murdered the previous king, Wittica, and some now planned to slay him in his turn.

The mountains were full of outlaws, the roads of brigands. In Africa a new and terrible army of men called Moors, who denied Christ, had come from the east, wading in blood, and possessed themselves even of the Pillar of Hercules upon that side; and no man knew what they intended to do, but each looked fearfully over his shoulder, for the strait between the two Pillars is very narrow.

As if these perils were not enough, in every court and palace of the Visigoths flourished all manner of abomination. No vice was too obscure or too bestial, the priest told me, but that it was practised by one and by many, not in secret and alone but together and in public. I asked the priest to describe these abominations to me, but he said I should ask Count Anseric and the Lady Hildoara; and yet, he said, our people – for he too was a Visigoth – have made good laws, and can live close to God's will, if they wish.

At the castle the state of the kingdom was laid before me in little, as though in a picture – for Count Theodomir lived like a saint, and his brother Count Anseric, my master, like a swine.

On a day in the middle of April Count Theodomir left on a long journey, to carry reports of the province to King Roderic, who was in the farthest north. That night the castle was filled with carousing and revelry. The next day Count Anseric sent for me, and I thought perhaps I should speak to him of my wish to continue my journey to Rome, for Torrox had begun to oppress me, more heavily now that Count Theodomir would be absent for many weeks.

But when I came to Count Anseric's chamber he said, 'We make a sea voyage tonight. Bring parchment and pen. Tell no one.'

The Count himself came to my cell soon after dark, and

we rode with two grooms to that ruined town on the bay below the Pillar of Hercules, which men called the Rock. There a vessel waited, we went aboard, the sailors cast off, and the rowers settled to their oars. The moon was high, and the face of the Rock shone very white on the left hand. Then Count Anseric said, 'We go to Septa. We will talk to Count Illan, the Governor, and others, about helping our king make order here in Hispania. What we agree, you write in Latin, we sign. You understand?'

My task was plain enough, and very usual, for only we of the Church can write, and until swords are drawn our help is necessary for every act of policy. Many had spoken of this Count Illan, in Torrox. It was said that King Roderic had violated his daughter Florinda while the maid was at court; but the Count had forgiven the king his sin, and only taken his wife and daughter away from the court that no more temptation might befall. So forgiving and Christian a nobleman I much looked forward to meeting.

God afflicted me with vomiting the rest of the journey across the strait to Septa, which we reached in the last hour before dawn. A man in a white cloak, which concealed his face, awaited us on the shore, and led us quickly through the city to a great villa set behind a high wall. A strange music, as of plucked lutes, filled the air even at that hour, and I heard water tinkling. I was shown to a large room full of cushions, where I soon fell asleep.

The man who aroused me wore a grey robe and a black cloth wound many times around his head. He was dark of skin but his hair was the colour of dull copper, and his eyes were blue. He was near thirty years of age. He spoke to me in excellent Latin, calling me by my name, which surprised me. He said 'I am David ha-Cohen, secretary to the general Abd-al-Malik. We meet in the centre chamber at noon.'

He bowed, and made to leave me, but I cried out, for a shrunken man, hairy and misshapen of face, ran in upon four legs from the garden, screeching and gibbering. David ha-Cohen laughed and said, 'That is an ape. The owner of this palace keeps a dozen here, well fed.' He waved his hand and the beast ran out, chattering.

Then he left me, and young boys waited upon me with spiced food, and sweetmeats in silver dishes, and wine, and iced sherbet. When all was done one boy stayed, an affectionate lad who curled up against me as a son or brother might, and showed me a wound upon his thigh, but I saw no wound, and gently bade him go and play at balls outside as I must prepare myself for the conference.

When I joined Count Anseric in the centre chamber I saw that the boys had served him, too, for he was very red of face, and sat down most heavily upon the cushions. In that place there were marble pillars, and many spread cushions, and a pool of clear water, and mosaic figures dancing under the water. Now came a tall, thin, grey man in a Visigothic tunic, like Count Anseric's but more splendid, and this was Count Illan himself. His eyes were deep sunk, and envenomed, his mouth wide and thin. He did not look at all forgiving.

We three Christians waited, not speaking, and suddenly a mighty blast of trumpets almost in our ears set us on our feet. The silk curtains shivered and three Moors strode in, followed by David, the scribe. He in the centre was a dark prince, with a forked beard and a cunning eye, dressed all in black, and he came on alone. Count Illan muttered, 'It is Musa-ibn-Nusayr, Governor of Africa for the Caliph.'

The Governor spoke sharply, pushing his hand flat towards the floor. I dropped to my knees, for his meaning was clear, and Count Anseric with me. Count Illan hesitated, but at the Governor's frown he too knelt. Then the Governor smiled and embraced us all, and introduced the other two Moors with him: Tarik, who was dark and wide and short and wore a green robe; and Abd-al-Malik, David's master, who was tall and young and fair, and wore white and gold.

Musa spoke a few sentences, then turned upon his heel and left, all bowing again. David translated, 'The Governor of Africa bids you make speed with your talk as he must leave in the morning. Let no foolish splitting of hairs delay agreement.'

The talking began. I had little to do, for David's Latin was better than mine, and beside Arabic he also spoke Visigothic. However, I listened diligently, and learned that Count Illan and Count Anseric meant to invite an army of 5,000 Moors to help King Roderic make peace in Hispania. The Counts would have to pretend to fight against the Moors, at first, it was agreed, though I did not understand why. And if, as some said, the King was the prisoner of Arian heretics and other evil forces, then his army must be attacked, and Count Illan would be Regent until the King could be released. The wages of the Moors was soon agreed, this to be freedom to sack Asido and two other towns, together with ten thousand pieces of silver. This Tarik of the green robe was to be the general, with Abd-al-Malik under him. The Counts swore to obey Tarik in all that pertained to waging war, and the Moors swore to return to Africa, after they had been paid, whenever Count Illan asked them.

In Hispania the Moors would land in the shelter of that Rock where I was shipwrecked. For the journey across the narrow sea they had four big boats. Each boat held 100 soldiers, and should be able to cross the strait once coming and once going each day. So it should take two weeks to transport the army to Hispania, if the weather remained fair.

When we ended our talking it was arranged that we should return to Torrox that very night, bearing with us Count Illan and his family, and also Abd-al-Malik, who would make arrangements on the very place for the arrival of the army.

Then the lords went away and David and I worked together to prepare the agreement, in four copies. When all was done, and we had read each aloud, that none might differ from another, we took the parchment to our masters, and our work was done.

I returned to my chamber, and David with me. He lowered himself to the cushions, sitting cross legged in a manner I never learned to follow, for it made my knees ache, also it is ill suited to the damp floors of Wessex. David said we had some hours to pass and since he had heard I did not care for other entertainment we would do well to converse together. Time spent in acquiring knowledge is never wasted, he said. He asked me many questions about Torrox, and about Count Theodomir – he seemed relieved when I told him I had seen the Count leave, with my own eyes – and about the Jews. When I said I had never met a Jew he answered shortly, 'You are talking to one. Did you expect us to have horns and a tail?'

I apologized for my ignorance, and he said, 'Aethelred, I don't know why, but I like you. Listen to me. You are in danger. Now, slip out through yonder arch. Across the street there is a blue door. It is the synagogue. Enter there, cover your head, and pass the time in meditation until tomorrow, when I shall come for you. Count Anseric will think that you have run off with one of the boys. He will not worry, as long as you stay in Africa.'

I said, 'I do not understand.'

David walked up and down several minutes. Then he spoke slowly to me – 'Aethelred, only seven people know of the agreement just made: the Governor, the two Muslim generals, the two Counts, we two secretaries. Of these, we four Moors are obeying the command of our Caliph. None of *us* stand in any danger should the agreement be revealed. Think you the same is true of the Counts? Think you that their king, Roderic, knows of the agreement?'

I thought that David was trying to warn me, but though I was troubled, what could I do? I said, 'Count Anseric sheltered me when I came in, near drowned, from the sea. I can not desert him. As for the king, he is a prisoner of Arian heretics. The Counts plan to free him from that thrall. It is so written.'

David struck his clenched fists upon his temples and cried aloud in his own tongue, and then said, 'What must be, must be . . . How do you like the Lady Hildoara? The scent of her doings carries across the Straits, even against the wind.'

I told him of her summons to me, and how I had saved her embarrassment, and he fell on the cushions and lay there a long time, struggling and gasping for breath He rose at last, weeping, and said, 'Farewell, Aethelred . . . farewell.' He embraced me, and in a moment was gone.

The rowers thrust our vessel from the shore after dark that night Abd-al-Malik stood silent in the stern, wrapped in a cloak. Count Anseric fell asleep at the mast. Count Illan's lady sat in the waist of the vessel, her arm round their daughter, Florinda, she whom the king was said to have defiled. The wind blew hot from Africa and clouds hid stars and moon. Faint light seemed to come from under the water.

I heard a tread behind me on the creaking deck, and turned to see Count Illan. He peered at me and said, 'Ah, it is the Saxon . . .' He seemed then to speak to himself, as though forgetting that I was at his side. 'What do they know, who have never left Europe? *I* have been to Damascus. I have spoken to the Caliph Walid. It is three thousand miles to Damascus, and all the way the banner of Islam waves over city and village, field and forest, desert and shore. And beyond Damascus, three thousand miles more. And all this in ninety years, since their Prophet launched them upon the world.'

'A mighty people,' I said wonderingly. 'And of a surety, if anyone can restore King Roderic to the peaceful possession of his throne and his rights, they can.'

The Count muttered a prayer and left me. At dawn we landed by the ruined town, and went at once to Torrox. Count Anseric announced a great feast, and all day the castle and village bustled with preparations. By the fourth hour after noon, all was ready. Soon after, the feast began.

It was as though I slid from the top of a mountain, where it was cool and clear, ever faster down a slope, the air growing thicker, the light more lurid. At first musicians played, men and women bowed and spoke politely one to another, and ate daintily. Soon the platters of lamb and fowl and boar, of fish and mussel and oyster, passed more quickly and more quickly emptied the wine flagons. From music, it passed to singing, and from that to shouting. The Lady Hildoara's robe was but ill-fastened, so that unknowingly she displayed her breasts to the Moor, Abd-al-Malik. All round men began to fondle women. By the time darkness came scores of the Visigoths were lying on the floor in their own vomit. Others pulled servant wenches to their laps, threw up their skirts, and shamelessly stroked and entered upon their privy parts like rutting animals. Count Anseric, Lady Hildoara, and Abd-al-Malik were not to be seen and soon I left too, for the sights of that place were an abomination. But, in the courtyard I stumbled upon Count Anseric engaged in vile concourse with a stable boy. Running in horror away from them towards my cell, I opened a wrong door by mistake and found Abd-al-Malik and Lady Hildoara, naked, watching a great wolfhound that was mounted upon a servant girl.

I ran out then, blind with terror, past the sentries, out of the courtyard, into the village, for God must surely be preparing his lightning against such people. A man stepped out of a dark doorway in front of me and held my arm. 'It is the Saxon,' he said, 'God be praised!'

I stared. 'Lord Theodomir! The Lord be praised, indeed! What I have seen . . .'

'I know,' he said abruptly. 'Their punishment will come. But you have been on a journey. I must know what passed. For the sake of our country, for our very Faith, Aethelred . . . tell me!'

I collected my wits. 'You must ask your brother, Count Anseric,' I said humbly. 'I am sworn to secrecy.'

'They will kill me, fool!' he snapped. 'Why do you think I creep around dark alleys under my own castle walls? In the name of our Saviour, tell me.'

My heart was ready to burst, for Count Theodomir was a saint among men. But I was his brother's servant. I could not break faith. I wrenched free, and before he could recover from his surprise, I was gone.

I ran out of the village, ran across moonlit fields, I knew

148

not where. Then a white light shone in the sky and I ran towards that, believing it was a sign from Christ, until, coming at last close to it, I saw it was the Rock. Then I slowed to a walk and the sand under my feet changed to sharp stones, and the moon hid itself. Careless of what might befall, I crawled under a great rock and curled up, shivering like a fevered animal. Sick and sore afraid I was, for in my marrow I felt the coming wrath of God. Ever more bright in the night I saw God, towering in almighty anger in the clouds, brightness about him, to destroy this world and all of us upon it. Then I prayed, gabbling words without sense, until at last, being very tired, I seemed to see a woman, long-haired and naked but with no lewdness, who cried for help; but I could not help her, and after a while, she left me, or I fell asleep, I know not which.

I awoke in the morning, feeling very weak. I began to think what I should do, for now I wanted nothing but to escape and go on to Rome. But before long Abd-al-Malik rode up with two Visigothic captains. I remained hidden until, at the hour of noon, I saw, half a league distant, four ships coming towards the land. I watched them without thinking what they might portend. Then I saw that each was crowded with men, and I saw the flash of spears, and horses I saw, and knew that these were the four ships of the Moors. It was a bright morning, the cloud gone from the Rock, and the wind fresh and clean from the ocean beyond the Pillars. Green banners covered in strange writing, floated from the mastheads. I held my breath, for these were they who had come thousands of miles across deserts and rivers, all-conquering. Now they were treading the sea, and would set foot in Europe here under the great Rock. Where would they stop?

I saw David ha-Cohen in the third vessel, and he

seemed then the only true friend I had in the world. Heedless of all else I jumped up and ran along the shore to meet the boats where they would come to land.

I was close as the bows ran up the sand. I saw General Tarik jump down and wade towards Abd-al-Malik, and behind him many soldiers splashed ashore, some with those strange apes on their shoulders, and then the horses were whipped so that they jumped into the sea, and came with their teeth bared to the shore. As David came up the beach, a big leathern satchel over one shoulder and a sword slung by a baldric from the other, a dozen black Moors ran upon me, curved swords flashing, and I fainted.

I awoke cold and wet. David was casting sea water upon me. He cried, 'I never thought to see *you* again, Aethelred! Was it luck, or are you not so innocent as you pretend?'

The vessels were still unloading men and baggage. General Tarik, at the head of a score of horsemen, had just set off along the sand towards Torrox. The other Moors, mostly foot soldiers, had begun to carry stones, under Abd-al-Malik's direction, to make a wall.

I said, unhappily, 'I want to go to Rome.'

David said, 'That is impossible, I fear, until what will come to pass here, has come. You must stay with me. I have told my master that you surrendered to my mercy. You are therefore my slave, which puts my protection over you, for what it is worth. . . . Come, let us put up a shelter. We may be living many weeks on this Rock.'

I knew nothing of war and listened with amazement, while we worked, as David explained to me the meaning of what I saw going on under my eyes, but, to my ignorance, without purpose

It was Abd-al-Malik's task to make a corner of this

Rock, where vessels could unload, secure against attack, so that the army coming from Africa could land whatever the Visigoths did, either the Counts or King Roderic. The Counts were supposed to pretend a resistance, and then flee. General Tarik had gone to see that they kept their word.

The coming of the Moors was, therefore, simple treason by Count Illan, helped by Count Anseric, to make himself king in Roderic's place. I wondered if Count Theodomir had been able to learn anything of this, and if he had escaped to carry the word to the betrayed King Roderic. Yet Roderic had murdered Wittica, and defiled the lady Florinda. The thought that they all pretended to share my Holy Faith shamed me.

So that evening, being the slave of David the Jew, who was servant to Abd-al-Malik the Infidel, I slept under a tent, on the ground, and drank fresh water and ate a fruit the Moors had brought, called 'dates', and felt almost that I was cleansed from the sins of the Visigoths.

The days passed. Numerous citizens, many of them Jews, came from far and near to offer their thanks and help, and to beg the Moors to advance with all speed. Abd-al-Malik's soldiers built their stone walls higher, and dug a well, and made a rough stone jetty into the bay. The vessels travelled back and forth from Africa, and now nearly all the soldiers who landed marched at once to join the general in Torrox. I went with him, as a slave, and saw his falcons strike down many of those red-legged partridges which abound on the Rock. At night we ate of the partridge, and they were very tender, but each time I saw one between Abd-al-Malik's fierce, bearded lips, I thought it was a little Christian.

After a month, I asked David why the Moors did not now march out upon the Visigoths, since all was ready. He said, 'King Roderic is in the Pyrenees. Think you we are going to march all that way, and fight six hundred miles from our boats? No, no, the king shall ride six hundred miles to us. The Governor of Africa has promised to send us more men. When we fight, it will not be far from here.'

Another month passed. As I had learned a few words of Visogothic before, now I learned a little Arabic, and, without meaning to, found myself laughing as they did, with a high-pitched loud sound, and David taught me to greet them properly, saying *Ia ilaha ill Allah, Muhammadur rasul Allah!* which pleased them mightily. And David told me that though the Moors were strong, yet might the Christians win the day, for the Moors had a most fatal weakness. It was their feuds, he said, which they took everywhere with them and cherished above women, above gold. The Governor of Africa, Musa, was of one party, Abd-al-Malik of another, and only common allegiance to the Caliph made them speak to each other. But Musa and Abd-al-Malik were Arabs while Tarik was a Berber, from this western Africa – and they despised each other. All this, and much more David ha-Cohen explained to me while we walked and climbed together all over that great Rock, and discovered many caves, and came upon dens of wild pig and lynx, and saw wolves, and found a big fallen stone, marked by the hand of man, but far from the shore.

At last word came that King Roderic had passed Hispalis with a host of 90,000 men. The trumpets sounded and the army gathered by the ruined city, being now 12,000 men. I rode out by David's side, I on a small grey donkey and he on a fierce horse with wide nostrils and turned-up nose and long tail and red eyes. As we rode round the bay upon the traces of an ancient road, such as we have in Wessex, and the Holy Abbot says were made by the Romans, I looked back at the silver Rock shining in the sun, and wondered if I would ever see it again.

The banners over us were green and black, and covered by that strange writing. Five times a day every man of the host, from the generals to the trumpeters, knelt down and prayed towards the east, striking their heads on the earth. Such devoutness I have never seen among Christians, saving a very few holy monks. But I was Christian, and we went to fight a Christian king, however deep in sin his people had fallen, and I was sore troubled in spirit.

We marched six days by forest and mountain and along the ocean shore. We marched among great trees whereof the bark may be cut off, and is indeed that cork used for shoe soles. The boughs cast a pleasant shade, and bards of the host sang wild songs. At camp and on the march spies came to tell General Tarik of the Christians' movements, and of fords and water and hidden food. In a thunderstorm of lightning and rain we came to a ridge, with a great marsh full of wild duck and wading birds to the right, and to the left a wide, fast flowing river which curved out of the marsh, passed round the ridge, and flowed by more marshland to the sea. Here General Tarik planted his standard, saying 'Here, we conquer.' To engage us King Roderic must pass the river, and the narrow ridge between the great marsh and the river would prevent him extending his host, much greater than ours, past our wings. And, as David muttered to me that first night, that place was as far as it was prudent for the Moors to go from the Rock, and their boats in shelter under it, until they had defeated King Roderic.

It was a purgatory to wait and hear every hour of the advance of King Roderic's host, and I dared not pray for fear the Moors would kill me. Nor did I know what I should pray for. On the second day in that place, which was the 16th day of July, the army of the Visigoths came down to the river from the north and began to cross. The Moorish horsemen rode out in readiness, but the Christians made camp, and set up their standards. 'Tomorrow will be the battle,' David said, 'and victory will be ours. A spy has just brought word that Count Illan commands the right wing of the Christians, and Archbishop Oppas the left. They are both sworn to us.'

While the soldiers began to whet their sword blades I walked away down the river, oppressed by my thoughts. I came after a time to the beach, where the river flowed into the ocean hard by a sandy cape, with a hill behind. I lay down and slept, and dreams came, for I saw the sand covered with dead men, and others rolling in the waves. I awoke with a cry, hearing my name called.

I got up, and saw Count Theodomir across the river. 'Aethelred,' he said, 'My brother Anseric is dead, choked in gluttony. You owe him nothing more. Come over the river, join us, and tell us all you know. Otherwise, I fear for the Cross in Hispania – aye, in all Europe, the world.'

I went to the river, and walked a little way in. Then I remembered that I was David's slave, and he had saved my life. I stepped back.

'Aethelred . . . we are *Christians*!' Theodomir called.

Again, I went into the water, a little farther this time. The current tugged at my legs to overthrow me, and suddenly I knew I could not go. I struggled back to the shore, and hurried to the camp, and the tent I shared with David. I did not speak, but lay shivering on the ground, my eyes closed.

The next morning the trumpets sounded early, and I rode out at David's side, and the army took its stand on the ridge between the marsh which is called Janda, and the river, and the Christians came against us. Behind the centre of their host I saw a domed litter, drawn by white donkeys, gold and silver glittering in the sun, and David said that was the litter of King Roderic. Then the battle began.

For a time I sat upon my donkey held in thrall by the spectacle before me – so many thousands of warriors under the bright sun upon the grass beside the marsh – the army of the infidels silent under the green banners, steel casques on their heads, their horses light-footed and flecked with nervous foam; the army of the Visigoths, under banners of boars and lions and eagles, and here and there a Cross. Their horses were mighty, and strode ponderously upon us, and their leaders wore long floating hair and carried two-handed swords, and wore horns or wolf-masks upon their helmets, like to the sea raiders who pillage our shores of Wessex. As the armies met I saw that on the right the Visigoths stopped many paces short of the Moors, and rested upon their swords, and to the left the same. Only in the centre did King Roderic's host fall upon us. It was all I could do to keep out of the warring, for the great horses reared over me and swords whistled, with a mighty shouting upon the summer air. I saw David smite a bishop so that his arm flew free of his shoulder, then a blow from behind knocked me off my ass, but David helped me again to the donkey's back, shouting, 'Not yet, Aethelred, such as you are immortal!'

Then the commanders of our right wing and our left wing, seeing that Count Illan and the Archbishop stood idle before them, swept round like the horns of a crescent moon, and fell upon King Roderic from left and right and behind. His men became affrighted, and fled, like an army of mice set upon by cats, and I saw many horses galloping away riderless, and the domed litter of King Roderic was abandoned upon the field, but none saw the King.

Then the soldiers of General Tarik again gathered together, and fell upon Count Illan's host. The Count rode towards us, his hand raised, but the Moors flew by him, like greyhounds unleashed and in a moment of wailing arose in his host as the Moors rent them, and soon they too broke and fled. On the other side Archbishop Oppas's men did not wait, but turned and ran, only the Archbishop coming forward to make obeisance before Tarik.

The battle was over, though for several hours more the Moors cut and hacked at the Christians as they tried to recross the river, until the ground and the bank squelched with blood and the water ran deep, dark red into the lower marsh, on its way to the sea. Then Tarik's trumpets sounded a halt and the Moors gathered their prisoners – to the number of twenty thousand, David said – and at the same time lit fires, set up spits, stripped a score of Christian corpses of their clothes, and set them to roast over the fires. The dusk was falling, and never have I heard, since, or hope to hear, such a wail of fear and horror as arose from the massed prisoners. Tarik gave an order then, and the prisoners were marched away.

I turned, blind, to run. I had betrayed Christ, for this! David's arm stopped me with a jerk. 'It is only to spread terror,' he said, 'When the prisoners are out of sight, the bodies will be decently buried.' Then Tarik called, and David hurried to him, I following more slowly. Count Illan and the Archbishop were there, and Tarik had just finished speaking. David translated: 'King Roderic is dead – or fled. I take possession of all this land in the name of the Commander of the Faithful, the Caliph Walid.'

He stooped, gathered a handful of dust and threw it in the air. Every Moor's sword flashed, and a great shout arose, beginning with those close by who had heard what the general said, and spreading as ripples on a pond so that there was still a distant shouting when David said, 'Thank the general's magnanimity for your life. Then go. He has no further use for you.'

Count Illan walked away, like a man dreaming, and disappeared in the dark, blood-soaked field. To the Archbishop, David said, 'Bring hither all those of quality who have surrendered, and all the women and baggage of the Visigoths. The general will give you his commands tomorrow.'

Gradually the space about the general's tent cleared. I had seen the wrath of God, and I still lived. Now I longed, I prayed, only for . . .

David ha-Cohen was beside me. 'My master, Abd-al-Malik, has been appointed Lord of Torrox, and Guardian of the Rock,' he said 'I am to be his chief minister. Stay with me. Be my friend, my companion in work and play, for I have come to hold a great love for you, Aethelred – and not such a love as Count Anseric's!'

The words rushed from my mouth, from my heart – 'I can not stay, David. I am sick at heart, for I have seen more than my spirit can encompass. I must to Rome to learn the Word, and take it back to Wessex.'

'Back to the land of fog and bog,' he said bitterly. 'You are a bigger fool than I believed, if that is possible.' He walked away, and round, then came back. 'Take this.' He pressed something hard into my hand and I saw the glint of gold by the starlight. 'Go now, down this valley to the sea, then follow the strand north to a little village of fishermen on an island called Gades. Ask there for Timothy Opadianus. He is of my faith. He will find you a vessel going to Rome. When you pass the Rock, think of me.' He embraced me suddenly, and cried *'Shalom!'* and was gone.

It came about as he had said. A month later I passed the Rock at high noon on a stormy day. The cloud streaming from its crest seemed to be green, like the standards of the Moors, and to have the word of that faith hidden in it in their long, slender writing. I gazed at the Rock until darkness hid it.

After five years in Rome I returned to Glastonbury on foot, and never saw David ha-Cohen, or the Rock, again.

Book Six

CALIPHS, EMIRS, AND KINGS

The Jewish years 4471–5222
A.U.C. 1464–2215
A.D. 711–1462
A.H. 92 866

AFTER the great battle, without waiting for Governor Musa's authorization, Tarik swept on northward, and was only halted by the arrival of the furiously jealous Musa, who publicly whipped him in Toledo. Musa then took up the pursuit and within a few years had conquered all of Spain, except the mountainous Asturias in the extreme north. The Pyrenees did not stop the Muslims' victorious advance and they were not finally turned back until 732, when the Frankish king Charles Martel defeated them outside Tours, in France. This was one of history's most important battles, for it decided whether Europe would become Muslim or remain Christian.

All the leaders of the invasion have their memorial. The Roman Traducta, in the gut of the Strait, was now named Tarifa, after the man who had made the first reconnaissance in 710; and, from the taxes levied there on goods from Africa, came the word *tariff*. Abd-al-Malik, one of the few Arabs in the invading army (most were North Africans), was given the Castle of Torasch or Torrox (since vanished; it was on the Guadiaro, about nine miles north of Gibraltar). The eighth in direct descent from him was Almanzor, the greatest ruler Muslim Spain ever knew.

The African Pillar of Hercules, known to the Romans as Mons Abyla, became Djebel Musa. The man himself paid the penalty of his success, and of a certain folly in marrying his son to Egilona, the widow of the lecherous but now vanished King Roderic, and then appointing him Governor of Andalusia. From Damascus this looked as though Musa was setting up his own dynasty in Spain. The Caliph recalled him, stripped him of his wealth and honours and soon afterwards, as a token of appreciation for all that he had done on behalf of his lord and his religion, sent him the head of his son.

In honour of Tarik, the leader who had actually taken the Rock, the old name of Calpe, though still known and used, was overshadowed by the new one of Tarik's Mountain, *Djebel Tarik* – Gibraltar.

Besides bringing their faith into Europe, the Muslims are also responsible, as I hinted in the previous tale, for introducing the famous apes. These animals, Barbary Apes, are in fact tail-less monkeys, macaques (*macaca sylvana, magus* or *inuus*). They cannot be descendants of the monkeys whose fossil bones have been found all over Europe, as far north as England, for they are of quite different species. Nor can they have come from Africa by a secret tunnel (the geological faulting under the Strait rules that out, even without the abstruse arguments of common sense). The Moors brought them, and the true oddity about them is that they have never spread into Southern Spain, but have remained confined to Gibraltar; also that though there are plenty still wild in North Africa, there are none in their original country of origin, Persia – where they have become extinct.

They are odd beasts, not very large ... but I cannot better the description of them by Mr Ivan Sanderson in his book *The Monkey Kingdom*: '... a beetle-browed, grumpy, greyish brown animal with rather long, thick, slightly wavy fur, expressive eyes and a wide vocabulary. It is a typical "slob" and aggresively obnoxious rather than just mischievous. ... None the less it has been repeatedly reported, and by totally unrelated sources, that these animals suffer loneliness acutely and will adopt all manner of small animals of other kinds and carry them about with them, stroking, caressing, even feeding them.'

Their numbers probably fluctuated considerably. All through Moorish times they were strengthened by the infusion of fresh blood from Africa. Then after two centuries of neglect and inbreeding under the Spanish they found themselves pampered and superstitiously nurtured as the alleged symbols of British power on the Rock. But from now on in this history they are there, with the Gibraltar candytuft and the Barbary partridge; from now on you should imagine them, an exotic and irrational part of the Gibraltar background, stealing fruit, fouling rooftops, grabbing baubles from children's hands, watching the bustle below from their fastnesses on top of the Rock and at the head of the eastern cliffs (a place here has long been called the Monkey's Alameda, or 'garden walk').

For the rest, the story of Gibraltar during these years is part of the story of Spain, and particularly of Andalusia. Spain remained subject to the Damascus Caliphs until the Omayyad family was overthrown by the Abbasids. In 756 a refugee of the Omayyads, Abd-er-Rahman, grandson of the Caliph Hisham, arrived in Spain and declared that he, not the usurper in Baghdad, was the true Commander of the Faithful. Thus began the independent Caliphate of Cordoba, which lasted, in great magnificence, until 1031. Cordoba became the intellectual capital of Europe, and one of the most civilized cities in the world. There was considerable religious tolerance, and many Jews reached prominence as scholars and statesmen. For these three centuries Gibraltar was either totally uninhabited, or nearly so.

When the Cordoba Caliphate collapsed it first broke up

into a number of independent emirates, until in 1080 these vanished under a new invasion from North Africa, by the fanatic Almoravides. The Almoravides lasted until 1145 when they in turn succumbed to the weakness of power and went under to the Almohades, also from Africa. All this time, the Visigothic-Celtiberian-Romans (that is, the Christians), starting in the unconquered Asturias, were slowly working their way southward, reconquering, uniting, consolidating, so that each successive wave of Muslims ruled over a smaller piece of Spain. The Almohades lasted until July 16, 1212, when they were defeated in the climactic battle of the whole 700-year reconquest, at Navas de Tolosa in the Guadalquivir valley. King Alfonso VIII's victory was largely due to a shepherd, Martin Alhaja Gontran, who led the Christians by unknown tracks and unguarded paths to the attack. After the defeat the Muslims broke up into small kingdoms, of which the only one to affect Gibraltar was the Kingdom of Granada.

Although Tarik's invaders had landed at Gibraltar, it was at Algeciras and Tarifa that they made their first ports and fortresses. The provincial capital under the Visigoths had been Asido, and it remained so under the Moors, but now called Medina Sidonia. In spite of the remarkable incorporation of 'Asido' in this name, the title comes from the fact that new Muslim immigrants were allotted to that part of Spain most like their homeland; the ones who came here were from Sidon, and the whole area was known as Filistin (Palestine). Gibraltar was dependent on Algeciras during all the early years.

Having tried to fill in the sweep of the background, let us put the Rock in the foreground, and see what passed over and on it ... 844 – the Norsemen pass by in their long ships, after having sacked Cadiz ... 1003 – a great battle is fought on the River Miel, by Algeciras, between rival claimants for Almanzor's power (he had died the year before) ... After the fall of the Caliphate the Wali of Algeciras (Gibraltar's over-lord), sets himself up as independent ... but soon falls under the Emir of Malaga ... who soon falls under the Emir of Seville.

This last, hard pressed by the warlike King Alfonso VI, asked the Almoravide King of Morocco to come over and help him. Many, including his own son, warned him that one needed a long spoon to sup with King Yussuf, but the Emir made a famous answer – 'I would rather be the King of Morocco's camel herd than a vassal of the Christian dogs.'

He had his wish, for Yussuf came, seized Tarifa, Algeciras, and Gibraltar as bases for his invading armies, and soon ruled all Muslim Spain. The foolish Emir died in 1088, a beggar in exile in a Saharan oasis.

The Almoravides persecuted Christians, Jews, and other Muslims alike, and large numbers of all religions, especially Jews, fled to Christian Spain. For a time in the 13th century it looked as though Spain might forge the first free or open society of modern times and a Castilian king was proud to call himself King of the Three Faiths; but Navas de Tolosa so crushed the Muslim power that Christian bigots were able to say, we don't need help, and turn Spain upon the opposite and fatal course of 'unification', that is, exclusion of all but the official race, religion, and way of thought. Laws forcing Jews to wear distinguishing yellow patches were approved in 1370 and 1405. In 1412 savage edicts were promulgated excluding Jews from many trades, defining what they must wear, forbidding them to employ Christians, and worse anti-semitism was encouraged, and in 1391 over 4,000 Jews were murdered in Seville alone. When the Almohades came from Morocco to overthrow the Almoravides, they came to Gibraltar, seizing it in 1146. The Almohade Emperor, Abd-al-Mumin was the real founder of Gibraltar as a city and fortress. He decided that the Christians were now so strong that neither Tarifa nor Algeciras could be relied on to stay out of their hands much longer. A third and final strong point was needed at Gibraltar, and he called in a famous mathematician and engineer to design it. This man was Al-Hajj Yaish, who built the great mosque of Seville, now part of the cathedral.

The foundations were laid on May 19, 1160, and all essential work finished in six months, which is very fast work indeed. Abd-al-Mumin did not stay long, but came back in November to see the completion of the building, and stayed two months listening to poets, holding council with the Muslim governors of Andalusia, and presumably dallying with houris in the harem, though it is hard to associate such gentle activities with the Rock.

It is also hard to disentangle Yaish's city from the one built after the Moors had lost and regained Gibraltar, in 1333; but there was certainly a complex system of walls, keeps, and towers at the north-west corner of the Rock dominated by a fortified Qasabah and that by a Tower of Homage. Most of the town huddled under this, though there must have been a settlement far to the south, at Europa, for there was a Muslim shrine near the Point and close by there was – and still is – a remarkable underground reservoir, the roof supported by Moorish arches, later known as the Nuns' Well. Yaish also put in an aqueduct from the Red Sands to the town, and probably designed the Moorish baths under the present Gibraltar Museum. The 'Moorish Wall' which runs straight up the west face of the upper Rock is Yaish's, but the Moorish Castle is not. Yaish's Tower of Homage was destroyed in the seige of 1333 and the present one built by Abu 'l Hassan, 'King of Gibraltar', in about 1340. The Spaniards called it 'La Calahorra' and the British, the 'Moorish Castle'. The attribution of any works to the original Moorish invaders of 711 is an error due to misinterpretation of an inscription which was once over the gate of the Qasabah.

Abd-al-Mumin's forethought in fortifying Gibraltar bore its first fruit when Navas de Tolosa ended the Almohade power fifty years later, and they began to disengage from Spain. Tarifa did not fall until 1292 and the then King of Morocco took the opportunity to get out of Europe altogether, by selling Algeciras (with Gibraltar) to the King of Granada.

There now steps into our story the founder of a remarkable family which became the most powerful grandees and the largest landowners in Spain. This man, Alonso Perez de Guzman, was a knight from Leon in the north, who so distinguished himself in the taking of Tarifa that the king made him *señor*, or squire, of Sanlucar de Barrameda. Guzman *el Bueno*, the Good, as he was known, soon expanded his power and in 1309, partly from ambition and partly from genuine outrage that the Muslims still held parts of Spain, he attacked Gibraltar. He landed on the Red Sands, south of the wall that protected the town, and took up a position on the steep slope above the castle. There he erected catapults and war engines and started battering the defences. Near the end of August the Moors surrendered. This was the first of Gibraltar's fifteen sieges, and the first of its four major turn-overs of population, for nearly all the Muslims left.

Now that Guzman el Bueno held the Rock for King

Ferdinand IV of Castile, the problem was to repopulate it, and hold it. Being in the forefront of a never ending war, and subject to raids, sieges, and attacks, it was not a desirable place of residence, and King Ferdinand had to take extraordinary measures to attract a population. He gave Gibraltar a charter which in effect made it a sanctuary for thieves, murderers, and runaway wives: all would be pardoned if they would just come and live in Gibraltar for a few months. Prisoners were also sent there from the jails, and released to be free citizens. Gibraltar became, and must have resembled, a frontier fort-town of the badlands, complete with loose women, ne'er-do-wells, remittance men and, in place of the U.S. Cavalry, such knights and men-at-arms as Guzman could find for its defence.

The Moors tried to regain the Rock in 1315 (2nd Siege), but failed. In 1333 the King of Granada instituted the 3rd Siege. The Governor of the fortress was one Vasco Perez de Meiras, a nobleman, from Galicia in the north-west. Meiras had ambitions of founding a mighty family, and spent the funds allotted for the defence of Gibraltar in buying himself estates around Jerez, already rich and long since famous for its sherry wines. On June 17, after four-and-a-half months of siege, in which Meiras's heroism somewhat redeemed his venality, Gibraltar fell once more. The Christian convicts, strumpets, and knights marched out and the Muslims marched in, making the second population turnover. The King of Granada did not retain overlordship for long, as the Moroccans, whom he had called in to help during the siege decided to keep it for themselves – but few of the Muslim people would have left on this account.

Alfonso XI was now King of Castile, and the recapture of the Rock became his obsession. Indeed, with this second loss of it to the Moors the place became, in Spain, not just a port and fortress, but a holy cause. Alfonso at once began the 4th Siege and came very near to success, but in the end had to march his army away, defeated. Seven years later he inflicted a crushing defeat on the Muslims at Salado, just west of Tarifa. In the aftermath he could easily have retaken Gibraltar, but an unaccountable lethargy overcame him and he did nothing until it was too late. When he did begin operations once more it was against Algeciras, a famous siege which began in August 1342, lasted eighteen months, and brought down, as volunteers, the flower of Europe's chivalry, including King Edward III's grandson from England. During the siege the King of Morocco gathered 12,000 troops in Gibraltar to help drive away the Christians. Nevertheless Algeciras did at last fall, was later razed to the ground, and ceased to exist, as a town, for four centuries. Gibraltar was now the only port on the Spanish side of the straits left in Muslim hands, and in 1349 Alfonso XI returned to the attack, in the 5th Siege. His army soon began to suffer from the Black Death (bubonic or pneumonic plague) then ravaging Europe, and on March 26, 1350, the king died of it. The principal Moors went out from Gibraltar in mourning to pay their respects to their dead adversary.

At this time Gibraltar was visited by the famous Moroccan traveller Ibn Battutah. He went, he said, because he wanted to take part in the Holy War against the Christians. Of Gibraltar, then under the Moroccan king Abu Inan he wrote:

I walked round the mountain and saw the marvellous works executed on it by our master (the previous king and the armament with which he equipped it, together with the additions made thereto by our master Abu Inan,

may God strengthen him, and I should have liked to
remain as one of its defenders to the end of my days.

But he did not stay: he visited Malaga and Granada and
then returned to his home in Tangier, probably convinced
that nothing could save the Muslim cause in Spain.

The rotations of Gibraltar from the hands of the Kings
of Granada to the Kings of Emperors of Morocco and
back again make a dizzy story; but it is not important.
The grip of any central Muslim authority was fast slack-
ening; indeed, the man whom the Emperor of Morocco
appointed Wali, or governor, of Gibraltar in 350 at
once declared himself its king – this is the 'king' Ibu Battutah refers to – and no one seems to have cared very
much.

Apart from the 6th Siege, a confused civil war between
Granada and Morocco factions, Gibraltar relapsed into
comparative quiet and for eighty years the only other
mention of it in the records is the visit of a Castilian
admiral, who dropped in on his way to sweep Castilian
pirates out of the western Mediterranean, and was received with much courtesy and feasting, including plenty
of *cous cous*.

But if the kings were no longer very interested in Gibraltar, some private citizens were. The heirs of Guzman el
Bueno were now Counts of Niebla, and owned all the
fishing rights from Gibraltar to the Portugal border, about
150 miles. Muslim raiders were poaching in the Count's
seas, attacking his pickling and salting plants, and causing
him loss of revenue. When pursued the pirates took refuge
in Gibraltar. For glory and profit, therefore, the Count
decided to retake the Rock. In August 1436 he began the
7th Siege by landing at the Red Sands, south of the town
wall, with the intention of following time-honoured pre-

cedents – advance up the hill, install engines of war above the castle, batter and starve the defenders into submission.

Alas, no one had noticed that in the years between the dastardly Moors had extended the wall southward along the sea front. When the Count's forces landed they were still under it, with no way up, a murderous current strengthening, and the tide rising ... Many were killed and drowned in the debacle, including the Count. The Moors, among whom there were (as a Spanish historian remarks disdainfully) few well-bred chaps at this time, recovered his corpse, put it in a box, and hung it over a gate of the castle.

The Rock remained in Muslim hands. The defences can not have been strong nor the population numerous, for the Kingdom of Granada had neither the will nor the means to make them so. The pirates still raided the Christian fisheries. The count's son, who soon afterwards added the Dukedom of Medina Sidonia to the family titles, looked hungrily at Gibraltar from across the bay. So did others, both noble and simple. It could not be long now before some small event, some man's single-handed action, precipitated the next conflict . . .

A JEWEL FOR THE KING

THE captain of the *Gaditana* lashed down the tiller and looked at his owner. 'Start unloading at once, Judah?' he said. Judah nodded, glancing at the sun; it was past noon and they would have to make haste to be finished when the gate closed for the night. Well, they could finish tomorrow – the Moors were not very strict about Christian boats staying overnight these days.

He went forward to his two passengers, and put an arm round each, for they were also his friends, all three of an age – between twenty-five and thirty – and had grown up together in Tarifa. 'There,' he said, 'el *Peñon*, the Rock.'

At the end of the jetty the town wall began, pierced by the Water Gate. Behind, roofs and minarets, thickly jammed together, rose to the towers of the castle, aflutter with the green and black flags of the Kingdom of Granada. Above the castle the slope steepened, grey rock gleamed in great tilted slabs and, far above, a grey cloud hid the crest.

Manuel Barrachina said, 'I wish we could take that box down from the tower. I think the Duke would reward any servant of his well who brought him the remains of his father for proper burial.' Manuel was slight, and stooped, and fair skinned; he was clerk to the Duke of Medina Sidonia's agent in Tarifa.

Pedro Santangel said, 'I wish we could put the flag of Castile up there instead of the Moorish banner. I think the king would knight a man who did that . . .' He was tall and fair, with dark eyes, willowy, swooning handsome to the girls. His father was trying to make him follow the practice of the law, but all his desire was to be a knight and fight for Castile, King Enrique, and the Holy Catholic Church.

Judah said, 'I wish it were settled one way or the other, so that we know where we are. Sometimes you can bring a cargo in here peacefully, sometimes they fire a cannon at you. Sometimes you can wander all over the town, sometimes guards prevent you stepping off your ship. For trade we need peace and security.' He was short and square, with a wide mouth, a broken beak nose and two fingers gone from his left hand; big ears and hands, thick curly black hair, and startling blue eyes. He had run his own ship out of Tarifa since he was twenty, and now owned three, that plied in trade along the coast, up the Guadalquivir and, when conditions allowed, over to Africa. He was a Jew. In 1399 his grandfather's sister, Beulah Conquy, had married a young man called Jacob Azayal in Cordoba; the following year Jacob Azayal was converted to Christianity and became Luis Santangel – grandfather of the eager young would-be-knight of the Church now at Judah's side; Pedro Santangel was therefore a *marrano*, a New Christian, and Judah's second cousin – a fact which both knew, but never mentioned.

'Can we go ashore now?' Manuel Barrachina asked. 'I must get to the Governor's audience as soon as possible.'

Judah let down the gangplank. The sweating sailors were already passing sacks of wheat up from the hold to the deck, and Moorish labourers were waiting to take them ashore. At the Water Gate the Berber guard was talking to a fat turbanned merchant, and did not look up. The young men passed into the city of Gibraltar, and, at once, into Africa. Donkeys loaded with brass jars trot-

172

ted down the narrow alley towards the harbour, to load there with oil and wine from the ships. In the gutter lusty-voiced women sold fruit by the single stem, spices by the pinch, sherbet by the thimbleful. In all the shop fronts the merchants sat, with carpets and baskets and bolts of cloth and mounds of flour. Cobblers banged on their lasts, blacksmiths on their anvils, tinkers on pots, beggars on drums. The knifegrinder made tunes on a bamboo pipe, and from the minaret of the mosque the muezzin chanted the call to prayer.

Manuel Barrachina left them to go to the Castle, for his business was to deliver a note from the Duke's agent, informing the Governor that a fishing boat from Gibraltar had been taken poaching off Tarifa, and would be released on payment of the fine.

The levanter made the day close, and Judah and Pedro walked slowly, left hands resting on the hilts of their daggers. Judah had no business – his captain was in charge of the unloading – but had come because he wanted a change of air. Pedro only wanted to see Gibraltar while it was possible. So they strolled together towards the square block of the castle, and then southwards along shelf-like streets. They paused where a flight of steps crossed, going down towards the harbour, and looked out over the bay, and pointed out to each other the new aspect of hills and valleys which they knew well from the landward side. As they turned to walk on, Judah bumped into someone, hard. It was a Moorish woman, and he had knocked her over. As she fell, the black veil dropped from her face, and Judah looked into startled dark green eyes under strong, straight black brows. On her forehead hung a silver ornament in the shape of the Star of David. Her lips were thin but perfectly curved in an oval face. Judah's jaw dropped. He had never seen anything so beautiful. He stared into the green eyes, stunned. The girl lowered her lids and he recovered his wits. He knelt quickly beside her, muttering, 'Are you a Jewess?' She was fumbling for her veil. 'Yes,' she whispered.

'Woman!' an old voice was yelling in Berber, 'What doest thou, shameless?'

'It's the duenna,' Pedro said, laughing. 'Shall I hold her off?'

The girl was slight, her skin like an olive's, her hair blue-black – and she was pulling her veil up now, rising to her feet. The green eyes glowed above the black cloth. 'Are you a slave?' Judah whispered. The old woman panted up, screeching. The girl nodded. The old woman grabbed her by the wrist, pulled her away. 'I shall find you,' Judah said in Ladino, the Hebrew-tinged Spanish which was the *lingua franca* of the Sephardim. Then she was gone, hurrying down the steps beside the old scold, the black robe fluttering behind her.

'Let's follow them!' Pedro said, still chuckling. They started down the steps, but had not taken three strides when heavy hands fell on their shoulders, and a deep voice growled, 'Slow, there.' Three large Negroes, naked from the waist, curved scimitars stuck in their sashes, fell in beside them. 'Do you think our master sends out his women without protection?' one asked. 'Such as they are not for Christian dogs . . .' They were passing a large stable, and without warning the three seized them, threw them inside, and slammed the door shut. They heard the scrape of the bolts, and the Negroes go on laughing down the steps.

They scrambled out of the dung-littered straw and leaped at the window – but it was barred. They began to batter at the door with their fists. At last an old man came, mumbling, and let them out – but by then the steps were empty, and when they ran down to the street next below, so was that.

Pedro took Judah's arm and led him into a coffee shop. 'Sit down, friend,' he said. 'You look as if you've been hit on the head with a mace.'

Judah sat sipping his coffee, staring at the wall, seeing only those green eyes. He'd traversed the Mediterranean three times, gone once to England, and knew the stews of every port from Cadaques to Pasajes. He'd enjoyed scores of women of every colour, size, and quality, but he had never fallen in love. And now, at first sight! It was impossible, he told himself. Worse, it was ridiculous. But it was so. There was no escape from it.

'I shall find and buy her,' he said at last, 'Even if I have to come and live here and become a subject of the King of Granada.'

'I guessed somehow you wanted to see more of her,' Pedro Santangel said dryly 'If she wasn't a Jewess, I might challenge you myself—'

'I'll kill you if you do,' Judah said.

'—but she is, and, well . . . for such as we, that makes her impossible. But, I have an idea . . .'

An hour later a burly broken-nosed man passed slowly along the street below the wall of the Castle. He wore a dirty old brown djellabah with the hood up, and a pair of battered Moorish slippers. A big basket of green vegetables hung on his left arm, and as he shambled along he seemed to be chanting his wares; but in truth the tune that he sang was a phrase from the Song of Songs:

175

Shuvee, shuvee Hashulamit
Shuvee, shuvee v'nechez bach
Return, return, O Shulamite,
Return, return, that we may look upon thee.

There were a few Jews in Gibraltar – one, indeed, the banker Chaim Uziel, was a distant relative of the Santangels; but though they would understand what he was singing, they would be unlikely to betray him. Judah trudged on.

Return, return, O Shulamite . . .

It was hotter than ever inside this accursed stinking garment, he thought. Pedro Santangel, back on the ship, must be ill with laughing.

Up and down, along and across, all through the city Judah passed; and even into the fortress to cry his vegetables in the empty square under the Tower of Homage, until a sleepy soldier came, cursing, to drive him out. The walls of the narrow streets seemed to give off heat like ovens. On the south walls the awnings were out to keep the glare from the barred windows, and under the north walls dogs slept and men snored. Judah tramped on, chanting:

Return, return, that we may look upon thee . . .

His sweat soaked the djellabah. From the houses now and then a voice cried angrily, 'In the name of Allah, hold your tongue now, and let us sleep.' Once a woman came to her door, and spent five minutes picking over his wares; fortunately she did not buy, as he had no idea what price to ask.

He reached the height of the town, above and to the south of the Castle. Half a dozen apes played, dozed and scratched each other for fleas nearby. He picked a cabbage out of his basket and threw it at them, crying, 'Lead me to her, shameless ones!' An old dog ape grabbed the cabbage, and retreated with it. All the others dropped what they were doing and followed him. Judah's shoulder throbbed and he thought his left arm would drop off. She'd never hear him, or if she did, she'd only laugh. What would she want of a thirty-year-old man with half his fingers gone, broken nose, big ears . . .

He got up, hitched the basket into place, and started along the path. Something white gleamed at his feet and he stooped to pick it up. He turned it over curiously – an ivory statuette of a naked woman, her hair piled up to form a hole so it could be worn as an ornament; but what Moorish woman would wear a naked woman, her slit clearly showing, dangling round her neck? Still, it was well made. The apes must have been playing with it. He put it into the inner pocket of the djellabah and started back down the nearest flight of steps.

Return, return, O Shulamite . . .

Almost at once a girl's voice answered, with a cradle song that he remembered his mother singing to his youngest sister.

He listened, pressed close under the wall. The singer was inside a three-storeyed house, with a walled garden below and the open mountain above. The tower of the Castle was a quarter of a mile to the north, and at the same level. Steep steps, interspersed with sections of ramp, led down on either side of a deep gutter and water channel into the town, houses becoming thicker all the way.

Then he saw her at an upper window, behind bars. He called softly. 'What is your name?'

'Tova is my name. Tova Hassan they call me,' she answered in the lilt of the song.

'I will buy you. I am not really a seller of vegetables.'

'I did not think so.'

'I love you,' he said.

'How do I know what love is?' she sang. Her voice faded as she moved away from the window. Judah stared longingly for a moment more, then called, 'I will be back soon,' hitched the basket higher on his arm, and hurried down the steps.

The sun was sinking over the mountains across the bay when Judah presented himself again at the house on the hill, this time at the main door. He wore a richly embroidered Moorish robe of blue and gold, with a thick gold waistband and blue silk turban. He had never worn Muslim clothes before, but nothing else of quality was available in Gibraltar. Pedro Santangel stalked ceremoniously at his side, elegant as always, with a long sword added to his costume.

Judah knocked on the door with the hilt of his dagger. Two minutes later it opened suddenly and one of the large Negroes who had thrown them into the stable appeared. Judah spoke, in his sailor's Berber, 'I am Messer Judah Conquy, of Tarifa. Is your master, the honourable Suleiman Qureshi, in?'

'What has that to do with you?' the Negro growled. He stared at the two of them suspiciously, as though trying to remember where he had seen them before.

Judah snapped his fingers, and Pedro dropped a coin into the Negro's hand. 'Important business,' Judah said. 'I am a ship owner and merchant. It is urgent.'

The Negro disappeared. The door slammed. They waited.

'Perhaps she is like one of those loud-mouthed partridges men put out as decoys, to bring other game down,' Pedro said cheerfully, 'We shall get our throats cut.'

After five minutes the door opened, and the Negro reappeared with a brief, 'Come.' He led them down a passage and round an inner patio, where a fountain played, flowers grew in blue and yellow pots, and caged birds sang. There was also a red-legged partridge on a long tether, pecking for corn upon the grass. Pedro nudged Judah and muttered, 'See?' In a cool room the other side, under a gently waving palm fan worked by a young girl – black, lovely, unveiled – a thin man sat on a pile of leather cushions.

Judah bowed. 'The honourable Suleiman Qureshi? The great merchant, whose fame has spread to Fez and all the coasts of Africa?'

'I am Suleiman Qureshi,' the man answered. He was bald and grey-skinned, with a pendulous lower lip. His eyes were small, dark, and alert. 'You are the Jew shipowner of Tarifa. But how can you benefit me? We are rivals, not collaborators.'

Judah bowed again and came to the point. The worth of a female slave, young and in good condition, was about 120 dinars here or in Morocco, rather more in Granada. He must offer more, because the fact of his coming proved that he badly wanted the girl. He said, 'You have a slave of my faith here, called Tova Hassan. She has not betrayed you, but I chanced to see her. I wish to marry her, and will buy her from you for two hundred and fifty dinars.'

There was a long silence. The black fan-girl's eyes

rolled and her teeth flashed. The bodyguard moved his bare feet on the tiles. The water tinkled more loudly in the patio. A reflection from the sky glowed red on Qureshi's bald head.

'No,' he said.

Judah snapped a finger. Pedro pulled a silk purse out of his fob, opened it, and poured a torrent of heavy ten-dinar pieces on to the low table in front of Qureshi. Judah knew that there were fifty of them, 500 dinars in all, borrowed from Chaim Uziel the banker.

'No,' Qureshi said.

Pedro scraped up the coins, poured them back into the purse, and put the purse away. Judah said stolidly, 'You must love her very greatly.'

Qureshi smiled thinly – 'No, Jew, it's not that. Do you remember buying a number of singularly excellent carpets in Larache two years ago? In spite of being warned that they had been promised to the Wazir of the King of Granada?'

Judah remembered at once. The man who threatened him had obviously not expected any competition, and when Judah bought the carpets at a fair price he had gone off scowling and muttering about Jewish dogs. He must have been an agent of this Suleiman Qureshi. If Qureshi wanted revenge, it was no use offering him money, so Judah bowed, and said, 'I recall the occasion perfectly. Now, with your permission . . .'

The thin man's eyes glittered in the failing light. 'Are you sure you won't bid higher, Messer Conquy? She is small, but between the thighs, aiih, what a fire burns!'

Judah stepped forward and pushed the merchant backwards off his piled cushions. Pedro drew his sword and pointed it at the Negro. 'We go,' Judah snapped. 'Do not hinder us.' The merchant began to shout and rave, footsteps and answering shouts echoed high in the house. Judah and Pedro ran across the courtyard, down the passage, and out into the open.

The sun had set and in the town a few lamps showed against the twilight. 'That was a bold answer,' Pedro said, 'though it may lead us to the bastinado.'

'I couldn't help myself,' Judah said. They hurried on towards the harbour, walking now, but fast. The Water Gate was still open, and they went out on to the jetty. At the gangplank of the *Gaditana* the captain said, 'We've just finished unloading, Judah.'

Judah saw Manuel Barrachina on the deck. There was no reason to wait. 'Sail at once,' he said, and ran aboard.

A sailor was hauling the gangplank in when a figure appeared out of the gloom and called, 'Stay! Where are you bound?'

'Tarifa,' the captain answered.

'Allow me passage, please. I will pay well,' the man said. He was richly dressed in black, his face hidden.

'Come on, then. Five dirhams.'

The man stepped on board and paid the money. The captain pointed to the hatch and the passenger went below. Five minutes later, the sail billowing, the *Gaditana* slid past the end of the jetty, eastbound.

Judah called for wine and sat down on a coil of rope. 'What in the name of St Thomas were you doing all day?' Manuel Barrachina asked. 'The sailors have been telling me all manner of strange tales. What is the truth?'

'I'll tell you in a moment,' Judah said, 'but first what of you?'

'Nothing,' Manuel said. 'They kept me waiting two hours, then told me to come back, and when I did, said the Governor was sick, and asked me to give my message to an assistant. I refused. I think the Governor's not in Gibraltar at all. So I have wasted my day.'

'Except that you've seen El Peñon, which your master the Duke swears he's going to get back one day,' Pedro said. 'Now, *I'll* tell you what mad pranks this Judah Conquy, whom we all thought was just a rough merchant, with no thought in his head beyond trade, has been dragging me into . . .'

Judah drank, and watched the bulk of the Rock fade into the darkness, and the dim point of light on the southern point vanished while his friend, with great animation, told of their adventures and misadventures. But he was not listening. His mind was full of her, of how he could free her.

An oil lantern burned day and night on the end of the stone jetty at Tarifa. Shortly after it came into view the passenger appeared on deck and walked aft. He peered at them in the dark – 'Who is the principal authority in Tarifa, gentlemen?' He spoke a poor Castilian, but easy to understand.

'The Duke of Medina Sidonia's agent,' Manuel said.

'The Alcalde, the Mayor,' Pedro said. 'For he is a servant of the king.'

The Moor looked from one to another. 'The Alcalde,' Judah said, 'Don Alonzo Arcos, a most respected and honest gentleman. I'll guide you to his home.'

Shortly afterwards the captain brought the *Gaditana* alongside. Judah took the Moor to the Casa Consistorial – Don Alonzo lived behind it – and went back to his own rooms above the warehouse on the waterfront. His housekeeper tried to make him eat, but he would not. For hours he paced the floor, thinking of one plan after another to gain Tova Hassan and, one after another, rejecting them.

An hour before dawn he flung himself on his bed. Before his eyes closed someone knocked on the door and a voice called, 'Judah Conquy!' He leaned out of the window. The man said, 'Come at once to the Casa Consistorial.'

A dozen men were already gathered in the hall of audience upstairs, with lamps lit and curtains drawn. The Alcalde sat in his big chair, a tall, fork-bearded Moor beside him – the passenger from Gibraltar. Gathered round them were other ship owners, captains, a few knights, Manuel Barrachina, and the parish priest.

The Alcalde said, 'Come close, Messer Conquy. Pray silence, gentlemen ... An affair of great moment has come upon me. This Moor, Ali el Curro, is a nobleman of Gibraltar. Wronged by the Governor, the wrong not redressed by their king, he fled secretly today from his post as Deputy Commander of the Fortress. He wishes to become a Christian ...'

'The Holy Ghost be praised!' the priest cried, crossing himself.

'... and he says that if we act before the day after tomorrow, two hundred men can seize Gibraltar.'

A dead silence suddenly fell, louder than any noise. It lasted long seconds, then everyone spoke at once – *Impossible! ... A miracle ... A trick ... We must go at once ... Wait!*

The Alcalde raised his hand – 'The Governor of the fortress, all the knights except one, and most of the soldiers, have gone to Malaga to pay homage to their king, who is visiting there. Gibraltar is almost without defenders.'

The clamour broke out again, some arguing for, and some against the idea, but the Alcalde, a man who imposed by dignity rather than force, said quietly, 'A state of war exists between our king and the King of Granada, even though there are many peaceful exchanges. So we will not be committing any treachery in making a surprise attack. We have good reasons ... we all know of the losses suffered by the Duke, and many other citizens. But there is an object greater than gold here, gentlemen. Two jewels are missing from the circlet of Don Enrique's crown – Granada and Gibraltar. I can not sit idle here when the chance is offered to me of winning back one of them. I will therefore go to take Gibraltar, either tomorrow night or the next. I call upon you to provide men, for as you know, I can command no more than fifty of our own here. How many will each of you give, and when can they be here? And from you, shipmasters – how many ships, and how many men and horses will each carry?'

'I'll go!' Judah cried. 'I have two ships in port.' Here it was, the answer he had sought for in vain, presented to him like a gift from God! He jumped with excitement.

The Alcalde smiled, raising his hand slightly – 'Thank you, Messer Judah. But let us talk of the soldiers first ...'

Manuel Barrachina spoke up at once – 'The Duke has forty horse and forty foot here in his castle. In the absence of my master the Agent, who is with the Duke, I pledge them all. But I must add that Gibraltar is, and will be, a part of the Duke's domain, not of His Majesty's.'

'That is not for such as you and me to settle, Messer Barrachina,' the Alcalde said gravely. 'I have your promise of the soldiers. That is all I need.'

The old knight Don Carlos Fuentes then promised twenty men-at-arms, and the young knight Don Fernando Ponce de Leon, a nephew of the Count of Arcos, as many; and others promised horsemen until the total stood at eighty horse and 180 foot.

'That will be enough,' the Alcalde said. 'But I shall send messengers galloping to the King, the Duke, the Lord of Jerez, and the Count of Arcos, entreating all to send more men immediately. For once we have taken the fortress, we must be prepared to hold it against a counter-attack by the Moors.'

Young Ponce de Leon said 'My uncle the Count will not weaken himself by sending more soldiers unless the Duke sends as many.'

'The Lord of Jerez will say the same regarding the Count,' old Don Carlos said.

'For this jewel of Gibraltar, these feuds must be forgotten,' the Alcalde said. 'So, gentlemen, do you go to it that men and horses with their arms and food for three days may be gathered here by nightfall. And let no word be spoken abroad of this matter, or the reason for the movements ... Shipmasters and captains, pray come close. . . .'

Six ships sailed before midnight, having waited an hour for the wind to veer sufficiently into the south-west. The *Gaditana* led the little flotilla, with the Alcalde on board, also Ali el Curro the renegade Moor, Judah Conquy, and Pedro Santangel, full of excitement at the prospect of knightly action. The *Sevillana* followed with Manuel Barrachina and many of the Duke's men. Behind came the *Santa Cruz, Santa Fe, Tiburon,* and *Angula,* with the rest. The Atlantic swell steadily lessened as the vessels passed into the Gut of the Strait, but several soldiers were already seasick, and the horses on deck stamping and shifting their hoofs, unhappy with the constantly changing balance. The ships carried no riding lights, only a small lantern, shielded from the front, on the poop. The moon slid irregularly in and out of low, luminescent clouds. It was a hot night.

Judah stood in the bow, so that he could be nearer to Gibraltar and Tova Hassan, and though he knew he would not see the light on the point for two or three hours he kept staring into the darkness until when he did see it, not one but two lights wavered before his eyes. Gradually then the bulk of the Rock took shape, a black lion crouching against the sky. Three hours after leaving Tarifa, that is, at two o'clock on the morning of August 20, 1462, the captain of the *Gaditana* ran her up on to the sand of a cove on the western side of Gibraltar, near the southern point. The others followed to right and left, the sailors put out the improvised ramps, and men and horses began to splash ashore. An hour later, having scrambled up the steep slope out of the cove and mustered on the flatter ground above, the little force started north for the town and fortress. The Alcalde strode ahead, Ali el Curro as guide at his side, Judah and Pedro following, then the men-at-arms, the horsemen last.

After half an hour Ali el Curro said, 'We are close to the southern wall now, Acalde, and it is near dawn. Let us stop here in the woods, for at the first light three soldiers come out of the town – one high up the hill, one opposite here, one near the sea, to search the ground and report that no enemies are concealed close to the walls.'

The old knight Don Carlos said, 'Lay an ambush, Alcalde, and take these scouts prisoner. Torture them separately, as to the truth of what this Moor says. Then we shall know whether this tale of the few soldiers and one knight is true or false.'

'I speak the truth,' the Moor said stiffly, but the other knights and Manuel Barrachina all agreed with Don

186

Carlos. So it was done; men-at-arms went up and down, outside the wall, ready to seize the scouts when they came out. Then the light slowly spread, and Judah and the rest, hiding in the trees, saw in front of them the red wall climbing from the sea to the mountain, and gates in it, minarets and roofs beyond, and at the far side of the town Judah saw the house of Suleiman Qureshi, where Tova Hassan was, and gazed at it as though he could pierce the wall just by looking.

The Moorish soldiers came out, as Ali el Curro had said, and were taken prisoner, and tortured a little. All separately swore, weeping, that there were no knights but one, and few soldiers in the castle, and none in the town. Then the Alcalde marched his army out of the woods and ordered the standards to be set up – the flags of Castile; of the house of Medina Sidonia, borne by a soldier at Manuel Barrachina's side; of the Count of Arcos, borne by the squire of Don Fernando Ponce de Leon. The light glittered on iron helmet and cuirass, sword and mace and halberd. The Alcalde drew his sword and carried the hilt to his lips – 'For God and Castile,' he cried, 'Advance!'

The captured scouts ran to open the centre gate and the army marched in, though at the last moment the squire carrying Ponce de Leon's banner galloped ahead so that he was the first to enter the town. Once inside, Manuel Barrachina, his face dark with anger, sent the Duke's horsemen galloping pell mell through the narrow streets towards the Castle. The other knights followed and in a moment the Alcalde and his fifty men, the King's standard over them, were left alone.

'Folly!' the Alcalde muttered as he marched steadily on.

When Judah reached the castle wall at the Alcalde's side, the knights and horsemen were riding up and down

187

outside, flourishing their swords and shouting war cries, but the gate was closed, the drawbridge raised. A few Moors peered down from the battlements, and a trumpet was sounding from inside. Don Carlos Fuentes muttered, 'Treachery! A great host is hidden inside, preparing to rush out upon us . . .'

The Alcalde ignored him and advanced with the King's standard to the edge of the fosse. There he cried up, 'In the name of Don Enrique, King of Castile, I call upon you to surrender.'

An old man with a bright turban appeared in an embrasure and Ali el Curro said, 'That is Mohammed Caba, the only knight left here.'

The Alcalde repeated his call to surrender, and old Mohammed Caba quavered, 'We have no choice. I have but forty men-at-arms here. But the people will need four days to take out what they can carry.'

'Take it by storm!' young Ponce de Leon said. 'Why should we wait four days?'

For once Manuel Barrachina agreed with him, and a new clamour arose, while the old Moor looked down with amazement from the embrasure. Then the Alcalde raised his voice and shouted sternly, 'Silence! I speak for the king! . . . Come down, Messer Moor, and we will settle the details. Meantime, I grant an armistice.'

Then the gate creaked and slowly opened, the drawbridge clattered down on its chains, and the old Moor tottered out, bent and slow, unarmed. As he came Judah, a little to one side, heard Ponce de Leon muttering to Manuel Barrachina, 'Now is the moment! Don't heed the Alcalde. What honour will there be for us in a tame surrender?' Manuel nodded, and they looked around, and caught the eyes of their soldiers and horsemen. Suddenly Manuel shouted, 'For God and Guzman!' and Don Fernando cried, 'Arcos! Arcos!' and both charged towards the drawbridge, with many of their followers. Judah drew his dagger and ran to stop them, and the Alcalde cried, 'Stop! Shame, shame!' but all would have been in vain except for Pedro Santangel. He must have heard the whisperings too, for when the hotheads charged, he was already there, defending the narrow bridge. They ran at him and he pierced Don Fernando through the liver, wounded Manuel Barrachina in the arm, and stepped back, sword flickering. They surged on and he killed another knight and a man-at-arms. Slowly the Moors inside lowered the heavy gate behind him. Slowly the Alcalde's soldiers overcame and forced back the assailants.

The gate closed and the attempt was over. The attackers slunk away and the Alcalde said sternly to Manuel Barrachina – 'When I have given the king's word, to break it is high treason. The king shall hear of this. And you, Messer Santangel, you shall go to the king as soon as the fortress is in our hands, with my dispatch.'

Judah clapped his friend on the back, laughing with pleasure. The man chosen to convey such tidings would certainly be knighted, and perhaps given greater honours. Here in Gibraltar Pedro had won the prize he wanted in life; now there was no limit to what he and his descendants might become – marquis, grandee, count, cardinal.

But for himself he wanted another prize, and now was the time to seize it. He said, 'Alcalde, I have private business to attend to. May I take four soldiers with me?'

'Not for looting, I trust,' the Alcalde said.

'No, señor. For persuasion.'

He started up the hill outside the wall, the four men-at-arms following. Near the house of Suleiman Qureshi he looked back. The Alcalde, Ali el Curro, and Mohammed

Caba had disappeared. The Alcalde's soldiers blocked the way to the closed gate. Other horsemen and soldiers and knights stood in small groups, talking, gesticulating. The Christian banners were in disarray, some propped against the castle wall, some on the ground. The green and black of King Muley Hassan still flew from the tower. The box containing the body of Enrique de Guzman, father of the Duke of Medina Sidonia, still dangled from its chains below.

Judah turned and walked faster towards the tall house at the head of Gully Steps. He rapped loudly with the handle of his dagger, and called 'Open!' The sun was high, and birds chattered in the trees overhanging the garden wall.

'Shall we break in the door, master?' a soldier asked eagerly, unlimbering a heavy battle axe.

'No,' Judah said. 'This will soon be my property.' He raised the dagger to knock again, when the door suddenly opened. The Negro bowed low. Behind him four more, half naked, prostrated themselves and beat their heads on the floor.

The Negro said, 'Enter, lord. We are men of peace.'

Judah pushed through to the fountain patio, and looked up at the tiers of balconies. Veiled women watched from the upper one, half a dozen servants stood bowing on the lower. The tame partridge suddenly chattered, making him jump.

'Bring me the lady Tova Hassan,' he said.

No one spoke. He felt cold, and his hand began to tremble. He drew his dagger and turned slowly on the Negro. The soldier with the battle axe cried eagerly, 'Shall I have his head off, sir?'

The Negro flung himself to the floor, grasping Judah's ankles – 'Lord, she is not here. My master took her.'

Judah grabbed the man by his hair, jerked him upright and thrust the point of his dagger into the skin just below the ear – '*Where* has he taken her?'

'I don't ... d-d-don't know,' the Negro sobbed. 'No one knows.'

'It is true,' a voice called down from the second balcony. Judah looked up. A fat middle-aged Moorish woman, her veil thrown back, said, 'The master aroused us at dawn, when a lookout reported that the Christians were entering the city. He took Tova and Raza, the head eunuch.'

'Where?' Judah called.

The Negro answered, 'No one knows, lord. He loaded Raza with bags of gold and jewels, and himself with other bags, some full of food, and left by the garden, ordering none to follow.'

Judah looked slowly round the circles of faces – down here by the splashing fountains, on the balconies above. He turned to the soldiers – 'Search the house. Every cupboard, every hole and corner. Show them,' he called to the women.

He went quickly upstairs, past girls pressing themselves against the wall, past bowing servants, to the roof. From there he could see the harbour. No ship was sailing or making ready to sail, so Qureshi must have gone southward, or to another house in Gibraltar.

'Lord ...' it was the Negro, beside him. 'If I may speak ... I think he is hiding in a cave, expecting your attack to be beaten off, or bought off. Then he will return.'

Something in the man's voice made Judah turn quickly. 'You know!' he grated. 'Where are they? Tell me, or I swear I'll throw you off this roof.' He grabbed the man's throat and bent him over the parapet.

'I followed ... but Raza turned and saw me, I fled.'

Judah released his grip. 'How far did you go?'

'To the flat land at the foot of the southern cliff. They were crossing it, heading east.'

'East? To the back of the Rock? Are there caves on that side?'

'Many, lord. From sea level to the topmost crags. Small and large, some easy to see, some quite hidden.'

Judah groaned. 'Come with me, then. Show me where you turned back.' He hurried down the stairs, found a soldier, and said, 'Ask the Alcalde to see that no one leaves Gibraltar by land or sea until I return. Run! ... You three, come with me.'

He ran into the street calling impatiently to the Negro – 'Which way now? ... Hurry, hurry!'

They stumbled along the side of the mountain, past several groups of startled monkeys, until they reached the flat above the bay the Spanish called called Caleta Laudero, where the six ships of the invasion fleet were now anchored off shore. 'I turned here,' the Negro said, 'close by this old heathen stone. They were going that way.' He pointed east, where after another hundred yards the plateau ended in a sharp line. Judah moved forward, his heart sinking. The slope was very steep down to the sea. To the left the Rock rose in buttress and crag, tower and cliff, to the sky.

In that direction a goat track led along narrow ledges between great precipices. With the soldiers at his back, he hurried along it, past a dangerous beak-nosed projection of the cliff, until it ended at a big cave; but the cave was empty.

Back at the flat place he thought despairingly, I might pass close to her and she see me, but she would not dare to cry out.

To the right the flat place ended in a low cliff, then

there was another flat place, the brazier of the light beacon, a few houses, a shrine, and the point. Nothing there.

Straight ahead, the flat place ended in a steep drop to the east. He went forward carefully. There was no path here, only the jagged rock curving over and then the sea, two hundred feet below. No one could have gone down there.

As he turned away, despair gripping him, something moved on the slope he had just been looking down. He stared – it was a woman, nothing like Tova – short, red-haired, quite naked. He gasped, for she was running up the steep, straight at him, her mouth wide in a scream. She passed and he whipped round, but she was gone. 'Where did she go?' he asked the soldiers.

'Who, sir?'

'The woman – the naked woman!'

'What woman, sir?'

He stared at them, and they at each other. He muttered a prayer and turned back. If the woman could come up, where he had thought it impossible, there must be a way down. He started cautiously on down and after a few minutes found a tiny piece of green cloth caught in a projecting thorn bush. His excitement mounting, he signalled to the soldiers to follow and went on. Ten minutes later the four of them stood on a narrow strip of sand at the foot of the cliffs. The sea rolled in, in small waves, behind them. In front a vast overhanging arch led back and up, the base a steeply rising floor of sand, into the Rock. There were fresh footprints in the sand, two pairs large and one small. They started up, abreast. As the light grew dimmer, where the slope flattened and a strange, shiny column of stone joined floor to ceiling, a man sprang out of the shadows on the left, and struck downward with a scimitar. Judah hurled himself sideways, putting up his arm to protect himself. The blow struck his left wrist, severing the hand instantly. His missing hand throbbed, but there was no pain, and one of the soldiers, thrusting from behind him, struck his sword into their assailant's leg. He fell and the soldier with the battle axe shouted 'At last!', and clove his chest in two.

Judah moved forward, his left wrist raised above his head to lessen the bleeding.

A voice grated – 'Stop!'

He saw, dim in the last recess of the cave, two figures – Tova, unveiled, the Star of David at her forehead, her ankles bound; Suleiman Qureshi, beside her, his dagger at her throat. Leather and canvas bags were stacked behind.

Wearily Judah leaned on his sword. He held out his arm to a soldier and said, 'Bind this . . . Let her go, Suleiman. I guarantee your life.'

The merchant laughed without mirth. 'What use is life without money?'

'You can keep your gold, too . . . except for a hundred dinars to each of these soldiers. In return I want the keys of your house. We have taken Gibraltar.'

Suleiman Qureshi said, 'And you, a Jew, helped the Christians do it? Ah, they will reward you well.' His knife still hovered at Tova's bare throat. Her eyes glowed with a dark green fire. Judah felt dizzy.

'Come,' he said, 'free her.'

The merchant's hand moved, the blade sliced, her ropes fell to the sand. She came forward slowly, and Judah waited for her. When she reached him, he said, 'I brought something for you . . . gift . . .' He dropped his sword, fumbled in his inner pocket and brought out the carved woman he had found the monkeys playing with. The light was fading, growing before his eyes . . . . 'A charm, to make you fertile . . .' he said thickly. She took the figurine from him, and looked at it, smiling. He said, 'Fertile, because . . . will you be my wife, daughter of Israel?'

She said, *'Verastech li leolam.'*

His knees buckled and his strength ebbed, but her eyes were over him, and her arms, suddenly strong, supporting him as he sank to the sand.

Book Seven

SPANISH TOWN

The Jewish years 5222–5465
A.U.C. 2215–2457
A.D. 1462–1704
A.H. 866–1116

Sevilla

Jerez Arcos

Almoraima

Pto. S. Maria   Jimena

Cadiz   Medina Sidonia

S. Roque

THE ROCK

Tarifa

Tangier   Ceuta

Tetuan

Old Mole   North Face

S. Joaquin Bty.

Devil's Tongue Bty.   Wolf Leap

Lost Lamb Cave

Town

Charles V's   Wall   Almadrabilla

New Mole   Jumper's Bastion

Half Moon Bty.

Tuerto Tower

Tarfes Altos

Tarfes Bajos

Nun's Well

Our Lady of Europa

JUDAH CONQUY would have done well to take Tova back to Tarifa until the situation in Gibraltar stabilized – but he would have had to wait a long time . . .

The original Moorish offer to the Alcalde was to surrender, providing they were allowed four days to evacuate their people, and what goods they could take to Granada. The Alcalde wanted to accept this, but by now Rodrigo Ponce de Leon, the Count of Arcos's eldest son (no relation to the Alcalde) had arrived with 400 men in response to the Alcalde's call for assistance, and refused to accept the surrender. He wanted to take the fortress by storm, presumably to increase the glory and the loot. Next, a large body of soldiers from Jerez arrived under Gonzalo de Abila. The Duke of Medina Sidonia was on his way with more men. And so was the Count of Arcos, with still more. The Alcalde, who had taken the initative and deserved the credit, was now quite outgunned, and pushed helpless into the background while the grandees squabbled over the jewel that he had won.

Gonzalo de Abila planned to seize the fort secretly with his men. Rodrigo Ponce de Leon came to hear of it and, to forestall de Abila, himself attacked, but was repulsed. The Duke of Medina Sidonia arrived, and though begged by young Ponce de Leon to await the arrival of his father, marched firmly into the castle, announced that Gibraltar was now his, and took his own father's body down from its suspended box. Gibraltar was again in Spanish Christian hands, this time to be held for much longer than the twenty-four years after its first capture by the Duke's ancestor, Guzman el Bueno, in 1309.

When the Count of Arcos came up a day or two later, he found the Duke in possession, the Moors all gone (the third complete turnover of Gibraltar's population), and his son Rodrigo in such a state of passion that he tried to persuade his father to attack the castle, kill the Duke, and institute a regular civil war – though, indeed, at this time, under a weak king, and with the unifying threat of the Moors rapidly fading, civil war was the normal relation of Spain's barons with each other.

The Count of Arcos was as angry as his son but he decided to accept the situation, and he and all the other contestants marched away, leaving the Duke to gloat over his prize. He did not gloat for long ... but before turning to that story we might note that Alonzo Arcos, the Alcalde, later became Deputy Governor of Seville, where he died in 1477. Ali el Curro was baptized, became Diego del Curro, and, unlike Benedict Arnold, lived happily ever after in the esteem of the people for whom he had betrayed his own.

Spain was about to enter its period of greatness, but before that could happen it had to come into existence. We have talked of 'Spain' as a geographical entity, but politically it consisted at this time of three kingdoms: Navarre, Aragon, and Castile. In 1465 King Enrique IV of Castile's son, the Infante Alonzo, was set up as a puppet king by some rebellious barons, Fortunately for the kingdom the prince died in 1468. King Enrique's heir-presumptive was now his young sister, Isabella, and he arranged a dynastic marriage for her with Ferdinand, son of the King of Aragon. In 1474 he himself died, and Isabella became Queen of Castile. In 1479 the King of Aragon died, the crowns were united and Ferdinand and

Isabella ruled jointly over a new country – Spain. (Navarre, much smaller, was incorporated thirty-seven years later.)

Four events now took place which cast the mould of Spanish life for centuries to come, and affected every inhabitant of the world. All started or were based in Andalusia. Gibraltar was closely affected by all four.

First in time was the setting up of the Spanish Inquisition. Queen Isabella was a considerable statesman except in the area of religion; here she was a maniac. The barons found her a strong ruler, but she was little better than putty in the hands of the fanatic priests with whom she surrounded herself. The Inquisition was founded in Christian jealousy of the power and wealth attained by families converted from Judaism – mostly in the pogroms of a century earlier. These New Christians or *marranos* had become bishops, councillors, knights: for example, the Grand Master of the Order of Santiago was descended on both sides from the Jew Ruy Capon. In Aragon within a brief period the master of the royal household, the treasurer, several assessors, the chief justice, and the president of the Cortes (advisory parliament) were all *marranos*. *Marranos*, or *conversos,* as they were also called, held a monopoly of the banking and medical professions. They constituted almost the whole of the small Spanish middle-class.

Many *conversos* were devout Christians, but some secretly held their Jewish faith. On November 1, 1478 the Inquisition was founded, by order of Pope Sixtus IV at the request of Queen Isabella, to root out these false Christians. The first Commissioners of the Inquisition gathered in Seville on Christmas Day, 1480, and on February 6, 1481, in that city, burned several *marranos* who had been surprised secretly celebrating Passover the year before.

These were the first victims of an institution which blackened the name of Spain abroad, and held the national intelligence in chains of fear until 1834.

If there were Christians in Gibraltar, there were certainly *marranos*, too, and although the Inquisition never held its inquiries in small towns, it is reasonable to suppose that some of Gibraltar's *conversos* were denounced by jealous rivals and dragged off to suffer for what they may or may not have secretly believed in.

From the moment the Inquisition was founded, the Church had seen the fatal flaw of such action against heretics: it could not be used against avowed Jews. But there were savage penal laws and exclusions against Jews to hand, such as those of 1412, and the Church now moved to strengthen and enforce these, with the purpose of driving the Jews out of Spain. In April 1481, Jews were ordered to be confined to their ghettoes. In 1482 and 1483 Jews were expelled from most of Andalusia, and three years later from most of Aragon.

Now came the second great event, the fall of Granada, the last Muslim outpost left in Spain. Ferdinand and Isabella, *los Reyes Catolicos* as they are usually known in Spain, encamped themselves before Granada early in 1490, and after various skirmishes and mishaps succeeded in bringing the King of Granada to sign terms of capitulation. These terms were wise and liberal, and specifically stated that the Moors were to be regarded as free subjects of the Crown, with the free exercise of their religion. On January 2, 1492, Ferdinand and Isabella entered Granada. The Reconquest, began 774 years earlier in the remote Asturian gorge of Covadonga, was over.

Two Jews, Isaac Abarbanel and Abraham Senior, had provided the *Reyes Catolicos* with most of the money they needed for the long campaign, and the monarchs demurred – just a little – when the Church suggested that now was the time to press on with the unification of Spain by expelling the rest of the Jews. Hernando de Talavera, once the queen's confessor, and now the newly appointed Archbishop of Granada, soon cut off those qualms by storming into the royal presence, casting down thirty pieces of silver, and crying that they were betraying Christ's church, for money, even as Judas had betrayed Christ. The *Reyes Catolicos* quickly ordered the expulsion of the Jews from Spain, signing the edict in Granada on March 31, 1492. It gave the Jews four months to sell up what they could, and leave.

This cruel and foolish order – the third great event – lost to Spain nearly all that was left of her professional skills, learning, and independence of spirit and thought. So, on July 31, 1492, being the 9th day of Ab (the destruction of both the 1st and 2nd Temples of Jerusalem took place on this date) the last Sephardim left Spain, many from Gibraltar. The total of exiles numbered over quarter of a million. They left behind their houses, libraries, and lands, but took with them their keys (hoping that the order must soon be rescinded); such belongings as they could carry; the Ladino tongue; and a great love of a country where Jewish culture had reached its finest flower – now apparently gone mad. Many of these Jews went to Portugal, and from thence to Holland and England. Others went to Leghorn, Genoa, Minorca and all parts of Barbary. Still others went as far as Constantinople, where the Sultan welcomed them with pleasure, expressing his thanks to the generous sovereigns of Spain for sending him their most talented and industrious subjects.

So, if Judah Conquy had existed, he would have had to leave Gibraltar thirty years after he helped take it; and perhaps he would have gone with Tova and their family to Tangier, where, by climbing the hill above the old town, he could easily see the Rock on most days.

In Spain the campaign for 'unification' went on. Keeping more or less to the terms of the capitulation, Hernando de Talavera set about converting the Moors to Christianity by argument and reasoning. He was having some success when Ferdinand and Isabella invited another prelate, Cardinal Ximenez, to speed up the pace. A campaign of coercion began, in direct contravention of the terms of the capitulation. A small and quite natural rising against this treatment, in 1499, was taken as an excuse to declare that the capitulation itself was no longer valid. All Moors were ordered to be baptized or leave the country. Since every obstacle was thrown in the way of their departure, most were baptized. And now the Inquisition, and the greedy, bigoted aristocracy of Castile, whose economic weapon it was, looked hungrily at these Moriscos and began to plan how to drive them, too, out of Spain, making sure that they, too, must leave most of their wealth behind.

The fourth event, incomparably the most important, was the expedition of a Genoese sailor, probably of Catalan *converso* origin, financed by Queen Isabella (and certain Aragonese *conversos*) to discover a new route to the Indies. Christopher Columbus discovered or rediscovered America on October 12, 1492, with incalculable results for mankind. The immediate outcome, for Spain, was to provide the nation with a new outlet for its energy, to replace the Reconquest. Ferdinand and Isabella's grandson, Charles V, King and Emperor, put the Pillars of Hercules on to his coat of arms, but from the demi-god's original legend *Non plus ultra* ('nothing beyond') he removed the first word; the new motto can be freely interpreted either as 'Go west, young man', or 'The sky's the limit'. One of the first people to go and find out what really was 'out there', was Don Rodrigo Ponce de Leon's son, Don Juan, the one who searched all over Florida (of all places) for the fountain of youth.

Against this background the intimate history of Spanish Gibraltar takes on a sharper focus. King Enrique was overjoyed when he heard of its fall. He at once added 'King of Gibraltar' to his other titles, and by a royal order transferred to the jurisdiction of Gibraltar all territories that had previously been under Algeciras. As Algeciras had not existed for a century these territories had been quietly appropriated by neighbouring towns, and the King's order was not popular with them. The king also sent to order the Duke of Medina Sidonia to give up possession to his own appointed governor, Pedro de Porras. Either because the king was at the time strong, or he himself was weak, the Duke unwillingly obeyed. Two years later the King visited Gibraltar in person, and invited the King of Portugal (who was visiting Ceuta, across the Strait) to join him there. The two sovereigns spent eight days together in Gibraltar, talking politics and hunting in the forests of Almoraima on the mainland.

Soon rebellious barons and grandees broke into revolt all over Spain, and the Infante Alonzo was set up as king, rival to his father. The Duke seized his chance, forced the pretender, then aged 11, to acknowledge his right to Gibraltar, and in March 1466 demanded of the new Governor, Esteban de Villacreces, that he give up the place at once. Villacreces refused, and the 9th Siege began. The defence was long and heroic, but no help came from the king, who was fully engaged elsewhere, and July 26, 1467, starvation and weakness forced Villacreces to surrender. The Duke, a vengeful man, imprisoned him with many threats of worse to follow.

Next year the Duke died, to be succeeded by his legitimized son, Enrique de Guzman, as 4th Count of Niebla and 2nd Duke of Medina Sidonia. This young man, then twenty-six, was able to force the harassed king into a definite cession of Gibraltar, but – and this is most interesting, as a comparable situation holds today – the king retained sovereignty. The actual words of the grant, which is dated January 3, 1469, are *'reservando en mi . . . e para los reyes que despues de mi fueren en estos dichos reynos, el soberano señorio . . .'* ('reserving for myself . . . and for the kings who shall succeed me in these said kingdoms, the sovereign dominion . . .')

The Duke incorporated Gibraltar into the rest of his extensive domains and gave it a constitution more liberal than most, though not as privileged as the extraordinary charter of 1310. The inhabitants shared in the increase in the Duke's prosperity, caused by the removal of Gibraltar's Moorish pirates and poachers. Many probably worked in his timber, cooperage, and tunny processing monopolies. In 1477 they saw the last flurry of Moorish warlike activity when King Muley Hassan of Granada, raiding into Christian territory, was brought to battle in the forests of Almoraima, below Castellar, by two doughty warriors, Vargas of Gibraltar, and Vera of Jimena. These two cordially hated each other – Vargas was the Duke's man, Vera the King's; and Vera had seized Vargas and thrown him into prison when the latter was on his way to take over the governorship of Gibraltar for the Duke – but they sank their differences to smite the common enemy.

The next year, 1478, the Duke had himself named Marquis of Gibraltar, and was also able to compel the recently enthroned Ferdinand and Isabella to confirm him in all his rights and titles, including the ownership of Gibraltar. But the times were changing, as the *Reyes Cat-*

olicos gained a firmer grip on their unified country. In the next two years they severely curtailed the power of the grandees, and had several castles of the Guzman and Ponce de Leon families dismantled.

Duke Enrique died in 1492, having performed valiantly in the fall of Granda. He was succeeded by Duke Juan, who went, as was customary, to the sovereign and asked for an affirmation of his rights and titles. Ferdinand and Isabella refused to give it unless he surrendered Gibraltar to them. In vain the Duke protested that they themselves had specifically affirmed these rights fourteen years earlier. Ferdinand and Isabella were adamant: Isabella had a feeling for Gibraltar as strong as Mary of England's for Calais. The days of huge independent baronies were over: the Duke must give up Gibraltar. After sulking for several years he realized that times had indeed changed, and yielded. On the last day of 1501 Garcilaso de la Vega arrived to govern Gibraltar for Ferdinand and Isabella. The first thing he did, being a proper civil servant, was take an inventory. Copies are still extant. It is an amusing document, starting with the 2nd Count's sarcophagus (the one that hung from the tower), and ending with detailed lists of arquebuses (without stocks) and pikes (three with broken point).

In 1504 Isabella died, and in her testament stated that Gibraltar must never again be alienated from the Spanish Crown. But the Guzmans didn't give up easily, and in the period of confusion between her death and Ferdinand's, in 1516, the Duke tried to get Gibraltar back, blockading it for four months (the 10th Siege). It did not surrender, and under Charles V the Spanish monarchy and people stepped into their glory years.

For Gibraltar itself the end of the Reconquest meant a temporary end to its importance. In 1535 when Alvaro de

Bazan arrived to take over the governorship he found the town almost empty and the fortress abandoned. He managed to attract some citizens back, only to have them killed, looted, and pillaged in an attack by the Moorish corsair Barbarossa. Barbarossa was informed and guided by an Italian renegade, Caramanli . . . who had once been a slave of Bazan's! The raiders were caught by a Spanish admiral as they sailed away, and dispersed in a sea fight. Caramanli was killed by an arrow in the chest and two arquebus shots at close range.

This occurred in 1540 but – showing how little real value was now placed on Gibraltar – Charles V did nothing until 1552, when he appoined a Milanese engineer called Calvi to design and build new defences. The only part of these remaining or, perhaps, ever constructed, is Charles V's wall, the high wall which marks the southern limit of Gibraltar's built-up area, and climbs from sea level to the cliff line seven hundred feet higher. Above the cliff it continues to the crest, in a series of long angles, rather farther to the south.

In 1556 Charles, King of Spain, Holy Roman Emperor, the most powerful ruler the world had yet seen, abdicated to a monk's cell in Yuste, Philip II succeeded, and continued his father's policy of neglecting Gibraltar, whose few inhabitants were left at the mercy of the Barbary pirates. The Invincible Armada which Philip launched against England in 1588 had two odd connections with Gibraltar. The admiral he appointed to command it was the ageing but most capable and experienced Alvaro de Bazan; but he died before he could embark, and in his place the king appointed a proud, stupid grandee, a soldier with no experience of the sea – Alonso de Guzman, 7th Duke of Medina Sidonia and 6th Marquis of Gibraltar.

The years pass. . . . An autumn storm in Gibraltar Bay sinks a warship preparing to escort the galleons to America. . . . A king completes the evil work of the *Reyes Catolicos* by expelling all the *moriscos* (descendants of Moors forcibly converted to Christianity) from Spain; there are more than a million of them. Many concentrate in and sail from Gibraltar, as many Jews had done 120 years earlier. . . . The same king builds watch towers all along his southern coast: one actually on the Rock (on what was then called Tarfes Altos and now Windmill Hill Flats) – this tower rather mysteriously becomes known as the Genoese Tower; and another at the foot of the north face, on the isthmus – this one is called the Devil's Tower. . . . Another king visits Gibraltar but has to walk in because his carriage won't go through the gate. His courtiers upbraid the Governor, who replies coldly that the gate was not made to let carriages in but to keep enemies out. . . . A terrible pestilence attacks the town (it is the same Great Plague which struck London in 1665). . . . There is a lack of oil and wheat, though a surplus of fish; and it is ordained that no ship will be allowed to load fish for export unless it has brought in a cargo of wheat or oil. . . . a steady, slow recovery from the years of neglect, and a new large mole is built, thrusting out from the western shore beyond the old southern limit of the town.

While Gibraltar thought about its fisheries, and King Philip IV about the gold mines of Peru, some northern islanders were thinking about Gibraltar. In 1625 a Colonel Henry Bruce – apparently with no particular emergency in mind – presented a plan for the seizure of Gibraltar to Charles, Prince of Wales. Charles did nothing and in 1649 (the years of the Gibraltar plague) lost his head on the block, as King Charles I. His successor, Cromwell, was a military genius and on April 28,

1656, wrote to Admiral Montague on the advantages to England and the disadvantages that could be imposed on Spain if England were to gain possession of Gibraltar. The matter was further discussed and investigated but Cromwell never took any action, either. His successor, Charles II of England, married a Portuguese princess, who brought him Tangier as part of her dowry. Tangier was not as easy to defend as Gibraltar, but it did give England a naval outpost at the mouth of the Mediterranean, threateningly close to Spain, and so met some of the needs which had made Cromwell think of the Rock. But in 1684 England abandoned Tangier, which again became part of the Moroccan Empire.

Spain's two centuries as the most powerful nation in the world were coming to an end. Its king, Carlos II was a sick man with no direct heirs. France was rising fast under the unscrupulous and ambitious Louis XIV. England, recovered from its civil wars, only awaited a favourable wind to spread its sails. None of this might have directly affected Gibraltar except for the chance of a sea fight off Cape St Vincent in 1693. The English admiral, Sir George Rooke, was severely handled by a French squadron (one of the century's small, purposeless wars was in progress). Spain happened to be allied with England in that war, and Rooke sailed his battered ships through the Strait and took shelter under the Rock. The Spanish only had a few guns mounted but they fired on the French, who veered off. Rooke was able to stay ten days, rest, and refit. The circumstance made a deep impression on him.

Before relating Gibraltar's next, and critical appearance on the world stage, in a starring role, let us look at the Rock more closely in these final years of the 17th century.

The larger wild animals listed on page 24 had fled,

though there were still wild pig. The ape population was large, perhaps 300, as they had the whole Rock to roam over, except for the town itself. The human population, about 6,000 was all white, and all Spanish-Catholic, except for a few Genoese, some of whom lived on the east side of the Rock, round the little bay at the foot of the great sand slope. This settlement (modern Catalan Bay) was called Almadrabilla, as the Genoese worked a tunny factory there. Ferdinand and Isabella had sent prisoners into Gibraltar, partly to increase the population, but it was no longer as necessary to people the Rock as it had once been, and thieves, murderers and runaway women no longer formed a large part of the population.

Nearly everyone lived inside the walls in the three joined 'neighbourhoods' which constituted Gibraltar – Villa Vieja to the north, under the Moorish castle; Barcina in the middle; Turba to the south; the whole being tucked into the northwest angle of the peninsula. The chief Moorish mosque had been converted into a church, and there were four other churches, together with a monastery, two convents, and the friars who manned the Hospital of San Juan de Dios. A public-spirited citizen had built this in 1587, in the upper part of Barcina, for patients suffering from the new scourge brought back from the Americas along with tomatoes, potatoes, turkeys and maize: syphilis.

A small chapel and shrine to Our Lady of Europa stood at the southern tip of the Rock, and over the years had been richly endowed with silver crucifixes, candlesticks, and ornaments. The Nuns' Well does not seem to have been used, and there was no other settlement on the southern plateau (Tarfes Bajos, or Europa Flats).

For defence there was the Devil's Tongue Battery on the Old Mole, Tuerto Battery on the New Mole, San

Joaquin Battery below the Moorish castle, facing over the isthmus, Half Moon Battery near the foot of Charles V's wall, plus various towers, bastions, small isolated forts and, of course, the walls. The Governor was Diego Salinas, an able and conscientious general of artillery. To man his batteries, towers, bastions, forts, and walls he could count on sixty infantry, six cavalry (without horses), 140 military pensioners, and about 220 citizen-militia. Many of the guns were dismounted, and for others there was no powder or shot. Blinded by the westward glare of the gold from Potosi, Spain had left its back door open.

As the unhappy King Carlos II of Spain drew to his death, the manoeuvrings in the courts of Europe to influence the choice of his successor became more frantic and unprincipled. Carlos himself wanted to name his nephew Charles, an Archduke of the Holy Roman Empire. Louis XIV wanted him to name another nephew, the Duke of Anjou, who was Louis' grandson. The wretched dying king turned to the Pope for advice. The Pope supported Louis, and Carlos gave in. On November 1, 1700, he died. Louis XIV made two famous remarks: first, to his grandson 'You are now King of Spain, but never forget that you are also a prince of France'; second, to the world at large, and Spain in particular: 'There are no more Pyrenees' – which, in practice, meant that Spain would be tied to the French chariot wheels for the next century, the century of England's great overseas drive.

England, Holland, and the Holy Roman Empire (its capital was Vienna) did not acquiesce in the accession of the Duke of Anjou, as Philip V, to the Spanish throne. They supported the Archduke Charles, who styled himself King Charles III. The War of the Spanish Succession began. The English and Dutch sent a combined fleet and

marines to seize Cadiz. Repulsed there, they landed at
Puerto Santa Maria across the bay and raped, killed,
sacked and pillaged the undefended town in a strenuous
effort to win over the Spanish people to the Archduke
Charles. Don Diego Salinas, feeling exposed and abandoned on his Rock, started pestering Madrid for more
men, guns, powder, and money. Madrid made urgent and
successful preparations to do nothing. The Archduke
Charles's agent, Prince George of Hesse, supported by
another large Anglo-Dutch fleet, set up headquarters in
Lisbon, rather to the embarrassment of the Portuguese.

There have always been separatist tendencies in Spain,
where at least two of the principal cultures, those of the
Basques and Catalans, are alien to the Castilian tradition
of the central power; and the Prince of Hesse thought he
could raise Catalonia for the Archduke if he landed in
sufficient strength in Barcelona, its capital. The large fleet
therefore sailed, made its landing, seized and held Barcelona, and waited for the popular rising. The Catalans
conspicuously failed to rise.

The fleet re-embarked its marines, and sailed away.
The naval commander-in-chief must have been racking
his brains, thinking what he could do to wipe out the setback. He had, after all, been entrusted with some sixty
warships and seventy transports for many months, and
what did he have to show for it?

As the fleet headed into the Strait of Gibraltar the
admiral, contemplating the grey lion-rock on his starboard bow, had an idea – for his name was George Rooke.
He quickly hove the fleet to off Tetuan and held a council
of war. All agreed to seize Gibraltar. The fleet sailed
again and on August 1, 1704 (N.S.), anchored off the
Rock. At 3 p.m. 1,800 marines of the battalions of
Colonels Sanderson, Villars, and Fox (later the 30th,

31st, and 32nd Foot), landed on the isthmus, cutting off Gibraltar from land contact with the rest of Spain. The 11th Siege had begun.

It did not last long. The Prince sent a demand to the governor to surrender to him as the representative of Gibraltar's lawful sovereign, Charles III. The governor replied stoutly that they were loyal subjects of Philip V. The surrender demand was repeated, and again rejected. Contrary winds prevented the fleet moving into position until August 3, when they anchored close in and opened fire. The warships mustered about 4,000 guns and 25,000 sailors; the transports held 9,000 troops. Even if Don Diego Salinas's six cavalrymen had had horses, they could only have used them to fade more rapidly from such a bad scene.

Later that day sailors assaulted direct from the ships. Captain Jumper of H.M.S. *Lennox* led one party ashore inside the foot of the New Mole (modern Jumper's Bastion). The Tuerto fort was blown up, and 100 English sailors with it, but these were almost the only allied casualties, and next day the Governor asked for an armistice while the terms of capitulation were worked out.

Some of the English ran amok, pillaging, looting, and raping – the worst excess being committed at the Shrine of Our Lady of Europa. Here they raped a number of nuns and girls sent there from the Convent of Santa Clara in the town for safety from the bombardments. They also smashed the images, stole the relics, and defiled the sanctuary. They were Protestants – the Inquisition had taught the rest of Europe to translate 'Spaniards' as 'cruel fiends' – they had been a long time at sea – they were following a hallowed tradition of how the English behave in victory (some of them must have taken part in the picnic at Puerto Santa Maria): but their actions did little to advance the reputation of their country or the cause of the Arch-duke.

On August 5 the governor signed the surrender. One of the terms was that any Spanish inhabitants of Gibraltar who took the oath of allegiance to Charles as the true king of Spain could stay, and keep his house and all his possessions. Few did, and those mostly Genoese. The exodus – the fourth in Gibraltar's recorded history – began. For days the people, carrying what they could, straggled across the isthmus, past the ruins of Carteia, into the hills above the Guadarranque. Here they founded the new town of San Roque 'in which is incorporated that of Gibraltar'. Over the weeks the intrepid priest of St Mary's Church, Father Juan Romero de Figueroa, smuggled church valuables and town records out to San Roque. One large image of St Anthony is legendarily said to have been taken out on a donkey's back, clothed and supported as a sick man.

But the Key of Spain, as King Enrique IV had called Gibraltar, was in the hands of the Pretender, the Arch-duke Charles ... for a few minutes. At the surrender ceremony the Spanish flag was lowered (a mistake of pro-tocol, this: if Charles claimed to be King of Spain, it should have been left flying) – and Charles's personal standard, a modification of the Imperial flag, raised.

Admiral Sir George Rooke looked at it, and decided that it would not do. This was not what he had in mind when he proposed the seizure of Gibraltar. He ordered Charles's flag taken down and the English flag run up instead. Gibraltar now belonged to Queen Anne.

Bad feeling spread quickly. Some admirals stole guns, some stole wine. Dutch squabbled with English, sailors with marines. Admiral Rooke sailed out and met a French fleet off Malaga. It was a hard fought day, and the

French might have had a clear victory but for the 'advice' of Louis XIV's personal representatives afloat, who, of course, had to be obeyed. As it was, Rooke was very early able to prove the value of his capture, as he once more limped into the shelter of its guns to repair and refit. Then he sailed again, with all the warships and transports.

The force ashore, left to wait the inevitable counter-attack, looted the empty houses, found hidden wine and brandy, and, sometimes, paid for the excesses they or their comrades had committed in assault. The Spanish sprang into galvanic action to regain what, with a little care, they need never have lost. An army of 9,000 Spanish and 3,000 French soldiers (these latter under General Cavanne) began to gather on the mainland opposite Gibraltar, under the overall command of the Marquis of Villadarias. The British now had some 3,000 men in permanent garrison, with many guns, all in working order. They had begun to dig inundations on the sandy isthmus, to canalize any attack still more narrowly. On October 8, 1740, the Spanish began to dig their siege trenches.

Inside the besieged town and fortress of Gibraltar then, the night of October 25th, about midnight ...

WEEP FOR JERUSALEM!

RAFAEL SANTANGEL waited, pressed back into the angle where two houses met, outside the lower wall of the Moor-ish castle. It was a redcoat coming, and alone – he had seen that much as the man passed the glimmer from a lighted window lower down the ramp. It might have been an officer, for few soldiers were permitted to wander round the town alone at this hour – though no one had taken much notice of the curfew while the wine lasted in the taverns.

He saw the man in silhouette against a white wall and gently put himself in balance for the thrust. It was an officer – tricornered hat, sword slung, no musket or bayonet. Quite old by the slow pace and the loud breathing. On his way up to the castle picquets probably. He passed, and Rafael stepped out, caught him under the chin with his left arm, and ripped the long knife across under his arm, opening the Englishman's throat to the bone, from ear to ear. There was no cry, only a faint bubbling cough. Rafael let the body fall, and stopped to wipe his knife on the tunic. That would show, he thought, smiling grimly. Blood was a different red.

He put on his shirt and the old jacket, glanced at his trousers to make sure they were free of blood, and slipped quickly down the ramp. He had thought once, earlier, when he began this work of vengeance, that he should shuffle to and from each murder like an old, bent man: but since the Spanish had opened their trenches any civilian caught out at night would be imprisoned and interrogated. The only hope was not to be caught.

He waited in the dark at each crossing of street or alley, then moved quickly to the next. Ne never stopped in the open, only in doorways. His knife was in his hand, but hidden.

The Fuentes' house was near the centre of Villa Vieja. He moved quickly down the last alley, waited for a pair of patrolling sentries to pass below, then crossed the street and opened the door. This was always a bad moment, for if Amelia had not been able to open it again, after Señor Fuentes had shut it for the night; or if someone had come along later, and rebolted it, he would be left out all night, sure to be discovered in the morning.

But it opened. He locked it carefully and turned to go upstairs. The girl came flitting down and put a hand on his arm. She usually waited in the attic: but now she led him up and at the head of the stairs turned left instead of right. There were two tiny attics up there – the left over the room where Señora Fuentes slept, the right over Amelia's room. Ever since the day of the surrender he'd been living in the one on the right. Now he followed Amelia through the low hatch into the other attic, closed it behind him and waited till she had lit the lamp.

'What's happened?' he muttered. He saw that she had brought his clothes, mattress, basin and bucket from the other attic.

'The English major put a Jew from Barbary to live with us,' she said. 'He wanted my room. I just had time to move everything across while he went back to his ship to bring his trunk.'

'What's he doing?'

'Buying and selling provisions for the English, he said.'

Rafael sat down on a wooden chest, and she set out food on another chest. She was a strong-limbed peasant girl from Castellar, wide mouth and eyes, seventeen years old, the Fuentes' servant for four years now; but getting restive to find a man, marry, and return to her village – so Maria Cruz had told him, the last time he saw her alive.

'I got one,' he said, drinking some wine. 'An old officer. That makes twenty-four. Seventy-six to go.' When he found Maria Cruz's body out there by the shrine, the novice's habit round her neck, and all her young woman's secrets, that were to be his, bared, bloody, defiled, her eyes

open, the livid marks of crazed hands round her throat, he
. . . he . . .

He put down the flagon and buried his face in his
hands.

After a time he felt the girl's hand gently on his forehead. 'Do it no more, master,' she said. 'I saw you from
that window, in the moonlight. Skulking down like a
thief, like a rat, in the shadows. And you to be the Count
of Grazalema. Man, it is not right.'

'I have sworn,' he said, 'one hundred lives for hers.'

'At first I said, 'tis good,' she said. 'After I saw how the
devils treated the women folk, aye, and had one up my
skirt when I was kneeling, scrubbing, but I kicked him in
the balls and ran in . . . But, master 'tis not right. Your
face is changing. It is not good for a great lord to want to
kill.'

'But it's all right for such as you?' he said, smiling, his
arm round her hips.

'Aye,' she said soberly. 'Sometimes the likes of us has to.
But not you. A lord can harm too many . . . Besides, I
think you must leave now.'

'Never!' he said.

'That Jew will be coming and going at all hours,' she
said. 'And he has a sharp eye . . . Father Romero gave me
a message to pass to you.'

'What?' Rafael asked. Father Romero was the parish
priest, and so far still permitted to travel to and fro between Gibraltar and the new town of tents and shacks
rising on the hill beyond the isthmus, where the fugitives
from Gibraltar were being settled.

'Our general – I can't remember his name—'

'Villadarias.'

'Yes – he wants to send many men up the back of the
Rock, at night, to take the English by surprise.'

219

'But it's all cliffs and precipices.'

'Not quite, master. A few shepherds know a path. Like my uncle.'

'Simeon!' Rafael exclaimed. 'Yes, he'd know.' Simeon Susarte was a small, wizened, 40-year-old mountain man who herded sheep and goats for their rich owners, all over the Rock. Rafael remembered seeing him at a boar hunt not long before the British attack.

Amelia Susarte said, 'The general. I can't remember his name, wants to send a lot of soldiers up and make a big attack, but first he wants to know what the English are doing on the upper Rock, and he wants to know whether ordinary soldiers will be able to get up the Shepherd's Path. So Father Romero thought you had better leave this house and live in a cave on the upper Rock somewhere, where you can spy on the English. And on the fourth night from tonight my uncle will come up to the Wolf Leap with an officer, to show him that the Shepherd's Path is all right for soldiers. And you should meet them there two hours after midnight and tell them what you have seen.'

Rafael got up and paced up and down the attic, his head down. He remembered that he was not over her bedroom now but over Señora Fuentes who did not sleep well because she was worried about the wound her husband had received in the English attack.

He sat down again. He'd been born in his family's Gibraltar house and as a boy, during frequent visits, he'd run all over the Rock, and later hunted boar and hare and partridge. He knew it well. There were a hundred caves where a man could hide for ever, if he could get food and water. But he'd have to give up his campaign of vengeance for his betrothed, with only twenty-four of the English gone to rot in hell for their crimes.

Amelia said, 'I'll bring food and water, every night.'

'Once a week will be enough,' he said. 'But . . .'

' 'Tis for Spain,' she said, 'and you'll get back Gibraltar for the king, and the church.'

'Not I,' he said. 'Your uncle Simeon. Then the king'll make him a count, and you and I could get married.'

She turned away and said after a time, 'Don't speak like that, master.'

'I'm sorry,' he said, remembering that his bethrothed was not yet three months in the grave. 'It was a bad joke . . . I'll do it. I'll leave as soon as I've eaten. Now, you know the Rock, too, don't you?'

'Aye,' she said. 'I've often looked after the sheep with my uncle when I was a little girl.' She was very subdued, her eyes red. He thought, she has run as much risk as he, hiding him, bringing him food, washing his bloody clothes, emptying the bucket that served for a commode; and she had her normal work as well – cleaning, sewing and washing.

'You're a good girl,' he said. 'I don't know how I'll ever be able to thank you for what you've done. But you'll never want as long as you live, I promise.'

'Let's talk about the caves, master,' she said wearily, '—and where I shall bring the food, or leave messages from Father Romero, perhaps . . .'

The Jew was about thirty, she thought, a strong square-built man with a long face, black jaw, and odd pale blue eyes that gave her shivers when she thought about them. She was very much aware of him, for she was kneeling on a pad scrubbing the tiled floor of the dining-room, and he was behind her, sprawled in one of the master's good chairs, looking at her legs.

'So the master got wounded the day the English came,

did he?' he said. 'That was a long time ago. Why hasn't he gone to Spain, like all the other gentry?' He spoke Spanish with an odd accent, using some words that she had hardly ever heard.

She answered him – 'He had his leg shot off. He nearly died. He'll leave as soon as he can, have no fear.'

'H'm.' The Jew got up and wandered round, picking up things and putting them down again. 'Who do you spend your nights with?'

'Alone,' she snapped.

'Why do you look so tired, then? . . . But you're a woman, aren't you? You wouldn't go out stabbing soldiers at night, would you? Though you're strong enough. A good, strong girl.' He passed his hand over her buttock. She knocked the bucket of dirty water over his feet.

He laughed. 'And good spirit, too . . . Do you know there have been no more murders since the night I arrived, three days ago? . . . What happened to Don Rafael Santangel? He was staying here, wasn't he, before the English came?'

She bent, and began to mop up the mess. 'He left the next day,' she said.

'Why was he here?'

'He was betrothed to marry Señor Fuentes' daughter when she finished her studies in the convent, next year. And now, if you will leave me to my work . . .'

'Not yet . . . Was she hurt when the English came?'

'Raped and strangled,' she said coldly. 'No more.'

'Ah. Are you sure Don Rafael left?' She saw that her bitterness had given him a clue, and resolved to keep a closer curb on herself. He was waiting for her when she came back, the bucket refilled. She knelt again. He said, 'What's he like?'

'Who?'

'Don Rafael. How old?'

'Twenty-one.'

'Good looking?'

'Yes. Tall, fair skinned. His eyes are dark. He is heir to a great name and estate.'

'Too high for you. But he used to steal a kiss now and then, perhaps.' She felt the tears stinging her eyes, and with effort kept to the rhythm of her scrubbing.

He said, 'Where did you get this?'

She looked round, and jumped up. In his hand he held the naked woman, carved of ivory, that Simeon found on the Rock years ago, and gave, laughing, to her, saying, 'One day you'll be like that, little one.' It had big breasts and a deep-cut *coño* and she did not let visitors see it, but kept it in a drawer, and sometimes found herself praying to it as though it had been a sacred Virgin. But because it was not a Virgin she only prayed to it for pretty clothes, and a high comb to put in her hair, and such.

The Jew was saying, 'This is old, my girl, valuable perhaps. See this stand, and the ring on her head. They're gold.'

'You stole it from my room,' she cried. 'You had no right to go in there!'

'I was just interested,' he said. 'You are a brave girl, loyal, and probably in love. A dangerous mixture.' He gave her back the figurine. 'I'd like to see *you* like that.'

She tossed her head, and as though it had been a signal, the house shook and a dull thudding rattled the window panes.

'The Spanish have opened fire,' the Jew said softly. 'They are making their next move. No more than a pawn, I think. They won't risk much for a barren rock like this.'

'You talk of us as pieces in a game?' she said angrily.

'We are people, not chessmen. This is our home, not a pawn.'

'This is how *you* see it,' he said. 'But you are in a minority are you not? A very small minority.' He smiled, suddenly kissed her, but gently, and went out.

*   *   *

From his place between two rocks, in a thorn bush, Rafael watched the English ships sweep into the bay, watched the French squadron try to escape, then the battle. The thunder of the cannon came up surprisingly loud and sonorous, though the billows of smoke sometimes hid all but the topmasts of the ships. When the smoke cleared the French had vanished – burning, beached, sunk. The English squadron hove to under the guns of the fortress below him.

He moved his position slightly, and grimaced with pain. It was not by sea that the English would be thrown off the Rock.

It was a cool day, with occasional drops of rain from the cloud hanging low over the Wolf Leap far above him. He had been in position since before dawn, and could not move till dusk, for he was almost in the middle of the upper defences, close above San Joaquin's battery. He could easily hear the English soldiers' voices as they talked. Sometimes, as they passed along the slope, they seemed to look straight at him; but his face was daubed with mud, his clothes drab and streaked, and they had not seen him.

This was his fourth day. The English had occupied and improved all the defences along this north face, from the water as far as the beginning of the cliff above the Moorish

Castle. They put out pickets along the foot of the slope, but they were far apart, and certainly men could pass undetected between them to seize the main works, where all but a sentry or two would be asleep. The chief defence was the inundation, which left only a narrow track for approach to the Landgate; but the inundation ended below the cliff, so men could pass to the east of it to the back of the Rock. If Simeon Susarte could really guide a large number of soldiers from there to the crest . . . the English had no defences at all facing upwards, except a post of a dozen soldiers close above the Hospital of San Juan de Dios.

The light began to fade, and rain fell more heavily. The redcoats scurried to the shelter of their lean-tos. Smoke of cooking fires rose. The sun gleamed once over the bay and the wreckage of the French ships, then hid, and soon it was dark. Rafael moved carefully, standing, stretching, taking the stiffness out of one limb at a time, then set off along the slope for the Lost Lamb Cave, his home.

It was on the slope, five hundred feet above the town, and hidden from it by an outjutting shelf of the limestone. Low holly oaks obscured the narrow sand-filled entrance. After a long crawl, it widened out into a big chamber.

He went in, lay down on the bed of heather, and fell asleep.

He awoke, knife in hand, at the clink of stone, and stared towards the entrance. Though there was no light he could see her plainly, naked, her hair streaming, running, her mouth open, but he could hear nothing. She vanished. He lay, sweating, afraid.

A long time later stones clinked again and Amelia Susarte's voice whispered, 'Master, 'tis I, Amelia.' She came in, and he heard her put down a heavy basket. He put out

225

his hand to feel her, and touched her breast. Her breathing stopped. He muttered, 'You are dressed ... I saw a woman naked. Running. Afraid.'

'You had a dream,' she said, her voice trembling.

The breast was full and round under his hand, and slowly he slid his hand round to her back. She sighed, and all the stiffness went out of her body. Her lips were warm and wet, her body trembling with love. Until the final ecstasies, when she cried out under him, he could not erase from his mind the fear in that other face, for it had been like hers, but not the same. But at last, spent, the apparition and the fear faded, and it was Amelia Susarte, the shepherd's niece, beside him.

'I love thee, master,' she said softly. 'I always have.'

He sat up, but held her hand. She kissed it, and held it to her cheek. 'I mean you no harm,' he said. 'It is not that I think so little of you. It is only . . .'

'Say nothing,' she said. 'There is no need ... I have a letter for you, from Father Romero, to give to Simeon.'

He took it. 'What time is it? I shall have to go up soon.'

She took his hand again – 'Are you tired? Is it bad, and dangerous, by day?'

'Sometimes,' he said. 'Yesterday a partridge nearly gave me away. It was walking under the bushes, feeding on fallen berries, and stepped near on my hand before it saw me, and let out such a squawk, and burst up through the bushes into flight with so sudden and loud a drumming that I thought I was lost, for two English soldiers were watching, not fifty feet away. But they had no interest. They see nothing except rum barrels ... What of the town? Señor Fuentes?'

'Well. He threatens to leave tomorrow, but I think the señora will keep him another week. The Jew – he is called Asher Conquy – puts his nose in everything. No one can go round a corner but he is there. I am afraid of him, master.'

He said, 'You don't have to come up again. There's plenty of food and drink here . . . I must go.'

Outside the cave, in the rain, she turned to him and put up her face. He kissed her, found his desire and affection rising, and stepped back abruptly. What could he bring but shame to a girl such as her?

'Go,' he said. 'Be careful.'

He turned and started up the slope. There were no English up here by day, and there would be none by night. The only paths were narrow winding tracks made by goats and sheep and wild pig. Sometimes he climbed across bare wet sheets of limestone, faintly gleaming, sometimes burrowed up on hands and knees under thorn and scrub. Suddenly, there was nothing ahead. On three sides the void opened before him. He was on the northern pinnacle of the Rock, the Wolf Leap. A few lights glimmered in the town, a few towards Spain. Cloud wraiths drifted past. He sat, waiting, fearing that the naked woman would come again in her terror.

He heard the crunch of stone before he saw the men, and then Simeon Susarte was over him. 'Don Rafael?' he muttered, 'This is Colonel Figueroa. He will bring up 500 men the night after tomorrow – if he found the path to his liking.' The colonel was short, one-armed, and heavy-breathing. 'It's the devil,' he said. 'But if I can get up, my lads certainly can. And you, Simeon, shall be as great in honour as Martin Alhaja Gontran, the shepherd of Navas de Tolosa. Now, my lord, what can you tell me about the English dispositions . . .'

Amelia went quickly down from the Lost Lamb Cave,

227

her heart light. She was a woman, at last. It had hurt, but the joy of giving had in a moment buried that pain. Perhaps even now she carried his child – though the women said it never happened the first time. Her lover could never be her husband, but that came to many girls. It was done. She was happy.

She reached the top of the town and went more carefully, for the English had increased the strictness of their curfew since the cannonading began. Even so, she heard roistering and shouting from farther down, and thought, some of the sailors are ashore and celebrating their victory of the afternoon.

The outer door opened squeakily, she closed it and locked it and went to return the key to its proper place in the hall. Then she crept along to her new bedroom, a tiny room beyond the kitchen, that had been a pantry.

As soon as she closed the door, she knew she was not alone. A man's voice said, 'Have no fear, pretty.'

She recognized the thick accent at once. 'The Jew,' she whispered. She heard the scratch of flint. A light glowed, the candle flame sputtered, towered, steadied. 'What do you want?'

'You, pretty,' he said. The pale eyes had a touch of yellow in them from the candle flame.

'Lay no finger on me!' she said fiercely, 'or I'll . . .'

'I said, have no fear,' he said. 'I see you love another. It is written in your eyes, your face . . . not to mention the heather in your skirt and hair.'

He was half smiling a little grim, his eyes wandering over her figure. He said, 'It's time you put some more oil on that lock. You might waken poor Señor Fuentes.'

She waited, head up. He said, 'An extraordinary amount of food seems to have disappeared from the kitchen. Two or three loaves. About two pounds of smoked ham. Three bottles of wine. There must be a burglar about . . . Or a thief, like the man who seems to have lived a long time in the attics here. There are cracks in the floorboards there, over your – my – room. Do you realize that a man might have been peering down and watching you undress? . . . The question is, shall I search you?'

'No!' she gasped.

He stared straight into her eyes, for a long time. 'Well, you might be carrying a message,' he said at last, 'but I don't think so. And the murders seem to have stopped.'

'Is that what you really came for?' she asked. 'To find the man who was killing the soldiers?'

'Ah, so it is only one man, is it?'

'I didn't say . . .'

'I am a humble merchant, señorita, a poor Jew, buying here, selling there . . . Sleep well. I certainly wish it was I who had pressed your pretty head into the heather.' He moved past her, and as before, kissed her. She was expecting it, and made no move, but let him. When he had gone, she began slowly to undress, not thinking, only remembering.

She was dozing in her little room when she heard Asher Conquy's voice saying 'It's a secret, but . . .' She sat up quietly. It was five in the afternoon, near the end of siesta time. Another man, also a Jew from his accent, was saying, 'How many? We have to know if we are to bring fresh beef over.' They were in the alley below the house.

'Two battalions,' Conquy said. 'One thousand five hundred men, in two ships. They'll be here soon after dark, with this wind.'

'What are they going to do with them?'

'The Prince said one battalion would go to strengthen the north defences, from San Joaquin's Battery to the

229

Landport, and the other, well, he wasn't sure – or he wouldn't tell – but he did hint he might send it right to the top, where it could look down on the whole Rock. Then . . .'

'Shhh. We'd better get down to the harbour, Asher, and finish our talk there.' Their voices faded.

Amelia slipped her feet into her shoes. Fifteen hundred men! And half of them perhaps going to the top of the Rock just before Uncle Simeon came up with the Spanish soldiers. And Don Rafael in mortal danger, too. She should tell Señor Fuentes. But he was still weak, and knew nothing of what was happening. The señora – still less. Father Romero . . .

She hurried to the outer door and looked both ways. Señora de Fuentes called, 'Amelia, where are you?' She did not answer. The street was empty, and she went out, and walked hurriedly to the church. She found Father Romero in the vestry and quickly whispered her news. He threw up his hands – 'What can we do, child? The English have closed all passage to and fro. They will not let anyone pass.'

'Does anyone here know the way down the back of the Rock?' she asked.

'None of us,' he said. 'Remember there are barely a score of us left now, and you and Señora Fuentes the only women.'

She said, 'I must tell Don Rafael then. At once.'

'Should you not wait till dark, child?'

'That will be too late, father. By the time he can get to them they will be half-way up the path.'

She returned to the house, slipped in, and went to Señora de Fuentes. The old woman was in full mourning, her face ravaged and haggard since the loss of her daughter. She seemed relieved to see Amelia – 'I

230

thought ... I dare not say what I thought. But now I want you to ...'

Amelia interrupted her – 'I must go, señora. It is for Spain. Say only, if the Jew or any of the English ask where I am, that I ran away to Barbary, on a ship.'

It was near six by now. She forgot the fearful, stricken face of Señora de Fuentes and again left the house. A few soldiers were about, but many houses stood empty for most of the English were quartered in the lower part of the town. As she climbed, all human sounds faded behind her. Her dress was plain dark grey cotton, and would not be easy to see if anyone were watching. But the English must have sent up scouts ahead to make a place for the soldiers who were to come. She must be careful not to betray Don Rafael's hiding place by carelessness.

The Lost Lamb Cave was straight above her now, over the ledge of rock and another hundred feet. Don Rafael might not be in it, but along towards the batteries, where he said he spent his days, on watch. She moved left, and instead of scrambling up one of the gullies which cut through the limestone platform, kept below it, and headed for the slope above San Joaquin's Battery. She saw Rafael in the same moment that he saw her. She signalled urgently to him – Come. No English were visible from where she was, crouched now close under a low tree, but he must be able to see some, for he did not move but kept his head turned away, and very still.

A glint of light caught the very outside of her left eye, and she whipped round, just in time to see a man with a musket sink down behind a rock, barely sixty feet from her.

They were following her. In a moment Don Rafael would come back in response to her signal. She stood up and walked towards the man with a gun, shouting at the top of her voice. 'Stand up, you with the gun! What do you want?'

The man jumped up, his face red with anger, and yelled at her in English. Then Asher Conquy came forward from the scrub behind her, and he was carrying a gun, too. The Englishman grabbed her by the throat and shook her violently. Conquy spoke a word and he let her go, but raised his gun menacingly. Conquy scanned the hill ahead. 'I suppose he's somewhere out there. If you don't show me, I'll tell the Englishman to blow your pretty guts all over that rock you're standing on.'

She shuddered involuntarily, but tightened her lips.

Conquy said, 'Come on down, then. We'll see if we can persuade you to talk to us in more comfortable surroundings.'

He sat opposite her in the big front parlour. Señora de Fuentes had started to protest when he marched her in there but he had silenced her with a curt – 'She will either talk or hang. Leave us.'

The shutters were closed and the tall candles burning. They were the last in the house, she remembered. Tonight was the Eve of Allhallows. In other years some of the children ran about shrieking of magic, and an old woman in the village said that witches rode the sky, she knew because she had seen one.

'My English friend is more used to stalking trollops in London than Spanish shepherd girls on the mountain,' Asher Conquy said. 'Otherwise . . . He was near, wasn't he? And it is Rafael Santangel?' She looked past him, at the windows, silent.

'It does not matter much,' he said. 'Certainly not as to who he is. But . . .'

'Why are you helping the English?' she said fiercely.

232

'What has this to do with you? Or do you try to betray us just for money?'

The half smile vanished from his swarthy face, and the pale eyes snapped. He said, 'Wait,' went out, and came back in a moment, his right hand behind him. He thrust it under her nose and opened it. A big rusty key lay across the square, calloused palm. 'That's the key of our house,' he said.

'In Barbary?'

'Here.'

'Here,' she faltered, '. . . but how . . .?'

'We Jews were expelled from Spain many, many years ago. Without reason. Without recompense. We have not forgotten. Why do you think we speak Ladino? It is Spanish, as your ancestors used to speak it . . . Some of our forefathers locked their houses and took the key, thinking the Christian king would recover soon from his madness. But he did not. So why should we not recover our own? You robbed – now you are being robbed. Good!' He shook the key at her. 'See that Señor Fuentes takes the key to this house when he goes. Perhaps he too will wait 212 years to come back.'

He saw her look of consternation, put away the key in the skirt of his coat, and sat down. 'What do you know of all this?' he said. 'You are a country girl. Can you read?'

She shook her head.

He said, 'I want to know what is the reason for haste. When you heard me talk about the English reinforcements, you—'

'That was a trap?' she cried.

'I fear so . . . You rushed hither and thither like a mad thing. I had expected you to wait until dark. Why did you hurry so?'

233

She pressed her lips together and looked past him.

'What would you say to ten maravedis? You know, the English hang spies. Even women. Do you want me to take you to the Town Major? He has a gallows set up ready.'

She knew, for half a dozen soldiers had dangled from it in the past month, convicted of looting.

It was a matter of time. This devil would find out, or guess, if he kept at her much longer. He liked her, or perhaps he liked all girls. It was her only chance. She burst into tears, only half voluntarily, and sunk her head in her hands. He had a habit of standing close, bending over her. He came now, one hand dropped gently to her shoulder, his voice was low and close, 'Don't cry, pretty, just . . .' She jerked her head up and back with all her strength. She felt a smashing thump, and heard a cry, and sprang for the heavy candlestick. He was reeling, blood spouting like a fountain from his nose. She hit him as hard as she could with the base of the candlestick, and hit him again and he collapsed.

She flew out of the room and the house and into the stable, and in a moment back with rope. She had tied up many sheep and goats and in five minutes he was well trussed, a cloth tied in his mouth. Then she wondered if he was dead, and listened. In the silence she heard his breathing, and sighed with relief. She ran out and found Señora de Fuentes. 'Help me drag the Jew to the cellar, señora,' she said. 'Then – clean the blood off the tiles. Hear nothing. Know nothing.'

She went to the outer door. It was dark. She started up the street.

It was moonless and cold on top of the ridge. They were burning the heath on the sierra to the north, and a fire glowed from the fishermen's huts across the bay. Rafael

Santangel sat huddled close to Amelia in the darkness, waiting. A bush stirred, and he strained his eyes to peer down the eastern steep, but saw nothing. The wind soughed in the spiny grass and made a thousand tiny flutes of the pitted, holed surface of the limestone. Lights shone in the harbour, and . . .

A man stood over him, dagger gleaming. 'The pass word!'

'All Saints,' he muttered.

'Don Rafael . . . and is that you, Amelia? What are you doing here?'

Colonel Figueroa came up, gasping for breath, and smelling of sweat and old wine. 'Mother of sin, I wouldn't come up there in daylight for all the gold in Potosi. Lead on, Simeon, for I have 500 men huddled like sheep on that infernal path, only they have but two legs each.'

Simeon said, 'I'll guide this party to St. Michael's Cave, Don Rafael. They'll all shelter there till dawn. Will you wait here for the next party, and bring them along. Five hundred more.'

'Very well,' Rafael said. Simeon moved off and the soldiers followed, passing in an endless line. He counted – 506 men went by: then he sat down to wait. The second party should be close behind.

Half an hour passed; then an hour; an hour and a half; two hours. The wind sawed into his bones, and the thin shirt gave no protection.

'Should I go to the cave and tell the colonel?' Amelia asked.

Rafael said, 'No. He will realize that something's gone wrong. We must stay here. The second party might come any moment.'

This time he saw Simeon coming from full ten paces off. 'No one?' the shepherd asked.

'No one.'

'The colonel asks that you join him at the Cave. I'll go back down the path and see whether they are stuck somewhere. Will you come with me, Amelia?'

'I'd be afraid, in the dark,' she said. 'I'll stay with Don Rafael.'

Simeon Susarte dropped over the edge like a falling stone. Rafael led down and across the great face of the Rock to St. Michael's Cave.

There was no light, and once inside the arch, after answering a quiet challenge, they had to step carefully among men sprawled asleep all over the damp floor and propped like sacks against every stalagmite.

Colonel Figueroa seemed unconcerned at the delay – 'It's 500 French who are supposed to be following, and to tell the truth I'd just as soon they didn't come. More honour for us, you understand? If 500 Spaniards – and we all took the Holy Sacrament before we set out – can't beat 3,000 drunken English and Dutch heretics . . .' There was a whirr of metal as he half drew his sword and slammed it back into the scabbard. Brave but stupid, Rafael thought glumly.

They sat down among the soldiers. 'How was it, coming up the Rock?' Rafael asked the nearest shape.

'Ah, that? Nothing,' the man answered in a strong accent. "We're from the Asturias. *Coño*. I've come up worse than that carrying a sick ewe, and in a rainstorm, man—' The voices murmured all round in agreement. 'Me, too . . . me too . . . Aye . . . We're shepherds, all . . . 'Twas nothing . . .'

'But this is something,' another rough voice cut in – 'Do you know how much ammunition we have? Three rounds each.'

'Quiet there!' an officer's voice was sharp.

Three rounds a man, Rafael thought angrily. It was fortunate indeed they had all taken the Sacrament and were shriven.

The time passed. Amelia was warm beside him. He found he was holding her hand, but did not let go. 'You should stay here when we go,' he said.

'Let me come with you,' she said. 'I am not afraid.' He squeezed her hand.

A little later – 'Don Rafael,' Colonel Figueroa said, 'time to go, I think. If you will be so good as to lead me to the nearest English outpost...'

In the first grey of dawn they passed over the ruined Moorish wall, and five minutes later came in sight of Middle Hill. The bay was dull green below, the western mountains just beginning to glow with light. 'The English have a guard there,' he said, pointing. 'They sleep under that bit of sailcloth.'

The colonel drew his sword. 'Ready, men?' The soldiers crowded up and around. 'Charge!'

They swept past, breaking into a shambling trot and then into a full run. A musket went off, close, with a sudden nervous bang. The yell arose – *Santiago! España!* – more shouts, shots, confusion. Rafael found himself running forward in the middle of the pack, his dagger in his hand. Ahead, the yellow and white tide swept over the Englishmen's hill, then swirled round but did not advance.

When Rafael came up he saw a dozen English soldiers lying about in the grotesque contortions of violent death. Colonel Figueroa was shouting, 'Take position here! Captain, you go there ...' The Spanish soldiers formed up, marching hither and thither.

'Go on down,' Rafael cried, suddenly aboil with fury. 'Don't stop here, colonel! The English don't have a single man on this side. Down into the town!'

The one-armed colonel awkwardly straightened his powdered wig – 'Do you look to your duty, Don Rafael, and I will look to mine. What is that girl doing here? Take her away at once . . . Steady, there, men!'

A bugle in the town began to blow hysterical calls. A couple of musket balls whistled overhead. The Spanish force gave no reply – only one or two rounds per man left now, Rafael thought. But, mother of God, if they attacked now they could seize powder and ball from the English! He looked up the slope. Simeon came running down the mountain, bounding from rock to rock in huge leaps. He was alone.

A column of redcoats marched out of the town, and began to deploy into line. Bugles blew, officers shouted incomprehensible orders. Rafael counted quickly . . . about eight hundred men. Simeon Susarte arrived, breathing evenly. 'No more soldiers are coming,' he said. 'And no more ammunition. I have been back to the camp. General Villadarias said the French colonel refused to follow you, because it was his right to go before you. Also, he thought the enterprise foolish.'

'Trust a viper sooner than a woman, and a woman sooner than a Frenchman,' Colonel Figueroa said pleasantly. 'Well then, we must die alone. *Viva la muerte!*'

'Go back, man,' Simeon said, violently. 'Nearly all will be saved.'

A storm of musket balls struck the hilltop. A dozen Spanish soldiers fell. The colonel smoothed his wig. 'You go, Simeon, and you, Don Rafael, with the girl. Tell the Marquis that we die like Spaniards. Give my compliments to the Frenchman . . . Now, my chicks, face the front.'

The musket balls flew thicker. Simeon Susarte's hand was on his arm, tugging – 'Come, master.' Then Amelia had his other arm, and he began to walk, then run, scrambling up the long slope with them.

He felt no emotion until they were down the tremendous path, where they would have fallen, many times, a thousand feet to death but for Simeon Susarte's sure hand and steady voice. He felt nothing until they had hurried along the eastern beach, past the end of the Spanish trenches. Then they turned and looked at the great grey tower of the north face.

Amelia suddenly said, 'Asher Conquy will take my ivory woman . . . Let him. I owe him something.'

'I'm thinking we've lost more than a little piece of bone,' Simeon said sombrely. 'We've lost the Rock. It'll be many a year before my sheep set foot on there again. When Englishmen and Jews get together, the rest of us stand little chance.'

Then Rafael felt the tears hot behind his eyes, and they flowed, silently, until he found Amelia's hand, and she took his and pressed it to her cheek without speaking. When they moved on, at length, she tried to free her hand, for her uncle was staring strangely at them, but he held her the tighter.

Book Eight

ENGLISH OUTPOST

The Jewish years 5465–5539
A.U.C. 2457–2532
A.D. 1704–1779
A.H. 1116–1193

SIMEON SUSARTE survived to tend his sheep on the mountains of the mainland, and so did Colonel Figueroa, though he was wounded three times more in this attack – twice in the chest and once in the leg; but most of his gallant 500 were killed. Before another assault could be made the English had discovered the Shepherd's Path and scarped it to make it impassable even for mountain goats or Andalusians.

In the following month, November, vile weather, good gunnery, and starvation almost succeeded where Figueroa had failed. Food ran low and the number of men fit for duty fell to 1,300, which was not enough to man all the guards. Then, as so often in the future, the Royal Navy came to the rescue, bringing in nine ships on December 7. Through December and January the siege continued under incessant cold rain, which was now beginning to hurt the Spanish in their encampments more than the British in their houses and fortifications. Becoming impatient, the Spanish king told Villadarias that he was to be replaced by a Frenchman especially lent by Louis XIV for the task. Since this man, Marshal Tessé, was to arrive on February 9, 1705, Villadarias naturally staged a massive attack on February 7. In spite of the inundation and the seemingly impregnable fortifications the stubborn Spanish infantry nearly forced a success, and probably would have but for the long and heroic stand, in an isolated outpost, of sixteen men of the 4th Foot. But fail they did, and Villadarias went, and Tessé came. After he had sat under that North Face for a few weeks he reported to his royal master that the Spanish were incompetent and improvident. On April 18, under cover of this verbal smoke screen, he raised the siege and marched his armies away, having achieved much less than the despised Spanish, in fact exactly nothing.

Late that year the Archduke Charles visited the Rock which his English allies had so obligingly seized for themselves in his name, and they permitted him to appoint a loyal Spaniard, Ramos, to succeed Prince George of Hesse as the Governor. But Ramos was soon succeeded by Colonel Roger Elliot, and from then on the governors were British. The war dragged on with, inside Spain, remarkably poor results for the Archduke. Queen Anne of England, moved by what whim or logic has never been clear, made Gibraltar a free port, decreeing that no manner of tax or impost was to be levied there on goods whether coming, going, or in transit. This free-port status has been the source of much of Gibraltar's wealth, although from the very beginning it has been eroded, at first by the greed of the governors, and later by the local administration's need to raise revenue.

The former inhabitants of the Rock waited in the 'most Noble, Most Loyal City of San Roque, in which resides that of Gibraltar' for a peace treaty which would return them to their homes. But the negotiations moved very slowly – because England was beginning to feel its rising power – because France, though financially weakened by Louis' megalomania, was still militarily strong – and because it was always to France's interest that England and Spain should not become allies; so, France always tried to prevent or delay solution of the Gibraltar problem.

Then the war became more complicated. The Emperor died and the Archduke Charles succeeded him on the throne in Vienna, as the Emperor Charles VI. The powers which had been supporting Charles now cooled off, as success in Spain would make him almost a Universal Monarch. The war finally ended when Charles renounced all claim to the Spanish throne ... and Britain insisted on keeping Gibraltar.

In the Treaty of Utrecht (1718) Spain unwillingly but formally granted Britain possession of it. Article X of that Treaty, which is the basis of all Britain's claims and Spain's counter claims, deserves to be set out here in full, in the English translation from the original official Latin:

X. The Catholic King does hereby, for Himself, His heirs and successors, yield to the Crown of Great Britain the full and intire propriety of the Town and Castle of Gibraltar, together with the port, fortifications and forts thereunto belonging; and He gives up the said propriety, to be held and enjoyed absolutely with all manner of right for ever, without any exception or impediment whatsoever.

But that abuses and frauds may be avoided by importing any kind of goods, the Catholic King wills, and takes it to be understood, that the above-named propriety be yielded to Great Britain without any territorial jurisdiction, and without any open communication by land with the country round about.

Yet whereas the communication by sea with the coast of Spain may not at all times be safe or open, and thereby it may happen that the garrison, and other inhabitants of Gibraltar may be brought to great straits; and as it is the intention of the Catholic King, only that fraudulent importations of goods should, as is above said, be hindered by an inland communication, it is therefore provided that in such cases it may be lawful to purchase, for ready

money, in the neighbouring territories of Spain, pro-
visions, and other things necessary for the use of the gar-
rison, the inhabitants and the ships which lie in the
harbour.

But if any goods be found imported by Gibraltar, either
by way of barter for purchasing provisions, or under any
other pretence, the same shall be confiscated, and com-
plaint being made thereof, those persons who have acted
contrary to the faith of this Treaty shall be severely pun-
ished.

And Her Britannic Majesty, at the request of the Cath-
olic King, does consent and agree, that no leave shall be
given under any pretence whatsoever, either to Jews or
Moors, to reside or have their dwellings in the said town of
Gibraltar.

Follow clauses about permitting trade between Gibraltar and Morocco and ensuring that Roman Catholic
residents shall be freely permitted to practise their religion. The last clause of Article X follows:

And in case it shall hereafter seem meet to the Crown of
Great Britain to grant, sell, or by any means to alienate
therefrom the propriety of the said town of Gibraltar, it is
hereby agreed and concluded, that in preference of
having the same shall always be given to the Crown of
Spain, before any others.

There it is; and if you wonder what full propriety without any manner of territorial jurisdiction is, so do I. The
wording has been used to assert and rebut all sorts of
claims and rights, but it seems clear to me that the fun-
damental purpose of Spain's reservations was to prevent
smuggling, by ensuring that there should be no land trade

between Spain and Gibraltar; and that Spain retained certain territorial sovereignty to prevent this, i.e. she wrote her terms into the infinite-year head lease.

Semantics apart, it was a bad treaty. It did not correct an injustice but legalized it. Both parties signed it in bad faith. Neither had any intention of keeping its side of the bargain. The Spanish immediately started harassing tactics which prevented Gibraltar buying goods in Spain; the British had no alternative but to turn to Morocco, a trade which was specifically allowed in the treaty. But many of the Moroccan traders were Jews, and the rest were Moors; and the Emperor of Morocco refused to allow trading unless his subjects were given full freedom to come, go, and reside in Gibraltar. Jews and Moors also bribed the governors to permit them to live in Gibraltar. Several provisions of Article X were thus being broken before the ink was dry on the Treaty ... and the Treaty itself was never considered by the European powers as a proper peace, but rather as a pause for regrouping and making fresh plans.

The next spasm of the general war which took up most of the 18th century came in 1727, and the Spanish instituted the 13th Siege of Gibraltar. This lasted from February to June of that year, vast quantities of powder and shot were fired off, and two or three abortive attacks made. The siege failed, the Rock continued in British hands.

The century stumbled on. The War of the Quadruple Alliance was succeeded by the War of the Austrian Succession, i.e. over who should succeed our old friend the Archduke Charles, later Charles VI, now dead, as Holy Roman Emperor. The Spanish king kept his country out of that one and the Rock saw no action. Then followed the Seven Years War, in which France finally persuaded

Spain to join, with the usual calamitous results for Spain, which suffered heavily in the Americas and in trade; but, again, there was no action at Gibraltar.

In 1759 Carlos III succeeded to the throne of Spain. Probably the best Bourbon in history, he was an appallingly ugly man (painted with ruthless sympathy by Goya) who spent his reign trying to drag Spain out of the middle ages, to modernize and reform her institutions, financial structure, industry, trade, and outlook. The recovery of Gibraltar was by no means his only aim, but it was very close to his heart. It was he who said the cardinal object of Spanish policy should be 'Peace with England – though war with the rest of the world, if necessary'. But it was he, drawn on by the French, who was to break his own dictum and make the most determined attemps to recapture the Rock.

Before returning to the large stage of world politics and European alliances, let us look more minutely at that Rock, the object of so much intrigue. ... When the dust had settled after Rooke's seizure, a report to London showed that some fifteen single individuals and thirty females (most Genoese) had stayed and some sixty Jews had arrived. By fifteen years later the civilian men capable of bearing arms were reported to number 45 English, 96 Spanish, and 169 Genoese: this would represent a total population of about 1,500. This dropped to 800 at the end of the 13th Siege, but then began to climb as England's continuing presence in Gibraltar, and all that it meant of creditable and disreputable, came to be accepted. By 1753 the civilian population was some 1,800, as against 4,500 military. Of the civilians about 800 were Roman Catholic (Genoese and Spanish), 60 Jewish, and barely 400 British Protestant. From this time on the Governors were continually concerned to attract more British settlers of

247

Protestant religion to Gibraltar; there was always the fear that a religious cause might unite the preponderant Catholic elements, which, combined with a mutiny or riot among the perpetually unruly soldiery, could mean disaster.

At first the civil population lived entirely by serving and providing the garrison. There was very little trade, as Spain kept Gibraltar in fever quarantine (a pretext for closing sea traffic as well as land traffic) almost continuously for half a century. But about 1750, with the advent of the neutralist Ferdinand VI, communications were opened, something like normal relations established, and trade began. The chief items shipped through Gibraltar were wine from Spain and France; and wine, wax, hides and brass from Morocco – all mainly consigned to Britain and North America.

In 1777 the population was about 3,100, of whom some 1,800 were Catholics, 800 Jews, and 500 Protestants (British). The Jews had established their first two synagogues, the Shaar Hashamayim and the Es Hayim. The Catholics kept the use of the churches built in the Spanish period, and remained nominally under the jurisdiction of the Bishop of Cadiz; but wars were more powerful than ecclesiastical hierarchies, and the Bishop and his Gibraltarian communicants saw little of each other. The Protestants could worship in the small chapel attached to the Governor's lodging (it had once been the Franciscan Convent) but there was no room for them on Sundays as the available pews were taken up by the military.

This population had watched the re-establishment in 1760, on its ancient site across the bay, of Gibraltar's old rival and one time overlord – Algeciras. It had suffered – civilians, military families, and military alike – under

Governors of a venality conspicuous even in that venal age. These gentlemen regularly made twice as much as their considerable salaries, in graft, known politely as licensing – they alone had the right to license porters, butchers, cow herds, goat herds, dairymen, bakers, chandlers, fishermen, bar keepers, wine merchants, and, I am sure, strumpets. The people had seen the state of their defences wax and wane according to the attitude of Spain and the greed or energy of the Governor; and they had come remarkably close, on several occasions, to losing their snug little home in the Gut.

Well documented offers – secret at the time – to restore Gibraltar to Spain were made in 1715, 1718, 1721, 1728, and 1757. One of them was a personal letter from George I to the Spanish king. In each case a *quid pro quo* was, of course, required. Sometimes the Spanish thought the price was too high; once they agreed, but by then the British had raised it. The Spanish, driven on by a daemonic desire to recover their territory, were always in the worst bargaining position, especially as British power grew relatively to their own. British ministers, sometimes with intent to deceive but usually with genuine concern, frequently took shelter behind 'Parliament' or 'the people', factors which a Bourbon despot could not appreciate; but they were real enough, and anyone who gave away Gibraltar against the wishes of the British people stood in danger of losing his head. It was barely a century since the same people had proved that whether the head wore a crown or not would be quite immaterial to them.

However shakily (even Pitt the Elder at one time wanted to exchange Gibraltar as an inducement for Spain to come into a war against France), the British connection survived these perils.

And the menace of 1720, when a large Spanish force

249

gathering in Gibraltar Bay, supposedly to sail to the relief of Ceuta (besieged by the Moroccans) across the Strait, was suddenly suspected of a closer task: a *coup de main* against Gibraltar. A hurried message brought ships and troops from Minorca (then British held), and the Spanish moved on.

And in 1761 when two regiments, bored, mutinous, or both, planned to rise, kill their officers, seize the treasure chests, and sell the Fortress to Spain.

And on January 31, 1766, when a storm of fantastic intensity struck Gibraltar; thirty-three inches of rain fell in twenty-six hours, over fifty lives were lost, and slides of mud, rock, and stone from the upper Rock buried houses, churches, barracks . . . and fortifications. The commander of the Spanish forces opposite was Duc de Crillon, a Frenchman in the Spanish service. He suggested that an immediate attack, before the British had recovered, would regain Gibraltar. He should, of course, have attacked first and asked permission later, for Carlos II was an honour-able man; he was not at war with England at that moment and he refused permission; and by the time the messengers had ridden to Madrid and back the British would have had time to build new fortifications, let alone clean up old ones.

In 1775 the embattled farmers of Lexington and Con-cord fired the shot heard round the world, but with par-ticular dismay by Carlos III. War against England promised an opportunity to even many old scores, in par-ticular to get back Minorca and Gibraltar; but to help the American rebels was almost certainly to establish them in power as a regime, and an example, which would soon cause the loss of Spain's own huge American empire.

But, reluctantly, he was dragged in. In 1778 France

agreed to help the Americans and declared war against England. In May of that year Spain offered to act as a peace maker, suggesting, as a stipend – Gibraltar. The brilliant French diplomat Vergennes finessed that offer out of court, and in the following April succeeded in leading Carlos III over the brink. Under the secret Convention of Aranjuez Spain agreed to declare war against England, and France agreed not to sign a separate peace until Gibraltar was again Spanish. The fate of the Rock was thus linked with the outcome of the American war, which was rapidly spreading to every place where France, England, and Spain could attack each other's interests, that is, the whole world.

On June 4, 1779, the Governor of Gibraltar, General Augustus Eliott, entertained his Spanish opposite number, General Mendoza, the Military Governor of San Roque, to dinner in honour of King George III's birthday. There was much bonhomie, friendship, and good cheer; the politicians had not yet told the soldiery of their secret negotiations.

On June 16 the Spanish Ambassador in London suddenly presented a list of complaints and accusations amounting to a declaration of war against England. Simultaneously, orders were sent from Madrid to close all communications between Spain and Gibraltar. Information about the artificially planned break must have reached San Roque by June 19, for when Eliott made a formal call that day to congratulate Mendoza on a recent promotion, he was surprised to find himself and his party treated with marked coldness and a most untypical lack of courtesy.

The courier carrying the detailed orders had been delayed on the road from Madrid and did not arrive until two days later, or Eliott might have been seized then and there. When the orders did arrive on June 21, 1779, Mendoza at once closed the land frontier on the isthmus. At sea the few Spanish ships in the bay began to enforce a strict blockade, under the command of Admiral Barcello, a man with a particularly virulent hatred of Britain and her usurpation of the holy soil of his fatherland.

The Great Siege began. . . .

THE GREAT SIEGE

(in contrast to the method followed in
the rest of the work, this section is
wholly factual)

> *Guarded by British Arms! Gibraltar Rock,*
> *Of France and Spain, sustains the hostile shock;*
> *See them in vain their arts and arms employ*
> *The vet'ran fortress proves a second Troy;*
> *Though that the Greeks by ten years siege could gain*
> *Here Bourbon and Iberia strove in vain.*
>
> (S. Ancell, 58th Foot)

THE GREAT SIEGE began . . . with a deafening silence. Except at sea no one fired a shot. So, while the British peer down from their eyrie and the Spanish look for a general who owns a copy of Vauban's *Handbook of Practical Siegecraft*, let us examine the military details of the confrontation now set up. At the time no one could have forecast how the light of history would fall. We, looking back, can see that the match was between an ill-harnessed mob of dukes, counts, generals, admirals, mad scientists, and cloaked agents on one side – and on the other, the excessively John-Bull-like shape of the British governor.

There is a famous portrait of him by Reynolds, cannon smoke billowing behind him and the sacred Key of Gibraltar firmly grasped in his right hand, its chain twined twice around the hand. Apart from two factors that were beyond his control – the cession of the Rock by negotiation, or the loss of all sea communication – the fate of Gibraltar came to depend centrally on this man. Seldom do those holding the highest positions at the beginning of a long campaign emerge from it with the most credit – or, indeed, any credit – at the end; but Eliott did, and it is essential to know him well.

George Augustus Eliott was born in the Scottish Lowlands in 1717, so was nearly sixty-two when the siege began, and had been Governor two years, long enough to show the first of his qualities, sheer military professionalism. He had already counted the stores, inspected the troops, examined the defences and put in hand a programme to get them back into shape after the neglect, embezzlement, and incompetence normal to peacetime. His military education had included training at a French academy, volunteer service in the Prussian Army, and further study at the British engineering establishment at Woolwich. In consequence he spoke French and German fluently. He had seen much active service, including Dettingen, Minden, and Havana. In politics he was a King's man, that is, of the Tory party which supported Lord North, George III, and the American War. He was addicted to formality but not form: he didn't care too much what the soldiers wore as long as they obeyed orders, performed the proper salutes and evolutions efficiently, and even used a little imagination. He was strict but humanitarian when he could be, in terms of the age, the sort of men he commanded, and the general conditions of a beleaguered fortress. He was bigoted in his attitude towards all new ideas except military ones: here he was a profound thinker and a restless innovator, always experimenting. He was a superb administrator and a master of logistics: supply, transport, and the administration of justice were alike rapid, effective, and sound. He had the memory of a top-grade inventory clerk, and always knew exactly how much of everything there was in Gibraltar, and where it was stored. He was not a good delegator of responsibility except – perforce – in naval matters, preferring, like Wellington, to make sure that he himself was always at the decisive spot at the decisive moment.

So far, so good – nothing incongruous with that great red face and beak nose of Reynolds'; but Eliott was also a teetotaller, a vegetarian, and, very probably, a homosexual – in this respect resembling his hero Frederick the Great.

The problem facing Eliott – to hold Gibraltar – was shaped by a number of factors, mostly unfavourable. The general war situation ensured that troops could not easily be found to reinforce or relieve his garrison. For several months, indeed, a huge Franco-Spanish fleet stood ready off Brittany to carry French invasion troops into England, and while that threat lasted the British government could hardly be expected to worry much about Gibraltar. The same bad political situation could at any moment decide the Emperor of Morocco, Gibraltar's nearest source of supply and intelligence, to give up his nominal neutrality. In the immediate neighbourhood of the Rock the Spanish were able to dominate, though not totally control, sea communications. Finally, the garrison was under strength (about 5,300 men against the 7,000 Eliott considered necessary).

On the other side of the ledger, the Spanish army, once the finest in Europe, was, like the country itself, in process of decline. Eliott's British and German troops were no braver but they were much better led. The same applied with even greater force to the two navies (though Eliott's local naval commander, Admiral Duff, must be excluded from this generalization: he was weak, slow, obstinate, and fearful).

And there was the North Front, towering 1,349 feet above the only land approach; the defences strengthened since the siege of 1727 and further improved by Eliott; the rest of the fortress out of artillery range except from the isthmus, and the whole of it not in range for the weapons of the time even from there; a general air of frowning impregnability, which imposed a sense of hopelessness, of futility, in the minds of any soldier sent against it or remaining long under the grey crown of its levanter cloud.

Eliott faced six specific main dangers. Assuming normal competence the Rock was unassailable by direct land attack, such as that of January 1705; but a combined attack from sea and land – prompt use of opportunities that might arise in fog, storm, or night – the turning of small mishaps to practical use through a good and rapid spy service – any of these, amounting to really good generalship, was the first danger.

Then there was pestilence. Minorca was soon to be lost, not by the defeat of British forces, but through blockade causing the soldiers to go down with scurvy, until it was not an army but a charnel house that surrendered to

Crillon. Pestilence had already struck Gibraltar several times, and a severe epidemic would obviously be very dangerous.

The third was starvation – and to this the Spanish originally pinned their hopes.

The fourth was treachery – the surrender of the garrison by its own soldiers. As we have seen, this nearly happened in 1761. Some particular discontent or grievance, aggravated by the conditions of a long siege – boredam, over-close contact, discomfort, fatigue, claustrophobia (endemic in Gibraltar at the best of times), and by the then-current custom of leaving regiments on the same foreign stations for inordinate lengths of time – could easily produce a similar situation.

Fifth, there was what we might call 'disaster', some piece of ill-luck which trumps good management. An enemy hit on one of the two major magazines could have rendered the garrison unable to resist. The magazines were well protected but there is ultimately no protection against chance, stupidity, or carelessness. Again, a very dry winter might have failed to replenish the Rock's subterranean supplies of water, which must have led to capitulation. I suppose that the chance of Spain or Royalist France turning up a Napoleon for command should also be reckoned under this heading.

Sixth and last, and the most likely of all, was the possibility of Gibraltar being ceded back to Spain in return for some other piece of territory less dear to Spanish pride, or more profitable to the British exchequer.

Armed then with some 663 pieces of artillery, served and defended by 485 artillerymen; 112 engineers and artificers; and 4,775 infantry (five British and three Hanoverian regiments of the line); facing an army of indeterminate size – but larger, and growing until in October it numbered 14,000 men, Eliott set to work.

He saw at once that he did not have enough trained gunners and matrosses to man the numerous cannon and mortars, and drafted strong and intelligent men from the infantry to bring the artillery up to strength. He had the paving stones of the streets removed and the earth ploughed, so that shot and shell would bury themselves instead of ricocheting or bursting and hurling the paving stones about with an effect as devastating as the shards of iron. On the isthmus and all over the Rock gardens were ordered to be cultivated, to supplement the stocks of food.

The military experimenting began. Mercier of the 39th Foot invented time fuses, so that shells could be burst in air over the enemy instead of sinking into the sand before going off: this was the forerunner of the device now known by the name of Major Shrapnel, who later perfected it. Witham of the artillery started his flashy campaign for prominence with the singularly appropriate invention of a light flare, to be fired from the mortars. Eliott ordered a gun to be emplaced on the very point of cliff over the North Face, the place the Spanish had called Wolf Leap, but ever after called Rock Gun – and with incredible effort it was done.

There were political as well as military considerations. The Emperor of Morocco had several warships being fitted out for him in Gibraltar. Admiral Duff now refused to provide naval stores to finish the job. Eliott was the Governor, but, as has been British custom since the time of King Canute, the admiral was under the orders of the Admiralty, not of the Governor. Eliott had to send for the British consul in Tangier, Logie, to come over and explain to Duff that the goodwill of the Emperor, on which depended the garrison's ability to buy food, mattered more than a few lengths of cable in his warehouses. The Emperor got his ships, Logie slipped back to Tangier in a Moorish galley, which was caught by Spanish cruisers; but Logie himself hid in a small scuttle for ten hours, with Eliott's dispatch and their secret code list concealed in a loaf of new baked bread, and finally reached Tangier safe.

Eliott now took a long look at the isthmus, where the new Spanish general, Alvarez, had reached page 23 of Vauban, and was throwing up his first breastwork about a mile from the North Front. The breastwork would be followed by parallels, batteries, and traverses, and thus, advancing by zig-zags in order not to be enfiladed, protected by merlons, fleches, barbets, and curtains, the works would steadily move forward until they were close enough for an assault. Then scaling ladders would be collected to climb the wall, the fascines to fill the ditch . . . but there was nothing in Vauban to say how you crossed an inundation, assaulted along a causeway ten feet wide, or climbed a cliff thirteen hundred feet high. Still, Eliott decided that he could not permit the enemy to carry out these engineering works as a parade ground exercise, so on September 12 he climbed up to the batteries with a large retinue, presented a Mrs. Skinner with a slow match, indicated the touch hole of a primed, loaded, and aimed cannon, and invited her to touch the match to the hole. A band struck up, Eliott removed his hat and cried *Britons, strike home!*, the lady's white hand descended, and the trim plans of Vauban gave way to the horrid manglings of war, where issues were decided not by diagrams but by flesh, blood, and brains.

Apart from the soldiers, Gibraltar contained about 1,500 military wives and children and 3,200 civilians, of whom 500 were British, 1,800 Roman Catholic (mainly Genoese), and 900 Jews. The contemporary historians and diarists lead one to wonder whether the non-Jewish people disappeared or made themselves invisible, for there is the barest mention of them, whereas Jews are perpetually being harassed, killed, beaten up, suing – in one way or another, making the scene. One, Abraham Hassan, volunteered for service and fought as an infantryman throughout the siege. When the bombardment began the civilians naturally expected the enemy to return the fire, and, encouraged by Eliott, many moved south, where a new town of makeshift huts grew up above the Naval Hospital. It was variously called New Jerusalem, Black Town, Jews' Town, or Hardy Town. Eliott also tried to get rid of all the 'useless mouths' he could, and what ships managed to run the blockade left loaded with 'Jews' (the Genoese were presumably under the floorboards).

General Alvarez advanced steadily through the pages of Vauban. Eliott cut the rations and his troops tightened their belts. There were no rations at all for civilians, who were in much worse case than the military. Besides this omission, which was the fault of the age rather than of Eliott, his passion for fairness led him to another anomaly: he ordered that after the government had bought whatever it needed of any imported food, all the rest – including presents received by anyone in the garrison – must be sold at public auction. This ensured that there should be no favoured people ... except those with enough money; who bought, and then usually sold again at a much enhanced price. In modern times such a system would have led to mutiny or treachery, but the only results then were a concentration of misery and an increase of robbery.

Another of the demons which haunted Eliott's pillow now assumed reality – a case of smallpox broke out in the town (a Jew, naturally), and Eliott ordered all civilians who had not already had the disease to move to Hardy Town.

Civilians began to starve, and the military to go very hungry. Eliott, in order to find out just how far a belt could be tightened lived for eight days on a diet of 4oz. of rice per day, with nothing else. The soldiers talked in awe of the governor's feat and simultaneously grumbled that it was all very well for *him*: he didn't eat meat anyway. Eliott riposted by ordering that soldiers were no longer to powder their queues with flour: it was wanted for food.

The situation was bleak, but people's nerves were rather more tightly drawn than conditions really warranted. At this time no one knew how long Gibraltar could hold out, or how long it would have to; there had not yet developed a semi-mystical faith that old Eliott would always think up something; worst of all, no one was sure that England knew or cared a damn what happened to them. It was to counteract these inner doubts that Eliott encouraged a regular routine. On September 13, for instance, the American Gentlemen had their usual annual dinner: these were officers who had been with Wolfe on the Heights of Abraham on September 13, 1759.

The appearance of a sail on January 17, 1780, was thus hailed with great enthusiasm; and the arrival two days later of the first ships of Admiral Rodney's relieving fleet, with something like hysteria.

Food and ammunition were replenished and Eliott took two important steps to improve his position. First, the fleet was transporting the 73rd Highlanders to the defence of Minorca; but Eliott decided that his need was greater than Minorca's, and took them off the transports. Second, when Rodney sailed away, Admiral Duff sailed with him.

The second phase of the siege began. The main activity was on the medical and diplomatic fronts. Scurvy increased and smallpox raged more widely, striking particularly at the children. Eliott refused to allow any inoculations; his conscience would not permit such a thing. A lady diarist wrote that an Eminent Personage seemed to think the deaths of the children a good thing, since there were too many of them anyway, and I fear she would have given the Eminent Personage's initials as G.A.E. Rations were still further reduced. Everything began to run short, especially leather; the soldiery wore all kinds of rag and makeshift foot coverings, and leather fetched as high a price as food, relatively.

Far from the Rock the diplomatic marching and counter-marching quickened, normal secrecy enhanced by the fear of some British politicians that their own common people were taking Gibraltar and its defiant governor even more closely to their hearts. The ministers stayed in their capitals and issued denials, while negotiations were carried out by obscure priests, playwrights, and naval commodores. There is no doubt that the British government would have traded Gibraltar at this time if they could have got a high enough price for it. The terms the Spanish were willing to offer depended on how they assessed their chances of getting it for nothing, by conquest, or by the total collapse of Great Britain. The Gordon riots of June 1780, for instance, caused them to lower their offer at a time when agreement was within a hair's breadth. It must also be remembered that though France wanted the war to end – she was going bankrupt – she also wanted to ensure that Gibraltar should remain as a perpetual hindrance to friendship between two countries which would normally have been natural allies against French aggression – Spain and England.

Logie, whose intelligence system was always excellent, sent warning that the Spanish were going to try a fireship attack. In June 1780, they did, and in spite of the warning only a providential failure of the wind saved the British ships in harbour from severe loss, and a conflagration which might have threatened the magazines and other defences. Barcello, who had been lurking in the bay waiting for the British to flee from the fire into the frying pan of his warships, withdrew, gnashing his teeth, to meditate fresh mischief, which he soon came up with – gunboats. These were about sixty feet long by twenty feet broad, mounting one large cannon in the bow. They had a lateen-type sail cocked from a forward-leaning mast, but the main propulsion was by oars. The Royal Navy considered the gunboats very unseamanlike and rather unsporting. The garrison, taking its cue from the sailors, attempted to sneer them out of existence; but they were most effective. They could hit at any part of Gibraltar, wind direction and strength were immaterial to them, they could move at night as easily as by day, and at night they could not be seen to hit back at. They made a large addition to the garrison's casualties, misery, and general discomfort.

Summer came, with tremendous heat. The food went bad in the stores, the officers started to bicker. Colonel Ross called Lieutenant-General Boyd 'a storekeeper's general'. (This was true, for Boyd had once been in the Commissariat; but it was of him that a German general had said, *The British send us commissaries fit to be generals, and generals only fit to be commissaries*.) Smallpox dead reached 500. The Emperor of Morocco first announced that as far as he cared the warring nations could sink and kill each other actually in his ports; and then leased the ports (Tangier, Larache, and Tetuan) to the Spanish. These steps removed the last shreds of protection afforded by his technical neutrality. The noose on Gibraltar jerked tighter.

The officers rioted 'a little', and a small steady trickle of desertion continued, in both directions. The worsening of the garrison's situation did not seem to make much difference – the stream of deserters was more or less constant in good times and bad; nor did the fearsome cliffs deter them, although most of the attemped desertions ended in mangled corpses at the foot of those great precipices 'at the back of the Rock'. The flow in the opposite direction was more surprising, except that many of the Spanish deserters were in fact Walloon mercenaries, relics of Spain's imperial past.

Scurvy grew so bad that Eliott was near the edge of another of those foreseeable but unpreventable disasters, when chance threw in his way a Dutch boat loaded with lemons. He seized it, used some lemons to treat the scurvy cases actually in hospital and had the rest pressed, the juice mixed with brandy in the proportions 5:60 in order to preserve it, and gave that to the troops as a scurvy-preventative.

Scurvy retreated, like Barcello, gnashing its teeth, but the gunboats advanced, now coming out by day to fire at the garrison's fishing boats, thus closing another source of supply. Their night attacks also continued and Eliott ordered a blackout from 7 p.m. every evening, so that they would find it more difficult to aim their shots. The weather grew appalling. Floods poured down the steep gullies, destroying houses, choking streets, and washing one gunner clean out of his battery. Holland and

Morocco, feeling out of step with the rest of the world, declared war on England. Logie, with 110 others, arrived as a refugee from Tangier. More civilians left Gibraltar and restiveness increased in the one body of men who could really nullify Eliott's skill – the corps of officers.

Their service in the already famous siege was far from benefiting them; just the opposite, it tended to disadvantage them in many ways. The army was expanding to fight all over the world. Anywhere else officers were being promoted and posted at high speed; but no one could leave the Rock, so officers there were not considered. Their pay was given to them in local Spanish currency at a variable exchange rate, which was considerably lower than par due to the poor opinion generally held of Britain's prospects. So they petitioned the Governor for redress, but did nothing more except riot 'a little' again, and beat up some Jews. (This was because the Jews wickedly claimed repayment of debts incurred by the officers; after the beating-up the officers concerned were summarily punished and fined by Eliott – 'The first time the Jews have ever found protection in this place,' a diarist reports acidly.)

On April 5, 1781, Lieutenant Burleigh of the Infantry (a consistent rival of Captain Witham for public attention and applause) took a few boatloads of men and tried to cut out some Spanish warships under Point Cabrita across the bay; but the moon inopportunely came out, the attempt failed, and Burleigh returned to the shelter of the New Mole.

Exactly a week later the garrison awoke to see a forest of masts bearing down upon them. A second relief fleet had arrived, bringing to an end the second phase of the siege. Simultaneously the third phase began with tremendous uproar, noise, confusion and damage. The dastardly Dons opened fire on the town at the moment that Admiral Darby's ships were anchoring.

Eliott's stores were again replenished, the dangers of starvation or lack of powder again pushed back, but the character of the siege changed. Life became much more unpleasant. The Spanish bombardment of the town was considered even more unsporting than their attack on the fishing boats, and it meant that most of the garrison were now forced, like the inhabitants, into tents, caves, and rough shelters; and danger was present everywhere, for the bombardment continued day and night, week after week, with tremendous intensity.

The immediate result was to bring to the surface another of Eliott's perils – the danger of disaffection; for the enemy shells blew down walls and floors concealing large stocks of food and liquor which civilians had been hoarding to increase prices. The soldiers did not actually mutiny but they were in a most unruly state for several days. The wise officer kept out of the way while his men drank themselves insensible, ate till they burst (one group barbecued a whole pig over a fire of cinnamon), ransacked, pillaged, blasphemed (they tried the image of the Virgin for high crimes and sentenced her to a spell in the whirligig), and in general acted as only the British soldier could. Eliott observed that the Germans took no part in this debauchery.

After allowing a few days for satiation to set in, Eliott appointed a Provost Marshal, had several looters hanged (only if they were looting the King's Stores, though), and discipline was restored. His principal accretion of strength at this time was the arrival from Minorca of a new naval chief, Captain Curtis. Curtis was a young social and pro-

S–TR–M

fessional climber, very brave, imaginative, efficient, un-scrupulous — and good looking. He became Eliott's greatest confidant and friend.

The inhabitants, who had been creeping back to their houses before the bombardment, again headed south where only the gunboats could reach them. Eliott this time provided some tentage for them; in return they threatened to sue him for knocking down their houses and using them for storage. Eliott, who had not yet received permission from the Horse Guards to issue extra pay to staff officers he had appointed in 1779, smiled grimly. The floods and the cannonades uncovered many bones of men and strange animals, encalcified in the rocks and gullies. Captain Drinkwater made a collection of these strange objects — which any anthropologist of the next century would have given an arm and a leg to see, for they were probably remains of prehistoric man and animals — but it was destroyed in the bombardment, most likely when Captain Witham had the batteries, for that indefatigable young gentleman was never content to let sleeping Dons lie. When it was his turn for duty everyone headed for Europa, as hell was sure to break loose in town. Witham didn't like to let *anyone* sleep, apparently, for he also found time to dig up the Jewish cemetery one night, in order to make a vegetable garden for himself.

The gunboats continued their harassment, killing chil-dren, blowing women naked and dead out of their shelters, reducing everyone's small ration of rest. Eliott ordered the batteries to reply, not at the gunboats but at the enemy camp, in the expectation that the sleepless Spanish soldiers would force their sailors to desist.

The endless experiments continued; what was the mini-mum amount of powder that would cause a shell to burst? Could the navy's rope ramrods be used instead of the army's iron ones? What was the difference in range of a musket when the powder used had or had not been dried? Could mortars, with their larger shells, be altered to reach the Spanish camp? What about using round stones instead of cannon balls? To deal with the shortage of medical staff, how about giving infantry sergeants medical and first-aid training? . . . There were many complaints against the doctors at this time and it is clear that the soldiery thought the medics, on the whole, were only interested in saving their own skins, and that with a minimum of discomfort. One surgeon, for instance, had to be turned out of a whole hospital ward that he was using for his own private quarters.

October 1781 was a bad month – the scurvy returned with increased virulence, the soldiers rioted, a naval crew mutinied, men killed themselves at a depressing rate, the fall of Minorca was momentarily expected, and Cornwallis surrendered at Yorktown.

Whether it was a reaction against this surfeit of gloom, or the fact that the enemy on the isthmus had now come uncomfortably close, Eliott decided to reimpose his will upon them. First, he tried a tremendous surprise bombardment with red hot shot. Some damage was done, but the works continued to advance. He thought again.

He and others had noticed that if one harassed the Spanish they resisted with increasing skill and obstinacy; but when left alone they tended to become careless and uninterested. Eliott, spying on them from the heights, noticed that although they clearly had their Vauban beside them they were beginning to omit several precautions that the master had laid down as indispensable. For example, when a siege work reached within a certain distance of the besieged, it must be protected by flanking redans and there must be adequate troops on the spot to protect it at night, against the danger of a sally by the besieged garrison. Such a sally was almost obligatory if all precautions were not observed; indeed regulations laid down that defensive works must have a special gate through which the sally should issue – the sallyport.

Eliott saw that the Spanish were not obeying the rules. He conferred long, in the evenings, in locked rooms with Curtis and enemy deserters, but said no word to a soul about the subject of the conferences. On November 26, when everyone was safely inside the walls, he issued orders for a sortie against the Spanish works. The plan was simple, clear, and admirable, being an advance in three columns with an ample and well placed reserve behind. Such a sortie should not have been particularly dangerous in view of the very detailed observation the British had of the enemy's works, and the exact accounts given by the deserters; but there was always the chance of something going wrong, of some last minute enemy reinforcement, of the intention being guessed, an ambush laid – and Eliott's real genius for command shows in his allotment of no less than 2,000 men, more than half his total fit strength, to the task. This was taking a sledgehammer to crack a nut, which is the right way to set about such affairs. So, at 2.45 a.m. on November 27, the columns filed out through the barriers, led by Lieutenant Colonels Hugo, Dachenhausen, and Trigge. The overall commander was officially Brigadier General Ross, but a large John-Bull-like figure, carring a sword in a sling over his shoulder, went along too, *incognito*.

The few enemy in the works fled or were killed, and the British set fire to the batteries, spiked the guns, and blew up the magazines. It was, of course, Captain Witham who formally presented the keys of the magazines to the incognito Eliott. Witham also captured a prisoner and behaved in a markedly dashing manner in all directions. The last of the British were back inside their fortress by 5 a.m., having lost five men killed and twenty-five wounded. They also brought back all their tools, weapons, clothing and equipment, except one kilt belonging to a soldier of the 73rd. How he came to mislay that, seeing what a man can do without taking his kilt off, must remain a mystery.

The siege continued. The purists among the students of war murmured that it was a gross breach of Vauban's rules for a commander-in-chief to go out on a sortie himself . . . but Eliott hadn't been there, had he? At least, his dispatch never mentioned his presence, but gave credit and chief command to Ross. (There is here a small piece of internal politics: Eliott's real deputy was the aged Lieutenant-General Boyd, but Boyd was a Whig while Ross and Eliott were Tories. To help Ross, Eliott had already markedly reduced the punishment a court martial imposed on him for insulting Boyd the year before.)

The siege continued. The officers presented another petition of grievance. The weeks dragged by in an endless procession: endless cannonading – sometimes up to 13,000 shot and shell a month from the enemy alone: endless scurvy – 400 and 500 regularly in hospital: endless guards and fatigues – some 2,500 men on duty every day, which officially gave a man every other night in bed, but in fact the calls for extra guards, working parties, and ammunition carrying fatigues, and the number of sick and wounded, meant that most men went nine or ten nights on duty for every one in bed.

In March, 1782, a number of breaks occurred. Another regiment, the 97th, was slipped in, and with it ten gunboats from England, in parts, plus instructions on how to put them together. With these Eliott was now able to hit back at his tormentors. The 97th however, was riddled with sickness. A hundred of its men went into hospital at once, nor could it find any guards. Its women and baggage had been captured by the Spanish in another ship and did not arrive for some time, which turned out to be fortunate.

And Eliott got some more lemons, by a ruse. He sent for the master of the ship *Mercury*, clearing for England, and gave him secret orders to stop in Lisbon, load up with lemons, and return to Gibraltar, but on no account to tell *anyone* he was doing so. The skipper obeyed his orders to the letter, though in Lisbon he did urge his passengers to continue their voyage to England in other vessels. Few of them did, since they could see no reason to do so . . . until they found themselves back under the hated Rock. This was considered a scurvy trick.

In Minorca, Murray surrendered. The enemy soldiers wept when they saw the skeletons they had been fighting. But good cheer was at hand: in England the army pay office allowed Eliott's extra staff their pay for the second half of 1779.

The siege continued, but soon with another change of atmosphere. The Spanish were seen to be doing something strange in Algeciras across the bay, and on April 1, 1782, Eliott's spies brought him exact word of what it was; but let us for a moment step back, and look at Gibraltar from farther off.

From London, Gibraltar was beginning to look very valuable. The disasters in North America caused the fall of North's ministry, and the new ministry wanted peace. In May peace commissioners went to Paris to open negotiations. The French badly needed peace as they were in worse financial shape than ever. The Americans had won all that they wanted: with them it was merely a question of formally agreeing that they had it. But Spain did not have what she wanted, and until she got it the war had to drag on because of that Convention of Aranjuez in April 1779. The British government were quite willing to give up Gibraltar for a suitable consideration, but by now the British people were definitely not. The war had been one long embarrassment and shame except for a sea battle in the West Indies and a generally good performance in India; but here on Europe's doorsteps a British garrison was cocking a three-year-long snook at the filthy Mounseers and Dons, and doing it alone. Several cabinet ministers believed that the sensible thing to do was to hand over Gibraltar, for which Carlos III would give fantastically good terms, but public opinion would not permit it. The British government being thus estopped from doing what it would dearly have loved to do, and not having sunk quite low enough, not even Lord George Germaine, to replace Eliott with someone who would betray Gibraltar, there was nothing for it, if the war was to be ended – but for the Spanish to take it by force. And now the French were going to see that it was done, by assisting and supervising.

That Frenchman in the Spanish service, the Duc de Crillon, who had thought of seizing Gibraltar in the aftermath of the great storm of 1766, more recently the conqueror of Minorca, was appointed to supreme command. Enormous naval and military reinforcements began to move to the scene. A general air of confidence and determination was inculcated: *this time we are going to show the perfidious English a thing or two,* the preparations seemed to say.

The principal cause of the confidence was a new and 'infallible' method of reducing the fortress. Carlos III's obsession with Gibraltar was so well known that for years military men, inventors, and plain lunatics had been bombarding Madrid with plans and suggestions. One method, the brain child of a French engineer called d'Arcon, was submitted in 1780 and had so much merit that in 1781 both Spanish and French ministries accepted it, and in February 1782 work on it was definitely put in hand.

From that date the British watched with awe the build-up of the preparations against them. Soldiers arrived by the boat-load, by the scores of boatloads, by the tens of thousands, disembarking at Algeciras or at a jetty built out from the Orange Grove, near the old site of Carteia and just beyond the reach of British guns. The enemy camp grew and grew. Crillon arrived, Alvarez went. Crillon peremptorily ordered his batteries to cease their bombardment of the rock pile, he would have other uses for them soon. The ships of war anchored in squadrons, until there were fourteen admirals' flags in sight. Word of the day chosen for the grand assault – August 25 – spread through Europe, and everyone who had nothing better to do set off to make sure of a grandstand seat. Every inn within forty miles filled up, and food prices rose as high outside as inside the garrison.

Though apprehensive, the British were also rather pleased that at least they were attracting the attention they felt they deserved. Eliott, stamping up and down and thinking of ways to do the enemy mischief, wondered how he could get a gun to an excellent enfilading position called the Notch, 800 feet up on the North Face and totally inaccessible. Sergeant Major Ince of the Military Artificers overheard, and suggested blasting a tunnel 500 feet through the solid rock to reach it. Eliott gave permission, all the miners in the garrison were posted to Ince, and he started work with crowbars, black powder and presumably the fire-and-water method, too.

Lieutenant Koehler invented a gun carriage that enabled cannons to be loaded, aimed, and fired quickly at extreme depressions – of great value in most of Gibraltar's batteries.

Captain Witham fought a duel with Lieutenant Burleigh, perhaps to decide who was the most dashing of them all.

Eliott overlooked nothing. The troops' quarters were regularly changed so that periods under close fire in the forward batteries and lines were interspersed with periods of comparative rest at Windmill Hill and South Barracks. Deducing that a bombardment would be made from the sea, he replaced the guns in the seaward facing batteries with guns removed from captured Spanish men-of-war, so that shot fired in the new attack could be fired right back. . . .

A magazine was hit, but it was not one of the two main ones, only a daily expense magazine, fairly close to the front. The enemy cheered but no real harm was done. Ince's gallery advanced a yard a day, but they were choking in there every time they fired a charge, until Ince had the idea of blasting a hole through the side wall to get a flow of air; which, when done, revealed a superb view of the Spanish works. The ventilation hole became a gun position, and as the tunnel advanced more were blasted. (It is these black holes spaced along the North Face of the Rock, about half-way up the sheer cliff, which attract the attention of every visitor to Gibraltar.)

Influenza struck the garrison, though not seriously. Eliott and Curtis agreed that since their few small ships were blockaded in, the sailors might be removed from them and made into a land force (Commander: Brigadier-General Curtis); which was done, and the soldiers laughed themselves sick watching the tars try to carry out

273

simple parade ground manoeuvres. Two French princes arrived — the Comte d'Artois (Louis XVI's brother and himself later King as Charles X), and his cousin the Duc de Bourbon. To greet them Crillon's Spaniards performed a feat which must have made old Eliott review his defences very carefully indeed. Between dusk on 5th August and dawn on 16th August, at a distance of less than 1,000 yards from British posts which had been put out specially to listen for unusual activity, being directly under the great Rock, ten thousand Spanish soldiers passed through their foremost lines and took up a defensive position close to the British. Behind them followed fifteen thousand labourers with sandbags and casks. In the six hours available for work they erected a defensive wall 1,500 feet long, 9 feet high, and 10 feet thick (this part contained over half a million filled sandbags); and in addition another wall, for communication, this one 3,900 feet long and 6 feet high (this one was built of casks full of sand). Not a shot was fired at them, and it was with unmistakable acerbity, remembering all the night bombardments and the handing over of keys and the duelling and the taking of prisoners, that the diarist of the siege wrote: *Captain Witham had the batteries.*

The last spectators have filed into their seats. The Comte d'Artois has visited a moored battleship but has soon had to return to land, seasick. Crillon has sent Eliott a handsome present of food and Eliott, a notable gamesman, has sent back an even more handsome one, also of food. The curtain is about to rise and we should now go backstage, and look at d'Arcon's secret weapon, about which Eliott received full details in April.

It was not cork horses on which real cavalry would charge across the sea; nor vast hoses to wash away the Rock and its garrison; nor a poisonous drug attack from balloons – all these, and many, many, much more fantastical had been suggested – but the relatively simple and sound idea of attacking the sea defences by armed floating batteries. The batteries were ships stripped, cut down, and altered so that they could only fire one way. In that direction they were protected by a thick sloped roof, extra timber 'armour' up to five feet thick, separated by layers of wet sand, and a system of water pipes to douse any fire caused inside the timber by red hot shot. They had sails but were of course very unwieldy.

It was a good idea, in itself, but it had been approved and put in hand before the Duc de Crillon was chosen as commander-in-chief. Crillon thought it a terrible idea, partly because it did have some drawbacks but mainly because if it were successful the main glory of taking Gibraltar would fall on d'Arcon, and not on him. He tried to have the plan abandoned, but too much time and money had been put into it. He thought of refusing his appointment, but then the world would think he was afraid to tackle Eliott. He solved his quandary in a thoroughly cheap and dishonourable way: before leaving Madrid for the south he inscribed a dated letter recording that in his opinion d'Arcon's plan was disastrous, and he, Crillon, was only putting it into effect because the king ordered him to. This letter, of which he left many copies, was to be made public the instant he sent word that the floating-battery attack had been made. Since he also stated in it what was already self-evident, that all the glory of success would be d'Arcon's, it was now quite clear that his own personal interests demanded that the floating batteries should *not* succeed.

The naval arrangements seemed designed to cause friction. Barcello still had his gunboats, but nothing more. Rear Admiral Moreno was put in command of the ten floating batteries. Admiral Cordova commanded over all – he had forty-seven French and Spanish battleships under him, with many lesser craft. But Barcello did not like being superseded in the campaign against Gibraltar, which had for so long been his own. Moreno was furious at finding himself cast as chauffeur for d'Arcon's inventions. Cordova was, in some ways, the most skilful admiral of his generation: he had an unbroken record of avoiding the squalor of battle in circumstances where anyone else would have found it unavoidable, or even sought it ... and now this upstart French mechanic looked like forcing the issue on the sea, perhaps involving Cordova's beautiful but fragile ships.

When the crews of the floating batteries had been escorted on board (at bayonet point), and after a couple of postponements, Crillon fixed 13th September as the day. On 8th September the British opened a tremendous fire of red hot shot from the North Face on to the new works which had been so miraculously put up the night of 15th/16th August. They set them on fire and the gallantry of the French and Spanish gunners, who suffered murderous casualties, could not prevent great damage. The incensed Crillon, much aware of the princes at his elbow, fired back heavily on 9th September, inflicting some casualties and damage, but enabling the British to locate and protect themselves against the new guns now unmasked.

On 10th September some of Cordova's battleships bombarded the fortress, sailing up and down and firing broadsides. One ship was set on fire by a red hot shot, but the attacks were effective, and they forced Eliott to keep his own men dispersed all over the Rock. But another card had been prematurely exposed.

On 12th September, the floating batteries were not quite ready. The secondary water-pipe and fire prevention system was not installed, and the vital test of actually firing redhot into the 'armour', to see how the whole design stood up, had not been carried out. Nor had anyone taken soundings at the places where the batteries were to be anchored for the Grand Assault. D'Arcon, ordered to make the attack on 13th September regardless, rushed out, jumped into a rowboat, and made the soundings himself. He found that there was a sandbank on the route to the batteries' firing positions, and planned a deviation to avoid it.

At dawn on 13th September, 1782, in the presence of some 150 warships, 35,000 soldiers and perhaps as many more spectators on the encircling hills, the Grand Assault began. The floating batteries sailed sluggishly out to take up their positions, Moreno leading in *Pastora*, the Prince of Nassau following in *Talla Piedra*, with D'Arcon on board. D'Arcon had the *Talla Piedra* thrust ahead to show the way round the sandbank . . . Moreno held course and speed, thinking the upstart *franchutta* was trying to take the lead . . . the other ships spread to right and left, conforming. When they dropped anchor some were too far south to be opposite any worthwhile target; the northernmost ones were fast on the sandbank and out of effective range; only *Pastora* and *Talla Piedra* could really engage Gibraltar's defences, or be engaged by them.

The fire fight began: the floating batteries and all the guns on the isthmus opened fire. All morning the British did little damage to the batteries – the shot was not hot enough till 2 p.m., but soon after that smoke was seen escaping from *Talla Piedra*. The crews of the batteries ran about the sloping roof putting out fires under a hail of shot and shell. All day the fight raged. Though there were casualties on the British side it slowly began to appear that thirst and exhaustion were more to be feared than the enemy's guns. Towards evening, the source of the smoke on *Talla Piedra* was discovered – a concealed fire in the timbers; the noble Prince of Nassau ordered his firefighters into action, not to douse the fire, but to damp the gunpowder. His vessel being thus put out of action he very properly took its only boat and rowed ashore, where the other thirteen admirals, with their 150 warships, were watching the scene with distaste.

From *Pastora* Admiral Moreno suggested that this fleet might come to his assistance. It was too rough, Cordova answered. Barcello, whose little gunboats had bombarded Gibraltar in much worse weather, agreed. If the floating batteries could not be towed out of danger, they must be sunk, Crillon reasoned; and gave the order. Boats went out from the fleet with a double purpose – first, to give each floating-battery captain a direct order to burn his vessel; and secondly, to take off what gunners and sailors they could. There were not enough boats, and panic began. The frantic D'Arcon rowed himself to Cordova – to Crillon – to get the suicidal orders rescinded, but it was too late. It would always have been too late, for Crillon's reputation depended on total disaster to the floating batteries.

At 1 a.m. the batteries began to burn like huge torches, with thousands of men still aboard. The British gunners reopened fire on the plainly displayed targets. Curtis ran down with his men from Windmill Hill, reconverted them into sailors, and set out in the British gunboats. Their fire drove off the Spanish boats, and then Curtis himself tried to rescue the crews from the floating batteries, which were burning so furiously that the whole Rock glowed red and orange. Curtis's coxswain was killed by flying wreckage, his boat holed, and saved by stuffing seamen's jackets into the holes. At last, with the battery magazines blowing up, he could do no more. He returned to land with a royal standard of Spain, taken from *Pastora*, that was to have been flown over the Rock.

On 14th September, dawn broke over total disaster – sunken ships, blackened hulks, burning hulls, corpses by the hundred rolling on the rocks below the Line Wall. The spectators on the hills had certainly had their money's worth.

The British losses in the assault were 16 killed and 68 wounded; the allies lost about 1,400 killed and 350 taken prisoner, nearly all in the floating batteries. Spain had suffered a shock and a wound to national pride greater even than the defeat of the Armada two centuries before.

The unharnessed herd of dukes, counts, etc., had failed, and the fairy John Bull had won. Reverting to my list of real dangers, we can see that pestilence and famine were kept at arms' length throughout – but only just, and by a combination of good management and good luck. Treachery never took root in the presence of Eliott's remarkable character: no one liked him, but everybody trusted and respected him. There was no major unforeseeable disaster; the rains did not fail, the main magazines were never hit, no Napoleon appeared to lead the enemy. Political surrender did indeed come very close, and although technically Eliott had no power to affect it, in fact his long and successful resistance caught the people's and the world's fancy, and so limited the politicians' freedom of action.

The danger – really good generalship – was obviously never present, though the component parts of it were displayed at various times. The great work of 15th/16th August, 1782, proved that the Spanish could move and work secretly and efficiently by night, and conceal all their enormous necessary preparations from a watchful enemy looking straight down on them. At one time or another great ingenuity was displayed: for instance, special craft with drop noses to land assaulting troops were designed, to support the floating batteries – but were not used. The ships and men were there to make a combined simultaneous assault all over the Rock, forcing Eliott to disperse his men. But everything went off at half cock, independently, or not at all. There was even a rumoured plan to attack in force the day following the disaster, to take advantage of the well known British custom of getting dead drunk after a victory. It was a good idea, and with any sort of co-ordination could have succeeded; but, as so often, nothing was done. In truth, the inherent capacity to lose or to take Gibraltar was always there: Eliott had the generalship to avoid the one, his opponents never found the generalship to achieve the other.

The peace negotiations in Paris, held up while the French and Spanish waited for the fall of Gibraltar, now went forward fast. In November preliminary articles of peace were signed between Britain and the United States. In December the Spanish accepted that Gibraltar would remain British (to the secret delight of the French), and in January 1783, peace was signed between France, Spain and Britain.

None of this was known on the Rock, where the formal end of Phase 3 of the siege was marked by the third sea relief, under Lord Howe, in October. Howe brought supplies, ammunition, two more regiments (the 25th and 59th Foot), and many more military artificers. Cordova set sail with his forty-seven ships to tackle Howe's thirty-three, but managed to avoid a serious engagement even in the narrow gut of the Strait, a considerable feat of seamanship. Curtis sailed with Howe to make sure that Eliott's account of his victory reached London before anyone else's. The garrison returned to its diet of scurvy, semi-starvation, quarrels, dysentery, and suicide, with a couple more tribulations thrown in for good measures – rabies among the dogs, and trouble in the hospital where seventeen of the 97th's recently arrived women had been shut up with venereal disease – but not soon enough, apparently, for a number of officers broke in and caused a riot there.

Crillon sent his engineers forward to locate a tunnel that had been started in the siege of 1727, to blow up the whole North Face. The British officers put on a play and Eliott promptly closed it. On 2nd February, 1783, news of peace reached San Roque, and from their works the Spanish sentries shouted, 'We are all friends now.' The Great Siege was over.

From the first to last the garrison had suffered 333 killed and 1,008 wounded – about 870 of these fairly lightly. Sickness, as in every war before the Great War, was much worse – about 1,000 dead, half from scurvy. There are no figures for the civilian population but it was probably not dissimilar, since the conditions were about equal for all: the civilians had worse food and quartering, but less exposure to enemy action and more rest.

The best estimates of ordnance expenditure give the British as having fired 205,000 shot and shell, using 8,000 barrels of gunpowder. The Spanish/French fired 260,000 missiles.

The necessary formalities began. Crillon and Eliott paid reciprocal calls, with much fulsome mutual congratulation. Crillon explained that it had all been d'Arçon's fault. The British army pay office were said to be thinking of authorizing pay for Eliott's extra staff for the first half of 1780. The garrison was voted the thanks of both Houses of Parliament, and Eliott was made a Knight of the Bath. The king appointed as his representative for the investiture the Lieutenant Governor, Boyd – who hated Eliott's guts – and vice versa. The ceremony was conducted under conditions that could not have been bettered in England. Continuous rain ruined the ceremonial arches and dripped down the spectators' necks, and everyone got drunk. The wonderful diarist Captain Spilsbury reports:

Never was a worse salute performed by the Artillery they not being able to fire a salute of 21 guns from 6 they had in the field, two of them being so neglected as to have a shot in each, left at the bottom before their loading was put in, and their tubes were in general too long; a worse feu de joie fired by troops, worse weather, worse musick, worse fireworks or worse entertainment . . .

The soldiery reverted to peacetime habits. Rape, murder, adultery, suicide, venereal disease, drunkenness, and indiscipline increased. The inhabitants trickled back from all over Europe – again, only Jews are named – many of them now destitute and homeless. Eliott, whose dislike of Gibraltarian civilians was only exceeded by his dislike of the British soldier (his praise was reserved for the Hanoverians), ordered that no civilian should be permitted to make lime, or employ a soldier in rebuilding his house. But he did overcome his feelings enough to give public praise to Volunteer Abraham Hassan on his release from the colours, and award him a house and premises for twenty-one years, as reward. Hassan soon exchanged this for ownership of another property in perpetuity. (Gibraltar's Major and Chief Minister from 1953–1969,

Sir Joshua Hassan, is a collateral descendant from Abraham.)

Smuggling began again, full swing. The Spanish seized a Gibraltar boat laden with goods being smuggled into Spain; the British governor demanded, and got, the boat's release. Spanish deserters and refugees from an unpopular régime crowded into Gibraltar. The situation was again fully normal. Peace reigned.

There was, however, a new factor in the Gibraltar equation. Strategy, commerce, politics were still there. The bitterness at Britain's usurpation was still there among the Spanish governing and aristocratic classes. But now there was also the Gibraltar Legend: for the place-name had become synonymous in the hearts of the British people, and in all languages, with *impregnable, defiant, reliable, unconquerable*. After 1783 the cession of Gibraltar would have been regarded as a cession of those qualities in the British people, i.e. as a collapse of the national character.

Book Nine

NELSON'S PORT

The Jewish years 5539–5564
A.U.C. 2532–2557
A.D. 1779–1804
A.H. 1193–1219

ELIOTT became Lord Heathfield and died of palsy in 1790. Admiral Sir Roger Curtis died in 1816 without adding to his already considerable fame. The three Hanoverian regiments that went through the siege took the battle honour *Gibraltar* and the motto *Mit Eliott Ruhm und Sieg*: and this led to much astonishment in later wars when British soldiers met the descendants of these regiments, by then incorporated in the German Army, in battle, and found them wearing *Gibraltar* on their sleeves.

Gibraltar itself was a wreck, not a house within range of the enemy standing and the ground so thick in cannon balls that they were still being picked up a century later. The population, which had fled (encouraged to do so by Eliott, as we have seen) returned to its prewar size remarkably soon, considering the unstable nature of the peace. The British people, admiring their new hero from a thousand miles away, were given advice about it by well informed and clear thinking Members of Parliament, e.g. '*Gibraltar . . . is the most valuable and important fortress of all the foreign territories belonging to Great Britain*'; and, '*Gibraltar always hung like a dead weight round the neck of Great Britain.*'

By 1787 the population was back to 3,400, then it fell but by 1804 it was over 6,000, with the largest element being Genoese, and after them Jews and Spanish about equal. The Jews had built another synagogue, the Nefusot Yehudah on Line Wall Road, and some were among the most prominent and influential men in Gibraltar, notably

Isaac Cardozo, Judah Benoliel, and Abraham Hassan the Volunteer. I have tried hard to find out just what Cardozo's business was – and so have other historians, notably Mrs. Dorothy Ellicott, who has written perceptively about Gibraltar through the ages – but there are no records, and it remains a mystery; yet he was very rich; organized the first Gibraltar police; acted as agent for the Governors in negotiating treaties with Moroccan beys and kings; and, after the Spanish rose against the French, supplied their armies with money and clothes. Benoliel was known as the King of Gibraltar, and was a friend of the priest later to become Pope Pius IX.

If there was boredom, a sense of let-down after the Great Siege, the Governors did their best to alleviate it. One, General O'Hara, nicknamed the Cock of the Rock, kept two mistresses in different establishments in a feeble attempt to outdo his father, a previous governor, who had had three, and fourteen illegitimate children by them. O'Hara also believed that if he could stand just a few feet higher on the high point of the Rock he could see into Cadiz Harbour (sixty-five miles to the north west). Military surveyors assured him he was mistaken, but he built a large tower up there anyway. The surveyors were right, he was wrong, and the tower was called O'Hara's Folly.

Then in 1802 the Rock received its first and only royal governor, the Duke of Kent, fourth son of George III. He had been there once already, when he was banished to Gibraltar at the age of twenty-two for running away from his military training in Germany, to the fury of his father. He soon drove the regiment of which he was colonel, the 7th Fusiliers, to mutiny; but he went with them to Nova Scotia and stayed there nearly nine years, consoling himself for the Arctic exile with a Mme de St. Laurent, who became his great and good friend for the rest of his life. She accompanied in 1802 when the king appointed him to govern the Rock. They sailed from England in H.M.S. *Isis*, commanded by Captain Thomas Hardy, who started by grumbling about all the royal hoopla but ended much taken with the Duke's charm.

The Duke discreetly installed Mme de St. Laurent in a farm in the Guadarranque valley below San Roque, for many years known as the Duke of Kent's Farm. He visited her there when he could spare time from his work in causing more mutinies among the soldiery. The trouble was that the Duke had a considerable sense of duty but no sense of proportion. His brothers, the Heir Apparent and the Commander-in-Chief, had told him to restore the shattered discipline of the garrison. He saw at once that the trouble was due to excessive drunkenness – there were ninety wine houses in operation – and began to take direct action. He closed the wine houses. The soldiers, who had no other release but drink, and no charming mistresses to keep their minds off the lack of alcohol, mutinied. The Duke's deputy, General Barnett, was delighted – this would get the Duke dismissed, he thought; and he was right. The Duke was recalled 'for consultation', but never replaced, so that until his death in 1820 the men actually bearing responsibility in Gibraltar were Lieutenant Governors. (All the Duke's elder brothers being without legitimate offspring, he was finally compelled to marry, and did so in 1818, marrying a depressing German princess called Victoria Mary Louisa, sister of King Leopold I of the Belgians. They had one child – Victoria.)

In these, its last few years, the eighteenth century's interminable war-game was swept away by a genuine conflict, the French Revolution; and that outburst of fervour was soon harnessed to the ambitions of Napoleon Bonaparte.

Spain, still tied to France's chariot wheels, and without a strong king (Carlos III had died in 1788), was dragged into the wars on France's side, although, as usual, it was in her national interest to treat France as an enemy, not a friend.

It is unnecessary to describe here all the manoeuvrings and counter-manoeuvrings, all the treaties and breaking of treaties, all the combinations and machinations, of each side. It is enough to note that the war was fundamentally between England and France; that France at one time or another persuaded, conquered, cajoled, or threatened the whole continent of Europe on to her side; and that with this overwhelming land power, Napoleon only needed to gain control of the Channel for a short time to destroy the one nation that stood between him and world hegemony. The Rock was, as always, in a position to hinder or prevent French and Spanish naval combinations. On this depended England's existence.

It is proper, then, that the outstanding personalities of the period should not be eccentric or royal governors, but sailors. Three in particular dominated the sea war, and Gibraltar.

First in point of time was Sir John Jervis, 'Black Jack' Jervis, later Earl of St. Vincent: disciplinarian, organizer, driver of men and ships. As admiral at Gibraltar he was always up at 2 a.m., made the rounds of every ship, then to the dockyard to see that the workmen clocked in on time, then to check the supply of fresh water. Jervis won one great battle; trained the Mediterranean Fleet into an image of himself – iron, tireless, ruthless; and made Gibraltar an efficient naval base.

Second was Sir James Saumarez, who, with a small force, attacked a French squadron that had taken shelter actually under the guns of Algeciras. The Rock scorpions had a grandstand view (6th July, 1701) of Sir James getting rather the worst of it, as was to be expected. The French admiral ran his ships aground, and Saumarez took a hammering from the shore batteries, with one ship grounded and taken, another put out of action and a third, his flagship, severely damaged. Saumarez limped back into Gibraltar and began a frantic refit, as the enemy would obviously try to take advantage of the British setback. Sure enough, the French refloated their ships, and a few days later H.M.S. *Superb* flew in from watch off Cadiz to report that six Spanish ships of the line were on their way. They sailed into the bay soon after, and next day sailed out again, escorting the French squadron. They were now also carrying many women and children from Algeciras who had thought this an easy and comfortable way to return to Cadiz.

Saumarez had only four ships partially ready, and with these he set sail in pursuit later that day; but unrepaired battle damage delayed all ships of his squadron except *Superb*. Saumarez sent her on ahead, alone. She caught up with the enemy in the night off Trafalgar and, unobserved, put three broadsides into the *Real Carlos* at 11 p.m. The *Real Carlos* – where the officers were at dinner with their lady guests and passengers – opened fire in all directions, notably on the *Hormenegildo*, her companion ship. After an hour or two of furious battle with each other both Spanish three-deckers blew up, with a loss of 1,700 lives. Meantime *Superb* slipped on ahead, captured the *San Antoine* and took her back to Gibraltar. Quite a night's work. . . .

When the report of what had been done to get the ships ready after the first battle reached the old perfectionist St. Vincent, by now First Sea Lord at the Admiralty, he wrote:

*The astonishing efforts made to refit the crippled ships at
Gibraltar Mole surpasses everything of the kind within
my experience, and the final success in making so great an
impression on the very superior force of the enemy crowns
the whole.* It was perhaps the most lavish praise Black
Jack Jervis ever bestowed in his life.

The third sailor was Horatio Nelson, probably the
greatest sea commander of history, a man who combined
fantastic courage with a woman's gentleness (to all except
Frenchmen or republicans). Nelson was commander-in-
chief of the Mediterranean Fleet when Napoleon put in
motion the vast plan aimed at gathering, in the Channel,
sufficient naval strength to force a passage across for his
invasion army.

As a first step the French admiral in Toulon, Villeneuve, succeeded in getting out and passing through the
straits of Gibraltar into the Atlantic on 8th April, 1805. It
was only by chance that his ships were seen at all and the
news passed by frigate to Nelson who was at the far end of
the Mediterranean. Nelson arrived a month later, guessed
that Villeneuve's destination was the West Indies, and
though considerably smaller in force, sailed after him.
Nelson was right but Napoleon's plan was precisely to lure
the British fleets westward while the French and Spanish,
having drawn them out, doubled back, concentrated, and
forced the Channel crossing before the British could re-
group.

Alas for the landsman's calculations – Nelson was there
and back before Villeneuve, having started a month later.
Villeneuve did indeed combine with the Spanish admiral,
Gravina, and bring a British fleet to action off Brest, but
the action was a draw. The grandiose plan having fallen
to pieces the combined fleets returned first to Brest, then
to Ferrol, and finally to Cadiz, where they holed up, ready

to rot, while their imperial master stormed from Paris that they should get out and fight.

Before this, on 18th July, Nelson stepped ashore at Gibraltar, the first time he had set foot on land for just over two years. He stayed only the inside of a day then returned on board; but first he gave a gold medal commemorative of the Battle of the Nile to his friend and admirer Aaron Cardozo, and patted him on the shoulder, and said, 'If I survive, Cardozo, you shall no longer remain in this dark corner of the world.' Gibraltarians are not quite sure how to take that remark. . . .

Nelson returned to England for a much needed leave. He had a month, and then on 14th September, the rumours of Napoleon planning fresh combinations, he was recalled. He said good-byes to Lady Hamilton and little Horatia, whom he never directly acknowledged as his own, and took carriage to Portsmouth. There he boarded, as his flagship, the old three-decker *Victory* (Captain Thomas Hardy). She had worn St. Vincent's flag too, and had first arrived in Gibraltar in Rodney's fleet during the Great Siege. Nelson did not go to Gibraltar but met his fleet at sea off Cadiz, sending a frigate ahead to order that no salutes should be given to him. He was vain but not modest, and he well knew that Villeneuve would think a long time before leaving Cadiz if he knew that Nelson was waiting for him outside.

Villeneuve may have heard from other sources, or suspected: but a motive stronger than fear was driving him to sea. As so often before, the spur to fatal action was the news that a replacement was on the way. Napoleon had named Admiral Rosilly to supersede Villeneuve in supreme command. Rosilly reached Madrid on 18th October: that day Villeneuve held a council of war in Cadiz, at which all his admirals vehemently disagreed with each other and with him. Villeneuve ordered his combined fleet to sea. It took them nearly thirty-six hours to get out of the harbour and bay, but they were finally clear at 8.30 a.m. on Sunday, 20th October. The wind was slight from the east-south-east. Later the wind freshened and veered into the south-west. The huge fleet of thirty-three ships, French and Spanish muddled together, sailed slowly south-eastward. Nelson's frigates signalled to him, where he waited over the horizon with twenty-seven ships of the line, that the enemy were out. During the night he moved slowly in. At dawn on Monday, 21st October, 1805, the two fleets saw each other. . . .

But let us go back now to the previous year: 3rd August, 1804, was the one hundredth anniversary of the British seizure of the Rock. It was about to face the most severe test of its history – far worse than Caramanli's raid, or the storm of 1766, or the Great Siege. . . .

THE EDUCATION OF ELIOTT CONQUY

'I CLOSE now,' Old Joe the publican growled. 'You go.' He rattled his keys menacingly. Eliott Conquy rose to his feet, stifling a yawn. His table companion called 'Stow your blather, man, d'you think I'd be staying where I'm not wanted?' He rose, weaving, and fumbled in his fob. Eliott said, 'It's paid for, Mr. O'Brien.' He swept several pieces of paper off the table, stuffed them into his pocket, and left the tavern at O'Brien's heels.

They started along Engineer Lane, O'Brien continuing his discourse from the tavern as though he had not been interrupted – 'So ye see, me boy, that stuff I'm telling you about the heart and the spleen and the kidneys is just what we know now, and if that's all we know, that's all we can teach, isn't that right? But because it's what we teach doesn't make it right, d'ye see? Because . . .' He stopped, teetering, and pointed – 'There! That's disease. That's where it's bred.' Eliott started, for they were at the corner of Bell Lane and O'Brien was pointing at the Shaar Ash-anayin synagoguge. Old Mr. Aboab's scandalized face, under a nightcap, was peering down at them from an upper window.

'I'm not pointing only at your religion, Eliott,' O'Brien said. 'Mine's as bad . . . worse . . . I mean that in religion, it's a matter of *believing*. In medicine it's a matter of *not* believing, but of finding out. But why do I tell you, who want to be a rabbi?'

'I don't know what I want,' Eliott said.

'Well, you're young. Holy Mother of Mary, I want to piss.'

'Here,' Eliott said. They were by Mr. Pitt's new Garrison Library. Behind it, the garden sloped steeply uphill under scattered trees. O'Brien went up a few paces and Eliott waited, looking into the garden and listening with amused affection to the torrential sound of Mr. O'Brien's relief. O'Brien was a square, short man with a big mouth and ears, and a trembling hand. He was surgeon to the 54th Foot, and in his forties: he might have been great and rich, but for the curse of the Irish.

It was a night of the levanter, mid-August, hot, close, the grey cloud mass stifling the town. Eliott was sweating, though wearing only a thin shirt, cotton trousers, and sandals. The moon gave a hazy dispersed light, shining through the cloud, and by it he now saw a dark shape under a fig tree in the library garden, and two more beside. They were men, one lying and two standing.

'There's a man ill there,' he said.

'Ill, or drunk,' O'Brien said. He staggered a few steps up the garden. One of the men came down at once, stopped a few paces off and said, *'Para, para, señor. No se acerca mas.'*

Eliott saw by his leather leggings, deep sash, and the Huelva hat perched over a bandanna that he was an Andalusian. He answered in Spanish, 'We thought we saw a man down. This gentleman is a doctor.'

The Andalusian said, 'Our friend has drunk too much, nothing more.'

'What's he saying?' O'Brien demanded. Eliott told him, and moved away. O'Brien joined him a few moments later. He said, 'I wonder where those fellows come from?'

'Spain,' Eliott said, for of course the men were smugglers: that is, they were agents of Spanish merchants come to buy tobacco. England was at war with Spain, and the land frontier was closed, but the Gibraltar merchants saw to it that the smugglers could come in and out of the garrison at will, war or no war, regardless of what orders the Governor gave.

'Does it not worry you that these men come and go as they please?' O'Brien said.

'It's not our business,' Eliott said.

'Ah, you scorpions!' O'Brien said, 'Nothing that does not happen on the Rock exists for you. But, man, there's a world outside, and you're tied to it, for better or worse, in a hundred ways. If you're to be a physician, you have to think, always, ask yourself, why is this happening? where has this come from? where is it going? . . . But you're not going to be a physician, are you?'

'I don't know, Mr. O'Brien,' Eliott said, 'Good night, Mr. O'Brien.' He turned up Forty Steps and a minute later let himself into the family house on Flat Bastion Road, and crept up to his room as silently as the creaking stairs would allow. He drew the curtains, lit the lamp, and sat down at the table. A copy of Albo's *Book of Principles* lay open at the section denouncing heresy, with on one side a torn volume of Maimonides' *Guide for the Perplexed*, and on the other the *Book of Criticism* by Abraham ben David of Posquieres. Pages of notes in his own careful but ill-formed Hebrew, written with a scratchy quill and spotted with ink where the quill had spluttered, littered the table. Every time his teacher came in, the old man shook his head sadly to see the word of G*D so disfigured, and said, 'If it weren't for the spirit in you, David, I'd think you had no respect for the word'; and he'd stoop and pick up the sheets that had blown to the floor.

From his pocket David Eliott Conquy pulled the sheets he had swept up from the tavern table and spread them over the Hebrew texts. Here was a diagram of the heart; Mr. O'Brien must have had a half-a-dozen glasses of brandy by the time he drew that, for it would not have been very clear even in a good light. Even so it was hard to imagine just how the heart functioned. He would have to see a heart, a real one, to know what these muscles and arteries looked like. He turned to the next sheet: the digestive system. . . .

He looked at the medical drawings, and the half hidden texts. Which was it to be? Sometimes the Word of G*D filled his thoughts, sometimes the formation and function of the human body. Or should he give them both up, and

296

learn to be a merchant, worthy of his employer, and future father-in-law? But did he want to marry Esther, or was he doing it only because the fathers had arranged it? . . .

The lamp was guttering when Nahum Conquy quietly opened the door two hours later, at three in the morning, and came in. He looked down at his son, head on the table, arms spread, asleep. He looked at the medical drawings that covered the sacred Hebrew books and the copied sections of the Torah, and raised his eyes to heaven. Then he touched his son's shoulder and said, 'Come, David . . . it is time you slept. What will Mr. Matania think if you appear before him red eyed and haggard?'

David Eliott stumbled to his bed, flopped flat, and returned at once to sleep. His father noticed that there was no smell of alcohol on his breath. That craving, at least, he had not learned from the Irish surgeon. He looked again at the medical drawings, muttered 'Blasphemy', and pushed them all into a drawer, leaving the religious works displayed on the table.

Eliott sat on a high stool in Baruch Matania's counting house on Bomb House Lane, looking out of the window. The blue water danced in the sun. The wind blew gustily, and he watched a young woman's light dress blowing about her as she walked along the Line Wall. The dresses of the officers' ladies scandalized his mother, for they wore only a single thickness of muslin, often damped, and now the wind was pressing it to their bodies. He yawned.

The familiar sharp nasal voice aroused him with a jerk. 'Would it not be more comfortable if I were to provide you with a bed here, Mr. Conquy?'

Baruch Matania was small and hunchbacked and heavily perfumed. He wore a black wig to hide his thin grey hair, and held a silk handkerchief to his lips when in the presence of young women, to catch the saliva that then dripped, uncontrollable, from his jaws.

Eliott stood up. He said, 'I'm sorry.'

Mr. Matania limped to the window, his gold-handled cane tapping – 'Sit down, David. I know why you're tired. Your father's told me . . . Let us make a bargain. I will release you from this clerkship if you will promise to give up the medical studies, and concentrate on the rabbinate. And marry Esther at once, as soon as the Teacher gives us a date. I'll settle five hundred pounds a year on you. I have made all the money I need, and it is time I paid some back to bring forth a respected Teacher in Israel. You shall be that Teacher, David.'

'Thank you, sir,' Eliott muttered. ' 'Tis most generous of you. I'm not worthy.'

'I often have doubts myself, on that score,' Mr. Matania said testily. 'Well, consider my proposal carefully.'

He tapped out. Sighing, Eliott returned to the ledgers . . . bill of lading, tobacco, Wilmington, North Carolina . . . Sight draft, Navy Victualling Commissioner, £13,000 . . . His head drooped.

Theodore Whittle, master of the schooner *Partridge*, shifted his quid from the left cheek to the right and shot a stream of tobacco juice over the side into the harbour. 'Come aboard, Eliott,' he called '—always welcome.'

Eliott hesitated. He had been getting manifests from a ship at the New Mole and was on his way back to Mr. Matania's; but Mr. Whittle was an old friend, English, an ex-Navy boatswain settled now on the Rock, and doing well by running cargoes between Gibraltar, Moroccan ports, and England.

Mr Whittle called again, and Eliott went on board. Mr

Whittle knew better than to offer him liquor, but gave him limejuice instead. Mr. Whittle settled himself on the upturned dinghy and looked up the grey-green slope of the Rock to the levanter cloud hiding the crest. He shook his head – 'It'll be worse tomorrow. I hate the levanter – masters run their vessels aground, husbands and wives fight . . . Do you have the fever ashore?'

Eliott said, 'Not that I have heard. Why?'

Mr. Whittle said, 'Three days ago *Dido* stopped a xebec but the crew shouted they was from Malaga, and the fever was killing off three hundred people every day there, so the captain said shove them off, don't touch them.'

Eliott said, 'Why would he do that?'

'Because there's some believe the fevers and pestilence is passed from one man to another, contagious-like, and doesn't breed by itself.'

Eliott thought, that would mean the fever could come here from somewhere else. From Malaga. And if it could come by sea, then it could come by land. Mr. O'Brien's interest in the smugglers in the Library Garden, of two weeks ago, suddenly became understandable; as also his upbraiding of Eliott's insularity.

Mr. Whittle said, 'Mind, I don't know about this contagion, myself. I think there has to be conditions that the fever likes, and then it comes of its own accord.'

Eliott wondered whether Mr. O'Brien had heard about the pestilence in Malaga. He thought he ought to tell him, and after a few more minutes' gossip excused himself and hurried along the mole. On reaching the shore he did not go to Mr. Matania's establishment but to Town Range Barracks, where the 54th Foot were quartered. He found O'Brien in his little room off the Sick ward. Fifty men of the regiment were drilling on the tiny square inside the buildings, sweating profusely in their heavy scarlet coats and high leather stocks. O'Brien glanced up from a thick book he was writing in and said, 'Eliott, me boy! I was just going to ask you to come. I'm thinking we have some cases of the Bulam fever, and I'm thinking, if that's true, I'm going to be terrible short-handed. I was going to ask, could you come and give me a hand an hour or two a day? Ye said once ye'd give an eye to work with me, so . . .'

Eliott felt the manifests in his pocket. The hard edges of them suddenly made up his mind for him. He gave them to O'Brien, and said, 'Just send a man with these to Mr. Matania, and I'll stay with you as long as you need me.'

O'Brien clapped his hands eagerly — 'That's me boy! Now I want you to help me get a full record of everything we can about the patients. Everything! I wish we had time to put down all about their fathers and mothers and where they spent every hour of the past thirty years . . . and that's what we're going to have to do one day . . . but with only you and me and Thompson the hospital mate we'll just have to do what we can.' He gave Eliott the book and went into the sick ward. 'Now write this down, Eliott . . . *Pte. Richard Tamlyn, 54th. Born Haworth, Yorks. Age 24. Town Range Barracks, in Cpl. Lindwall's room. Admitted August 31, 1804, 10 a.m.* . . . . Got it? Now write that Tamlyn was in here with ophthalmia from the 7th to the 14th of August. We've had a deal of ophthalmia in the garrison and there just may be a connection with the fever. We don't know. We don't know *anything*, Eliott, always mind that. Now let's go and see the man. He's in the end bed there. I'll speak, and you write down.'

The ward was an ordinary barrack room, with ten beds on either side. The floor was of stone paving, well scrubbed. One sick man slept, a couple of others sat on the edge of their beds, in trousers and shirts, playing cards on an empty barrel between them. The thud of the drum beating time for the drilling soldiers echoed loudly between the white-washed walls.

The man in the end bed was tall and lantern-jawed, with thin, lank brown hair. 'Write that down, how he looks,' O'Brien said. He turned to the patient – 'Now, Tamlyn, how d'ye feel?'

'Bad, sir, bad,' the man replied in a scratchy voice, 'Sir, am I . . .'

'Where's the pain now?'

'All over . . . like I'd been beat, doctor. Ooh, ooh.'

O'Brien laid a hand on his forehead and said, 'Chill . . . write it down, Eliott . . . 31st August, 11 a.m. Chill. Violent pains back and limbs. Throat sore . . . Stick your tongue out . . . tongue furred, whiteish. You look queasy . . . Head, stomach? Both. When was your last stool? . . . Shit, Tamlyn. Last stool yesterday, can't remember what it was like, didn't look . . . but we have to, Eliott, it's very important, especially in fevers . . . Urine – piss?'

'I wants to, but I can't. I wants to now.'

'Under the bed. Hold it for him, Eliott. There. Let it go . . . Hm. Not much. Write – wants to urinate often but with little success; urine produced is thick, high coloured. Pulse – 100, full.'

'Doctor, am I going to die?'

'Of course not. Cheer up, man. Holy Mary, let's have some air to breathe in here.' He walked down the ward to the far door and opened it. The thudding of the drum and the yelling of the sergeants burst in louder. 'That noise won't disturb *our* patients,' he said, 'They'd think they was dead without it. Write, in Tamlyn's report, "very nervous". That's a common symptom in the beginning of this fever. Depression, nervousness, fear.'

Eliott said, 'I see.'

O'Brien poked a finger into his chest – 'Don't you want

to know what the treatment is? Ask, ask, Eliott, or you'll never be a physician ... And now I'll tell ye, we have no idea what the treatment should be. Some of us do one thing and some another. The first thing I do, if the patient's not too weak, is to purge him. This is what we'll give him.' He took the book and wrote: *Ordered ipecac, gr xv. antimon. tartar, gr j to be wrought off with 2 quarts of water.* 'Now take that to Thompson, watch him make it up, then you give it to the patient. I have to go to a soldier's wife who I'm afraid ...' He hurried away, shaking his head.

Hospital Mate Thompson was a thin rheumy soldier who seemed to fear that Eliott was after his job, but when Eliott insisted, he grumblingly allowed him to watch the mixing of the ingredients. Eliott then took the medicine to Private Tamlyn, who had hardly swallowed it before he was sitting up, retching and straining, convulsed. Just in time Eliott got the bucket out from under the cot.

O'Brien returned as Eliott was taking the pot out to the latrines. He said, 'Stop there, boy. What's in it? ... Just his porridge, beer, tea, bread ... Write it all down. Now listen. There's two soldiers coming in, complaining of pains and don't feel well and their heads splitting open. You take all particulars. I must go back to Mrs. Cropley. Aye, she has the fever.'

Eliott took off his coat and hung it on the wooden peg behind the door in the surgeon's little office. ....

Pvt. Tamlyn. 3 pm: Emetic operated well. 2 copious fetid black stools. Body heat increased, tongue same, pains in back and loins worse, stomach easy. Face flushed. Pulse 104, weak. Ordered oatmeal gruel with a little wine.

There were four other soldiers in the ward by then, and

Mrs. Cropley in her married quarter behind. The lieutenant-colonel of the battalion came and walked the ward with O'Brien. They stopped near Eliott and the colonel said, 'If it gets worse I'll speak to the Governor about taking the men out to camp.'

Pvt. Tamlyn. 6 p.m. 1 black stool: urine free, slight pain forehead. Thirsty, eyes red, tongue more furred, mouth dry. Took tea and toast. Pulse 108, moderately full. Ordered 1 gr James' powder, at once, and if no effect another in 6 hours.

Eliott followed O'Brien to the next bed. And the next. And the next ... At midnight he was asleep on the floor of the surgeon's office, a blanket under him, when he heard his name called – 'David, David?'

He awoke, groaning, trying to unstick his eyes. It was his father – 'David, what are you doing here? We've been searching all the town, and the ships, for you. I feared you'd been pressed into the navy. Come home now.'

'I can't, father.'

The groans and sighs and mutterings of the ward sounded like low laughter in a charnel house. The smell of vomit and sickness and faeces lay thick and sweet under the acrid stink of the feathers Thompson had burned in the evening, to kill it.

'This is my place,' Eliott said.

'Ay, *que miseria!*' his father groaned. 'It's safer with us, son. None of *us* have it.'

Pvt. Tamlyn, September 1, 8 am: The dose of James' powder operated violently as emetic and purgative: now easy but thirsty; face swelled. Took tea and toast, drank toast and water. Fearful of not recovering. Pulse 104 but very soft. Ordered 2 gills wine in gruel through the day.

O'Brien said, 'Ye recall that night we saw the Andalusians in the Library garden? 'Twas 10th August. Now a merchant called Bresciano – ye know him? – has come forward to tell that the priest of the Spanish church here, Don Francisco Hoyera, was dining with him that night, and was called out to give the last sacrament to a dying man. He found the sick man under a fig tree in the Library Garden, and as soon as he was dead his friends buried him there. They were smugglers from Malaga, but before they smuggled the tobacco out they had smuggled death in. Aye, death, and ye see that what we have to thank this cursed fever for is greed ... How many more cases in the night? None? Well, 'tis early yet to say one thing or another. Now, Eliott, I'm going to do a very improper thing here. I'm going to experiment with these wretched men's lives. I'll give Tamlyn and the fellow next to him the regular treatment, but with others I'll try out different ideas. Ye've heard of the vaccination against smallpox, which is giving the person a dose of a similar but less dangerous disease? Now the remittent fever's like the Bulam, but it's not so strong. So I'm going to give two patients a vaccination of urine from that man Hallam, who has the remittent fever, ye see, to learn whether that protects them from getting it later. And I'm going to boil the stool of a patient who has recovered from the fever, and ...

Pvt. Tamlyn, Sep. 1, 6 p.m.: Took 1 gill wine, tea, toast; vomited; head well, back and limbs painful; tongue very furred. Pulse 100 weak; feels chill, but body heat moderate. Ordered 1 gill extra wine before morning, and to

take every hour 1 large spoonful of R.Decoct. Cort. Peruv.
zviij. Tinct ditto. zj.spt aether. vit.c.zjtinct. op ii.
gr.xl.M.

Pvt. Tamlyn Sep. 2, 8 a.m.: Slept very well; 2 fetid
black stools, vomited a little early; tea and toast since,
which is still sitting in him; some pains in limbs and
throat. Pulse 100, moderately full but feeble; forward half
of tongue towards tip clear and shining. Ordered medi-
cines continued and to have 4 gills wine, with sago and
tapioca.

'Eliott, there's a message for you here, to go to Mr.
Matania's place of business at once. Me boy, are ye still
supposed to be . . .?'

'Tell him I'm sorry. I'm busy, I can't come.'

'Aye, but listen to me, boy, you know 'tis dangerous
work looking after patients with the Bulam fever?'

Eliott nodded without speaking. He knew, too well.
Fear of the disease sometimes paralysed him, now that he
was seeing its course at close hand and knew that all the
surgeon's treatments amounted to no more than a pious
wish; but that was only when he was not actually in the
ward – once there, he became absorbed in his task of
recording the symptoms and the treatment. Several times,
feeling an onset of panic, he had gone to the ward to calm
himself.

Pvt. Tamlyn, Sep. 2, 3 pm: Thinks himself well; free of
pain; vomited much, ate 1 oz. meat (given him without
leave by a soldier friend) face pale, tongue not so shiny,
hawks bloody slimy matter, eyes clearer. Pulse 106, rather
feeble. Has had 2 gills wine. Ordered 4 more, and to
continue medicine.

'Ah, Eliott, come in, come in. I've asked the surgeons of the other regiments to have a look at our ward here, and then we'll have a talk, and I'm hoping we can speak with one voice to the Garrison Surgeon, and he to the Governor. This is Mr. Ashland of the 2nd, Mr. Greatorex of the 10th, Mr. Mackenzie of the 13th. Gentlemen, this is Mr. Eliott Conquy, my assistant. Now, if you'll follow me . . . This patient was admitted – read from the book, Eliott . . .'

They went down the ward, and an hour later crowded into O'Brien's office, all standing, for there was only one chair. O'Brien said, 'There you are, gentlemen. D'ye not agree that we must urge the Garrison Surgeon to go to the Governor and declare an emergency? By God, we are at war! If the fever strikes us very heavily, the Spaniards could walk in, and seize the fortress.'

'Quite right,' Greatorex said. 'We should fumigate the whole of Gibraltar immediately. The air is foul and the pestilence is breeding in it. There should be fires in the streets, especially at night. Find the most pestilential areas and move the troops from those areas out into camp. Or into caves. St. Michael's Cave would make an excellent site for several hundred men.'

MacKenzie said, 'By your leave, your proposals are nothing short of disastrous. The only help is isolation. The Bulam fever is contagious, and is passed by physical contact, or breathing common air, between the fit and the sick, in which I include those in whom the disease is not yet fully incubated, that is to say, persons whom we have no means of knowing are about to become stricken. Everyone, therefore, is a potential danger, and everyone must be prevented from giving the disease to others.'

'What evidence do you have, pray, that the fever is contagious? It is well established that this fever is spontaneously generated in certain climates and places, such as that very island of Bulam off the Guinea Coast.'

'Rubbish, Mr. Ashland.'

'Mr. Greatorex, fiddlesticks to you, sir.'

'Sir!'

'Gentlemen, gentlemen, can we not agree on one thing, just one recommendation?'

'Provided it is agreed that contagion is not . . .'

'Contagion must be treated as the one, the only . . .'

Pvt. Tamlyn. Sept. 2, 6 pm: vomited, continues easy. Tongue not so shiny, pulse 102, feeble. Ordered continued wine and medicine.

Pvt. Tamlyn. Sept. 3, 8 am: bad night, delirious, 1 stool; vomited twice, comatose, tongue dry, very weak, no appetite. Pulse 90, feeble. Ordered bottle sherry wine, and to continue medicine with aether vitriol zj to ziv of the bark, M.

3 pm. No alteration.

7 pm. Vomited about one quart of matter resembling coffee grounds; no pain, delirious. Pulse 102, v feeble. Ordered continue wine and medicine with a tablespoon of water, strongly acidulated with elixir of vitriol, every half hour.

Sep. 4, 8 am: Slept little, was delirious, feels easy, vomited black fluid very often, had half hour of hiccups; took medicine regularly, also 2 bottles white wine; pulse hard to perceive. Ordered continue all medicines and apply sinapsisms to feet.

'Eliott, you look like a ghost walking.'

'Yes, Mr. O'Brien.'

'Yeoman's well on the way to recovery. The other three . . .' O'Brien took another swig from the rum bottle on his desk. His skin was grey and his breath rank with liquor. 'Mrs. Cropley died last night.'

Pvt. Tamlyn. Sep. 4, 2 pm: Died an hour ago. Bled profusely from nose and mouth.

Eliott drew a line under the entry and looked at O'Brien. 'Next patient,' O'Brien said harshly. 'How do you feel, sergeant? Vomit? Stool . . . ?'

Eliott usually enjoyed Succoth, the Feast of Tabernacles, more than any other religious occasion of the year. But today he felt nervous and uncomfortable.

The cantor and the rabbi led the service, their three-cornered hats bobbing and bowing. Eliott took the pointed palm and the citrus offered to him by his neighbour and stepped into the side aisle to find space. He bowed his body forward and began to thrust out the palm and citrus . . . but should he be here at all, with Mr. O'Brien's certainty that the fever was contagious? Should any of them be here? Surely the Parnassim should have cancelled the service and closed the synagogue? But *could* they?

Twice to the east, twice to the south, twice to the west, twice to the north: then twice upward and twice downward. He gave the palm and citrus to another. The singing became more intense.

> *Hosha-na, Hosha-na,*
> *Save us, we beseech Thee*
> *Save us, we beseech Thee,*
> *For Thy sake, if not for ours, save us,*
> *O Lord, save us we beseech Thee, we beseech*
> *   Thee.*

The president drew back the curtains of the Ark, and Levantadores went forward, brought out two Torah scrolls, raised them, and carried them down the steps. Eliott bowed his head, carried out his prayer shawl, touched the case of a Torah with it, and kissed its fringes where they had touched.

When they had carried it slowly all round the synagogue, and were again in front of the Ark, the Levantadores faced the congregation, suddenly raised high a heavy Torah, and unwound the scrolls so that three columns of the Word showed. In front of Eliott Mr. Matania half stretched out his arms, tears rolling down his cheeks. He believes, Eliott thought, so he is not a hypocrite, even though he is an unscrupulous old lecher. My father and young brother Hillel here beside me, believe. But I? I am here, I perform the functions laid down, carry out the appointed rites, but do I *believe*? If not, how can I become a Teacher?

He glanced up at the balcony, where his mother and three sisters watched intently, their faces half covered, wigs hiding their hair. Three hundred deaths a day in Malaga. What if the Law said one thing and Medicine another? The teachers were calling for a Cohen to read the Word, as was his right. Old Jacob Cohen hobbled up, and read. When he had finished, the Teacher beckoned to Eliott, and he went up. He read from Leviticus 22, carefully, for he always found the un-pointed Hebrew difficult to read:

These are the appointed seasons of the Lord, even holy convocations, which ye shall proclaim in their appointed season ... And ye shall offer an offering made by fire under the Lord, seven days: in the seventh day is a holy convocation, ye shall do no servile work.

Afterwards Mr. Matania met him outside the Tabernacle set up in the synagogue garden. He said, 'You read well, David. But then you go and "do servile work" in the soldier's hospital ... Are you ready to come back to the counting house now? Or to start serious study?'

'There are still many sick among the soldiers,' Eliott said. 'It is getting worse. Afterwards ... when it dies down....'

'All *our* people are well,' Mr. Matania said. 'None has taken the fever. It breeds in dirt, and to avoid it, only cleanliness and clean living according to the Law are needed.'

But it was not true. Succoth fell on September 23 that year. On October 3rd Eliott's father was stricken with fever, and the same day, Esther Matania and five other Jews. The pestilence continued among the military, but now also moved full force upon the civilians. It crept out of the soil and shook down from the sky. It was breathed in the air, drunk with the water, eaten with the food. Day followed night followed day in a slow procession of nightmarish unreality, of fear that spread and grew like cancer in the body, bursting out in sudden blossoms of violent pain and worse, despair. There was a certainty of being unwanted, doomed. Twice Eliott saw men hurl themselves from upper windows, and twice into the sea, and make no attempt to swim.

Eliott left the 54th and moved out to the fever 'ward' of tents and shelters set up on Windmill Hill. His daily hours of sleep dropped from six to four to two. In succession he nursed, and buried, five members of his family – all, except his mother. The rich of all religions left Gibraltar, the Jews to Morocco, the rest to Genoa, a few to England. The poor stayed and died with the garrison.

Towards the end of the year the pestilence began to

abate. In the first months of 1805 those who had fled began to return. The narrow streets of the town had become silent corridors, the houses silent but for the squeaking of rats. On Windmill Hill and by Black Town hundreds of vultures feasted on the ill-buried bodies.

Eliott Conquy returned to work for Mr. Matania, because he needed money to support his mother, and because Mr. Matania, who had lost seven out of nine clerks, begged him to. In the evenings he studied medicine with O'Brien, or the Law with the Teacher of the congregation; but more and more now, when he finished for the night, it was the sacred books that lay on top, obscuring the medical notes below. Many who had known him for all the twenty-one years he had lived before the pestilence, did not recognize him; for he had lost thirty pounds in weight, and developed a stoop, so that he looked like a black-avised heron, the dark blue eyes deep sunk under the bony overhang of his forehead. He believed that YHWH had shown him His terrible face and commanded him; for Eliott had turned away from Him and now his father, his brother, and his three sisters were dead, taken in agony. Eliott knew he must obey YHWH ... yet he had come to hate Him.

O'Brien rocked back in his chair, the grog glass shaking in his hand. He had not been able to drink heavily during the epidemic, but had made up for it in the ten months since. Eliott did not think he would last much longer. It was Friday – October 18th – four o'clock in the afternoon.

'Do you have a shilling to spare, Eliott?' O'Brien said, 'The navy officers here are having a sweepstake on how long it will take the new Governor to discover about Signalman Dacres. D'ye not know about that? Well, there's a post for a common sailor to be naval signaller on the Rock, that's been filled and the pay drawn for the past twenty-four years by Admiral Dacres, and him retired in England since 1788! Old Tommy Trigge never did find out!'

Eliott did not smile. The minor rascalities of the Christian military seemed very unimportant against life's permanent background of death and fear, and the menace of YHWH, as real and as toweringly present as the Rock above these barracks.

O'Brien cleared his throat nervously, 'Well, I mustn't be wasting your time, must I? ... I've been making out a summary of the epidemic from the regimental reports, and the civilian figures you gave me. Take a look at that, me boy ... Well, Jasus, I shouldn't be calling you "me boy" any more, should I?'

Eliott picked up the paper. On it was written:

(Rank and File)

Corps.	Admitted Hosp.	Died, all causes
Artillery	462	201
Engineers	229	123
Military Artificers		15
2nd Foot	300	131
10th Foot	419	22
13th Foot	479	130
54th Foot	456	100
De Roll's Regt. Hanoverians	414	187
Officers, all corps		54
Military women and children		164
Civilians, all		4,864
		———
Total		5,991

O'Brien leaned forward and tapped the paper with his finger. 'Two things stick out like a sore thumb, Eliott. We had 4,864 civilian deaths. That's about half the civilian population of before the epidemic. But many civilians left Gibraltar, so the mortality among those who stayed must have been near eighty-five per cent ... compared with fifty per cent in the Engineers and only thirty per cent in the infantry. And the infantry is the worst disciplined, the most crowded, and the dirtiest of all. What do you think of that?'

Eliott said nothing. O'Brien was a good man, but blind.

O'Brien went on quickly. 'The other item is this – look at the figures for the 10th Foot. They have as many admissions as the others ... but barely one-fifth of the mortality! Now what can that mean? That the 10th have acquired a resistance? Where? They've come from India. Is that it?'

Eliott stood up. He said, 'None of these things matter. I can not be interested in your medicine any more, Mr O'Brien. Thank you for what you have done, but I shall not be back.'

O'Brien stared up at him open-mouthed. The glass rattled on the table. Eliott turned and went out, hearing one baffled hurt cry behind – 'Eliott!'

He went straight to Mr. Matania's house, where the merchant now lived alone with his only surviving daughter. He was in the parlour, and stood up carefully when Eliott entered. 'David,' he said formally. 'What can I do for you?' His manner to Eliott had changed greatly since the epidemic; but then, everything had.

Eliott said, 'I have decided to become a Teacher.'

'The Lord be praised,' Mr. Matania exclaimed.

'I have come to accept your offer. I shall go to England to study.'

'The Lord be praised!' Mr. Matania cried again. 'David, this is wonderful! When are you leaving?'

'As soon as I can get passage.'

Mr. Matania hurried out, calling, 'Wait there.' His cane tapped away, and in a few minutes returned. 'There's fifty sovereigns for your passage, and to fit yourself out in London,' he said. 'And here's a banker's order on Mr. Rothschild for twenty pounds a month. If you need more, you have only to write. And . . . you'll come back to us, to be our Teacher and guide?'

He looked up, anxious and subservient.

'I shall come back,' Eliott said sombrely. He went out, the merchant's final 'The Lord be praised', still echoing in his ears. Now he had to tell his mother. She would faint for joy, for she had been pestering him to take this step ever since the end of the epidemic.

He bumped into someone and a voice cried, 'Hey, hey, look where you're going, you walking beanpole . . .' It was Mr. Whittle. He recognized Eliott – 'Why, Eliott, damn my eyes, I haven't seen you in an age, and now I'm off again – but there's just time for a quick one afore we sail.'

'Where are you going?' Eliott asked quickly.

'Bristol.'

'I'll come.' He looked at the sun – still an hour or more before the beginning of the Sabbath. 'I'll be on board in half an hour.' He ran away down the street, the tails of his black coat flying.

'Sail-ho!' a sailor at the bow cried, 'Two points off the port bow.'

Mr. Whittle leaped nimbly into the portside rigging

and peered forward. 'Thank God!' he said. 'It's one of ours.' He jumped down and glanced astern, where a brown-sailed black-hulled sloop was hauling up fast on the *Partridge*. A few minutes later the sloop's captain saw the new sail, and put down his helm. Two puffs of smoke blossomed on his flank, two columns of water leaped out of the sea, far short, and then two thuds of cannon. The sloop, a Spanish privateer, turned and headed back for Cadiz, just out of sight over the eastern horizon.

Mr. Whittle laughed and cocked a snook at it. To the helmsman he called, 'Steer for the man o' war, George. We'll sell 'em some vegetables.'

The ship bore down upon them, all sail set before a north-west wind. When the black hull and yellow gun-ports and waving ensigns seemed to be right on top of them, sailors scrambled like squirrels up the rigging, and she backed top-sails. A boat smacked into the water almost simultaneously, and Mr. Whittle said, 'It's the *Ark Royal*. Best handled ship in the fleet. She was fitting a new mainmast in Rosia 'till a few days ago. But . . . hold hard! What do they want to send an officer and marines for? Put up the helm, George, quick!'

An officer on the poop of the warship shouted through a speaking trumpet – 'Put down your helm, master, or I fire.' Eliott saw that half a dozen guns on that side had been run out to the ports.

The boat rowed alongside and a lieutenant came aboard. 'Captain Burleigh's compliments, and he must press any able-bodied men aboard for the King's Service.'

Mr. Whittle shouted, 'You can't press my crew, lieutenant.'

'Oh, yes, he can, master. It's Mr. Whittle, isn't it? We sailed forty short and now we've lost ten more down with fever. And the enemy are reported to be warping out of harbour.'

Red-coated marines scrambled aboard the sloop, and Mr. Whittle called up resignedly, 'All right, Captain Burleigh. But leave me five sailors.'

A marine jogged Eliott's arm and pointed to the boat. Eliott said, 'I'm a Jew.'

The marine said, 'All right, Moses, into the boat.'

'But . . . this is not my business. This is nothing to do with me.' Eliott cried. 'I'm a passenger, going to England for rabbinical studies.'

Two marines seized him and dragged him, struggling and shouting, to the boat. 'Go along easy,' Mr. Whittle called anxiously. 'It can't be helped, Eliott. The fleet needs men . . . He's a doctor, lieutenant.'

Twenty minutes later Eliott stood on the deck of the battleship with a dozen other sailors and passengers taken off Mr. Whittle's ship. The *Partridge* itself was just beginning to make headway towards the north-west, on the starboard tack. A tall, dark jowled man in blue, with much gold lace, stood in front of them and said, 'Seamen, one step forward. Mr. Trott, distribute them . . . Bos'n, take charge of the rest. Give 'em some gun drill at once.'

Eliott said, 'I want to go to England.'

A nearby group of sailors began to titter. The lieutenant said, 'The master said this one was a doctor, sir.'

Captain Burleigh said, 'Ah, then down to the orlop with you, and report to Surgeon Halford.'

Eliott said obstinately, 'I am not a physician. I want to go to England.'

Captain Burleigh glared at him, the dark eyes snapping. They stood alone on the poop, for everyone else had gone about his business. Two marine sentries, guarding

316

the companion up from the main deck, stared woodenly ahead.

The Captain said, 'You speak very good English for a Rock scorpion. You are a Gibraltarian, aren't you?'

'Yes.'

'Try saying "Yes, Sir".'

'Why? I am not in the military.'

Captain Burleigh said, 'You are now . . . You are an educated man or you wouldn't speak English. And yet, you seem to know nothing . . . This ship is about to rejoin Lord Nelson's fleet. Tomorrow that fleet will fight the French and Spanish, somewhere near here. Do you know what will happen if we lose?'

Eliott shook his head. It was none of his affair, this business of fleets and armies and battles.

'The enemy will be able to invade England. And Gibraltar will go back to Spain.'

'Gibraltar?' Eliott exclaimed. 'Here?'

'Here!' the captain said.

Eliott looked out over the heaving tumbling waste of blue and white. Specks of sails had begun to show along the western horizon. If Gibraltar became Spanish, what would happen to the Jews? It seemed unbelievable, and unjust, that such a question should be decided miles away, upon another element, by men from other countries. But so it was. And the movements of these forces, which he had lived with all his life, but ignored, would now also decide his own career, and his fate.

'Take me to the surgeon,' he said, 'I will do what I can.'

The next morning was Monday, October 21st. Shortly after dawn a sailor found Eliott killing cockroaches in the orlop, and told him the captain wanted him. 'Bring a sharp knife, captain says,' the sailor added. Eliott worked his way up narrow ladders, through long, low-roofed spaces crowded with chattering men and silent guns, to the open air. Captain Burleigh was sitting on a barrel on the poop. The rising sun shone on his worn blue coat and tarnished gold lace. He thrust his hand out – 'See that splinter? Cut it out.' The splinter was at least an inch long, and had been driven hard into the palm of the captain's hand. Eliott said, 'But . . .'

'From Commander-in-Chief, sir – form order of sail in two columns,' an officer nearby called out, the telescope still to his eye.

'Acknowledge, Mr. Ponsonby . . . Don't "but" me, surgeon, do as I say.'

Elliott took the hand, and probed gingerly with his scalpel. He began to sweat and his own hand became slippery.

'From Commander-in-Chief, sir – course east by south. Masthead reports enemy fleet wearing in succession from rear.'

The sun shone on blue heaving water, the sweat glazed in Eliott's eyes, his wrist trembled.

'From Commander-in-Chief, sir: prepare for battle.'

Battle, Eliott thought. Soon, and he was to be in it. His trembling stopped, he gripped the captain's hand firmly with his left, and cut deep along the line of the splinter with the point of the scalpel. The hand tightened, but did not move. Blood flowed freely, as he slipped the scalpel under the splinter and eased it out.

'Water, someone,' the captain said. 'Wash it. Didn't you bring a bandage, surgeon? Think, man think!' He peered at Eliott more closely, meanwhile wrapping his own handkerchief around his hand – 'By God, you look as if you need a tot more than I do. And I certainly do.' He prised up the lid of the barrel, dipped in the ladle hanging at the side, and gave it to Eliott. Eliott drank, coughed, choked and drank again. The captain clapped him on the back. 'Sit down a minute, man. If blood affects you that much are you sure you wouldn't rather serve a gun?'

'No, sir,' Eliott muttered. 'I've never worked with the wounded or hurt, only the sick. It's different.'

'It is indeed,' Captain Burleigh said. 'Take a look round while you can.'

Eliott looked ahead and saw in the eye of the low sun a long line of sails, stretching across from horizon to horizon. The Andalusian mountains rose hazy behind them. 'That's the enemy,' Captain Burleigh said. 'About fifteen miles away. They're turning to try to get back to Cadiz before we can cut into them but they won't do it.'

A column of ships stretched ahead and astern of the *Ark Royal*, and a mile to the left there was another column, the two heading for the middle of the enemy line. 'That's the Commander-in-Chief's column,' the captain said. 'He's in the van, in *Victory*.'

'From flag, sir – course east by north.'

'Acknowledge . . . You'd better get below now, surgeon. Mr. Halford will need your help. Tell him we'll probably engage about noon – say, in four hours – if the wind holds.'

Eliott took a long look round the circle of sea and sky, filled now with ships. From all the English ships huge white and red ensigns streamed out ahead in the breeze. Then he went below.

The orlop deck was a part of the the third deck down, on the port side, forward. It was below the water line and had no ports. Flimsy wood partitions shut it off from the rest of the deck, which contained powder magazines, huge water butts, and bins of 32-pound cannon balls. Oil lanterns swung from the beams, and there was a mixed smell of tar, rum, and sweat. Mr. Halford, the surgeon, was gaunt and harried, with pale eyes and gingery whiskers. 'Set to, set to, Mr. Conquy,' he said, 'Arrange, put out, stack . . .' There were four or five seamen-mates, and with them Eliott began to get ready. In the orlop 'Prepare for battle' was a grim business indeed: scrubbing a heavy table for operations, laying out knives, saws, pincers, and a padded hammer; broaching a small cask of rum; setting out buckets of pitch, buckets of water, and just buckets – several of them, empty; a wooden bin, for legs and arms; miles of bandage . . . Eliott worked with his jaw set. He felt uneasy in the pit of his stomach, but hoped it would go when the firing actually began.

They finished at last. Halford sat down on the table with a sigh and helped himself to a mug of rum. He drank, shaking his head, 'There'll be a big butcher's bill today, if Lord Nelson gets his teeth into them.' He drank again.

At half past eleven the pipes shrilled and Mr. Halford said, 'All hands on deck.' Eliott followed him up through the decks – empty of men now, the guns standing in long rows on either side, to the top. There, he gasped, for the line of enemy ships seemed very close. The lead ship of the *Ark Royal*'s column must be no more than a quarter of a mile from them. Eliott, from the sixth ship of the line, felt he could almost recognize men's features in the enemy vessels.

Captain Burleigh stood on the break of the *Ark Royal*'s poop, the crew massed below, a few officers behind. Eliott climbed into the rigging close to the poop, the better to see, and looked out over a sea of blue, white, striped jerseys, and black bandannas of the sailors, mixed with the red coats and cockaded black top hats of the marines.

The officer with the telescope said, 'From Commander-in-Chief, sir – intend to pass through enemy line, make all sail with safety to masts.'

Captain Burleigh said, 'Acknowledge,' and turned to face the crew – 'Men,' he began. 'On this auspicious occasion, I feel it is my duty to address a few words to you. We are about to engage the enemies of God, of the King, and of mankind. Let it never . . .'

'From Commander-in-Chief, sir—' the signal officer interrupted.

'God damn it!' Captain Burleigh exploded – 'We don't need any more signals!'

'England expects that every man will do his duty.'

The captain's raised, bandaged hand sank. After a long pause he turned to the crew and said quietly, 'Did you hear that, men? There's nothing more to be said.'

'From Commander-in-Chief, sir – close action! . . . The signal is being kept flying.'

'Except that!' Captain Burleigh cried. 'Three cheers, men, then to your action stations. Hip, hip . . .!'

Eliott found himself cheering with the rest, and though all the hundreds of mouths were open, bellowing lustily, the sound came out thin in the open air, against the creak of the masts, and the slat of the sails and the surge of the sea. The upper deck began to empty. Eliott gazed ahead, fascinated, as the leading ship of the column suddenly vanished in a huge cloud of white smoke. Seconds later a thunderous booming reached him. Very quickly the thunder was repeated, and Captain Burleigh shouted to his signal officer, 'Eighteen seconds between broadsides! *Royal Sovereign*'s outdoing herself . . . Can you see who we're likely to draw, Mr. Ponsonby?'

'*Bellerophon*'s going to get *Monarca*, sir. I think the next ship is *Covadonga*, 74. That'll be ours.'

The white smoke ahead billowed higher and wider. More and more of the centre of the enemy line was vanishing in the smoke. Over to the left smoke began to hide the head of the other English column, as it too engaged. Ahead of the *Ark Royal* ship after ship sailed steadily into the white murk, all but their topsails vanishing. One by one Lieutenant Ponsonby muttered their names as they went: *Royal Sovereign, Belle Isle, Mars, Tonnant, Bellerophon* ... The thunder of cannon grew into a continuous battering.

'Our turn now, sir,' Ponsonby said.

Captain Burleigh said, 'Good luck, Mr. Ponsonby ... Good God, surgeon, what in hell are you still doing up here? Get to your post!'

Then they were in the smoke, the fumes caught at Eliott's throat, a great bow loomed over, and pair by pair the guns on both sides of the ship began to fire, from bow to stern. The deck jumped, the masts groaned, the whole ship shook. Eliott ran for the ladder, filled with a wild, fearful exhilaration.

They started coming into the orlop at once – men with chests crushed, knees smashed, arms gone: 32-lb cannon balls fired at forty feet range or less made no small wounds. *Crash ... crash ... crash ... crash ...* the explosions of the guns never paused, and under them there was a heavy, hollow rumbling – 'the guns recoiling and being run back, sir,' a sailor with a pulped left hand told him – 'Can I have a little water please, sir. God bless you, sir. Thank you, sir.' *Crash ... crash ... crash ...* The ship jarred and grated ... 'rammed someone,' a seaman-mate said. *Crash ... crash ... crash ...* The minutes accumulated into hours, the pile of legs and arms grew in the bin. The operating table and the deck all round was red and slippery Every few minutes the mates carried off men who had died, to throw them through a port, and came back staggering under new cases. Powder burns, amputations, disembowellings, deep gouges from flying splinters, Eliott saw them all, wept inwardly over them all, and did his best for all; and below the sadness at the horrors men were inflicting on each other he recognized a steadily growing assurance, a contentment of discovery. Whether he liked it or not, he *was* a surgeon. It was, and must be, in this way that he would serve his God.

Crash . . . crash . . . crash: and always the faint voices – Water . . . thank you, sir. God bless you . . . I'm all right, look after my mate, sir . . . Those he heard louder, in his mind, than the helpless screams and groans.

'Are we winning, sir?' a sailor asked, pale as death with a splinter clean through his body.

'I don't know,' Eliott said.

Captain Burleigh stooped under the beam beside him – 'Yes, we're winning, Muggeridge,' the captain said, speaking loud so that all in the orlop would hear, 'The *Covadonga*'s struck to us, and *Monarca* to the *Bellerophon*. But we're badly holed below the water line. Get everyone on deck, Mr. Halford.'

He left, and Eliott realized then that the ship was tilted slightly to the starboard. He began to support and carry the wounded men to the upper deck. The noise was as great as ever, though only the port side guns were firing. When he returned to the orlop after his second trip the list had increased visibly. On deck the masts were only stumps, and all the sails hanging over the side. Sailors were cutting loose spars and barrels, anything that would float. Eliott went down once more, to make sure no one was left in the orlop. It was empty, the buckets and barrels beginning to slide down the tilted deck, and legs and arms rolling out of the bin after them. He started back up. As he passed the empty lower gun deck he looked down it and stopped, gripped with a paralysis of horror. He had not paused in the gun decks as he ran up and down with the wounded. Now he was seeing one, after battle, for the first time. He thought the sight would remain burned on to his eyes for the rest of his life, a permanent background for all else that ever passed before them.

The deck was only empty of the living. The dead lay in drifts and piles, a hundred, two hundred, mixed red, white, blue, yellow. Heads rolled in scuppers awash with blood and tripes. Under the bodies the teak deck was inches deep in blood, ears, fingers, entrails, and eyes. The thick bulwarks of the ship were smashed and splintered the whole way down both sides. Many of the square gun ports had become gaping raw-edged holes. Several of the upper deck beams had been smashed, to fall angled across the deck. Some of the cannon had broken free from the restraining ropes. One by one they thundered down the slope, mashing the bodies under their wheels, to stop with a deafening crash against the lower bulwark, or smash through a huge hole into the sea.

Eliott muttered a prayer, then went slowly up the last ladder. A few minutes after he reached the upper deck *Ark Royal*'s list increased suddenly and, as she went over, he jumped into the sea. Ten minutes later he found himself almost alone on the water, sharing a spar with three sailors. It was late afternoon, the sea was rising, and the warring ships fading to the west.

One by one the three sailors slipped, exhausted, off the spar and vanished into the sea, their mouths open, but Eliott heard nothing. Near dark the waves became shorter and steeper, and he felt sand under his feet. Holding to the spar, swimming, trying to walk, being knocked down, rising again, he struggled at last to the shore. On hands and knees he crawled up the beach till he felt sharp reed grass, and the slope of a high dune. There he fell, lay down, and slept.

He awoke screaming, for in his sleep he had seen the sand covered with dead men, and others rolling in the waves, and men on land hacking each other with swords and spears. He staggered to his feet, for an elderly man in torn and soaked uniform was coming towards him, barefoot. A river ran into the sea on the right, and beyond there was a low sandy cape and a steep green hill behind. Dead men, mostly naked, did indeed cover the sand, and others rolled in the waves; but of the warriors with swords there was no trace.

'You cried out?' the other man said in classical Castilian. 'You are wounded?'

'No,' Eliott said. 'I was deafened yesterday, but now I can hear . . . I was going to England to study to be a rabbi.'

'You are a Jewish priest?' the grey-haired man said, still polite, but obviously baffled. 'Spanish?'

'I was. I thought I was,' Eliott said. 'But I'm not. I'm a physician. Gibraltarian. I was Assistant Surgeon on *Ark Royal*.'

The other's face cleared, and he bowed. 'You have won a famous victory, sir. I am Luis Santangel, Count of Grazalema and lately Captain of His Catholic Majesty's ship *Covadonga*. I own an estate near here. We will go there, and . . .'

'Where are we?' Eliott interrupted.

The Count pointed. 'That low cape is Trafalgar. This is the River Barbate. You must be my guest for as long as you wish. I shall be honoured to show you . . .'

'Thank you, sir, thank you,' Eliott said, 'but I must get back to Gibraltar at once. I have to start all over again, properly.'

Book Ten

VICTORIAN HEYDAY

The Jewish years 5564–5662
A.U.C. 2557–2655
A.D. 1804–1902
A.H. 1219–1320

NELSON was killed in the battle. They cut off his hair to give to Lady Hamilton, put his body in a large barrel, filled it with brandy and lashed it to *Victory*'s mainmast below decks, with a sentry over it. On the slow stormy voyage back to Gibraltar the body rose and lifted the lid in the night. The sentry's thoughts are not recorded. In Gibraltar, alongside the Rosia Bay, the brandy was drawn off and replaced by less volatile spirits of wine. *Victory*, her wounds patched, sailed for England with her much loved admiral, neither ever to see the Rock again.

The four chief admirals at Trafalgar were Nelson; Collingwood, who succeeded him and died at sea five years later, without ever again setting foot ashore; Villeneuve, who committed suicide before reaching Paris; and Gravina, the Spanish commander – he died of wounds received at Trafalgar. On his deathbed he said, referring to his conqueror that day, *I go now to join the greatest hero the world has ever known*. Over 8,500 men were killed, wounded, or drowned in the battle.

But the glory must be shared by others. There was Black Jack Jervis and the nameless officers and boatswains who had forged the weapon that Nelson so terribly wielded. It took Spanish ships of the line 24 hours to unmoor – a British ship as many minutes; when Spanish ships had to cross their yards for a harbour ceremony they started the day before – the crew of a British man-of-war did it in one minute from the deck. After Trafalgar a tremendous storm blew up, but Collingwood stayed on his post, reporting 'I kept the sea after the action with the least injured ships. I had another view in keeping the sea at that time (which had a little of pride in it) and that was to show the enemy, that it was not a battle or a storm which could remove a British Squadron from the station they were directed to hold.'

And there was the common sailor, the brutalized, press-ganged, subhuman who yet at such times became super-human. During all that week in 1801 when the Gibraltar dockyard maties were working night and day to get Saumarez's squadron ready for action again there were no drunks and no desertions in the fleet – except several wounded and sick sailors who 'deserted' from hospital to rejoin their ships. During and after Trafalgar the sailors not only did their duty, as the famous signal expected of them, but in their conduct towards each other and towards wounded and defeated enemies they lived up to the far more severe standards Nelson had set in his noble and moving prayer before battle (written into his diary an hour before action was joined):

May the Great God whom I worship Grant to my Country and for the benefit of Europe in General a great and Glorious Victory, and may no misconduct in anyone tarnish it, and may humanity after Victory be the predominant feature in the British Fleet.

The only permanent relics of Trafalgar at Gibraltar are in the so-called Trafalgar Cemetery, where among victims of other battles and fevers, lie buried two men who died of wounds received at Trafalgar; and the huge figure of Sir Augustus Eliott in the patio of the Convent. This was carved from the bowsprit of the *San Juan Nepomuceno*, one of the four prizes which reached Gibraltar (the other sixteen were all wrecked or driven ashore in the storm).

Captain Churruca fought the *San Juan Nepomuceno* until she was a shattered hulk, her decks in the state I have described in my imaginary *Ark Royal*. When dying, he was asked which of the six ships engaging him he wished to surrender to, he said, 'To all, for surely no one of them alone could have brought us down.' His ship was a prison hulk in Gibraltar harbour for many years, the captain's cabin locked and left as it was in memory of Churruca's gallantry.

When my Eliott Conquy returned to Gibraltar from his adventures he would have found the epidemic just past its worst, but by no means over yet. Its effects were so shattering that the Spanish general Castaños had arranged a conference of French, Spanish and British medical officers, on the neutral ground outside Gibraltar, to discuss measures that might be jointly taken to prevent a recurrence. Nothing seems to have been decided except the usual arrangements for quarantine, which the Spanish had used and were to use so often for non-medical reasons; and the failure is not surprising when there was as yet no knowledge of the cause of the disease. This particular epidemic finally faded, having killed off some 6,000 people in four months, as against the Great Siege's loss of 300 in four years.

The war continued, bringing Gibraltar an increased prosperity. One chief cause was the establishment of an Admiralty Court there, which enabled merchants based on Gibraltar to buy – often at bargain prices – ships and cargoes seized by British warships and privateers operating in the western Mediterranean and central Atlantic. This prosperity increased still more when on May 2, 1808, the Spanish people rose against Napoleon. There was now plenty of scope for legitimate trade, but that was never enough for Gibraltar, and on July 12, 1808, we find the Governor issuing a proclamation:

His Excellency (the Spanish Governor of Algeciras) having complained that much smuggling of tobacco and other goods has been carried on between this place and Algeciras and St Roque by inhabitants of Gibraltar: This is to give notice that any persons so transgressing against the laws of Spain are not to expect any Protection from the passport granted them by (the British Governor); nor are they to suppose that His Excellency wishes to screen inhabitants of this place who have made so unworthy a use of the indulgence granted them . . .

Three years earlier, replying to London about some Gibraltar merchants' complaints against the imposition of quarantine, the then Governor, General Fox (brother of Charles James), had written:

About the letters from Messrs Faulkner and Turnbull, I will pay great attention to the matter, but I am much afraid Mr. Turnbull and the merchants and traders of Gibraltar are inclined to expect such Facility to their Comercial Intercourse as is inconsistent with the Safety of the Garrison either with regard to the Enemy or the prevention of the return of the Disease; and are more indifferent than they ought to be to the King's Service where there is a possibility of its interfering with their smuggling goods into Spain.

The previous chancellor of Spain was Godoy, who had taken the unusual title of Prince of Peace, which is usually reserved, in England at least, for Jesus Christ. He had worked out an ingenious scheme to get back Gibraltar by arranging for it to be attacked by an Irish Army, while Irish regiments were serving in the garrison; in return Spain would back and guarantee the setting up of an independent Irish State.

But that was all past and now Spain and England were friends, on the surface. Forts San Felipe and Santa Barbara, which had guarded the isthmus for so long, were levelled and the fortifications between them razed. Spanish armies were supported and supplied from Gibraltar, and British soldiers went out from there to fight against the French invaders. Particularly heroic actions were fought at Tarifa and Barossa. Yet it was, alas, only a surface friendliness. England's aim was certainly not the emergence of a free and powerful Spain; nor Spain's the strengthening of England's grip on Gibraltar; and when the histories came to be written the English consistently underrated the enormous sacrifice of the Spanish people in the war against Napoleon; while the Spanish, going farther, gave the impression that no English troops fought in their War of Independence at all, whereas all but one of the successful actions were fought with a majority of British troops, and British casualties.

When Napoleon fled from Waterloo in 1815, the Victorian Era began, though she herself was not yet born. It was the century of the Pax Britannica, the British Empire, and Laissez Faire. Peace reigned, with the usual unsettling effects on Gibraltar's role as a trading entrepot, for there was now no need for ships to change or pick up cargoes there, as there had been when most of Europe was under blockade. Politically England was steady as another rock, Spain unstable as a weathervane. Time and again through the century Gibraltar was to give shelter to victims of failed or successful coups, of the right, left, and centre.

In the town itself the population rose steadily from about 7,500 after the effects of the fever had been overcome, to 17,000 in 1831 (nearly 2,000 Jews), and stayed close to that figure to the end of the century. Spaniards began to enter as the Napoleonic Wars ended, until by the end of the century there were 1,900 of them out of a total population of 19,000. The largest single group of Spaniards were females, who came in as servants to prosperous Gibraltarians. The prosperity seems to have been based on cigar making. There were only a handful of cigarmakers in 1800, but 2,000 by 1900; and cigarmaking was an excellent cover for tobacco smuggling.

There was also much work at the dockyard, but it did not benefit the Gibraltarians directly. The headquarters of the Mediterranean Fleet moved to Malta in 1833, but at the same time plans were made to enlarge the facilities at Gibraltar, and this work was put in hand about 1842. For some unclear reason convict labour was imported for the job. Barracks for 1,000 convicts were built, and soon 600 were actually at work. They worked with notable inefficiency, and they had an effect on the Gibraltarian outlook that has not yet died: an association of manual labour with degradation. When convict labour was ended in the 1870s it was not Gibraltarians who filled the vacancy, but Spaniards.

About the middle of the century the population of some 15,500 was occupied as follows:

Local Government	132
Professions	72
Commerce	681
Trade	1,297

Agriculture	28
Miscellaneous	5,565
At School	2,633
Unemployed	4,994
Paupers	60

As for revenue, Gibraltar was still nominally a free port, and most of the local government revenue came from wine and spirit duties, liquor licences, and the like. A considerable number of ships passed through Gibraltar – about 3,300 a year in the 1850s – but they cannot have caused a general prosperity, when the figures for unemployed are considered. When the high prices of food, rent, and clothes (endemic in Gibraltar) are thrown in, the Rock is seen as a depressed area, for the poor; yet – and this must never be forgotten – it was a paradise of luxury compared with the Andalusia that bordered it. There, entrenched in their latifundias, the Spanish rich could starve whole villages into accepting disgraceful wages by leaving acreage out of cultivation until the peasants accepted the wages offered.

In 1869 the Suez Canal was opened and Gibraltar's strategic and mercantile importance still further increased. Though individual fortunes were being made there was still no general prosperity; but a stable government and at least a chance of something better than most of Europe knew kept the immigrants coming – Dutch, Belgian, Russian, and Maltese. These last started arriving in 1871 and were particularly unwelcome to the resident Gibraltarian, for their skills and ways of life were in direct competition with his own.

The Jewish population reached its height about the middle of the century and then declined. The great families began to go; by 1900 there were no Benoliels, and no

Cardozos (of the latter some had gone to London, some to Portugal, and thence to the United States).

But one famous Jew had visited Gibraltar, the 25-year-old young dandy, Benjamin Disraeli. He went there on part of a 'Grand Tour', in 1830. His letters to his father are as informative as a contemporary print:

This Rock is a wonderful place, with a population infinitely diversified. Moors with costumes radiant as a rainbow or an Eastern melodrama: Jews with gaberdines and skull-caps; Genoese, Highlanders, and Spaniards, whose dress is as picturesque as that of the sons of Ivor ... We were presented to the Governor, Sir George Don, a general and G.C.B., a very fine old gentleman, of the Windsor Terrace school, courtly, almost regal in his manner, paternal, almost officious in his temper ... His palace, the Government House, is an old convent, and one of the most delightful residences I know, with a garden under the superintendence of Lady Don, full of rare exotics, with a beautiful terrace over the sea, a berceau of vines, and other delicacies which would quite delight you ... Tell Washington) Irving he has left a golden name in Spain ...

And two weeks later:

After dinner ... it was the fate of Meredith and myself to be lionised to some cave or other with Sir George. What a scene and what a procession! First came two grooms on two Barbs; then a carriage with four horses; at the window at which H.E. sits, a walking footman, and then an outrider, all at a funeral pace ... In spite of his infirmities he will get out to lionise; but before he disembarks, he changes his foraging cap for a full general's cock

*with a plume as big as the Otranto one; and this because
the hero will never be seen in public in undress, although
we were in a solitary cave looking over the ocean, and inhabited only by monkeys. The cave is shown, and we all
get into the carriage, because he is sure we are tired; the
foraging cap is again assumed, and we travel back ...
Meredith, myself, the Governor, and the cocked hat, each
in a seat.*

A little later (in 1844) another famous man visited it –
William Makepeace Thackeray. His comments, too, are
sharply evocative, particularly of the 'feel' of Gibraltar to
a civilian:

*If one had a right to break the sacred confidence of the
mahogany, I could entertain you with many queer stories
of Gibraltar life, gathered from the lips of the gentlemen
who enjoyed themselves round the dingy table cloth of the
club-house coffee-room, richly decorated with cold gravy
and spilt beer ... All the while these conversations were
going on, a strange scene of noise and bustle was passing in
the market-place in front of the window, where Moors,
Jews, Spaniards, soldiers were thronging in the sun; and a
ragged fat fellow, mounted on a tobacco barrel, with his
hat cocked on his ear, was holding an auction, and roaring
with an energy and impudence that would have done
credit to Covent Garden.*

*'All's Well' is very pleasant when sung decently in tune;
and inspires noble and poetic ideas of duty, courage, and
danger; but when you hear it shouted all the night
through, accompanied by a clapping of muskets in a time
of profound peace, the sentinel's cry becomes no more
romantic to the hearer than it is to the sandy Connaught-
man or the bare-legged Highlander who delivers it ...*

336

Men of a different way of thinking, however, can suit themselves perfectly at Gibraltar; where there is marching and countermarching, challenging and relieving guard all the night through. And not here in Commercial-square alone, but all over the huge rock in the darkness – all through the mysterious zigzags, and round the dark cannon-ball pyramids, and along the vast rock-galleries, and up to the topmost flagstaff where the sentry can look out over two seas, poor fellows are marching and clapping muskets, and crying 'All's Well' . . . The young men in the coffee-room tell me he (the Governor) goes to sleep every night with the keys of Gibraltar under his pillow. It is an awful image, and somehow completes the notion of the slumbering fortress. Fancy Sir Robert Wilson, his nose just visible above the sheets, his night-cap and the huge key (you see the very identical one in Reynolds's portrait of Lord Heathfield) peeping out from under the bolster . . .

Though I have freely used the word 'Gibraltarian' the sense of community was only slowly beginning to develop, at this time. Below and alongside the governors, officers, staffs, troops and sailors, all of whom were on passage, Gibraltarians began to merge as a people; and the Town, or Colony, began to compete and conflict with the Fortress. Civil rights and a civil magistracy were granted in 1830 (Jews were put on the jury lists in 1878); and the governments in London and on the Rock began to exercise themselves over a problem which they should have tackled a hundred years earlier. Now the Maltese immigration forced them to ask, and answer, the question: What is a Gibraltarian, that is, who has the right to live on the Rock, and under what terms?

From the beginning Governors had influenced the

answer by the way they had attracted one sort of person and discouraged another, given one certain rights, and denied them to others. The census of 1871 shows a population of 18,700. A couple of years later an order in Council made 'better provisions to prevent the entry into and residence in Gibraltar of unauthorized persons not being British subjects and to prevent the further increase of the overcrowded condition of Gibraltar.' This was the thin edge of the wedge, though London does not seem to have realized it, for if you define whom you can keep out, you define who has the right to stay in – thus creating something which is separate from the military complex. The Governor in 1849, Gardiner, had already seen this and represented to the government that Gibraltar was and must be solely a fortress. The present problems would be much simpler if his opinion had been taken – but it aroused an enormous outcry from people whose human and financial interests were threatened, so the report was shelved, and Gardiner removed.

Town and Garrison together became the parents of the institutions British take or found wherever they go. First, of course, a pack of fox hounds. When the last British regiment (24th, South Wales Borderers), came out of Cadiz in 1814 at the end of the war, it brought with it a pack of fox hounds belonging to the Real Isla de Leon Hunt (this is the old name of San Fernando, the military town at the head of the Cadiz peninsula). The pack, descended from hounds originally brought from England by the Duke of Wellington to while away the time between battles – (see Conan Doyle's marvellous exploit of Brigadier Gerard, *How the Brigadier slew the Fox*) – was taken to Gibraltar to found the Calpe Hunt and so give Spanish peasants and landowners the privilege of watching the unspeakable pursue the uneatable over their crops and through their cork oaks and olive groves.

After the hunt, the ornithological society, the horticultural society, the philosophical, the Garrison Library – a most important and permanent addition to Gibraltar's facilities this; founded by Captain Drinkwater, historian of the Great Siege, and financed by Pitt, it is a fine building with a fine garden (which we have already met), and provides the Garrison not only with books, but much of the attributes of a quiet club. The *Gibraltar Chronicle*, later published by the Library, in its early issues seldom bothered itself with local happenings – its eyes were focused on far places and imperial themes – but every now and then a snippet of news tells us more about life on the Rock than a thousand statistics.

8th June, 1805 – Captain Fuller of the 20th Light Dragoons, is drowned sailing behind the Rock, when his boat capsizes. This was in the middle of the Napoleonic Wars, which obviously did not seriously interfere with the normal amenities ... 6th July, same year – a woman of character drinks herself to death in a shed near the Castle; the shed, furniture, and clothes are destroyed by the Authorities 'as a useful lesson to the lower Classes for them to obey the regulations of the Board of Health respecting cleanliness of homes and persons.' ... After 1806 there is a dentist advertising himself, Peter Seminara: before that, the blacksmith? ... H.M.S. *Beagle*, the ship in which Darwin later sailed, serves from Gibraltar ... there is a fire in Mr. Israel's house in Engineer Lane: it was a Friday night of course, for Sephardic housewives put the Sabbath *adafina* in the oven before sundown on Friday and do not touch it or look at it before noon the next day: so, frequently there are runaway ovens, and

339

'Jewish' fires, on Friday nights . . . The venereal hospital
of San Juan de Dios, which has become first an ordinary
hospital and then a British barracks (Blue Barracks) is now
pulled down and again becomes a hospital, successively
called the Civil, the Colonial, and St. Bernard's . . . A
naval captain on his way to China with his ship bets a
friend, after a late night, that he can knock down
O'Hara's Folly in three shots. Next dawn he sails, and,
hangover notwithstanding, hits the tower with his third
shot.

The most important event of Gibraltar's century was
not much remarked at the time. In 1848 in the course of
normal operations at Forbes Quarry, a smugglers'
rendezvous at the foot of the North Face, a human skull
was found. It seemed to be of great antiquity, and so was
shown to the Gibraltar Society (this was one of those so-
cieties which in a small place keep forming and fading
according as interested personalities come and go). The
Society thought it was 'an old skull' and as such sent it to
the Royal College of Surgeons. They didn't show much
interest in it, either, although it had features markedly
different from those of modern man or of any known
previous race of man.

In 1859 German archaeologists – the science was in its
infancy – discovered a skull and parts of a skeleton which
they could attribute to no known race of man. They therefore named this newly discovered race of prehistoric man
after the place where the remains were found – Neanderthal. Now the Royal College of Surgeons took
another look at the Forbes Quarry skull, and found it was
of a woman of the same race, a race – as I tried to show in
Book One – driven to extinction by Cro-Magnon man. If
the Gibraltar Society in 1848 had numbered even one
archaeologist, that race would now be called Gibraltar

Man, not Neanderthal. Whatever we call him, he certainly used Gibraltar for a long time. The events of 'The Woman' are to be read as occurring about 33,500 years before the present; but recent researches by Dr. Waechter have unearthed Neanderthal bone relics which can be carbon-14 dated to 47,700 B.C.

Cave exploring became fashionable. Two officers set out to explore St. Michael's Cave. They never came back, nor has any trace of them ever been found, though St. Michael's Cave has since been explored to a distance of 1,700 feet from the entrance, and to depths of 600 feet below the entrance, which is 937 feet above sea level. But, as to the vanished officers, some believe that they had troublesome wives or debts in England which a judicious 'disappearance' would have much eased.

The most devoted cave explorer and scientist of the period was a Captain Brome, who was in charge of the convict labour. The prisoners did not work well for the navy, but they did marvels for Brome in helping to find and explore caves. His most notable find was a series of four, separate, on Windmill Hill Flats. They were later named Genista One, Two, Three, and Four in honour of their discoverer (*genista* is the Latin for 'broom').

Genista One, of which Brome released full details to the *Gibraltar Chronicle* on January 23, 1865, is 200 feet deep and full of animal fossils, including rhinoceros, horse, pig, deer, aurochs, leopard, hyena, innumerable kinds of birds, fish, and shells; and man. Genista Two is a small cave, at the foot of a steep ramp, which the reader may think he has already seen.

Brome's work soon received its just reward from a government always alert to reward scholarly initiative: he was fired.

341

Militarily the fortress attained its zenith of usefulness about 1870 when enemy artillery could reach it, but not shatter its defences, while its guns could nearly reach across the Strait. The largest gun installed, at the end of the muzzle loading era, was called the 100 Ton Gun. It is still there, on a semi-circular railed mount near Rosia Bay. It fired a one-ton shell about eight miles, at the rate of one round every four minutes. The traversing, elevation, and loading were worked by steam but the firing cartridge was electrical – the first in the world. It was never fired in anger and seldom in play. At a visit by an artillery general in 1902, a full-charge practice was arranged. The electric cartridge fired, but the main charge, of God knows how many hundredweights of powder, did not. After the compulsory wait of half an hour under cover, the general asked for a volunteer to extract the shell. This meant sliding head first down the barrel (about eighteen inches in diameter) and attaching a rope to the ring in the nose of the shell. Behind the shell was all that powder. The general's request evoked a clamorous silence. Finally a thin trumpeter volunteered and the general, who was probably thirty inches in diameter, said 'There's no danger.' The trumpeter replied, in an excess of military effusiveness, 'If you say so, sir!' – slid down and attached the cord. The general, in one of those scenes beloved of Victorian lithographers, pointed to him when he came out, and cried, 'This man's promotion to bombardier is to appear in orders tonight!'

It was a beautiful gun, but of course, by the thin trumpeter's day quite useless. The time for a testing of Gibraltar's defences was not yet to hand, fortunately. The British Navy was modern, reasonably efficient (though far from being the terrible instrument of Nelson's day), and enormously numerous; but by the end of the century the

ground defences were out of date, and faced with an insoluble problem. The main line of defence had been
drawn back from the sea wall to half-way up the Rock,
where several modern big guns were installed; but other
batteries looked like something left over from the Am-
ercian Civil War: and in some of the galleries cannon and
cannon balls which had seen service in the Great Siege
were still in position and on the strength. Still, the fortress
could throw a powerful weight of metal on to attacking
ships or the Spanish mainland. The insoluble problem was that the Spanish mainland could now throw a
powerful weight of metal back, not at the fortress's
guns – they couldn't harm them much – but at the
harbour.

To question the impregnability of Gibraltar at this
time, after all it had been through, was, as someone said,
equivalent to speaking disrespectfully about the Equator.
There is little doubt that it was in fact impregnable; but if
it could not be used as a naval base and port, its impregnability was of no value. Nevertheless, when the navy
surveyed its world wide position in 1890, it decided to put
larger and more modern facilities into Gibraltar to service
and repair warships, and to protect ships in harbour
against mines, torpedoes, and submarine, etc. As soon as
the plans for the new dockyard on the western side were
announced and work begun in 1895, anxious critics
pointed out that the facilities and any ships using them
would be subject to the direct fire of Spanish guns mounted on the semi-circle of hills all round, and now all within
easy range. Parliament appointed a committee under
Admiral Sir Harry Rawson to investigate. The committee
concluded that the new dockyard was wrongly sited, and
that another one must be built at once on the east side of
Gibraltar, where the mass of the rock itself would protect

it from everything except perhaps high-angle howitzers. The government took careful note of this view, and went on with the western site, the work being done by Spanish labourers under the supervision of British technicians. The only concession to the 'western' threat was to put the oil fuel tanks on the east side, and run a rail tunnel clear through the Rock near sea level, linking them with the harbour.

The critics now raised again the general question of Gibraltar's real value to England, there were again discussions about exchanging it for Minorca, one of the Canary Islands, or Ceuta.

Nothing came of any of it. The New Dockyard was completed – 308 acres of sheltered anchorage, coaling facilities, three dry docks, all kinds of cranes, shops, forges. In view of its total vulnerability to Spanish fire one must assume that its defence, in 1902, rested on a tit-for-tat threat, i.e., if Spain bombarded Gibraltar, the British fleet would bombard Santander, Cadiz, Cartagena, Barcelona, Bilbao, San Sebastian, Malaga, and a dozen other cities vulnerable to sea power. In other words, Gibraltar was to be protected by the general power of England, not the other way round.

In 1902 the Boer War – a focal theme for much of the long-massing anti-British sentiment in Europe – came to an end. England was again at peace. In Gibraltar officers, soldiers, merchants, traders, labourers, and petty bourgeois lived their ordinary lives in an extraordinary place. Though there were still brothels on the Rock, many favoured the more open and *alegre* atmosphere of the establishments in La Linea, a city grown up, just across the Neutral Ground, for the sole purpose of feeding off, and on, Gibraltar's needs. Some of the girls of La Linea were public, and cheap. Some were private and ex-

pensive. From there one got an extraordinarily clear view
of Gibraltar close-up, seen from below . . .

AUTHOR'S SPECIAL NOTE:

*Now that we are approaching the present time I will em-
phasize that from here to the end of* THE ROCK *none of the
characters mentioned in the fictional sections have any relation to, or are intended to represent, any real person
living or dead, except that passing mention is made of the
following, who are or were living people: Don Pablo
Larios, King Alfonso XIII of Spain, Calvo Sotelo, Sergt.
Major Ince, Winston Churchill, Hitler, Nurse Cavell,
Napoleon, Carlos III, General Eliott.*

A VIEW FROM LA LINEA

THE ivory figurine of a naked woman, which hung over
the head of her bed where the devout often had a crucifix,
blurred and enlarged before her eyes. It always did in
these final seconds of ecstasy, seeming to bless her lust. She
spread herself, crying out, took him into her heart with a
convulsion of her muscles, wrapped arms and legs about
him, and immediately began to come, in shivering transports. She felt his teeth in her neck, a sharp pain, and held
him tighter. Minutes, hours later, the spasms calmed into
long trembling waves. He was rolling off her. She held

345

him, whispering – 'Stay,' but he got up, lit a cigarette, and inhaled deeply.

She could see him, back and front and side, in four full length mirrors on the wall, and herself in another on the ceiling. He plucked her dress off a chair and slowly swirled it around him in a *paso natural*. He was insolently graceful, with narrow hips and long gypsy hair. Her neck hurt where he had bitten her.

'I need money, Dolores,' he said.

'Again?'

'I have no work now. The Count dismissed fifty of us. He needs more money to serve the king, he said, so he could not afford to pay us.

She sighed and slipped out of bed, found a key in her purse and opened a drawer of the ornate escritoire. 'I will give you a hundred pesetas,' she said.

'Make it two hundred,' he said. 'I have to live.'

She shrugged, and gave him the money. He was pulling on his trousers. She stood naked in front of him, wishing he would touch her breasts, or enter again into the aching emptiness. But he sprawled in a chair, the cigarette dangling from his lower lip. 'Put on my shoes,' he commanded.

She knelt before him, and slipped one battered, cracked brown shoe on to his bare foot. 'You should go to Pablo Larios's stables,' she said. 'I heard he needs a man to look after the English hounds. You are good with dogs.'

She picked up his other foot.

'I might,' he said. 'Just to get a little money, so I can leave La Linea for good.' He put his foot on her shoulder, and pushed hard, sending her flying over backwards. 'I'm going to be *torero*!' he cried, striding away from her with the exaggerated mincing walk a matador uses in the ring to show his dominance over the bull, '*El Gato Moreno* – the Black Cat.'

'You're nothing but a gypsy,' she said.

He brought the lighted end of his cigarette close to her nipple, so close that she felt the heat of it. She did not cringe, and he suddenly stooped, kissed the nipple, and swaggered out.

She went slowly to the window, pulled back the edge of one long velvet curtain an inch, and watched him leave the front door. She heard him calling his dog, 'Cabo? Cabo! Come!' Beyond the lights of the last house of La Linea, beyond the lights at the frontier, Gibraltar glittered like a magic city in the sky.

She drew the curtain, and said in an ordinary speaking voice – 'Who's first, Juana?' She looked at the calendar: January 8, 1902. It would be . . .

The old maid waddled in from a side door – 'Tomas Lopez. He's waiting.'

'Ten minutes, Juana.' She douched herself in the ornate bathroom, using a herbal concoction an old gypsy woman had recommended to her. It had not failed her yet, either with disease or pregnancy, and she had been at this trade thirteen years now – just half her life.

She dressed again, and then went through the side door into another bedroom identical with the first, even to the maroon curtains and the precise pattern of the heavy frames of the mirrors. Juana set to cleaning the bathroom and remaking the bed in the first room. These details cost money, and took trouble, but they marked the difference between a whore and a courtesan.

Tomas Lopez was solid, square, about forty, a little grizzled. He liked a glass of wine and a little conversation before attending to business. Dolores did not mind

347

humouring him, as his more particular demands, unlike those of most of her clients, were very simple.

He sipped the wine carefully. 'That Court of Inquiry the English sent out are said to think that the dockyard could be made useless by our Spanish guns. That is a serious matter.'

'Yes?' she said. 'You mean, they have wasted all that money?'

'Of course, yes. But perhaps they will close it. We will lose our positions. Not everyone can say, I work in the English dockyard, I receive so many pounds a week, you understand.'

'Naturally,' she said. Tomas Lopez was Andalusian and poor, so the appearance, the position, mattered more to him than the reality.

'It is from my wages, and the goods I smuggle out every day, that I am able to visit you once a month. And that is known to all the men, of course. It is not everyone who can afford your kindness.'

'You are generous. All know it.'

'A man's position, his wife's virtue, these have value. The Gibraltarians look down their noses at us because we work with our hands, and go home dirty. To them it is only valuable that the wife should employ a cleaning woman. A Spanish woman, naturally, for *their* women won't demean themselves.'

He got up and took off his coat. He had to have the lights out, and would only approach her from behind. She pulled off her drawers, flipped up the back of her skirt, leaned over the bed, and waited.

Afterwards, he paid, and gave her a bottle of Scotch whisky, his usual gift, smuggled out of Gibraltar. She poured him another glass of wine.

'I shall win the dog show,' he said. He saw her look of

348

mystification, and said, 'The English Prince and Princess are visiting Gibraltar, to attend the dog show. The important class is for smooth-haired fox terriers. My Manolo is of pure race, and he will win, Unless the Freemasons rob us. Father O'Callaghan of the Gibraltar church says the Freemasons are at the bottom of all our troubles. He says they sent out the Court of Inquiry to do away with our positions ... The prize is fifty English pounds.'

'Enough to buy a nice little bit of land,' she said.

'Yes,' he said. 'And to improve the situation still further, my wife is going to seek work as a cleaning woman on the Rock. Unfortunately, my dog Manolo has not been well. There is time for him to recover. Nevertheless I am looking for another dog, in case Manolo should still be showing the effects of his sickness. And there is the judge to be taken into consideration, of course.'

She said, 'But the judge is Don Pablo Larios. There's not enough money in the world to bribe Don Pablo, especially in anything to do with sport, or the English.'

'Money is not the only value in a gentleman's eyes,' Tomas said. 'Indeed, with a rich and great *caballero* like Don Pablo, it is the least ... But what is Don Pablo's passion? Rare books? A new plant? Old wine? I must find out. But my position in the dockyard does not throw me much into his company.'

'There's a young fellow called Paco Santangel who's going to work quite closely with him, at the Hunt stables,' she said. 'I imagine he could find out, for a consideration.'

Tomas Lopez shot her a shrewd peasant look. 'I see. Well, perhaps. Though I am not a rich man.' He drained the wine, got up, and bowed formally. 'Señorita, a thousand thanks.'

349

She said mischievously, 'If the English prince and princess are coming to Gibraltar, perhaps it is to close the dockyard and give the Rock back to Spain.'

'No, no, they are coming for the dog show,' he said firmly.

Señorita Falcon was a superb-looking woman, the Deputy Chief of Police thought – high-bridge aquiline nose, strong eyebrows, oval face, good lips and intense, deep blue eyes. He'd seen her naked, too, when duty had made him burst in to 'surprise' her with a man they wanted – her breasts were high and a little small, but some liked them that way. Her hair was dense, strong, almost blue black. When it fell to her shoulders it looked like black wine on the thick, creamy white of her skin. The same with her pubic hair, a thick black pelt, clearly limited, and the strong tufts in her armpits, all amazingly definite against the skin. If she had not chosen this profession, she could have married almost anyone in Spain. Well, 'chosen' was a cruel word. No one knew her past, or where she came from, but there would certainly have been a seduction, a child perhaps, banishment, disgrace. That was, sadly, the way of the world.

He rose to go, saying, 'You are a very beautiful woman, señorita.'

'Not that it ever stirs you,' she pouted, tapping him with the envelope. He took it and dropped it into his pocket. His hand was on the door. 'By the way, young Paco Santangel is not, how shall I say? – threatening you, is he? He has no money. He visits. One wonders . . .'

'No,' she said. 'He is a friend.'

The Deputy Chief of Police bowed himself out. Poor woman. They all had one, usually six or seven years

350

younger, like this half-gypsy lad. It was, sadly, the way of the world.

Dolores yawned. She knew who was coming – Carlos Firpo, the Gibraltarian – because Juana had reminded her to drink an extra two glasses of lemonade, and not relieve herself. Juana showed him in five minutes later. At once he started to pant and slaver and undo his trousers, as he always did. And she, as always, held out her hand, and waited. Only after he gave her the money, and she had put it away did she respond to his urgency. She spread a heavy towel on the tiled floor at the foot of the bed, and he lay down quickly on it, muttering obscene words in Spanish and English. She took off her drawers, and danced around him, holding up her skirt. His eyes glazed, and he spoke louder.

After a time he sighed, 'Marvellous! You must have drunk a barrelful.'

'I try to please,' she said.

He went into the bathroom and began washing himself with great energy, as though to eradicate any trace of what, so recently, he had craved for. 'I've got a job,' he said. 'Crewman on one of Mr. Torrenti's fast new steamers.'

She said, 'Doesn't your brother the shopkeeper still support you?'

'Oh yes, but with the new child my wife needs a cleaning woman, and now we can afford it. We got one today. A woman called Maria Lopez.'

He came out and began to dress. He was short, with a long nose and wide mouth, and a little pot belly, though he was only thirty-three. He spoke Gibraltarian-Spanish, with many English words. He always seemed aggrieved and ready to take offence.

'Mr. Torrenti used to play safe,' he said. 'Just import the tobacco in bulk from America, and sell it to the shippers—'

'You mean the actual smugglers?' she said smiling.

'They're not smugglers when they buy the tobacco,' he said, with a little heat – 'Just merchants. The Spanish can call them smugglers if they catch them taking the tobacco into Spain ... Well, you'd think Mr. Torrenti was making enough money with that and his cigar factory, but no, he wants to send his sons to Eton, and have the Governor invite him to tea, so he's going into the shipping end as well. He'll be richer than the Jews soon.'

He paused in the act of pulling on one sock. 'You know what some of the young fellows are going to do this Easter Saturday? ... Throw a dummy with a top hat over the wall into the synagogue. Only it will be on fire, see. A good joke.'

'Don't people get hurt?' she asked.

'Sometimes. A Jew girl got burned a bit last year ... How about a little champagne, eh? Put it back in so it can come out again!' He gave her a nudge in the ribs.

She called – 'Juana – a half of champagne.'

Carlos Firpo was dressed now. He fumbled in his pocket and gave her a small box of cigars. 'Brought them out for you,' he said.

Juana opened the champagne, and poured expertly, and disappeared, Firpo sat back, glass in hand – 'Did you know the Prince and Princess are visiting Gibraltar? In March. There's going to be a dog show. I'm going to enter my fox terrier, Fido. He won't win the first prize, but as long as he does better than Mr. Torrenti's, that's all I ask.'

'It will be a great honour for Gibraltar,' she said. 'The Prince and Princess visiting.'

Carlos Firpo shook his head – 'Perhaps. But you know what I think—' he lowered his voice. 'England's finished. Look at the Boer War. Couldn't beat a few Dutchmen. Every country in Europe hating her. If you ask me, we should get someone else to take over Gibraltar.'

'Spain?' she asked.

'Mother of God, no! We're not Spaniards.'

'A great many of your mothers are,' she said.

'No, no. What we want is someone like Germany. They'd take it like a shot. Father O'Callaghan says it's the Freemasons and the Jews behind it all.'

'Behind what, Señor Firpo?'

'The Boer War, and England going downhill. My wife's sister's walking out with an English private, a fellow called Tamlyn. When it began we were all congratulating ourselves, because although he's only a private he's *English*, and would take her to England. Now, we don't know.' He drained his glass and pulled out his watch. 'Time to go, or the wife will be wondering where I've got to.'

Juana said, 'He doesn't speak any Spanish. He just says, "Dolores", and holds out money.'

'Enough?'

'More than your lowest, much less than your highest. I think he is a soldier.' She squared her shoulders and indicated a short haircut.

'Is he drunk?' Dolores asked. 'Alone? Show him in then.'

He was a tall man, nearly thirty, with a long, sad, bony face, dull red hair, and big, horny hands. He stood, awkward but determined, in a cheap brown suit and huge ammunition boots, in the centre of her little reception parlour.

'You speak English?' he said. His voice was deep, and accented, but she did not know enough about England to be able to place him.

'Yes,' she said. 'My mother taught me. You are a soldier, aren't you?'

'Private Richard Tamlyn, Royal Berkshire Regiment,' he said.

'How did you get this money? It is a lot for a simple soldier.'

'Stole a dog,' he said. 'There's to be a dog show, and a Spanish dockyard workman gave me ten pounds for it. The Prince and Princess are going to give the prizes for that show, did 'ee know, miss?'

'Perhaps they'll give all you soldiers extra pay in honour of their visit.'

'Nay, miss, they'll never do that. Just extra parades, drill, and such. We did three hours today.'

'Goodness, and the visit nearly two months away still. You must get bored with it.'

His pale, distant blue eyes looked down into hers – ' 'Tis better than sitting in the barrack room, staring at the wall,' he said. 'Hours on end. Aye, soldiers go mad here. No one wants us. No one speaks to us. 'Cept to take our pay on Fridays. I hate 'em.'

'The Rock scorpions?' she said.

'Aye, that's what they are . . . I got one of them into trouble, she says.'

He sounded almost pleased. What a life it must be on that gaunt rock for such as these, she thought. He spoke as though he had got the girl 'into trouble' not out of love but out of boredom, almost as an act of revenge.

'Before I stole the dog I got drunk, thinking of you. What I heard about you, miss. The colonel gave me fourteen days C.B. and said he'd a good mind not to let me go on the parade for Their Royal Highnesses.'

'And you would have minded that?' she said fascinated.

'Aye, miss. I'm the flank man of No. 3 Double Company.'

'Oh . . . Do you find people unpleasant to you, because of the Boer War?'

'All the niggers and frogs and wops are yapping, miss. The colonel says the whole lot of 'em's not worth a pint of 49th piss . . . begging your pardon, miss.'

'49th?'

'That's us. The 49th Foot. The Royal Berkshire Regiment, though I'm from Yorksheer, myself.'

She was feeling a little dazed, so she held out a hand – 'Come.'

He was a normal lover, and after some initial awkwardness took her firmly and manfully. If any of her clients could arouse her, she thought, he might, when they came to know each other better. And he, to her surprise, rapidly passed from a stolid lust to an almost poetic rapture of passion.

He had hard, strong muscles, and the outdoorman's sharp colour lines at neck and wrists, brown on one side, white on the other. He had reddish hair, a man's good phallus, and a bullet scar in his right shoulder.

Long after he had spent his strength in her, he kissed her breast, and lay on his back, and said, 'I wor a shepherd when I wor a boy. On the dales, by Haworth. Sometimes, when I'd been alone a long time, and it wor cold, and a full moon, and all the sheep around me, I'd feel I knew what we wor all doing here on earth . . . It's the same now, miss. You'll not go away from La Linea?'

355

'No.'

'Then I'll not go away from Gibraltar. Not as long as I live.'

George Torrenti, Esquire, was in his mid-forties: rather short, plump, swarthy, big nose, of a very Italian appearance except for the flowing silky moustache, which might have been borrowed from a caricature of a British Guards officer.

He was nervy, jumpy, fiddling with his glass of whisky (never touched anything else). He always was, through the half hour it took him to shed the layers of convention and shame separating him from what he really wanted.

'I thought my Baron would win the dog show,' he was saying, 'until some swine stole him. A soldier, I'll swear. Those brutes will do anything ... But the dog show's a minor matter, really, even though the Princess will be giving the prizes in person. The really important thing is the dinner party at the Convent. By the time you have counted the two Admirals, the General, the Brigadier, Lord Howard Kingsley, the Colonial Secretary, the artillery brigadier, the judge, the priest, the chairman of the City Council, and their wives ... there are only four places left. Two couples!' His prominent eyes bulged, and he had begun to sweat – 'One must be Haroldson, the lawyer. The other must be either me, or Joseph Aboab.'

'Oh, surely they would give you precedence over a Jew,' she said gravely.

'Of course, they *should*!' he said vehemently. 'But King Edward loves Jews. Father O'Callaghan says they're strong in the Freemasons, and you know the prince is a Mason.'

He drank some whisky and eyed her obliquely, licking his lips. He was uncomfortable on her chair, but she knew it would pass. 'Aboab's been made an honorary whip of the Calpe Hunt,' he went on. 'How can I compete with that? I hate riding. And then yesterday I shot a bird, and it turned out to be a Barbary partridge female, which was out of season. And the Governor's a keen ornithologist . . . What can I *do*?'

'Make a big contribution to some fund the Governor is interested in,' she said. 'Money is very persuasive.'

'I'll think about it,' he said. 'But I have very heavy expenses just now. I'm fitting out three new trading steamers.'

'Surely the Syndicate must have borne a share of that?' she said.

'What do you know of the Syndicate?' he said, suddenly suspicious – 'Well, it is not really very secret, is it? Old Bawltrum's the official owner of the ships, but he's only a dummy. The Syndicate really owns them – myself and three Spanish gentlemen.'

'Spaniards?' she said. 'Engaged in smuggling from Gibraltar?'

He laughed, without humour. He got up and began to pace the floor. It was getting close now. 'Lord Howard Kingsley's in charge of the invitations to the dinner. He'd give his eyes to be made Comptroller of the Royal Household in London. Looks the other way while the Admiral here sleeps with his wife. If King Edward wanted her, good God, he'd guide the royal cock in himself. But how can I help to become Comptroller?'

'I don't know,' she said.

'Nor do I. But he's taken to greeting me very cordially in the street. I think he's going to ask me for something. I wish I knew what.'

His eyes were glazed, and he stopped pacing. He suddenly undid his fly.

She got up – 'Disgusting man,' she said, and slapped

him on the cheek. 'For that you must be punished. Go into the bedroom, sir!' She pointed imperiously.

He hurried through. She followed, and while he undressed she selected a few canes. Juana was tying him expertly, head to knee, in the middle of the floor. 'Kiss my boot,' Dolores said, thrusting it into his face. She took a cane, stepped away, and gave him a swishing blow on the buttocks, as hard as she could. 'Disgusting,' she cried. 'Kiss Juana's stinking foot. Lick her shoes.' Swish! Swish! The red weals leaped up across his buttocks. 'No, no!' he cried. 'Enough. Let me up!'

Swish! Swish! She wondered how he kept his wife from seeing the marks. Swish! They had probably never seen each other undressed.

'Oh, oh! Mercy!'

The cane whistled more fiercely.

The next visitor would not arrive for half an hour. Dolores put her feet up on the couch and rested – the whipping always tired her, though Torrenti was in many ways so despicable that she rather enjoyed it. When Juana signalled that the next client had arrived, she undressed and put on a man's suit. Then she lit a cigar, stuffed her hair under a bandanna, and waited, legs crossed, puffing nonchalantly.

Lt. Col. Lord Howard Kingsley, Grenadier Guards, was tall, broad-shouldered, narrow hipped. His fair hair was wavy and touched with grey, he had level grey eyes, a square jaw, slightly cleft, and an easy, effortless grace of movement. The first time he visited her she saw what he really wanted, and sent for a beautiful young public pederast; but the Oscar Wilde scandal had bitten too deep into his world, and she soon realized that he dared not admit to himself, let alone to anyone else, the true nature of his need. So he came to her, to prove that he was the same as other men; and she did her best.

They went into the bedroom and he undressed at once. In one respect he was not at all like most men; he was endowed with enormous sexual equipment, more like a horse's than a man's, she had thought, almost quailing, the first time she saw it. She had no fear now, for it would never serve her, or any other woman. She used her wiles, as always; as always nothing happened.

'I'm afraid it's no use, m'dear,' he said. 'I'm a little tired. Been overdoing it on the tennis court a bit.'

He rolled languidly over on the bed, and closed his eyes. She slipped out of her trousers, strapped on a large dildo, put a little vaseline on the end, and climbed up on to the bed behind him. He began to quiver and bulge . . .

When it was done she retired at once, washed, and dressed as a high-class courtesan – expensively, but a little garishly.

He wandered in a few minutes later, drank manzanilla, and talked of his brother, the Duke of Devizes; of his master, the Governor of Gibraltar; of his friend, the Count of Brazalema. 'Do you know him?' he asked.

'I've seen him,' Dolores said.

'A really delightful man,' Lord Howard said. 'His daughter's staying with us now, as a matter of fact. She and my own daughter are thick as thieves – both mad on horses – tireless – spend the nights dancing with the young officers, and the days galloping all over Andalusia exercising their horses.'

'The young ladies ride out unaccompanied?' she asked.

'Oh no. Pablo Larios lends them a stable lad, as groom . . . You know, the Count's very fond of England. Be-

tween you and me, he's hoping to become the next ambassador to London. All he has to do is manage a little
affair to King Alfonso's satisfaction, and it will be arranged. There's a damnable amount of smuggling goes on
out of Gibraltar into Spain, y'know. A lot of these Gibraltar tradespeople are up to their necks in it. Well, King
Alfonso's asked Grazalema to do something about it – in a
way to help England, y'see, because it'll stop the anti-
British complaints to his government. The Count doesn't
have any official position, of course, but he's the largest
landowner round here—'

'He can ride thirty miles in a straight line without leaving his land,' she said.

'Just so. Well, in a way it's better for him not to be in an
official position because so many of them are in it, too.' He
rubbed thumb and forefinger of his right hand together.
'Rotten with corruption, Spain is, y'know. Oh, by the by,
here's a little present for Juana.' He gave her a parcel he
had brought. 'Five yards of Harris tweed. I had to slip the
customs chap twenty pesetas not to see that . . . Did you
know our Prince and Princess are going to visit us?'

'I had heard something.'

'M'dear, you should see the intrigue that's going on
among the tradespeople to get invited to the big dinner.
There's a Jew who's pouring money into the Hunt. Torrenti's frantic. So frantic that I *think* I can get him to cut
off his own nose for us.'

'Cut off his nose?'

He laughed – 'Only metaphorically.'

'Is there not to be a dog show, too, for the Prince and
Princess?'

'Is there? Oh yes, I recall now, I asked Pablo Larios to
be judge. I have a pedigree fox terrier bitch that will win
that class. I didn't think it was quite cricket to enter her,

but H.E. said, No, no, let the best dog win. Ha ha.'

He waved his hand round the magnificence of her drawing-room – 'I've only had the honour of visiting you four times, m'dear, but you intrigue me. Such . . . splendour! Dare I ask, how did you achieve it? By what path did you attain these rarefied if, ah, a trifle *scandalous* heights?'

She looked surreptitiously at the grandfather clock in the corner. She'd give him the half-hour story. She dabbed a small handkerchief to her eyes, and began:

'I was born . . .'

One of the mirrors on one wall of the bedrooms was not a true mirror, but a glass through which one could watch the next room, without people in there knowing they were under observation. She stood in front of that mirror now, naked, her breasts cushioning the back of the head and neck of the client, who sat, also naked, in an upright chair close to the mirror. He was Don Pedro de Santangel y Barrachina, 28th Count of Grazalema, a Grandee of Spain with a tremendous lineage and a tiny penis.

In the next room a man and woman performed the acts of sexuality with slow deliberation, always ensuring that an observer behind the false mirror would get a good view of their sexual organs and the details of each act. The man was a powerfully built young fellow, available for any service Dolores would pay for; the girl was Juana's daughter, plump, large-breasted and large-eyed. She lay now on the side of the bed, one knee raised and bent aside. The young man lay across her other leg, teasing her sex.

Dolores raised a hand to her hair. From concealment Juana would see the sign, and whisper the word to the couple next door – 'Go to it now.'

The young man half rose, pushed the girl's other leg

aside, and rammed into her. The Count's view was from straight behind, and underneath. As the young man's powerful gluteal muscles contracted in his final spasms, the Count began to breathe deeply. Dolores guided him quickly to the bed and pulled him down on top of her. After a few rapid, trembling jerks, he burst into tears, and that, she knew, was the sign. She patted his head, and murmured, 'There, there! Lie still . . . You have exhausted me.' With the Count there was no sense of hurry, for on a day when he was to visit her he required that she saw no one else.

Later, he took coffee in her big drawing-room. Through a gap in the curtains they could see the lights of Gibraltar. The Count pointed – 'Do you see those lights, Señorita Falcon? Not the town – in the bay. Those are twelve British battleships. Twelve! Spain owns three, altogether. No, we shall never regain our Rock by force . . . but by generosity, I think we might. That is what I shall try to achieve in London.'

'You are going to London, Count?'

'As ambassador, I hope.' He was quite tall, slender, rather dark-skinned, with large sad, black eyes, the classical long Spanish face, and long hair, going grey.

'Do you pay to become an ambassador?'

'After,' he said, smiling slightly. 'Not usually before. A man of no family might have to buy the place. But many noblemen have had to pay considerable sums, under some other pretext of course, to persuade the king *not* to send them to such places as Siam or Paraguay or Ethiopa.' He shuddered delicately. 'I for one can not tolerate heat, or black men, or brown men – or Jews for that matter, but there is no Jewish capital. God be praised . . . In this matter of the ambassadorship – well, I will tell you – Don Alfonso has asked me to produce some spectacular success against the smuggling from Gibraltar. As you know, many agents of the Tobacco Monopoly, and the police and customs, are involved in it, so, to achieve success, one must go outside them. I am particularly interested in some fast steam vessels recently built for the trade. I believe I am a member of the syndicate owning them, but of course it would not do to make any direct inquiries in that capacity, so I have approached an important English officer to obtain precise information about their proposed activities for me. Then, with a little threatening and bribery on my part – we shall strike. There will be a great success, just as Don Alfonso asked, and I shall go to London . . .'

'More coffee, Count? A cake? . . . Have I not seen your daughter riding through La Linea with Miss Kingsley, the daughter of the Governor's Military Assistant, and a groom from the Calpe Hunt stables?'

The Count's eyes flickered in recognition of her subtle method of indicating that she could guess who the 'important English officer' was.

'Yes,' he said, 'Kitty is staying with Lord and Lady Howard for a week or two, to hunt with the Calpe. My wife is not entirely happy about it.'

'Lady Howard Kingsley is not as discreet as she might be.'

'Precisely. She will set Kitty a strange example . . . but I do need Lord Howard's help, so we could not refuse the invitation.'

Pleasantly, the talk drifted on. The Count's occasional visits were always cases of calm for her. His yellow Daimler in the driveway, the chauffeur and postilion sitting outside a nearby tavern, guaranteed that there would be no interruptions.

The hands of the clock came back to twelve, the pages of the calendar to one. It began again ... Paco her lover, a drunken *juerga* with half a dozen gypsies clapping and singing and herself dancing on the table, no drawers under her flaring skirt, and finally Paco taking her there, on the table in front of all of them ... Tomas Lopez, the dockyard labourer ... Carlos Firpo, the contraband crewman ... Private Tamlyn of the 49th ... George Torrenti, Esquire, importer ... Lieut. Col. Lord Howard Kingsley of the Guards ... Don Pedro de Santangel y Barrachina, Count of Grazalema ...

The hands of the clock came back to twelve, the pages of the calendar to one. . . .

'I've been staying with the Count,' Lord Howard said. 'Very pleasant, except that it was unseasonably hot. The Count can't stand heat, y'know. But that was the only fly in the ointment. Excellent partridge shooting, though not up to Yorkshire grouse, of course ... good riding ... came down for a day with the Calpe once ... rattling good day, too, with a five-mile point, which is rare in this country. Kitty Santangel fell into a ditch. That gypsy groom, Paco, was up with the second horses for her and Clara, that's my daughter, and pulled her out.'

'It was fortunate he was there,' she said.

'Fortunate for him, too – the Count gave him a hundred pesetas.'

He was silent, puffing on his cigar.

She opened a newspaper she had kept on the escritoire, and handed it to him. The headline was *British Smuggling Steamer Sunk. Captain killed, 2 crewmen wounded. 4 tons tobacco seized.* She said, 'How did you get the information?'

'Just asked Torrenti. The reward to be a place at the royal dinner.'

'It was a great success then, just as the Count needed.'

Lord Howard did not seem very cheerful. 'Not really, I fear. No one was supposed to open fire, but the Spanish had artillery ready, and sank the ship. Some tobacco she had already landed was seized, the rest went down with her, not far off shore. But too many people have been offended. The success may have been too spectacular. The Spanish politicians are crowing, but our admiral is threatening to bombard Malaga. And the Count has had to spend a vast sum of money in bribes...'

'I feel sorry for the wife of the poor man who was killed,' she said.

'Great pity, that, because the gutter press in England's taken it up... The ship should never have been lost, either. That was the captain's fault, backing off when he was holed, instead of running her farther ashore. Then we could have got her back.'

'Even though she was caught in the act of smuggling?'

'Good heavens, yes m'dear. We just send a strong note demanding the return of our ship, and have a battleship steam out of harbour. And the owners see that a suitable sum is passed to whoever's responsible for releasing the ship...'

She listened, thinking, perhaps I could hire two *maricons* to do it to each other in the little room, and get Lord Howard to watch through the secret mirror. If at the time he could be drunk, or could pretend to be drunk, then he could tell himself he was not responsible for what followed when the two men came in to join them. There'd be an

365

orgy of sodomy. She would have to be there at the beginning, then she could leave, and Lord Howard could discover his true love.

'. . . Pablo Larios wants me to get Aboab into the royal dinner because of the hounds he gave, but I can't squeeze him in unless I squeeze someone else out.'

Yes, there'd be a fine bout of buggery. Lord Howard would be deliriously happy, and the next day he'd shoot himself, and everyone would say he'd just discovered he had cancer. The English acted as though the fat writer Wilde had invented *mariconeria*.

She looked surreptitiously at the clock, keeping her smile alert and interested.

'It was insured!' George Torrenti shouted.

'Against theft? Of, you mean the ship, not your dog.'

'Of course! But the particulars weren't correct. You can't get insurance if you say what the ship's really going to be used for, and now . . .'

'A man killed,' she said.

'. . . Lloyd's won't pay. Do you realize how much we'll each lose? Thirty thousand pounds! And do you know who the papers say was behind the whole thing? The Count of Grazalema!'

'He is a great lord here,' she said.

'Yes, but I've also just found that the "Pedro Perez" who's a member of our syndicate, and who we all thought was the cover name for a group of officers in the Tabacalera headquarters in Madrid, is none other than the Count of Grazalema! The rotten, lying, intrigue of the Spaniards!'

'And the man killed,' she said.

'But Lord Howard Kingsley's the one who's responsible for the loss of the ship and cargo as far as I'm concerned.

Worming confidential information out of me and then passing it to the Spanish. Oh God, I should have stayed in the customs house side ... And he promised he would get the ship back, but she's sunk!'

'And the man killed.'

'Well, I'm sleeping with Lady Howard! That'll teach him. I approached her the next day. He was still up in Ronda with the Count. I was terrified, because, well, she is a duke's sister-in-law, but I was so angry that I could do it.'

'Does she – punish you?' Dolores asked.

'She'll do anything, as long as I make love to her, too ... And I'm getting half a dozen of us together, the most important merchants in Gibraltar, and we're going to write an official letter to the Admiralty in England, hinting that Lord Howard gave away British naval secrets to the Spanish. And we'll send a copy to *The Times*. The scandal will break while the Prince and Princess are here. He'll never be made Comptroller at Buckingham Palace.'

'And you'll never be invited to the Convent,' she said.

'Oh, God, I suppose not,' he said, relapsing into uncertainty. 'It's a ... a *damned bad show* all round.'

'Especially for the man killed,' she said.

Today her caning of him served as a release for a sudden venomous hatred of men in general and George Torrenti in particular. Further, she felt physically queasy. So, she whipped with tight-lipped, precise force, the cane whistling, the livid welts springing up exactly superimposed. She broke a cane, and took another. Torrenti's moans and prayers for release grew louder. She aimed carefully low, and hit his testicles twice, as he was ejaculating. He began to writhe and scream like a trapped animal then, but she took another cane, and kept up the savage, whistling cuts until his buttocks were purple and white, and dripping blood all the way across. Then she flung the cane away, rushed into the bathroom and vomited.

Dolores Falcon was not looking well, the Deputy Chief of Police thought. That young Paco Santangel had been beating her, probably. And her request was an unusual one. Still, it was not for him to inquire into the secret life of high-class courtesans, and on general grounds her request should be granted. She had been good to the police – paid well and punctually, given extra presents when there was sickness or a new baby, never caused scandal or noise except sometimes when Paco took his friends to the house.

'As long as it is no important official of the British Government, who could make trouble for us in his turn . . .' he said.

'No. It's a merchant, very rich,' she said, 'but that must be forgotten.'

'Perfectly. We shall hear from you?'

'In a week or so.'

The police officer smiled, pocketed the envelope – it was a good deal thicker than usual – and bowed out.

Private Tamlyn came half an hour later and Juana brought beer. 'I've asked for my discharge,' he said, almost before he had sat down. 'The colonel says he wouldn't stand in my way even if he could. I've done me time, and nobbut a week to go before I could sign on again, but I won't. An' the colonel says he'll recommend me for policeman in the dockyard. They like old soldiers there. They can't hire the Gibraltar folk because they'd never arrest each other. I saw the officer in charge of the police, and he said if I applied when I was discharged, he'd take me on, if the colonel recommended me.'

'So it's all arranged. When are you getting married?'

His long face set into a remote hardness. 'Next month,' he said.

'Did the colonel give you his blessing?'

'Lor' no! He called me everything but "darling", miss. Offered to send me back to Blighty, sick. Said these Gibraltar women were useless to man or beast. But I said I had to stay. He thought it was to do right by Luisa, and shook my hand and said I was only a private soldier but a natural gentleman.' His voice softened – 'But it's to be near you I'm staying, that's the only truth on it.'

She thought, that poor woman he marries is going to have a dreadful life. She had brought it on herself, but still . . .

'I was telling you about Tofrek last time,' he said. 'About the fuzzie wuzzies and how they couldn't break our square . . .'

'When was this?' she asked, a little dazed.

'I don't know, miss. Not long, 'cos there's plenty of long service men now was there. But it's the Frogs *I'd* like to fight. Wish I'd a few in front of my bayonet right now, that I do. I'd teach 'em to stick out their dirty tongues at England, and the King and Queen, and . . .'

She put out her hand to him, and said, 'Tell me later . . .'

But later he said little, only looked at her with his pale blue eyes glowing, and his bony face fallen into a deep calm. When it was nearly time for him to go, he said, 'Will you see me at the dinner? There's to be a Guard of Honour outside the Convent. I'm the left flank man, front rank.'

'I'll come,' she said, 'just to see you all.'

Carlos Firpo's right arm was in plaster-of-paris from the elbow down, the whole carried in a sling. Sexually he was even more frantic than usual, as though his brush with violent death had re-emphasized the real values in his life.

Later, he was more subdued. 'Smashed my arm,' he said, over and over. 'A shell splinter, it was. Another killed the captain. Blew his brains all over me. And that dirty, stuck-up swine Torrenti's refused to give me a pension, or a bonus, or anything.'

'What can have happened?' she asked. 'Juana, the champagne!'

'Someone got paid a lot of money, that's what's happened, he said bitterly. 'Probably Torrenti. He's capable of anything.'

'But it was his ship.'

'Yes, but . . . I don't know. Father O'Callaghan says it was the Freemasons fixed it, because everyone on the ships, and in the syndicate, is Catholic . . . And I promised Luisa, that's my wife's sister, twenty pounds for a wedding present, and now I can't give her two. And she's having hysterics because the fellow she's marrying, this Private Tamlyn, is not going to England at all but staying here as a dockyard policeman. Well, that'll be worth something to the family, I suppose.'

He got up moodily. The effects of the sexual therapy were wearing off fast.

'And your wife?' she asked.

'Bad backache, she has. And very upset, because the woman who was working for us, left. Maria Lopez. She and I were on the bed. Her husband came in, unexpected, from the dockyard. My wife came back at the same time, because she'd forgot something. So . . .'

'I understand perfectly. You could find another cleaning woman. Uglier, or older, perhaps?'

'Yes. But I can't afford it any more.'

Tomas Lopez sat on the edge of the straight-backed chair, drinking red wine, very correct in his grey cotton suit and white shirt buttoned up, with no tie. 'My wife, unfortunately, cut her nose, quite severely. The end cut off, in fact. Only a few days ago. Yes, she is recovering, thank you.'

He'd do that, she thought, the old Andalusian, Moorish way. There was a position to hold, a seat to be sat in, straight.

'The English Prince and Princess arrived yesterday, for the dog show,' he said. 'The soldiers lined the route when they paid a call on the Governor. They are living on the royal yacht in the harbour. It is all done properly, with much *señorio.*'

'And the dog show? Are you still confident your Manolo will win?'

'I am confident, señorita. As you suggested I paid Paco Santangel one hundred pesetas to inform me what was Don Pablo Lario's passion, or, as you might say, weakness; but after nearly a month he told me only that Don Pablo craved to own a full-blooded Arab stallion. I am not in a position to present Don Pablo with such a horse. That young man, is, perhaps, a scoundrel, señorita.'

She sighed, and said nothing.

'In the end I gave Don Pablo a perfect yellow rose. I could see that he recognized in me a person who knows the correct values.'

'Indeed yes.'

'It will not influence his judgment of the dogs ... but it will cause him to look very carefully at Manolo. A man who could select so perfect a rose ...'

371

'... would naturally have a perfect dog,' she finished.

'Precisely. Manolo is not perfect, but he is good. Very good. Indeed, his appearance and posture have changed, that is, improved, immensely in the past few weeks. Well, tomorrow at 2.30 of the afternoon is the "moment of truth" as they say in the bullring.'

She refilled his glass. He lit a 'black' cigarette and drew on it cautiously. 'There has been a considerable scandal in Gibraltar over the arrest of Mister Torrenti, a prominent merchant, the evening before last, in the house of a professional lady of La Linea. Many believe that the misfortune befell him because he shot a female Barbary partridge out of season, which is well known to be almost as fatal as catching the eye of our king, Don Alfonso.' The shrewd eyes surveyed her – 'It is said that the lady was yourself, though it has not been published.'

'That is so,' she said, nodding at the memory. The police had come while she was whipping him. She had wondered whether he would keep his appointment after the way she had beaten him the last time. If he failed to appear she had only to apologize to the police. But he had come, begging for more whipping – 'only let me loose when I ask you to.'

'Father O'Callaghan says it is the Freemasons who caused his arrest, in order that he should not be able to dine with the English prince and princess, for now, it is understood, he has been requested to return his invitation.'

When the police burst in, she recalled with pleasure, he had thought it was some exciting new continuation of the whipping, that they were going to do. Then, when they arrested him, he began to rave like a madman. She had to bury her face in the curtains, and pretend her laughter was sobbing, to see him shaking his fist, his pot belly quivering, his penis shrinking, his silky moustache puffing out. When they took him away he could no longer speak.

'What was the charge against him, that the police should follow him and enter here? It must have been serious,' Lopez said.

'Yes,' she said. 'It was smuggling. They found a packet of English cigarettes on him, that he had smuggled through the frontier.'

Lopez said, 'A serious matter, indeed. It is certainly true then, about the bad luck that will follow anyone who kills a Barbary partridge, for it was surely a very ill stroke of chance that reporters from the Gibraltar newspapers, and even the representative of Reuters, happened to be with the police when he was arrested.'

'Yes,' she said. 'Otherwise he might have persuaded the police, on the way to the jail, that there had been a mistake.'

'God preserve us all from such mistakes, Señorita Falcon,' he said meaningly. He gave her money and the usual bottle of whisky. 'I trust the police will not break in on account of this bottle, which certainly has not been seen by any customs officer.'

'There is no chance of that, Señor Lopez,' she said, and led the way to the bedroom.

The day of the dog show dawned, waxed, waned. She heard nothing. She had no clients, and went to bed early.

The clang of the front door bell awakened her. She sat up, wondering whether it could be day yet. But it was not. It was three o'clock in the morning. She heard Juana's shuffling feet, then distant murmuring. Shoes clattered up the marble stairs, the door burst open. She jumped out of bed, her arms wide – 'Paco!'

Juana waddled in, and lit the lamps, grumbling, 'Send him away, señorita. Before he causes any more trouble.'

He was wearing an expensive grey worsted jacket, incongruous over the patched blue cotton trousers. There was a big bulge inside the jacket. He dived in his hand and pulled out a fat, sleepy puppy. He pressed it into her hands. 'A fox-hound bitch,' he said. 'I stole it for you. It'll be a good guard dog when it grows up. Good-bye.'

He was going. She grabbed his arm – 'Paco!'

'Let him go,' Juana said, 'It'll be best.'

'Paco, what are you doing? What do you mean, good-bye?'

'My Cabo won the dog show, because he's really a pup of the Count's pedigree bitch, that I stole when I birthed her two years ago. So I won fifty pounds and I'm running away with Kitty, the Count's daughter. She's waiting in the carriage outside.'

'But . . . but . . .'

'The Count's been appointed ambassador to Ethiopia. Tomas Lopez was arrested and fined five pounds for dog stealing, right in front of the princess, because his dog wasn't his, but Torrenti's that he'd stolen, and painted.'

She sank on to the bed, looking at him as though he had come from another planet.

'We'll be married in Cadiz, then we're going to Peru. I'll come back when the excitement's died down. The Count will want to see his first grandson. Then I'll be a torero . . . *El Gato Moreno*!' He pirouetted on his toes, and ran out.

'Good riddance,' Juana said. She bustled over and fluffed up the pillow – 'You get back into bed.'

374

She said, 'The girl's going to have his baby.'

'Naturally,' Juana said. 'The English girl, also, I wouldn't be surprised. He will leave them all over the world.' Dolores felt pale and ill. Juana looked at her keenly. 'You, too?'

Dolores nodded – 'I'm sure.'

'It was the *juerga*. You were drunk.'

'Perhaps. But it might be anyone.'

'Well, we can get rid if it.'

'No, Juana. I'll keep it.'

'You're mad!'

'Perhaps. Good night.'

She had a good position near the front of the crowd opposite the Convent, to watch the ceremonies preceding the great dinner. She was wearing black, with a heavy veil. The sergeant of the police next to her was one of the few people in the world who knew her and her whole history; but he did not recognize her under the veil.

In the hiss of the gaslamps she watched the redcoats march down, the band playing, and take up their positions to the left of the main entrance. She saw Private Tamlyn, and thought that his wandering eye – his head and neck remained ramrod stiff throughout – detected her. In the crowd she saw Tomas Lopez and his wife, with a bandage over her nose; and Carlos Firpo, his arm in a sling, with his sour wife and depressed sister-in-law. And when the guests began to arrive she saw Father O'Callaghan, looking every which way to make sure his flock appreciated that he had been invited; and Mr. and Mrs. Joseph Aboab, Jews, invited at the last moment to take the place of the Torrentis, unhappily indisposed; and Don Pablo Larios and Pepita, who were warmly applauded by all; and Lt. Col. Lord Howard

Kingsley, and his thin, blonde, hungry-looking lady.

Finally the sound of cheering rolled up Main Street from the direction of Casemates, and the Governor came out to stand under the arch outside the Convent. Beside him a red-coated spike-helmeted sergeant held a velvet cushion, and on the cushion rested three huge, ancient keys, the Keys of the Fortress.

The royal carriage rolled up and the crowd surged forward, cheering. Dolores was left against the wall. She pushed up her veil and stood on tiptoe, trying to see. The sergeant of the police turned, stared, and said in a low voice, 'What are you doing here, Leah Conquy? What concern of yours is such an affair as this?'

Book Eleven

THE GREY DIPLOMATISTS

The Jewish years 5662–5696
A.U.C. 2655–2689
A.D. 1902–1936
A.H. 1320–1355

STORM clouds were gathering over La Linea, over Gibraltar, over all Europe, the sun of a brilliant, selfish young century already fading. In the chanceries the candles burned late as the politicians wove and rewove the alliances for the 'inevitable' conflict. In the shipyards arc lights sputtered and oxyacetylene torches glared twenty-four hours a day as ship after fighting ship joined the swelling navies.

Gibraltar showed its teeth in October 1904, when battleships put out into the Atlantic to intercept a Russian fleet heading from the Baltic clear round the world to fight Japan. The Russians, steaming down the North Sea earlier, had fired on a number of British fishing vessels. Britain demanded apologies and compensation – and sent out the Gibraltar fleet to enforce its demands. The Russians, who must indeed have been stricken with panic to imagine that British trawlers were Japanese destroyers, quickly made amends and Lord Charles Beresford steamed back to Gibraltar. The Russians sailed on to annihilation at Tsushima.

In January 1906, the representatives of the major European powers met at Algeciras, across the bay from Gibraltar, to divide up the Moroccan empire, and so complete the absorption of all Africa except Ethiopia. The convention being arranged was a piece of skulduggery of dubious antecedents and more dubious promise. Its main purpose was to keep out Germany. In return for concessions in Egypt and elsewhere England was to agree to a French take-over in Morocco, except that a part directly opposite Spain – and Gibraltar – should be allotted to the weakest and most ailing of the powers concerned – Spain. If it came to a vote Germany would stand almost alone, backed only by Austria, and Morocco itself. The British plenipotentiary, Sir Arthur Nicolson, was grave and anxious. The proposals held enormous possibilities for future disaster. Still worried, he went over and spent the night in Gibraltar. Harold Nicolson tells in his biography of his father what happened:

'The Atlantic and Mediterranean Fleets were there – thirty battleships, innumerable cruisers, countless destroyers. He dined with Lord Charles Beresford upon the flag-ship. Those great grey shapes lay around him under the great Rock: Illustrious, Indefatigable, Implacable, Indomitable. *Clearly there was no reason to be frightened of Count Tattenbach. (He) decided that at the very next meeting he would put things to the vote.*

The battleships, which at that time many Englishmen called 'grey diplomatists' had signed another treaty, and the Rock had witnessed it. The thoughtful observer would be tempted to quote Lord Rosebery's remark of half a generation earlier: 'Till I saw Gibraltar I never fully realized why we are so hated in Europe.'

The Edwardian period in Gibraltar itself was perhaps the finest heyday of snobbism. Queen Victoria had sent her third son, the Duke of Connaught, there for six months in 1875. The reason for his posting has escaped history, for he had no responsibilities and wasn't studying anything. As he was twenty-five and a bachelor one might suspect that the Queen sent him away from some petticoated menace in London. The Duke's elder brother, Edward, visited the Rock briefly as Prince of Wales, and again the year after he was crowned. He dined with the governor, and ordered that the name of the latter's official residence should be changed to Government House; it didn't seem right for a Governor to live in a Convent: all those nuns ... (The name was later changed back again.)

Queen Alexandra came: King Alfonso XIII came to Algeciras (not to Gibraltar, that would have been too much for a Spanish king): the new Prince and Princess of Wales (King George V and Queen Mary) came ... The link between the upper echelons of Spanish and Gibraltar society was the Larios family, Spanish landowners and aristocrats who also owned estates and houses in Gibraltar. It was Pablo Larios and his wife who escorted the kings, queens, and princesses through the cork woods of Almoraima, it was he who introduced the Spanish gentry to polo, it was he who became Master of the Calpe Hunt in 1890, and was still master in 1906 when King Edward and King Alfonso honoured it with their patronage, and its title changed to the *Royal* Calpe Hunt. The exaltation in royalty-worshipping Gibraltar knew no bounds.

More prosaically, the water problem was at last overcome. It had been so bad that Nelson once came out from England with a warship, loaded with nothing but water. Of old, convoys and fleets had to go over to Tetuan or Tangier to water. Jervis had inveighed furiously that he would eject all women from H.M. ships (many were then permitted on board) as *they would insist on washing*. Between 1898 and 1961, in three main spasms, thirteen reservoirs with a total capacity of 16,000,000 gallons, were constructed. All but one of these are deep inside the rock and are fed and serviced by a tunnel and railway of their own. Some of the water is collected on cemented-over outcrops of limestone on the west face, but the main catchment area is thirty-four acres of corrugated roofing material spread over the steep aeolian sand slope on the eastern side. It is this huge expanse of greyish white, the sheets screwed firmly into timbers driven into the sand, which every traveller from the east now sees before anything else of Gibraltar emerges from the haze: it is that that we saw, coming in by helicopter on the first page of the Foreword.

Archaeological research continued, and the first formal scientific exploration of a Gibraltar cave was made by Mr. Duckworth in 1910. He explored Cave S, at the top of the east face Water Catchment Area which I have just described; and found more bones and artifacts, to confirm that Gibraltar is an inexhaustible mine of material for the study of early man in a certain definite and plainly limited environment. Later Gibraltar also attracted the attention of the father and the dean of modern archaeology, the Abbé Breuil, but he made no remarkable discoveries.

Smuggling continued, limited only by the primitive means then available – sailing cutters and a few steam pinnaces for sea work (though the invention and use of radio at sea was soon seen to provide an excellent means of communicating between the smugglers and the *Tabacalera* operatives, so that unfortunate encounters between them might be avoided). On land, dogs wearing tobacco belts continued to trot back and forth across the neutral ground from the caves under the North Face where the tobacco was stored to their waiting masters in La Linea, until, at the request of the Spanish authorities, a dogproof fence was built from sea to sea across the isthmus.

In 1914 Princip shot the Archduke Ferdinand of Austria at Sarajevo, and the lights began to go out over Europe. War began. Spain remained neutral, though her royalty and court had strong ties to both sides – the queen was English, the queen-mother German – so Gibraltar did not have to face direct attack from the mainland. Gibraltar's situation made it an excellent place for gathering and 'mating' of convoys and escorts, when that system of anti-submarine defence was introduced. But it had remarkably little effect on the German submarine campaign in the Mediterranean. The first U-boat passed through the Strait in May 1915, and from then on shipping losses in the Mediterranean were very heavy. Submarines came and went almost at will, and to cock a final snook, one of them surfaced off Trafalgar two days before the war ended, and sank the battleship *Britannia*.

The guns of Gibraltar were fired in anger, for the first time since the Napoleonic Wars, against submarines. One, spotted on the surface on 31st December, 1915, was engaged and probably sunk by the Levant batteries on Windmill Hill; another was engaged in Gibraltar Bay during 1917 by the Devil's Gap Battery. Some say this submarine was sunk, some say it wasn't, some say it never existed. What is certain is that a number of shells ricocheted into 'neutral' Spain, which protested. Spain had no cause for complaint, as her official class much preferred Germany to England, and several damaged U-boats had secretly been repaired in Spanish harbours.

The war ended in November 1918, bringing a bad combination of circumstances for Gibraltar – the world was at peace, but depressed. The British forces, particularly the Navy, were ruthlessly cut down; and once again the value of Gibraltar had to be considered anew, the war had seen the birth, infancy, youth, and early manhood of a new force, air power, all compressed into four years. When it began pilots in fabric wings tied together with string fired pistols at each other and a strong wind caused the machine to go backwards. When it ended England had four-engine bombers capable of flying from London to Berlin and back, non-stop, with 4,000 lb. of bombs. Similar bombers could fly much more easily from Madrid, Mallorca, or Morocco to Gibraltar . . .

A post-war governor assured the populace that they had nothing to fear from aircraft. He had frequently sailed around the Rock in his little boat, he said, and all seafaring men would agree the air currents were very treacherous and unreliable, far too much so to permit the operation of flying machines. Nevertheless, as the smelly things seemed to have come to stay, a landing strip would be cleared in the middle of the race course. This race course was on the disputed area between the North Front and the sites of the forts of San Felipe and Santa Barbara. The Spanish said the land was not part of Gibraltar, it belonged to them. They had built the old forts that far back as it was customary not to put up any defence work within gunshot of a fortress (they were well within gunshot, even when built: about 450 yards from the North Face). They had permitted the British to use the land solely as an act of courtesy, first to build barracks for the care of fever cases after 1808, later for gardens and recreation purposes for the cooped-up garrison; but an airfield . . . no! The British, naturally, said the land was theirs, and always had been.

In the ruins of the old Europe, like poisonous glittering weeds, the tyrannies of communism and fascism flowered – Salazar, Lenin, Mussolini, Stalin, Hitler. . . .

Internal disease had wracked and rocked Spain throughout the 19th century. There is an old Spanish proverb relating how God, when allocating the virtues and qualities to the nations, asked each patron saint what he wanted for his country. St. George asked sea power for

England, and got it; St. Denis, good food for France, and got it; but when it came to Spain's turn Santiago wasn't there. He was off converting the heathen in Galicia, where some say he obviously never had a chance to finish the job, for God sent a messenger to fetch him, and meanwhile went on with the allocations. When Santiago arrived, panting, God asked him what he wanted for the Spanish people, and he replied – 'Just one thing, Lord – good government.' And God looked into his depleted sack, and shook his head and said, 'You can have the swiftest horses, the most passionate women, the bravest men, the clearest water, the most glorious sun, but what you ask ... never, never, never.'

The 19th century was one long demonstration of that proverb: anarchy, revolution, coup, counter-coup, counter-revolution; the monarchy overthrown and a Republic established in 1871; the Republic overthrown in 1873; bloody civil wars between followers of the regular and the Carlist lines of succession from 1833–1837 and 1870–1876; a bomb thrown at Alfonso XIII's wedding coach, many killed, blood spattering his bride's face and dress; in the 1920s military disaster in Morocco against Abd el Krim, and ignominious rescue by the French; a public clamour blaming the king, causing him to hand over power to a dictator, Primo de Rivera; the collapse of Primo de Rivera; the elections of 1931 won by left wing parties who set up another republic; the flight of Alfonso and his family (his eldest son escaped through Gibraltar).

The left-wing parties in the Republic held a paper-thin national majority, which its actions did nothing to increase. It was beset by riots, separatism, risings by the still-further-Left in Asturias, and the gradual coalition of all the interests in Spain which it had made its implacable enemies.

On 12th July, 1936, the right wing leader Calvo Sotelo, who had consistently spoken out in Parliament against the government, was murdered in Madrid by men of the Guardia Civil, acting on the orders of the government. Six days later the Right rose from end to end of the country, and all that had been hidden, all that had been deeply felt but unspoken, five centuries of repression on one side and five years of personal insult and national and religious degradation on the other, burst out into the Spanish Civil War. . . .

SANCTUARY

'THE shame of Spain, I agree,' Señor Porras said, 'but how can we get it back? England is much too strong for us to take it by force.'

'Even if that were legal,' Susana's father said. 'No, force will get us nowhere.'

'It's getting Mussolini what he wants in Abyssinia – in spite of the British.'

'Negotiation,' Susana's father said, 'A socialist government, with whom we can talk like reasonable people. . . .'

Susana, leaning over the parapet and gazing towards Gibraltar, switched off her attention. Her father always called it 'The shame of Spain', but she thought of it as the Red Prince's castle. Especially after dusk she liked to look at it, for it glittered then like a magic city hung in the night, and there, in the middle, among the brighter lights, the Red Prince had his palace. By day, just before dawn perhaps, a wizard came and transformed it all, taking the palace into the sky, while huge secret doors opened and the rest of the castle vanished inside the mountain, and instead the town came out, so that by day no one would know about the castle or palace.

'. . . I know well that you are not of our socialist camp, my friend. That is your privilege. But grant me that in this one matter of Gibraltar, which lies equally close to the heart of every Spaniard, royalist or socialist – the socialist attitude is more likely to achieve success. After all we have had kings of England arguing and fighting about it with kings of Spain for two hundred years now, without result. . . .'

She yawned, and was reverting to her daydream when her pigtails were sharply pulled from behind. She cried out, pleased but pretending to be angry. Jose Porras had left her brothers to come and play with her. She rushed shrieking round the rooftop after him, flailing with her arms at his back, until her father said, 'Susana, Jose, run out into the street now.'

The streets of Castellar were wonderful for playing, narrow, crooked and full of sharp corners and hidden arches, and she played with Jose and her brother David until it was time for supper. Her father did not come to the table, and they could all hear him fiddling with the radio in the sitting-room. She heard men shouting, screeches in the radio, music, more voices. Her father put his head round the door – 'There's been a military rising, Leah. In nearly all the capitals. I knew there'd be trouble

386

when those bloodthirsty fools had Calvo Sotelo murdered, but this . . .'

'Eat. Drink,' her mother said. 'Be quiet, boys. Your father is worried.'

'Don't worry, papa,' Susana said, and stood up to kiss him. She sat next to him at the table, and was his favourite, she knew, because she was a girl.

He hugged her tightly with one arm, 'It'll be all right,' he said. To her mother he said, 'I'll go and see Paco as soon as I've eaten, and I'll talk to the Cabo of the Guardia Civil, too. One report said the Government is arming the people in Madrid, to fight the army . . . Perhaps we ought to do that everywhere. Otherwise, what hope does any civilian government have against the military?'

'Don't go interfering,' her mother said, 'Paco's the mayor. Let him talk to the Cabo.'

'I must,' her father said, 'Otherwise, perhaps nothing will be done.'

Susana slept in the passage in a bed that was like a big drawer, and was turned up against the wall during the day. In Madrid she had a little room of her own, because she was a girl, but she liked the summers in Castellar better. When she felt sleepy she took Prince's cage down from its place in the patio, and hung it on the hook over the foot of her bed. Prince was a baby bird her eldest brother Saul had found with a broken wing just after they came down a month ago. He was still wild, really, but he would eat from her hand – pecking at her finger sometimes – and her father had set his wing. He said Prince was four months old, and was a Barbary partridge, and when he grew up they'd use him as a decoy to attract others, which they would shoot; but Susana cried No, no, you shan't!

She talked to him in whispers, and then said, 'Good

night, Prince. Sleep well,' and lay back to sleep. The door of the living-room was close, and she heard her father saying, 'I don't like it, Leah. Paco seems terrified. The Cabo said he'd had no orders, in any case they only have their own arms here, for the four of them. I'll go to Jimena soon, and see what I can do there. Or Algeciras. If we moderates don't show we're determined to support the elected government, the extremists will take over, and then . . .'

Susana yawned mightily, and heard no more.

On the third day after that she made a dress for her doll and a hood for Prince. It was a very hot day and her next older brother, David, didn't eat any dinner. He was always dreamy and had longer eyelashes than most girls. He was twelve and Susana was ten. Jose Porras was eleven, but he didn't come round today.

Her father came in late to supper. They heard him wheeling his bicycle into the hall, and then shutting the door. Her mother's head jerked up. He was bolting the door, though no one had gone to bed. He came in and her mother got up at once – 'What is it, Simon? What's happened?'

'Quiet,' he said, 'Lower your voice. Keep calm. You children . . . No, stay. You'll have to know. I've been shot at.'

'With a rifle? or a machine gun?' Saul the eldest asked. He was sixteen, and like her father but taller and he didn't have a droopy moustache.

Her father said, 'As I was coming up from the river. Wheeling the bicycle, of course. Someone fired two shots from bushes, quite close. . . . I heard them running away, so I kept on up the road.'

'Have you told the Cabo?' her mother said.

'Yes, and that's the worst part of it. He said he had other things to do than worry about the safety of Jews and Communists. My God, I'm not a Communist, and never have been, and never will be.' He tore off a piece of bread and went into the sitting-room, calling, 'Saul, bring me some wine.' The radio was clicked on, and soon the air was full of squeaks, shrieks, and shouts.

She was asleep, but a tapping on the side window nearly opposite her bed awakened her. Her father and mother were talking in the living-room, but in low voices. They stopped. The tapping came again. Her father came out, and muttered, 'Who is it?'

'A friend.' Susana, listening intently now, recognized Señor Porras's voice, and wondered why he didn't knock at the front door and come in. 'Listen. They are going to kill you tonight. Take your family and leave Castellar at once.'

'But . . .'

'Don't ask questions. Do you think I'm not risking my neck for you? Not because of your politics, God knows. Because you've spoken up for Spain. Don't go south, the road's picqueted. But go!'

She didn't hear him leaving then, but he must have. Her father and mother stood in the passage, almost over her. The light from the living-room slanted across the floor and up the wall behind them.

'It's . . . it's unbelievable! That was Fernando Porras! Who's "they"? Why . . .?'

Her mother said, 'Someone shot at you, didn't they? I'll get the children up. Where are we going? And take some money, hidden.'

Her father repeated, 'Where are we going? With Spain become mad? People you've known all your life shooting

389

at you from the dark? There's only one place to go. Only one sanctuary – the Rock!' He burst into a terrible laughing, until she jumped out of bed, and said, 'Move, papa, you're standing on my shoes.'

She was ready in three minutes, in her best dress, in spite of dressing in the dark, but then her mother made her change into her oldest and wear her worst, raggediest shoes. She heard her telling the boys the same, and understood that it was like a game, they were all to dress up like tinkers, and then her mother called her, and she helped pack bread, onions and sausage into little sacks.

Her father came into the living-room. She nearly cried out, putting her hand over her mouth, for he had shaved off his moustache. Then they all dirtied their faces, and her mother let out her hair from the pigtails and shook out her own.

They gathered in the parlour. Her father began to speak, choked, tried again. He said, 'We must be brave. Keep together. Make no noise. If anyone asks, our name is Garcia, and we are a poor family, labourers, from Ronda, going to join relatives in Algeciras, where we hear there's work. Our identity papers were burned in our house by a mob. Now open the back door, Saul. No, leave the lamp. Someone may be watching to see when we put it out.'

Ruy, her middle brother, who was red-haired and gawky because his voice was breaking, said 'Susana can't take the bird cage, can she?'

Susana cried out 'I will, I will! Prince shall come to the Rock!'

Her mother began to argue with her, but her father said, 'Leave her be. She can free him when she gets tired. He will be no worse off than he will be here.'

Then they left the house, and the village, and after a short pause at the orchard where their hired man kept the donkey, on northward along the ridge top, on a broad path now, Ruy leading the loaded donkey.

Susana looked over her shoulder, Castellar was dark, beyond it Gibraltar glittered and sparkled, the enchanted castle and palace of her dreams. And now she was going there at last, even though they had to start out in the wrong direction. Prince in the cage would meet the Red Prince of the Rock and the Red Prince would talk to her. She felt thrilled and frightened, together, and muttered to the bird, 'Be brave, Prince.'

They walked all night, slowly, along the sierra, curving steadily left-handed until when light came they were nearly level with Castellar but on the next ridge to the west, and facing Gibraltar. They crept in under the bushes, tethered the donkey, and lay down to rest.

The sun rose, and her father said in a troubled voice, 'It's going to be hot, Leah.' Her mother didn't like the heat, nor did David.

The sun climbed. It was always hot in the middle of July, but this was the hottest day she remembered. By noon her mother was beginning to moan, and David said he had a headache. Her own tongue hurt, and there was no water or spit in her mouth.

'Water, papa,' David croaked, 'I want water.'

Later in the afternoon her father said, 'Load the donkey. We must go down to the river.' They started down the side of the ridge, among the hollyoaks and gorse, but came to a cliff the donkey could not get down, so had to go back. Then Saul thought he saw men with guns, and they waited, keeping still, till it was dark, then tried again. At last they came to water and though it was still and rank, they all drank, then lay down. Susana gave Prince water, and then slept.

In the morning she did not feel well, but her father said,

'None of us do, little daughter. But we must get up to the ridge again.' They started back up, and soon Gibraltar climbed above the middle hills, and she looked at it longingly, set there in the blue and silver bay; but it did not seem any closer, for all the hours they had been struggling. Then she felt a gripe at her belly, and rushed into the bushes and pulled down her underpants. In a moment she was vomiting, too, and crying, for she had dirtied her clothes.

When she had finished they moved a hundred paces, then her father had to go. A hundred paces on and it was David. The next time it was her mother, and herself again. Her mother said, 'We stop here, Simon, until all this is over. It was the water.'

'We can't stop here,' he said. 'We must go on, or we'll never get there.' He was looking very tired. He was not fat, but he did not go out of doors much, either here or in Madrid, and he was not used to exertion.

They moved on thus all day, southward, stopping every few minutes for one or another of them to strain at their empty bowels or retch and moan at an empty stomach. It was as hot as the day before. By afternoon Susana felt strangely light, and stumbled sometimes though she thought she had raised her feet high. Her mother could not walk any more, and rode on the donkey. Her father walked very slowly, his face shiny and white. Sometimes they would stop because one or other of them saw trails of dust moving along the roads in the valley floor below, or men going out to the fields, for her father said, 'We can trust no one now – after a lifetime of trusting everyone!'

Darkness came before they had found any more water, and they stopped. Gibraltar shone there ahead, and Susana cried, 'Let's go on, papa. I'm not tired.'

'You're fainting, little daughter,' he said. 'We must stop.'

'I must have water,' her mother said. 'There's water in the valley just down there. That's where the river comes in.'

Her father hesitated, but her mother began to moan, so he said, 'Very well. Lead, Saul. I will hold your mother secure.'

They moved on. For the last hour clouds had hidden the sun, and it was close and dark. They wound downhill, over uneven rock, over steep-sided water runs – but dry; and along the side of a hill with lights below; and suddenly something jumped out of the gorse and dashed through the line of them. Susana thought it was a fox or a wild pig – but by then the donkey had snorted and broken free, and vanished with her mother in the dark. Her father ran after it. Saul cried 'Stop!' and there was a crashing, thump, repeated, another crash. Her mother screamed, cut off like a hiccup.

She went forward and found the boys on the lip of a quarry. She heard faint sounds from below. They hurried round the side and down. Her mother was lying on her side in the quarry, making a strange noise as she breathed. The donkey lay twenty feet away, and Saul said it was dead.

Her father crouched beside her mother, whispering to her, but she did not answer. After a time Saul said, 'Take the food off the donkey. We must carry it now. The water jar is smashed.'

Then they huddled together under the cliff, and ate a little. Susana went to sleep, and when she awoke it was daylight. David slept beside her. Her father, Saul and Ruy were coming back from a group of bushes at the far side of the quarry. All three were crying.

'Your mother's dead,' her father said.

Susana jumped up and hugged him. Her own tears mingled with his on her cheek, but she did not truly feel sad, for this was all too strange, too different from the time when Granny had died, slowly in bed. Then she had cried every day, for many days. Now she said, 'I can cook for you until you marry again, papa.'

Her father sat down, and she curled up in the crook of his arm. Saul said, 'We can't stay here, papa. We must cross the valley and get on the sierra the other side.'

'Very well,' her father said dully. They moved off, but now it was Saul who gave the orders, and her father walked like a man in a dream, holding Susana's hand.

A rough road, used by the stone carts, led from the quarry out to the road a quarter of a mile away. Before they reached it Saul crept on ahead, and came back to tell them that they could cross safely, as no one was in sight. When she reached the road, Susana saw that it ran straight in both directions for a long way, the hill on one side and a forest of cork oaks on the other. Opposite the track from the quarry a footpath led into the cork forest, and Saul took that, saying, 'This is going the right way, papa.'

Susana liked it among the corks, for there was a good shade, and no bushes or thorns under them. Prince in his cage had felt very heavy yesterday, and made her arms stiff from carrying him; but now he felt light, and she talked to him as they walked along. At noon her father fainted, and Saul said, 'He is tired. He didn't sleep all night. We must rest here until the evening.'

They rested where they were, and Prince ate some bread and Susana slept some more. Then her father sat up, saying, 'I can go on now,' and they started walking again. After sunset, in the dull twilight, Ruy said, 'This path is coming to a cork factory, Saul,' and her father said, 'Better turn right.'

Saul said, 'But that's the road again. It's curved round, and we've gone straight. We're going to join it just before a bridge and . . . soldiers!'

He stopped, and turned. Her father said, 'They've seen us . . . keep on . . . remember what I said.'

Susana saw the soldiers clearly; two men in brown and black with rifles and fixed bayonets. 'They're not real soldiers,' her father muttered.

The path left the cork oaks and led up a little bank to the bridge. The other side of the bridge there was a roadmen's hut, with half a dozen more men lounging about outside, and smoke curling from the chimney. The nearest sentry held up his hand – 'Stop!'

Her father said, 'What is this? We are going to Algeciras.' He spoke in a thick imitation of the accent ordinary people of Castellar spoke in.

A man from among the loungers outside the hut came across the bridge to them. A few of the men were really boys, no older than Ruy or Saul, the rest were as old as her father. They wore ordinary clothes, but mostly good, not peasants'; and they had ties on, and all wore a red and yellow armband on the left arm. The new soldier, who had a pistol, said, 'This is a Falange picquet. Have you seen any bands of Reds? Where are you going?'

Her father began his story. She and the boys stood close together, a little behind him. The men outside the hut had gone back to their cards, but another man had come out, and was standing in the doorway, staring at them and listening.

'We have no papers,' her father said. 'They were burned. We lost everything, everything . . . Because we are church goers! What can one do with such a government?'

'Well spoken,' the interrogator said. 'All right, move on. Keep your eyes open, and if you see or hear of any bands of Reds, tell the first army or Falange picquet you come to. *Arriba España!*'

'*Arriba España!*' her father responded. He beckoned to them – 'Come.' They walked out on to the bridge. It was almost dark now. The man from the hut doorway was standing there, waiting for them. He was wearing military uniform, but it hung loose on him, as though he had been bigger when it was made. He was tall, old, with grey hair and dark eyes and a very long, mournful face.

As they came up to him he peered closely and said, 'It's Señor Toledano, the lawyer and journalist, isn't it?'

'Toledano?' her father muttered. 'No, no – Garcia. A labourer, with no labour.' He made to pass by.

'Wait!' the officer said. 'You have shaved off your moustache, but I know you. We were on the platform together two years ago at the Gibraltar Protest Meeting in Madrid. I am the Count of Grazalema.'

The sergeant had joined them by then. 'Did you say this man was Señor Toledano, count? The Jewish Communist from Castellar?'

'I'm not a Communist,' her father shouted.

The sergeant drew his pistol, and said, 'We won't bother to . . .'

A shot cracked out by her ear. She jerked round and saw that Saul had grabbed the rifle from one of the bridge sentries, and fired. The sergeant's brains spattered the road and his body lay half over the parapet. 'Run!' Saul shrieked, 'Into the woods!' He fired again, and the other sentry collapsed. By then she was running hard, and did not look round till she reached the edge of the cork woods beyond the roadmen's hut. Her father and Saul were coming, running. It was too dark to see where the soldiers were, but a flurry of shots exploded around the roadmen's hut, and she heard bullets clattering overhead and slamming into the tree trunks. Beside her, David gasped – 'Someone hit me!' Her father stumbled out of the dark, crying, 'Where are you?'

'Here, papa.'

'Run,' he said. As he ran he gasped, 'Saul's dead ...'

David said, 'My side hurts, papa ... It's numb ...'

'Can you move, son? Just a bit farther.'

They stumbled on for twenty minutes, all sounds died behind them, and then, deep in the cork forest, David groaned, and fell.

They crouched beside him. Her father felt David's body and muttered, 'He's bleeding from the belly ... Oh God ... I must give myself up. Though to whom, and for what crime, I don't know. We can't go on.'

Ruy said, 'We could carry David back to the soldiers.'

Susana burst out, 'We are going to the Rock! You promised!'

From the ground David said, 'It doesn't hurt, papa. But ... I just can't walk ... Don't go back. That man was going to shoot you. He would shoot me, too – all of us!'

Her father said, 'Very well. We'll stop here. In the morning we can look at your wound and make up our minds then.'

When light came they found they were on the edge of a small stream that trickled through the cork woods towards the Guadarranque. The ground was uneven, and at the foot of a small hill nearby there were leaning rocks which, though they did not form a cave, gave shelter from view. They carried David there, and after Susana had washed his wound – it was in his back, low down, with another larger hole at the front – her father tore off his shirt and made a bandage. Then they waited.

They waited the rest of that day. At first Susana sat by her brother's head, watching his every movement, ready to run to fetch him water when he asked, while her father and Ruy slept. Then her father awoke, and Susana left Prince and his cage in Ruy's charge and went up the hill above the rocks. From the top, as she had thought, she could see Gibraltar. It was much closer now, and seen in a gap between the lacing tops of the trees, its head again crowned with cloud, it seemed to be staring back at her, and whispering, 'Come. Why are you so slow?'

They waited all that night, and the next day ... She asked her father who the Count of Grazalema was. 'A nobleman,' he said. 'Very rich. Very conservative. He served a few years in the cavalry as a young man. He and I would have nothing in common – though his estates surround us – but that we were on that accursed public meeting together to protest the British occupation of Gibraltar ... Intellectuals, military, land owners, church, merchants. I sat next to him on the dais, and spoke for the legal profession.'

'Who are the Falange, papa?'

'A political party, child – very much opposed to mine.'

She looked at David, dozing now a few feet from them, and said, 'Is David going to die, papa?' Her father sank his head between his hands and began to sob, silently, and she knew it would be no use trying to comfort him.

They waited all that night. Before dawn David began to talk, and when the light came she saw that his skin was dull grey, and his lips blue. Soon, he died. Her father knelt

398

and began to say a prayer in Hebrew, but Susana slipped away and hurried up the hill to see the Rock again, so that they would know which way to go when they moved on. The cloud had gone and the face shimmered pale grey towards her. 'I'm coming,' she whispered; and then she saw the soldiers, a line of about twenty of them coming round the base of the hill on the side farthest from the Rock. She ran quickly down the hill, bounding from rock to rock under the boughs. A bullet cracked over her head, and she saw her father and brother run out of the rock shelter where David had died.

'They're coming!' she screamed. 'Soldiers!' She reached them, scooped up the bird cage, and started to run back up the hill. Her father said, 'Stop, Susana. It's no use.'

She saw that he and Ruy had raised their hands, and the soldiers were coming. It was the same ones from the bridge, in the ordinary clothes, with the Count of Grazalema in the middle.

'If you have arms, lay them down,' the Count said.

'We have none,' her father said.

'Shoot the whole brood now, and have done with it,' a man muttered, glaring at her with a bloodshot eye.

'None of that, now!' the Count's voice was sharp – 'That's the way the Reds behave. That's what we're trying to wipe out in Spain ... Can you walk, Señor Toledano? You must come along with us, then.'

'Why?' her father burst out. 'By what right? In whose name are you acting? For what government?'

'For the soul of Spain,' the Count said. 'This is a rising of the old spirit, Señor Toledano. We have tolerated the filth of the Republic long enough ... Besides, your son killed my sergeant. He is – was – a prominent wine merchant of Algeciras.'

'He was going to murder me in cold blood,' her father said.

The Count said, 'Come, please. It is no use talking here. A court martial in Algeciras will see that justice is done to you.'

They started back through the cork woods then, the Count in front, then some soldiers, and then her father, Ruy, and herself, followed by more soldiers with bayonets fixed on their rifles. At the bridge there was an old motor bus, very small and battered, and more soldiers cooking food. Susana's mouth watered, and when a soldier gave her a plate of beans she ate greedily, but Prince would not touch them. He looked tired and small, and she said, to cheer him up, 'It won't be long now, Prince'; but she did not think the soldiers would take them to Gibraltar, or let them go there. She heard her father saying, 'My son, Count . . .?'

'Buried,' the Count said, 'under that tree. I am sorry. I will send men to bury the other, too, as soon as . . . Soon.'

'And our mother,' Susana said. 'She is dead in a quarry.'

The Count shook his head. 'Terrible . . . I will speak to them in Algeciras about you, Señor Toledano. My word may carry some weight, although . . .' he shook his head again. 'When the men hear what is being done in Madrid, all over Spain, it is hard to hold them. And we have had five years of this, this . . . rape, arson, murder, anarchy. If you will get into the bus now.'

They got into the bus. By the time her father and Ruy had got into the back, with half a dozen soldiers to guard them, and a few more who wanted to go to San Roque, Susana had to sit in front with the Count beside the driver.

After several swings the engine started, the driver jumped in, and they bumped off down the road, southwards. The railway line was on the left, cork woods beyond it, and a river close to the right. After a few minutes they turned a corner and there was Gibraltar straight in front, seeming to rise up out of the woods.

At another corner, the driver slammed on the brakes, and lurching forward Susana saw a tree across the road. She saw men, too, and before the bullets came knew what was going to happen. The bullets came in a wild crackle, glass shattered all round her, and the driver began to cough blood over the steering wheel. The bus ran into the tree and stopped with a crash. 'Out!' the Count cried, trying to clamber over her. She reached up her hand, took his little automatic pistol out of its holster, pressed the muzzle into his side, and pulled the trigger. The door swung open and he fell out, head first. He was looking towards the wood where men were coming, running. Then he saw Susana, the automatic in her hand and a wisp of smoke still curling from the muzzle. 'Spain!' he gasped. 'Oh, my God. My poor country.'

A short, square grizzled man wearing peasants' grey cotton, rope-soled shoes and a black cummerbund was standing over her, a rifle in his hand. 'Shall I finish this one off?' another asked, pointing at the Count.

'Don't waste a bullet on him,' the square man said. 'This little beanpole of a Pasionaria did his business. Get rid of the rest and set fire to the bus.'

'My father and brother are in the back,' she cried, 'Prisoners. That one's my father.' She pointed. 'Where's Ruy, papa?'

'Killed,' he said. 'Killed in the first burst.'

'I'm sorry,' the square man said gruffly. 'We didn't know there were any of ours with them. No more though?'

He waved a hand. His followers raised rifle and revolvers, and began to fire. In a moment six of the militiamen lay sprawled in the road, amid pools of blood. Two more, and Ruy, were dead in the bus.

The bus began to burn. 'I'm Manuel Susarte, once a shepherd, till I saw the light,' the square man said. 'Now I'm an Anarchist. I have three brothers. One's a Communist, one's a sergeant in Africa, and one's a priest. Can't be more Spanish than that, can you?' He laughed bitterly. 'Time to be going. They will have heard the shooting. Do you want to come with us? Though it's a hard life, and we'll have to farm out the little girl with some of our people. And it may go on a long time.' Thick clouds of oily acrid smoke enveloped them.

'We're going to the Rock,' Susanna said, pointing. 'Papa, and Prince and I.'

'Oh, you are,' Susarte said. 'Well, maybe that'd be best, if you can just get over the border. Or swim.' He pointed down the road – 'San Roque railway station's about two miles down – you know it? San Roque's on the hill above, a mile or more back. If I were you, I'd keep between the two, work down to La Linea, and try to steal a boat. Or get to the British wire in some sort of disturbance.' He raised a hand – *'Que siguen bien!'* and soon disappeared into the cork woods, his ragged band on his heels.

Her father looked at her, and the distorted corpses, and the wide-eyed Count. 'He was right,' he said. 'Poor Spain. Come, child, or they will find us here.'

They moved off in the direction indicated by Susarte. Half an hour later they saw soldiers marching along the road towards the scene of the ambush, and crouched in a thicket until they had passed. Then, walking on again together, they breasted a hill, and the woods ended. Before them lay the white houses of San Roque – and beyond, a narrow neck of land; and at the end of it, the Rock. They sat down side by side and stared. She saw a row of black holes high in the face of the Rock, and thought they must be windows of the inner castle. The palace clustered at the foot of the slope, washed by the sea. Her father interrupted her – 'That town close under the Rock, on our side, is La Linea. It will be full of soldiers. But do you see on the right where the river flows into the bay? There was a famous city there before anyone lived in Gibraltar. Now there are a few fishermen's huts. We shall go there, and buy or steal a boat. God knows what we will do when we get to Gibraltar. The only man I know is a jeweller called Conquy. I met him at a Freemasons' meeting in Algeciras a few years ago.'

'Shall we start now, papa?' He shook his head. 'Not until dark, Susana. It is . . .' A crackle of gunfire interrupted him. It seemed to be coming from San Roque, barely half a mile away.

'Look!' Susana pointed. Bands of men and women, some with firearms, some with billhooks and kitchen knives, were running across the heath from the left, towards San Roque. The firing increased, and a few bullets smacked over their heads.

'Those aren't soldiers, or Falangists,' her father muttered. 'They must be peasants, workers . . . they're attacking San Roque.'

Susana grabbed the bird cage, and stood up. 'Come then, papa! To the boats! That's what Señor Susarte said we should do.'

'Get to the British wire in some sort of disturbance,' her father said. 'Very well . . . You're braver than I am, Susana.'

He struggled to his feet, and they started diagonally down the slope, leaving San Roque, on their left.

Gradually, very slowly, the white town swung past, from in front, to the side, to behind. They saw soldiers at a distance, but running away from San Roque; and others, further on, walking towards it. They saw big guns, at a distance, and two dead men, close to. Women passed, carrying babies, hurrying aimlessly. All the time the rattle of firing sounded from the town irregularly – long periods of silence shattered by a few minutes of frenzy.

They came to a wide river – 'The Guadarranque,' her father muttered, and walked down the bank towards a clump of tall trees that sheltered half a dozen houses. They reached the trees in the middle of the afternoon, and her father knocked on the door of the first house. No one answered, and when he tried the door, it opened. They went in, and he said, 'We'll rest here till dark, Susana.' There was water in the jug, and half a ham hanging in the kitchen, and Prince ate better than he had for two days. She stroked his head with her finger through the bars, and said, 'Look, Prince, out of the window. There's your castle!' Then she curled up on the bed in another room, and went to sleep.

Her father was shaking her, and it was dark. 'We have a boat,' he said. 'I wanted to buy it, but the man said "What good is money now – take it." Are you ready?'

She felt a real excitement for the first time, and as she slipped down a narrow, dusty lane with him her heart pounded so loudly she could hear nothing else. There was the boat, under a tree on the sandy bank, where the river flowed into the sea. They pulled it out, and her father went away and came back with oars, then they launched it, and he started to row, while she sat in the back, looking towards Gibraltar. Prince's cage on the floorboards between her feet.

It was a dark night, and the pyramid of lights in the

Red Prince's castle and palace shone more brightly from the blackness of the land – not a light in San Roque behind or La Linea beside, or Algeciras to the right. The water made small, oily lapping sounds and even in the darkness some sparkle of light fell from the ends of the oars when her father pulled them out of the water.

Her feet began to get cold, and she put her hand down to them and found it wet. 'There's water in the boat, papa,' she said.

'Bail with your hands,' he gasped. 'We're half way.' He began to row harder, the oars creaking ever faster in the oarlocks. Susana put Prince's cage on the seat beside her, and knelt and began to scoop the water over the side as fast as she could. The magic city towered ever closer and she thought she heard the Red Prince's bands playing in it, but the water kept rising, and the boat went slower, and her father's groaning, frantic efforts became slower. Suddenly, they stopped, his head hit her knee as he fell forward. He was ill, and could not speak. A bright light bathed them, and she saw that the water was only two inches from the top of the sides. She scrambled over her father, pushed his body aside, and took the oars. A motor chugged close as she began to row. Then the sea was flooding in, and men were shouting in a foreign language. She leaped for the bird cage, and seized it, just as a strong arm pulled her out of the boat, and it vanished, with her father, under the black water, the oars floating free on the surface.

The motor boat went slowly round and round, its searchlight weaving back and forth over the water. Then someone gave an order and it turned towards the lights and increased speed. The tall, grizzled blue-uniformed old man with the big hands who had pulled her out of the boat said, in poor but understandable Spanish, 'Was that your

405

father?' She nodded. 'I'm afraid he's drowned.'

She nodded again. Her father had fallen forward before the boat sank. He was very tired, and had to row so hard. The lights were very close. Soon she would step ashore, with Prince, on to the enchanted land. To the old man in blue she said, 'Conquy?'

He said in surprise, 'Me? No. My name's Tamlyn, little miss – Dockyard Police, on special patrol, and lucky for you we are. But I know Conquy, same Lodge as me. He'll see you're looked after.'

Neutral Zone

Runway

North Mole

Forbes Quarry

North Front

Rock Gun

Waterworks Tunnel

Harbour

Detached Mole

Devil's Gap

Catalan Bay

New Dockyard

Main Water Catchment

South Mole

Admiralty Tunnel

Fuel Tanks

Windmill Hill Flats

||||| Cliffs

Built-up areas

Europa Flats

Europa Point and Light House

¼ 0   ½   1 Mile

Scale

Book Twelve

BETWEEN WARS

The Jewish years 5696–5700
A.U.C. 2689–2693
A.D. 1936–1940
A.H. 1355–1359

THE fighting which enabled Susana Toledano and her father to slip past San Roque took place on 27th July, 1936, when a Republican column 3,000 strong arrived from Malaga and retook the town. Troops from Algeciras and La Linea, who had joined the rebellion, soon drove them out, and the Campo de Gibraltar remained under the rebels' control until the end of the war.

Gibraltar saw many refugees those early days. Many more tried to get in than it could hold, or than was safe for its security. Throughout the war it was also used as a handing-over point for prisoners condemned to death by one side or the other, and here exchanged instead. It saw a little action, too, since the Republicans held control of the sea until near the end. Republican destroyers harried a rebel troop convoy all the way across the strait from Ceuta to Algeciras on 5th August, 1936, and next day the battle-ship *Jaime I* and the cruisers *Libertad* and *Miguel de Cervantes* bombarded Algeciras. Towards the end of 1938 the heavily damaged Republican destroyer *Jose Luis Diez* limped into Gibraltar for repair. She crept out on the night of 30th/31st December, hoping to evade the rebel ships waiting for her; but someone 'accidentally' fired a rocket from Gibraltar and she was attacked round the back of the Rock and driven ashore at Catalan Bay. The British later refloated her and interned her till the end of the war.

Most of the rest of the world had signed a pact of non-intervention in regard to this war, but the pact was observed only by the democracies, which alone had the

power to save the Republic from its internal and external enemies. The pact was ignored by Hitler, who wanted to test war theories and also attach an ally; by Mussolini, for the same reasons plus a wish to humiliate the British, who had organized sanctions against him for his Abyssinian aggression of the year before; and by Stalin, who wanted to ensure that the Republic should not be democratic or anarchist but Russian-Communist. These helping hands strangled Spain, slowly, until on 1st April, 1939, General-issimo Franco who had early succeeded Generals Mola and Sanjurjo (both killed in air crashes) as the head of the rising, was able to announce that the war was over.

The new Nationalist Spain was a country bankrupt, split, and shattered. It had suffered more casualties, pro-portionately, than England was to suffer in the coming Hitler's War, or than the U.S.A. had in its own Civil War; and incomparably more material damage. It needed enormous foreign aid, capital investment, and above all peace. . . .

Hitler armed, planned, and manoeuvred with fero-cious efficiency. France of the Third Republic staggered from one political crisis or scandal to the next. England dithered. The United States looked the other way.

The inhabitants of Gibraltar were in for a rough time . . . but let us pause, now; and examine apes. Later, we shall not have time.

As we have seen, these beasts must have been imported into Gibraltar by the Moors. I do not know when the legend arose that the British would leave Gibraltar when the rock apes did, but it sounds to me like a not-so-subtle Spanish joke. From the beginning of this century the huge new dockyard, increasing population, urbanization, and mechanization all worked to restrict the areas where they could live and to reduce the plants on which they fed.

Their numbers fell drastically until in 1924 only four apes could be found on the whole of Gibraltar. These had taken to raiding down into the town, fouling roofs (always used to collect drinking water), and stealing vegetables from barrows and back yards. The year before – whether moved by concern for the apes or for the people, I do not know – the Secretary of State for the Colonies applied for permission to have the remaining apes transported back to Africa. This was refused on account of the legend, and more attention was paid to the preservation of the surviving animals.

The 'Head Keeper' was the artillery general in Gibraltar who appointed one of his officers as Officer in charge of Rock Apes. A Master Gunner was appointed to see that they had enough to eat, supplementing their natural food with scraps and left-overs begged from military kitchens and civilian institutions. At last, the Colonial Office was persuaded to make an allowance for their care and feeding. The Master Gunner's post became that of cageman-cum-storeman. The 'cage' part of the title came in because by then covered cages had been built to provide shelter for the apes, who now consisted of two mutually hostile packs, one at Queen's Gate and one at Middle Hill.

When Winston Churchill began to take a personal interest in the apes, during Hitler's War, the numbers were again very low. By 1943 there were only seven, even after imports from North Africa. Gradually, with the devoted attention of the famous cagemen Gunner Portlock and his successors, the numbers increased. Now the apes have assumed an importance which makes a look at the *Ape* files like a glimpse into the mind of Edward Lear. . . .

(Telegram from the Secretary of State for the Colonies to the Governor of Gibraltar, 3rd February, 1951):

*Parliamentary question, APES: Following is text of ques-
tion down for oral reply 7th February: To ask S of S for
the C if he is satisfied that subsistence allowance of 4d a
day paid out of civil funds for maintenance each Barbary
ape at Gibraltar is still sufficient; when amount was fixed
at 4d; and to what extent the ape population has increased or decreased since the end of the war. . . .*

And in May 1953, after the Queen made Winston
Churchill a Knight of the Garter:

*After careful consideration the Commander Royal Artil-
lery has decided not to authorize a change in the name of
the ape 'Winston', Winston Churchill himself is still called
Winston, even though now knighted.*

About this time, with the population in the low thirties,
apes were offered to zoos all over the world, with free
transportation by Royal or United States Navy, although
a monkey expert thought that to keep the pack going
needed a strength of about 100. The reason for this apparently reckless generosity was that the Gibraltar civil
government, which had taken over financial responsibility
for the apes, announced that it would not pay the subsidy
of 4d a day for more than thirty apes.

The humourless Hitler, caring not a fig for the havoc he
would cause in the files and among the apes and their
keepers, invaded Poland on 31st August, 1939. At this
point Neville Chamberlain became suspicious of his inten-
tions, and preparations were hurriedly made to teach the
bounder a lesson. Gibraltar's days of leisure, hunting, and
upper-class dalliance were over, for ever, and Pablo
Larios had died with them.

Nothing much was done until the fall of France in June

1940. Then, with a thunderstroke of astonishment, Whitehall realized that only Spain lay between Hitler's armies and the Rock; and Spain's ruler in part owed his position to Hitler's help.

Between July and November, 1940, all male civilians except about 4,000 engaged in vital work, and all females, to the total number of 16,700 were evacuated. To be more precise, they were evacuated twice, first to Tangier and French Morocco, whence they soon had to return owing to the hostility of the Spanish and Vichy French governments installed there; and then re-evacuated to Britain, Jamaica, and Madeira. Those who went Home found it less homelike than it had seemed from the Rock; the Jamaican climate and landscape, which some have thought idyllic, were too lush and tropical for the Gibraltarians; only those who went to Madeira found anything to rejoice over – as much as anyone can rejoice uprooted from home and/or separated from husband, lover, family. The only women in Gibraltar were nurses, a few in the services, and the señoritas who still came every day to work from Spain; and could sometimes, by a well worded offer to carry their bag, be persuaded to spend the night in the fortress.

The civil population had been about 20,000. Britain now put in that number of troops. And the troops laid barbed wire and sandbags, and installed guns, mortars, machine guns: and above all, under all, they dug, like fear-crazed moles. Under the personal omnipresent drive of the Governor, Field Marshal Lord Gort, V.C. (recently defeated at Dunkirk) the engineers tunnelled and bored. Rock began to be thrown out, by thousands of tons. At first all the excavated stone went to make a runway, for when Hitler defeated France it was considered that even the racecourse would have to be sacrificed for the making of an all-weather airfield, large enough to take modern fighters. While this runway crept out westward into the bay from under the North Face (the Spanish protesting all the time that Gibraltar had no territorial waters and no right to build out from the isthmus) the tunnellers hammered and blasted and gouged deeper into the bowels of the Rock. . . .

INSIDE

1941

'Who are you?'

The man addressed started out of his study of the sheet metal ventilation ducting running along the side wall of the tunnel. It was a good question. What should he answer? . . . The late assistant manager of Coggershall Colliery Yorks? Samuel Chaddock, B.Sc. (Notts)? The only son of Joseph Chaddock (née Crapp) Esq., and of Mrs. Margaret Chaddock (née Akers-Carr), of Darley Court, near Pewsey, Wiltshire?

'Well, speak up, man.'

He stared at the speaker – a tall thin brigadier in well cut khaki battledress, a row and a half of ribbons, and a thin, greyish moustache. Chaddock's company commander was at the brigadier's elbow, and now cut in, frowning – 'This is Captain Chaddock, sir, my new second-in-command.'

The brigadier stuck out his hand. 'I'm Hamilton, Chief Engineer. Sorry I couldn't see you when you arrived. I was laid up with gippie tummy . . . What were you looking at?'

Chaddock said, 'The metal ducting. It's full of leaks, and it's very difficult to take down and put up for blasting. I was wondering whether rubberized canvas could be used.'

'Put in for some. Try it out. In your own time, of course. Make a report. In quadruplicate,' the brigadier said. They were walking fast along the tunnel now, the brigadier in the middle, Chaddock on one side, Major Hughes, commander of 177 Tunnelling Company, Royal Engineers, on the other. The racket of drilling increased. The brigadier shouted, 'Remember, that's for development heads only. We have natural ventilation in the main shafts . . . What are you? Coal?'

Chaddock nodded. 'Yorkshire.'

'This is quite different. Hard rock. Tunnelling, not mining. I keep asking for more hard-rock men. Quarry men. University?'

'B.Sc., Nottingham School of Mines, sir.'

The brigadier glanced at him curiously and yelled, 'School?'

Chaddock tensed. Why the hell couldn't a man who wanted to get out of some place he'd been put in be allowed to move without being pestered, reminded, firmly slammed back? 'Eton,' he said, 'and King's. I have a B.A. of a sort, too.'

'Thought so,' the brigadier shouted. 'Well, I won't hold it against you as long as you get your yards in. Four hundred and forty cubic yards per platoon per week.'

They were close behind the men drilling charge holes in the face now. The nearest drill coughed to a momentary

416

stop as the colonel shouted again 'Four hundred and forty yards!'

The man at the drill bellowed in a powerful Geordie accent 'Ah fucking know it's four hundred and and forty fucking yards, but we have to do it one fucking yard at a time!' He turned his head and saw the red tabs – 'Ma Goad!'

Major Hughes said, 'Sergeant, take that man's name.'

The brigardier waved his hand. 'No, no. What's a few kind words between miners. Keep that bloody thing going sapper, so we can't hear what you want to say next.'

They edged back from the clamorous work face, and walked back down the twin sets of rails to a row of waiting empty tubs. The noise faded. The brigadier said, 'You've come in at the beginning of a great game, Chaddock. Before this war began there were less than four miles of tunnel in the whole Rock. We plan to put in over twenty. We're going to make the Rock absolutely, finally, totally impregnable, to any assault, no matter how great the fire power. The Royal Engineers' motto is *Ubique*, 'everywhere', as you know. Well, here in the Tunnels we have a little extra motto. *Four hundred and forty or . . .*' He jerked his thumb. 'Off to the infantry you go.' He indicated the row of men sitting along the tunnel wall. '4th Black Watch, acting as muckers, to save our chaps for the technical jobs. We're getting some Eimco-Finlay loaders soon, though.' He slapped his swagger stick into his hand for emphasis. 'You've got to get the feel of this rock, Chaddock. This limestone is not like coal. It's hard as hell, but it's absolutely honest. No deception. No tricks. It'll give you fair warning, and then if you ignore it – wham! You've got to break it, but you've got to respect it . . . love it, *I* think.'

He strode away, tapping his leg with the swagger stick. When he was fifty feet away Hughes brought his hand down from the salute. 'You are supposed to salute, too, Chaddock,' he said. 'I know,' Chaddock said. 'I was thinking of something else.'

'It's better to concentrate on the work in hand,' the major said, 'and safer, too.'

'Yes, sir,' Chaddock answered formally. Hughes was Welsh, a colliery manager in peace time, careful, anxious to please owners or seniors. He said, 'By the way, Tunnelling H.Q. Mess is inviting all the army nurses to drinks tomorrow.' He nodded, and hurried off.

Chaddock began to walk back towards the face. The drills were making a lot of dust, yet they were drilling dry. Limestone was much safer than silicas, but he must find out whether X-rays were being taken, and how often. Surely they could wet-drill here, using sea water? Safety was poor all round. No one wore miner's helmets except the drillers. The infantry muckers didn't even wear their steel helmets.

The section sergeant fell in beside him, and he remembered the name – 'Gaffer' Farley, small, 50-ish, a coalmine foreman in peace. Chaddock started asking questions . . . were they using hole directors for the easers? What about the dry drilling? The helmets? How much air was reaching the face? What was the maximum capacity of the pump? How about exhaustion of fumes? The little sergeant answered patiently in an accent Chaddock could barely understand.

The blast master came and asked permission to blow the round. Chaddock walked back behind the safety line, his brow furrowed. 'Four hundred and forty cubic yards a week is a lot, sergeant,' he said. 'There's no allowance there for little errors. Corners are being cut, safety precautions are not being observed, in order to reach that figure, whereas we ought to be tightening up, and . . .'

The sergeant said, 'It's not easy, sir, but . . . Look, the army's a game, see, and it's best just to play the bloody game. It's not like trying to earn a living in Dipton in the depression. That's serious, see.'

Chaddock said, 'We've got to win the war, sergeant.'

'Aye, we will, but it'll be a long tram. For drills we're using these 25-pound jackhammers that the oldest colliery in County Durham would 'a thrown out twenty years back. Half a dozen portable 100-cubic foot compressors, that sound like my Aunt Jane dying of the pneumony. Then the bloody Eyeties drop a bomb slap on the R.E. stores depot and bang goes half our steels, cable, pulleys, clamps . . . You have to take it easy, captain, or they'll carry you out in a strait jacket.'

The sharp regular cracks of the exploding round echoed down the shaft.

In the saloon bar of the Star and Garter, the Flight Sergeant had a large audience of army corporals and sergeants. His R.A.F. Harrow-and-Stepney accent filled the room. 'This Jewish fellow goes to the magistrate and says he wants to have his name changed see. The beak fixes him up and out he goes, Clarence Fauntleroy, Esquire, instead of Joe Levy. A couple of months later, back he comes, and says he wants to change his name to Thompson. The beak scratches his head and says, aren't you the chap was in here a few weeks ago, changing his name to Fauntleroy? Don't you know who you are? Yes, your honner, the Jew says. Then why do you want to change your name again? And the Jew answers, Vell your honner, ven someone asks my name I say Thompson, and they vill look at me and my nose – he has a real Jewish

419

conk, see – and they vill say Ah, but vat was your name *before* it was Thompson, and I shall say, Fauntleroy!'

The soldiers laughed, the Ape Corporal frowned. Mr. Wardrop and old Sergeant Tamlyn stared into their glasses without expression. Chaddock took a draught from his glass. It was a filthy hot muggy Levanter day and the beer was heavy and livery, but that was what they had at the Star & Garter, and that's what you had to drink.

A naval petty officer said, 'And now we're fighting for the Jews.'

Joe Morello behind the bar spoke, half-aside, to the Ape Corporal – 'They not fighting for Gibraltar, *claro*. Sometimes before war, *sometimes*, maybe they ask us what we want, ask whether they can take this, blow down that. Not now. Just take. War on, they say. And no bloody civilian allowed into a service concert. They think we don't need amusement, too?' He murmured a Spanish obscenity.

Mr. Wardrop said, 'You scorpions would be on a better wicket about the service concerts if you'd ever raised a finger for the redcoats in the old days. You kept 'em out of *your* dances and bunfights, didn't you?'

The petty officer said, 'I'm not fighting for no fucking Jews, I tell you straight. I'm fighting for fucking England.'

Mr. Wardrop raised his gin glass. 'That's what I like to hear – patriotism. Talking of which, listen to this. This'll bring a lump to your throat, friends. Silence, for Mr. Disney-Roebuck's poem, which many connoisseurs consider the worst ever written:

> *Watchful and silent, wakeful and stern*
> *Frowns the great fortress . . .*
> *High o'er the sea in the midst of the Rock*

Grey guns point threateningly over the bay
Keen eyes peer into the fringe of the night
Gunners are patiently awaiting the day

'What the hell is this?' the petty officer muttered.

'Poem,' Joe behind the bar said. 'Mr. Wardrop often speak it. It's about when Devil's Gap battery fired at a German submarine, 1917 or 1918, about then.'

'Did they sink it?'

Mr. Wardrop paused in his declamation and said, 'No. But they did at least try to, which is more than the navy did when the French fleet passed through the straits in '40.'

The petty officer sprang to his feet. 'Now, look 'ere . . .'

But Mr. Wardrop was off again:

Governor's Lookout with a shattering roar
Hurls its vast projectiles into the black:
Shrieking they rush on their way overhead
Woe to the target they meet in their track.

'Sit down, chief,' Joe said, 'Mr. Wardrop don't mean any harm. He not sure what he say this time morning.'

Morning, Chaddock thought. What morning? How could anyone tell? He must be on the first shift, then.

'We're the only people doing any fighting now,' the petty officers said belligerently. 'Us, and the R.A.F.'

'It's going badly at sea,' Flight said, shaking his head. 'The shipping losses are much worse than we're being told, you mark my words.'

'It's going badly everywhere,' Mr. Wardrop intoned, speaking with the unnatural precision of the permanently drunk – 'On land, on sea, and in the air, we are being thoroughly defeated . . . You were arguing just now about

421

this war being fought for the Jews. Well, Corporal Pember here will tell you that's a damned lie. The war is being fought for the apes.'

'You will have your little joke,' the corporal said sullenly, 'But everyone in the world knows about the prophecy, now, and still the fucking civilians complain about them. There's this fellow . . .'

'Some fucking civilians think they have more rights than fucking monkeys,' Joe the owner muttered.

The Ape Corporal swept on: '. . . Pasarelli on Lopez's Ramp. An ape on his roof, he reports, and will we get it off because it's making messes on the roof where he collects his drinking water. So I go. To see on the roof they has to open a trap door and I stand on a toilet. The ape's there, it's Tony, one of the young males who's been kept off the females by Monty . . .'

'Don't talk to me about females,' Flight groaned. 'How many are there on this bloody Rock, not counting the señoritas? Twenty-seven, to twenty thousand men. All nurses, all look like the north end of a tram going south, and all bloody military. And even with that, every time I see one I get a hard on you could hang your hat on.'

Joe said, 'Our women all sent away 1940 – two years. You go back England this year, next year. Not us.'

'So Pasarelli claims I broke his toilet bowl with my hobnail boots, but I was wearing P.T. shoes, see?'

'Wouldn't matter what Pasarelli say,' Joe said. 'He only bloody Gibraltarian.'

'Rock scorpion,' Mr. Wardrop said. 'Great name. Be proud of it. Sting!'

The petty officer said, 'You bloody Brylcreem boys don't have much to boast about, come to that. The Jerries are dropping bombs on England just where they fucking like, and . . .'

'. . . So the Governor replies, no, in principle he has no objection to the next male apelet which is born to be called Anthony, after Anthony Eden. But the C.R.A. says . . .'

1942

'. . . never saw so many ruddy aeroplanes in one place in all my bleeding life. The ruddy airfield's full of them. You couldn't fit another in with a shoehorn.' The infantry sergeant drank thirstily.

'You're not supposed to see them,' Flight said brushing up his gingerish R.A.F. moustache.

'I'd have to be blind man! My platoon's on the Upper Galleries, and we're looking straight down on them. They've been flying off all day today.'

'No Spanish labourers in town. First time that happen, ever.'

'What! No señoritas, either? Christ, I've been saving up for a month to carry a bag tonight! Christ, I was going to fill one of them señoritas up to the ruddy brim tonight!'

'It's the invasion of North Africa,' Mr. Wardrop said.

'Here, here, *cuidado*,' Joe said, pointing to a sign tacked up behind the bar; *Loose talk costs lives*.

The Ape Corporal said, 'I knew it was coming. Had a Yank general up day before yesterday to inspect the apes. Didn't look too much different from one himself, if you ask me.'

Chaddock drank up. The first ten minutes every day in the Star and Garter were like a foreign holiday, a breath of fresh air, a dramatic change from the harsh tunnel and his barren quarters. But soon a sense of unease would begin to possess him, and then it was time to drink up and get out. Whatever it was they talked or fought about here was unreal; the people themselves were unreal ... they didn't exist, and being among them made him wonder whether he did. Only rock was real. He lit another cigarette, paid and went out. He was smoking too much. God, how long, how long?

Inside the Rock he tramped along the drive under the lights. Gradually the pub and its sounds faded into dream. A little diesel loco puttered past on its way to the spoil box with half a dozen tubs. Lieutenant Glass passed on his way out. 'We made eight feet on the shift,' he said triumphantly.

Major Hughes was watching the shifts hand over at the face. He came back to Chaddock, and said, 'Glass's lot made eight feet.'

'I know,' Chaddock said curtly. 'He just told me.'

Hughes said, 'You've got to increase your yardage overall, Chaddock. Tunnelling H.Q.'s on my back all the time. We've given you the loaders, and the yardage ought to go up fifty per cent, but you're only up twenty-three per cent.'

Chaddock's head ached, and he wanted to shout in the other's face, but he controlled himself and said, 'I'll improve the figures.'

'For all our sakes,' Hughes said, a little more gently. 'The C.E.'s biting Tunnelling H.Q., and the Governor's biting the C.E., and Winston's probably biting the Governor. You're just the chap at the bottom of the pile.'

He left and Chaddock went to look at the men working on development head No. 42, Black Watch Raise. What the hell could he do to increase the yardage? ... Train the men to work the new loaders more efficiently. Keep the drills sharper. Place and fire the charges more quickly.

424

Hughes had said he was at the bottom of the pile, but he wasn't – that man there was, the man with the drill at the face, the mucker, the loco driver . . . Those diesels cleaned their own exhausts of everything except carbon monoxide. That was O.K. for the face men as long as the ventilation, natural or artificial, was working well; but for the loco drivers, sitting right behind the exhaust, it must be different. And the ventilation *wasn't* working well, especially in the development heads. The metal ducts were not doing the job, and how the hell could man or machine work without air? At 300 feet from the air pump, rubberized canvas increased ventilation by 400 per cent. Quite apart from that, it could be taken down before blasting, and put together again afterwards, in a quarter the time of metal. How long since he had put all this in his report? Four months, three months? And still no canvas ducting.

'You look as though you just swallowed a dose of paregoric, captain.'

Sergeant Farley's face was dim under the helmet lamp. 'We had two men go to hospital yesterday,' Chaddock said, 'and the medical report says bronchitis for both of them.'

The sergeant said, 'It's just a chill on their chests.'

'Are you sure the doctors aren't lying?'

'Captain, what are you saying?'

'I'm saying they're so bloody keen to win their bloody K.C.B.'s that they may have told any doctor who finds a trace of silicosis in our men to say it's something else, so they won't have to start wet-drilling.'

The sergeant chuckled. 'Ee, that's a booger of a notion! . . . Praps ye'd better be taking a holiday, sir.'

Chaddock said, 'We've got to increase our yardage, sergeant. Come to my office after shift.' He walked back to the main drive. Some rails needed replacing before a loco got derailed. The concrete floor of the spoil box was getting damaged. It ought to be relaid before the rails came loose and caught a tub load, or they'd have hell's own job freeing it.

At the end of the drive he turned left, strode into the company offices, knocked on Major Hughes' door and walked in without waiting. 'When are we going to get the Meco rubberized ducting?' he snapped.

Major Hughes looked up frowning from a pile of papers on his table. He took off his glasses and his Welsh accent was strong. 'When we are sent it from U.K.' he said. 'And, Chaddock, it is customary to call your company commander "sir".'

'Fuck that,' Chaddock said. 'The C.E. told me to investigate the rubber ducting. I did. You saw my report. You saw the Tunnelling H.Q.'s forwarding letter, saying we must have the Meco at once. Why haven't we got it?'

'Because there isn't any for us, yet,' Hughes said. 'We have been allotted a priority below . . .'

'Below what, for Christ's sake? Are they tunnelling in the desert? . . . Another thing, here we are trying to improve our yardage a few per cent by cutting safety corners, fiddling about with old-fashioned methods. Is anyone investigating what we could do with diamond drill techniques?'

'That's only suitable for blasting big chambers.'

'That's what is said now, because that's what the Canadians did. But who knows what the limitations are? Who's been working to find out? Give me a diamond drill team and I'll . . .'

Hughes stood up. 'Look you, Chaddock, I have work to do, and I bloody know you have too. When you have done your own work, it is time to think about taking on other responsibilities, eh? Now get back . . .' He peered more closely at Chaddock. 'Look, man, I'm sorry. We are all tired. I have bad news, you know. My wife . . . well, that's war, too.'

'I'm sorry,' Chaddock muttered, because it was a reflex response to the other's tone. He had no idea what Hughes was talking about.

'Why don't you take a couple of days off? Sit on the beach behind the barbed wire, eh? Have your batman bring you tea in bed. Go along now.'

Joan was waiting for him when he arrived at the door of the nurses' quarters. It was a levanter day, sun shining everywhere but on Gibraltar. She was in Q.A. uniform, and examined him critically – 'You look tired. Are you suffering from night starvation?' She giggled and said, 'All you men are, really, aren't you?'

He tried to smile, but couldn't manage it. Her energy sometimes wearied him. They met soon after he arrived in Gibraltar, and something had clicked between them at once. Two or three times they had even managed to make love in the dark on the hillside, but it was not important for either of them, and Chaddock sometimes wondered why.

She rested her hand on his sleeve and then took it away. 'Oh dear, officers mustn't walk hand in hand, must they?'

'You look a little down yourself,' he said.

Her mouth tightened to the professional calm, cool feeling. 'Oh, we had some merchant seamen brought in,' she said, 'rather badly burned. There was no room for them in the naval hospital . . . It was quite exhausting and several of us were on extra shifts . . .'

427

He had heard a badly burned man once, for two days, and said, 'I don't know how you can . . .'

She interrupted brightly, 'Isn't Lower St. Michael's Cave marvellous?' They fell into step together and started down the road to Europa Point. She was tall, well made, and blonde, rather like his mother. 'The sapper officer who took us in said there are hundreds of caves on Gibraltar.'

He said, 'There must be. It's all Jurassic limestone, and there are a few minor faults, but nothing we can't get through, except one in there – 'he nodded at Windmill Hill '—where we've run into trouble, but . . .'

She said, 'Now don't talk shop, Sam. Look at the flowers. Look at that funny little cucumber.' She stooped to pick up a furry green cucumber three inches long. It leaped into the air with a sharp pop, and she jumped back with a gasp. A blob of creamy white liquid lay in her palm. She blushed and wiped it on the grass. 'Goodness, that gave me a turn. What is it?'

'I have no idea,' Sam said.

They walked on round the level Europa flat. 'Well,' she said, pointing, '*that*'s an autumn crocus. You know, if you dry those stamens, that's saffron.'

He smiled, more easily now. She smelled of soap and water, not very feminine, but at any rate different from miner's sweat and limestone dust and gelignite fumes. She was about thirty, and definitely in the marriage market. If he married her she'd be Mrs. Chaddock. Or should it be Mrs. Crapp? Perhaps she'd mind that as much as his mother had. He frowned, remembering the Flight Sergeant's story in the pub. Could his father have changed his name twice?

Joan said, 'You're not listening. You're always day-dreaming, Sam. What is it now?'

He said, 'I was wondering who I am.'

'What? ... Are you feeling all right, Sam?'

'My father changed his name right after he came to England from South Africa. Mother says she refused to marry him unless he did, but I think he may have done something disreputable in South Africa.'

'What was his name before?' she asked, suddenly suspicious.

He said, 'It took me ages before he'd tell me — Crapp.'

She laughed, obviously relieved. 'I thought for a moment he might have been a Jew. I can't stand Jews.'

'Nor can my mother,' he said. 'That's what makes me wonder.'

They walked on, round and round. Joan was fit and brave and clean and honest. She would face up to the Nazis come hell or high water. She was indomitable, admirable.

'Wonder what?'

He said, 'Whether my father had changed his name twice. Who he *really* is, in other words. So, who *I* am. One reason I think my father did something bad in South Africa is that he's always been a maniac for respectability, for doing the right thing. Of course my mother may have caused that ... He made his pile in gold and diamonds, but my God, he's turned himself into a country squire. He reads books, but pretends not to, so the foxhunting crowd will take to him. I was to inherit everything ... Darley Court, the squiredom, Joint Master of the Tedworth, the lot. I went through Eton and Cambridge, then I wanted to do something real ...' He was talking to himself now — 'Real, with my hands. With my brain. I went to mining school. I became a mining engineer. Father nearly died of chagrin. And, do you know, until I got my degree I didn't even know he had made his loot in mining! Am I me, or my father over again? Or someone else?'

They walked round and round. After two hours they returned to the quarters. When he kissed her good-bye, she said 'I think you'd better take a good dose of Epsom Salts, Sam, and ask for a couple of days off. I'll take two days at the same time, and we'll play tennis all day . . .'

Sam went to his quarters. Constipation as the root of all disquiet. It was an old female shibboleth, and Joan was female to the tips of her toes, in spite of the outward severities.

He sat down at his table and found his writing pad. He had to know. The doubt had been drilling into his mind all day – through the talk with Farley, through the scene with Hughes, all time with Joan; especially with Joan. After what she had said, if he cared for her, he must get down behind the face, tunnel through the dark, reach the open.

Dear Father, he wrote. *What was your name before it was Crapp?*

1943

> *Swift is the flash that lights up the obscurity*
> *Sudden in answer the echoing roar*
> *Where ye light hearted ones now your security*
> *Mind ye tonight the world is at war?*
> *Thunder the monsters aloft on the Ridge*
> *Echo the pop guns below the Moles,*
> *Jews, Buffadero, Levant . . .*

'What's that about Jews?' Chaddock snapped, thumping his tankard down on the counter, and half standing.

430

Mr. Wardrop eyed him owlishly – 'name of a battery, my boy. Jews' Battery. Joe, another gin for me, and a pint for Captain Whatsisname here. You're looking a mite distray tonight, captain.'

'I've got things on my mind,' Chaddock said shortly.

'Wouldn't you find it more congenial, shall we say, in the Piccadilly? That's the officers' pub.'

'I came here first with some Canadian's, officers and O.R.s together,' Chaddock said. 'They didn't give a damn for this separate officers'-pub business, and nor do I.' He turned his back.

'I hear you're importing apes from Morocco,' a petty officer said to the Ape Corporal.

The Ape Corporal nodded. 'Yes, we are. On Winston's orders, express. Though mind, getting the ones already here to accept the new ones so they can settle in, that's another kettle of fish. We put them together in threes, the ones from Morocco, 'cause their coats aren't so thick as ours, and they can huddle together for warmth . . .'

'It wasn't warmth I saw two of 'em huddling together for,' the petty officer said. 'It was you know what. So Gibraltar's safe again.

Old Sergeant Tamlyn said, 'Those monkeys are nobbut a damn nuisance. It's the Barbary partridge we ought to be saving. There are too many people on the Rock, so the hens can't sit.'

A sergeant-major of Signals turned to the petty officer – 'Had a little trouble with the Italians, haven't you?' he said.

The sailor said, 'No.'

'I see a ship's mast and funnels sticking out of the water outside the Detached Mole. What happened?'

The sailor ostentatiously turned his back. Flight said,

'Eyetie frogmen. It took our noble bluejackets rather a long time to find out.'

The petty officer said 'Fuck you', and stalked out, slamming the door behind him.

Mr. Wardrop said, 'Seeing that you Brylcreem boys can't fly a Polish general a hundred yards without killing him, I don't think you've got much to boast about.'

'Thank God for our allies. Look at the Russians! Look at Stalingrad!'

'What about Alamein?'

'What about Arakan?'

'Eighteen months and I haven't seen a bit of skirt.'

'Three and a half years for us,' Joe said. 'But things looking better, maybe. Today the army asked me if O.K. to strengthen my roof, to put anti-aircraft Bren gun up there. Last year, they do it, don't ask. Someone smell the end of war, maybe.'

'This is not the beginning of the end, but it is the end of the beginning.'

Mr. Wardrop said, 'This is better than any female in the world.' He raised his gin glass. 'What woman could have written

> *Down in the city, lights are a-twinkle,*
> *Hums the close hive with the evening's affairs . . .'*

'And they're *tough*! We had to put Monty down. Three bananas loaded with nembutal. Another shot full of cyanide. He just acted a little sozzled. A couple of days later . . .'

Chaddock slammed down his tankard so hard it shattered. Beer splashed his tunic and Joe's face and Flight's feet.

'Shut up, shut up!' he yelled.

'Here, here! What the . . .'

'Hey!'

The lights swung in front of Chaddock's eyes. 'Apes. Skirts. Stand here, filling your bellies with beer. We are in the presence of EVIL,' he shouted. 'This . . . Hitler . . . this is not a war for glory . . . not a cup final. We are fighting the most evil thing in the history of the world. Until it's burned out, it affects us all, we're all unclean because we're all human, too, like him.'

He stopped, his hands clenched at his side. Joe was mopping up the counter. Flight said awkwardly, 'We're all with you, sir . . . I mean, none of us want to invite Hitler to tea, you know. Here, take a seat.'

Chaddock stared at them, their faces wavering. The light grew bright, dim. He ran for the door, and out.

Chaddock felt a little more solid on his feet as soon as he entered the tunnel, and the gradually growing stutter of the drills acted to settle his jangling nerves. By the time he came near the face he felt sure of his balance, and did not wonder at every step why he was not falling.

The round of charges were set and the explosives were being tapped in. Three men were dismantling the last hundred feet of the ventilation ducting. He glowered at the work, for it was still the sheet-metal type.

'Who are you?'

The voice was in his ear. He wheeled round – 'Conquy,' he said.

Major Hughes frowned – 'This is Captain Chaddock, sir. My second-in-command.'

'Is your name Conquy or Chaddock? Or do you mean conky, C.O.N.K.Y.? . . . I'm Greenway, the new C.E.' Chaddock saluted.

The whistle blew for the safety check. Everyone started to move back behind the safety line. The new Chief Engineer was round and youngish and pop-eyed. 'What delays are you using?' he asked.

'Zero in the cut, one second easers, two top outers, three side outers, four bottom outers.'

'It works well? Leaves a clean advance?'

'Clean enough. There's no need to have the walls smooth as a house corridor, is there?'

The C.E. poked out a thick forefinger. 'What you civilian engineers have got to understand is that the basic principle of military mining is exactly the opposite of what you have been brought up in.'

'It's the time that matters, not the cost,' Major Hughes said, quoting the previous Chief Engineer's favourite dictum.

Chaddock said, 'Hole not string.'

'Eh? By God yes, that's it. In normal mining your object is to extract a valuable substance – coal, ore, whatever. The shape of the hole doesn't matter, *per se*. In military mining your object is to make a valuable hole. The shape or value of quantity of the extract doesn't matter, *per se* ... Hole, not string, like a net. Very good.'

A whistle blew again and Sergeant Farley intoned, 'Blasting. All clear?'

'All clear.'

Farley pressed the firing plunger. A series of cracks echoed sharply down the tunnel, followed by a short, heavy rumble. A cloud of grey dust and fumes hid the face. 'Nineteen fired,' a voice cried.

'Fuck!' Sergeant Farley said.

' 'Twas one of the easers missed, gaffer.'

Chaddock lit a cigarette. Now they had to find the

misfired detonator in the mass of fallen rubble, and extract it, and after it the actual charge.

'The detonator's in the top of the charge?' Hughes asked anxiously.

Chaddock said, 'That's where we always put it.'

'This is the sort of thing that makes six hundred cubic yards a week hard to keep up,' the C.E. said.

'There'd be fewer delays if we had electric detonators,' Chaddock said.

'We've asked for them.'

A miner standing close by, dragging at a tiny stub of cigarette said, 'It's nothin' to do with the bloody charges, man. It's the ghost.'

'Ghost?' the C.E. said cheerily. 'What ghost?'

'There's a naked woman runs about with her mouth open,' the miner said. 'She's the one who fucks up the drillpoints and derails the tubs and snuffs out the fuses.'

'Does she have a name?' the brigadier asked.

'Aye. The ghost of Thompson's Raise, we call her, 'cos that's where she were first saw. The officer had a dog with him, and suddenly the dog started whining and whimpering as though he'd seen ... a ghost. Since then that bloody woman's been seen in every raise and winze and drive in the Rock.'

Chaddock said, 'It's not a ghost holding us up. It's unnecessary delays. Spit and polish. Old-fashioned methods. Non-delivery of what we need. Look at these ventilator ducts. I put in a special urgent report in January 1942. The air flow at 300 feet from source is 630 cubic feet a minute with this stuff, and 2,600 *cubic feet* a minute with rubberized canvas. How the hell can the men be expected to work without enough air?'

'Chaddock!' Major Hughes said warningly.

'No, no, I like an officer to speak his mind,' the C.E.

said. 'I've got to go now. Walk back a little way with me, Chaddock.'

They started down the tunnel. Chaddock kept talking, because he could not stop. He was aware that the brigadier was looking at him under the passing lights, rather than listening, though every now and then he murmured Yes, or No, or Quite. 'One size rip bit only, one and a half inch diameter,' Chaddock babbled, 'no steel transport, use the drill sharpening shop only for reshanking the rip rods ... Hand drills, Holman SL 9 or something like, instead of the sledges ... compressors in banks, 3.5 gallons diesel oil per hour for the Ingersoll Rand ... drifters ... two fans in parallel, short Y junction ...'

'Are you a regular?' the C.E. said. 'I thought I only had three in Gib. Where were you at school?'

'Eton!' Chaddock shouted. His hands were shaking violently and he could not hold them still. 'What the hell does it matter where I went to school? We're in the presence of Evil! ... That's the ghost of Thompson's Raise – Evil, Evil! And all you can do is ask where I went to school. And in the pub, about monkeys ... the ... the ...'

The brigadier took his arm. Chaddock felt hot tears running down his cheek. 'Been overdoing it a bit, eh?' the brigadier said. 'Come along, old chap. Here, Fanshaw, give me a hand. There. Sit back.'

He sat in the back of the staff car, his hands held tight between his knees. A green room. Two years, three months, twenty-one days. Tunnelling all the time? Yes, sir. Tunnelling Company? Of course. Aeroplanes roaring overhead continuously. Must be imaginary. One hundred and seventy-five feet, 7/8 inch riprod, climax stopers and 1-inch steel, 4.9 tons, cubic yards, rock, rock ...

The window was open, and there were red flowers in a box outside. He sat in an armchair. They ought not to keep books away from him, surely? A man's mind couldn't be stopped turning by depriving him of books. That would only make it go round and round, instead of along the lines of the author's through. The Spanish hills were brown across the bay. A coastal steamer had just cleared Algeciras harbour, heading outside Europa Point, the Spanish colours of red and yellow painted huge on its side. The sky was still full of aircraft and their droning went on day and night.

Joan came in and sat beside him – 'Don't get up . . . How are we feeling this afternoon? Good. You look better too.'

She was nice, strong, no nonsense, everything clear: black, white – good, bad – us, them. Impossible to imagine her wondering who, or why, she was. Perhaps if you lived with her you wouldn't worry either, because she would tell you, and you'd believe.

'Everything's going well,' she said. 'Except at Casablanca.'

'Eh? What's that? . . . Oh, the African invasion.'

'You poor dear, there's a war on, you know. They thought that's what was on your mind. You were gabbling a lot about evil, you now.'

'Not the kind of thing one talks about,' Sam said. 'Sin. Crime. But not evil.'

She said, 'You've been working too hard. You didn't even know your own name, the nurse who admitted you told me. She said you kept telling her it was Conky.'

'It is,' he said. 'Or should be. C.O.N.Q.U.Y. An old Jewish family of Gibraltar.'

Her voice rose – 'You're joking.'

'You remember when I told you my father changed his

437

name? I wrote that same day asking him what it was before that.'

'And it was ... Conquy? I've seen the name on one of the houses here. Why didn't you tell me? Where's the letter?'

'I don't know,' he said. The light was growing bright, dim. 'Months ago. I ... thought I had the letter but then I couldn't find it. Must have torn it up, burned it, at once ...'

She said, 'So that's why you've been so odd. And I thought it was just overwork.'

His brain was missing its gears. He said, 'Overwork, yes. Turning my world, my views, upside down. Listening to all the talk about Jews, but I *am* one. Hitler. What happens if we lose ... Suddenly, Joan, I began to understand, to feel, evil.'

She was surreptitiously wiping tears from the corner of her eye with a handkerchief. 'Mustn't excite you, Major Borthwick told me,' she said. She got up to go.

He said, 'I'm not the same man I was, Joan, but I feel the same about you as I did before.'

She ran out of the room.

Patriotism is not enough, Sam repeated to himself. Nurse Cavell, 1915. I say unto you ... Blood toil sweat tears. Not enough either. Vengeance is mine saith the Lord. Suppose we tried wedge cuts instead of pyramid? Easers have a burden of three feet, yet they fall, so ...

1944

Chaddock nodded, and Joe refilled his glass. Chaddock took the letter from his pocket and read it again. It was plain enough. His father had many faults, but he'd never known him to lie. So it must be the truth.

'D Day at last!' a corporal of the Devons shouted, 'Now we'll show 'em.'

'Up the 49th,' shouted Sergeant Tamlyn, whom no one had ever seen drunk.

Roll out the barrel, we'll all have a barrel of fun.

'Hoo-bloody-ray, same again!'

'Make more quiet please, or M.P.s come.'

'Fuck the M.P.s. Another pint, Joe.'

Mr. Wardrop said, 'Perhaps within my life span on this accursed Rock we shall be getting some decent Holland Gin again, the best, the only *real* gin, my friend. Where was I?'

'*Death to the submarine . . .*'

'Ah yes.

> *Death to the submarine out in the night*
> *Death to the crafty piratical foe*
> *Swiftly we bring you the murderer's fate*
> *Death to the slayer of mother and babe*
> *Death to the Hun who has taught us to hate*

How's that for lambasting? They ought to recite that in the synagogue, eh, captain?'

Chaddock smiled faintly. He had told them all that his real name ought to be Conquy, though the Conquys in Gibraltar hadn't made any rush to claim him. In his only effort to establish contact, Mr. Conquy the jeweller had indicated politely that there was no trace of any member of the Gibraltar clan who could possibly have been his father, in South Africa or anywhere else. Well, that again tended to confirm this second letter. But what about the first? Had it not existed?

The Ape Corporal said, 'So you will all be glad to hear that the apes are increasing. We shall win the . . .'

'We *'ave* won!' a private yelled.

'Must have,' Joe said sourly. 'Yesterday an officer say he recommend me for medal. And Mr. Carlotti pay me back two pound he owe. Must be going to be an election soon.'

'These apes have got brains. On New Year's Eve last year, you know what one did? A young male called Pat. He tried to cross the boom that blocks the entrance to the Admiralty dockyard.'

'Must have been a skirt on the other side.'

'Gawd, that word's like a spanner. Every time someone says "skirt" me nuts tighten.'

'The Navy's better at keeping the ruddy apes where they belong than the ruddy French . . .'

His words ended in a yell, 'Here, what do you . . .?' and that in turn cut off by a fist smashed into his nose. The bar was full of bluejackets. Fists flew, glasses smashed, tables overturned. 'You dirty pongo,' a sailor near Chaddock snarled. His fist flashed out. Behind the bar Joe picked up the telephone and spoke a few words in it.

> *Narrows the circle of flashes and flame*
> *Closer and closer the columns of spray*

chanted Mr. Wardrop –

> *Whitey grey monsters from out of the deep.*
> *Ghosts of dead mariners claiming their prey.*

A voice in Chaddock's ear shouted, 'Here's another of them bastards in the shit-coloured suits.' A hand gripped his shoulder, then the voice said, 'Christ, it's a fucking officer.'

440

Chaddock felt suddenly hilarious. This was ridiculous and childish, and atavistic, but it wasn't evil. He jerked out of his battle dress blouse and said, 'Now I'm not an officer, you bloody matlo. I'm a Royal Jewish Engineer. Take that!' He landed a good solid blow on the sailor's nose. Then the M.P.s burst in.

Chaddock walked through the portal, went to the pick-up station, and waited. Half a dozen miners were waiting already for the lorries that shuttled up and down the sub-terranean Great North Road carrying men to their shifts. They talked and smoked quietly. More came in from the open. Chaddock read his letter again, under a bright bare bulb, shook his head and put it away.

He looked around. There was something strange about tonight. Coming into the tunnel had not made him feel secure, that was it. For weeks, months, years, entry into the Rock had been re-contact with reality, escape from an airy false world of emotions, of loyalties and jealousies, envies and fears, hunger and greed, hope and despair, all equally unreal.

Here inside the Rock – this very rock he leaned against, touching with his fingers – there were only air, light, heat, rock – reality, he had thought. But today it was the tunnel that seemed unreal, a glittering, beautiful, visionary elfland, and the lusts and angers and hilarity of the pub that were real. What was reality? Take the first letter from his father. Was that real or not? Had he imagined it? And if he had, did that make it unreal, for had it not changed his manner of living, his posture of being?

'Are ye no' coming, sir?'

The lorry was here and he climbed up into the back. He recognized Sapper Tim Althorne, a long cut over his right eye. Tim held up his hand, showing raw knuckles. 'That were a good fight in the Moon and Bloomers,' he said grinning. 'Best I seen since I left Blaydon . . . I saw you gi' that sailor something to remember you by!'

Sergeant Farley was already at the face, marking out the next round. Lieutenant Glass came away, lighting a cigarette. He was a tough capable young officer now – 'You'll reach daylight, Sam,' he said. 'The brass hats will be here in strength to watch.'

The drills started stammering, and Sam made a cursory tour of inspection. Methods had changed for the better, and he could take credit for a little of it. Holman hand drills instead of jackhammers; rip bits and studs, so the power tool could be worked longer hours: power loaders instead of picks and shovels: compressed air winches on the loaders when the gradient permitted, and static winches beyond that: and of course diesel locos instead of hand tramming to and from the spoil boxes – he could hear the steady chugging of one of them behind him now: electric detonation instead of fuse; good ventilation . . . that had been his real baby, the thing he had fought for all his time. He glanced up at the canvas ducting; that was the stuff, and to some extent he could take the credit. He coughed and mopped his face. It was hot here, near the surface. The drillers were resting more often than usual, too.

The telephone bell down the tunnel rang and a voice shouted, 'Captain Chaddock, Sergeant Farley, the major wants you both.'

Farley joined him with a cheerful, 'The buggers can only shoot us, sir.' They set off together down the long tunnel. The company offices were in a deep bay off the Street, designed for use as headquarters for combat commands under full siege conditions.

Major Hughes stood up as they came in. He smiled and put out his hand. 'Good news for both of you. You're both going on repat, on the next boat. They never say when that'll be, but between ourselves I hear a convoy'll be in the day after tomorrow.'

Chaddock shook the proffered hand automatically. 'Is that all?' he said. Had Hughes brought them away from the face just to hear this?

'No,' the major said with a little frown. 'You've been awarded the M.B.E., Chaddock, and, sergeant, you've got the B.E.M.'

Sergeant Farley made a comic face – 'Gaffer Farley, B.E.M.? The buggers'll laugh me out of the cage, back home.'

'Thanks,' Chaddock said absently. It was becoming more unreal every moment.

'You deserve it,' Hughes said. 'It's for your work to improve our methods here, of course, particularly in ventilation. Now, I want to go through the company stores list and a few other things with you while we're waiting for the C.E. and the Tunnelling Adviser. You'd better get back to the face, sergeant.'

They sat down and set to work.

After a couple of hours the telephone rang. Hughes picked it up. 'Company Commander. Yes. All right.' He said to Chaddock, 'They're ready to blast. I told them you'd be right along. But wait till we arrive before you fire.'

A couple of hundred yards before he reached the face Chaddock passed the diesel loco that trammed the tubs. The engine was running, but he could see no driver. Glancing back after he had passed, he stopped, stared, and ran.

The driver of the loco had fallen from his seat. His head

443

on the ground, his feet up on the machine's side. It was Tim Althorne. The diesel fut-futted steadily on. Four hundred feet away, the rest of the shift sat near the face, smoking, talking and laughing animatedly.

Chaddock felt the man's heart. It was beating, but faintly and irregularly. His own heart pounded painfully, for he knew at once what had happened. He yelled, 'Farley, send two men back to the loco, at the double. Phone for the oxygen crew.'

A voice spoke over Chaddock's shoulder. 'What's happened?'

He looked up. It was the brigadier, with Colonel Baines, the Tunnelling Adviser. 'Carbon monoxide,' he said.

Farley ran up – 'They're sending the oxygen right away, sir.'

The C.E. said, 'Turn off that damned thing.' The diesel puttering stopped. 'Don't move him for a moment, just lie him down properly. Disconnect those ducts, there, and let's have some air.'

They waited. A truck engine raced in the Great North Road, then they heard boots, running. The stretcher team with the doctor and the oxygen arrived.

The C.E. said, 'You'd better start an investigation as soon as we've blown, Hughes.'

Chaddock walked ahead of them towards the face. At the forward fans he said, 'Help me get these down, Farley.'

'But, sir . . .' Farley began.

Chaddock shook his head wearily. 'Thanks, sergeant, but I don't want to be protected.' They brought a fan down. Chaddock looked at it, knowing what he would find. It was clogged with dust and grease. The other one was the same. He showed them to the C.E. 'These fans

444

have to be cleaned every forty-eight hours, if there's to be proper ventilation at the face,' he said. 'I proved that in '42. I had it written into the regulations here. I'm responsible for seeing that it's done. Last time, I forgot. Everyone trusted me, because I'm the expert on ventilation ... If Althorne's dead, I've killed him.'

It was the business of the letter, he thought, that made his mind wander; but that was no excuse.

The C.E. said, 'You haven't killed anyone, Chaddock. You made a mistake, perhaps. We'll find out. Now blow the round. I want to see daylight.'

The others crowded round the exploder. Farley stayed behind with Chaddock. 'Don't take it so hard, sir,' he said. 'It's a bugger, but these things happen, tha' knows. Tim'll pull through.'

'No thanks to me,' Chaddock said.

The tunnel shook and shivered and rumbled. A current of strong, fresh air began to move up from behind. The miners raised a ragged cheer.

'Come on, Chaddock. Let's take a look. After fifteen thousand seven hundred and twenty-nine feet, that's the least we deserve.'

Chaddock crawled on hands and knees over the pile of rubble. The dawn light was spreading, and the sun was close below the rim of the violet sea. The drive had reached the open air.

'Look at this,' a miner said. 'The poor wee bugger.' He held up a small skull. 'A bairn. It's been here a long time, any road.'

'That's the ghost's baby,' the C.E. said jovially. 'Give it a decent burial and you'll have no more trouble.'

He held out his hand to Chaddock. 'Congratulations. I'll be sorry to lose you ... You've got to *care*, Chaddock, but not worry.'

The sun burst out of the sea, and Chaddock yawned mightily.

At Jews' Gate, when the sentry was checking their identity cards, Chaddock said, 'We're going to look at the cemetery first.'

'Very good, sir.' The soldier handed back the documents and saluted.

The flat tombstones were jammed together so tight that there was no path between. To get through the cemetery you had to walk on them. He peered down at the eroded Hebrew lettering, and Joan said, 'Good heavens, have you learned to read those squiggles?' He did not answer. The cemetery had been abandoned nearly thirty years earlier, the Conquys had told him. It lay on the hillside above Windmill Hill flats, looking towards Africa. Autumn crocus flowered in the crevices, and thorn bushes and scrub were creeping in to cover the stones.

After a time she led impatiently out of the cemetery and back on to Martin's Path. They walked one behind the other round the slope, past the deserted ancient gun of the Levant Battery, past tangles of rusty barbed wire, past empty sentry posts and unoccupied machine gun positions, dandelions and coarse grass growing in the torn sandbags.

'It looks as if they think it's all over,' he said to her back, 'but it may be a long time yet.'

She said, 'Last Tuesday the Matron asked me whether I wanted to go on repat. I'm past due, if I want to take it.'

He said, 'I'm going home.'

'Oh . . . You didn't tell me.'

'They only told me this morning . . . On the next boat. The day after tomorrow, perhaps.

She led up the narrow ledge to Martin's Cave, and turned. Her face was deep red. She said, 'What do you mean, you're going home? Isn't Gibraltar your home? Aren't your people here?'

He said, 'No, Joan, but—'

She said, 'I . . . I . . . said I'd stay on in Gib . . . because . . . oh damn . . . because of you . . . and now, and now . . . you're going away. I might have . . . expected it from a, a, a . . . dirty Jew!'

He said, 'Will you marry me, Joan?'

She turned her back violently. He took her shoulders, holding her gently and making no attempt to turn her to face him. 'Look, darling,' he said. 'If I've learned any-thing inside this Rock the last three and a half years, it is that if you're going to stay human, you have to hold on to what's good, even if it's stupid, and isn't working out right, and you have to reject what's evil, however well it works, however easy it is to take it, or let it take over. I think we love each other, or can, and that's good. I think we have had, and still have, fears and prejudices, and that's bad. Let's work out the good.'

He swung her round gently and lifted her chin. She was a big woman, and he knew she was surrendering, because he couldn't have pulled her round, or lifted her chin, if she didn't want him to. She looked past him at the vertiginous seven-hundred foot drop at his heels and jerked him to her, snapping 'Come *back*. Sam!'

He turned and looked down. There was the mouth of Arow Street, and there, just inside, was the end of the tunnel he'd been working in all the war; or should he say, trapped in, all his life?

They kissed, long and delicately. She was warm and experienced. He released her, and gave her the letter from his pocket. 'Read it.'

447

She read it, holding it up to the light; and again. 'I don't understand,' she said. 'Are you, or not?'

'Probably not. Does it matter?'

'Not the way it used to, but everyone ought to know who he is. I suppose that first letter you told us about, from your father, just didn't exist? It was part of your nervous breakdown?'

He pulled her to him, and said. 'If that was a nervous breakdown, then any time we look at misery and evil and say "that's *them*", not "that's *us*", then it'll be time to have another one.'

She hugged him with a bonebreaking eagerness that made him laugh, and they went slowly back to Jews' Gate.

Book Thirteen

FOREIGN FORTRESS?
PUPPET COLONY?
FREE PEOPLE?

The Jewish years 5700–5730
A.U.C. 2693–2723
A.D. 1940–1970
A.H. 1359–1390

DURING World War II the military tunnels in the Rock increased from a total length of four miles to over twenty-five miles. The biggest single work was the driving of the Great North Road, which runs the length of the Rock from north-west to south-east, about 400 feet above sea level. It is, like all the recent work, a vehicular tunnel, with passing places, light, power cables and water pipes. It is the spine of Gibraltar, with other tunnels (adits, winzes, raises, and galleries, in the delightful mining jargon) taking off on both sides, some to the open air, some to other tunnels at upper or lower levels, some to form great or small bays.

The object of these works, of course, was to enable Gibraltar to withstand a siege by modern weapons. To that end the engineers excavated sites for barracks, store-houses, magazines, power stations, headquarters, hospitals, offices – everything that would be needed under full siege conditions. The hardness of the limestone enabled very large galleries to be excavated without roof supports. One, containing vehicle workshops, is some 400 feet long by 80 feet wide. Inside these places you do not think you are in a cave because the engineers found that it paid to put up conventional walls, roof, and floor inside the tunnel – to keep out the damp, and to enable all the wiring, plumbing, lights, power outlets etc., to be hung, put, or fastened on something easier to work than the rock.

The names bestowed on these works often give a clue to their history: *Jock's Balcony* – built by the Black Watch:

Jellalabad Tunnel built by the Somerset Light Infantry (Jellalabad is their chief battle honour): *Arow Street* – which is not a misprint, but named after an engineer officer, Lt. Col. A. R. O. Williams, who is also commemorated in *Williams' Way.*

Together with the water tunnels, the Admiralty tunnel, and the old North Face galleries, these works make Gibraltar the most formidably honeycombed place on earth. And I refer only to the works of man. The number of natural caves seems to be without limit and the only boundary to the discovery of new ones is the number of man-hours Gibraltarians are disposed to put into the task. One of the finest was revealed by chance in 1940. It was planned to use St. Michael's Cave as an emergency hospital. A new operating theatre, with its own exit tunnel, had to be blasted out below. While making the tunnel the engineers found that they had blown in the roof of another huge cave system, hitherto unknown. The new cave, Lower St. Michael's, is a miracle of softly tinted limestone, shaped into a thousand forms. At the far end there is a pool of soft still water. The rock walls plunge sheer into the water, but just below the surface there is a hidden ledge of rim rock extending round the pool, and with a last secret grotto. It is a magnificent place, both in itself, and to see one's companions walking on the water!

A recently formed Cave Research Group of the Gibraltar Society is setting about its task with considerable scientific know-how and boundless enthusiasm. They are systematically mapping, exploring, and recording full details of the caves, categorizing them as Cavers' Caves, Archaeologists' Caves, or Anyone's Caves (meaning, anyone who wants them is welcome). The full report on each cave is pages long, with plans, elevations, and detailed descriptions of the cave's geology, biology, and history, but the brief notes are racy, to the point, and tell the interested person as much as he initially wants to know, thus:

Boathoist Cave: At sea level, and just north of Governor's Beach. Access from Boathoist Tunnel. Arow Street. Explored. Small. High roof-hole needs looking at (J.M. Note: This cave was prepared for use as a launching place for V.I.P.s in case they needed to get into or out of Gibraltar by submarine).

Diesel's Pot. Behind the fuel storage tanks in Glen Rocky distillery. Explored. Large and deep. (J.M. Note: Deep indeed . . . it has been explored to 100 feet below sea level: the mouth is about 250 feet above sea level. Glen Rocky Distillery, alas distils nothing healthier than fresh water from sea water.)

Devil's Dustbin. In the foot of the North Front Face. Extension in West Chamber. West wall not explored.

The Cave Researchers achieved their finest hour so far on 30th May, 1966, when they went to have another look at Cave S. first scientifically explored by the archaeologist W. H. Duckworth in 1910. The cave is now extremely difficult to get at, being under a cliff at the head of the east face catchment area, but George Palao, the group's surveyor, managed to climb up, and found prehistoric engravings on the cave wall. There were representations of men, fish, boars, and other living things, some covered in a thin layer of sinter. Precise dating of this art has not yet been done, but it has been tentatively assigned to between 30,000 and 40,000 B.C.

Perhaps one day, the Cavers will discover a bone-statuette of a naked woman, or a little bronze scarab brooch, lost by some woman in the endless past. But the Cave Research Group and its activities were still in the future while the war raged. The raging was mostly at a long distance from Gibraltar, although the Germans had an invasion plan, 'Felix', which depended on Franco's co-operation; he never gave it. Gibraltar's war role was as a way and staging station, and a headquarters for task forces, such as Force H. This small carrier-battleship-cruiser group was the force which relocated and crippled the *Bismarck* in April 1941. When the old Swordfish torpedo biplanes took off and landed on that operation, the *Ark Royal*'s flight deck was rising and falling 60 feet in heavy seas.

General Eisenhower's headquarters for the assault on Vichy-held North Africa on 8th November, 1942, was at Gibraltar. In return Gibraltar suffered three air raids, two by the Vichy French and one by the Italians. In anticipation of air raids a little booklet was prepared, giving both the English and Spanish names of streets, for use by fire wardens, etc. (Few Gibraltarians had much English at this time.) In that booklet you can see not only different names, but different ways of thinking. City Mill Lane is the *Calle de las Siete Revueltos* (Street of the Seven Turns): Flat Bastion Road is *La Cuesta de Mr. Bourne* (Mr. Bourne's Ramp): Fraser's Ramp is *Escalera de Benoliel* (Benoliel's Steps): New Passage is *Calle del Peligro* (Street of Danger), and Castle Steps is *Calle de Comedias* (Street of Comedies) ... these last two were the brothel areas.

Gibraltar's most interesting war was that fought in secret, under water, between the Italian and British navies, personified by Prince Valerio Borghese on one side and Commander Lionel Crabb on the other. Three times

453

between October 1940 and September 1941 Borghese took his submarine into Gibraltar Bay and from it launched piloted torpedoes. One of the torpedoes narrowly failed to get the battleship *Barham* inside the inner harbour, and later efforts did sink three ships, including a large armed motor ship. From mid-1942 Italian frogmen launched from submarines or from Spain placed limpet charges on the bottoms of merchant ships marshalling into convoys in the bay. Several ships were sunk. When the Italians swam ashore in Spain, to be captured by the Spanish police, they were at once released to repeat their gallant but not precisely 'neutral' feats.

The previous year the epic of the *Olterra* had begun. She was a small Italian tanker scuttled in Gibraltar harbour at the outbreak of war; later raised; bought by a Spanish firm or 'front'; towed across the bay; sold to an Italian firm and moored alongside the long outer mole of Algeciras. The Italian Navy, with great ingenuity, now turned her into a fitting-out basin and home port for their midget submarines. On 6th December, 1941 – one day before Pearl Harbor – the *Olterra*'s midgets set out for Gibraltar, where the battleship *Nelson* and the fleet carriers *Formidable* and *Furious* were in harbour. But Crabb had devised a system of random firing of depth charges into the harbour approaches, twenty-four hours a day. One of them hit a piloted torpedo killing its crew; the other attackers ran into bad luck; and the operation was an expensive failure for the Italians.

Midget attacks were made from the *Olterra* through August, 1943; all the time Crabb and his small team were also fighting the frogmen and their limpet charges. The Marshal Badoglio took Italy over to the Allied side. The underwater team in Algeciras, like their countrymen at home, were split down the middle in their loyalties, and broke up. By then Crabb and Intelligence had guessed that the derelict *Olterra*, apparently manned by a watch and ward crew of half a dozen scruffy Italian merchant seamen, was really the headquarters of the operations, which had been carried out under the noses of the Spanish authorities. Those noses began to be a little more aware of bad smells after Alamein and Stalingrad, but by then the worst was over. (Crabb died as he had lived. He vanished mysteriously on 19th April, 1956. He was last seen swimming in Portsmouth Harbour near the Russian cruiser *Ordzhonikidze*, which had brought Khruschev and Bulganin on a state visit to England.)

In 1945 the United States dropped nuclear bombs on Japan, and the war ended. Britain had already started to repatriate the civilian population of Gibraltar, but so slowly that the people began to stage mass protest meetings for the return of their families. The snail's pace of the repatriation was probably due to the British government's need for time to reassess its attitude to Gibraltar in the light of new conditions. For it was not only the weapons of war that there were changing. Britain led the way in a world-wide process of decolonialization. Gibraltar had been one of a number of strong points and fleet bases guarding the route to India, Australasia and the Far East. But now India became independent, Australasia turned towards America, and China dominated the Far East. England was still a great power, but clearly she was less powerful relative to others than she had been, and a combination of economic and political factors was hastening the decline. Could she still afford Gibraltar? Did she still need the Rock?

Many factors had to be considered in assessing the military worth of Gibraltar in the atomic age. In case of actual nuclear attack, the Rock must surely have been classified as 'Livable but unusuable'. Men and installations could probably survive inside the limestone, and rockets could probably be fired out, but no ships or aircraft could survive. This, as we have seen, was the situation even with conventional weapons, i.e. that Gibraltar can be held but not used against the enmity of Spain or some other power holding the Ceuta-Tangier area. To *use* Gibraltar a large area of Spain or Morocco would have to be cleared.

Provided Spain is neutral or friendly, Gibraltar has a role in non-nuclear war. By electronic gadgetry it is probably possible for Gibraltar to detect and prevent all sea passage – submarine and surface – through the Strait. Modern aircraft can fly comfortably from Gibraltar to, say, Israel or Turkey at the other end of the Mediterranean, thus enabling Gibraltar to be used as a staging base for operations throughout the Mediterranean, and also in the area Morocco-Canaries-Azores, which has always been a focal point of world shipping lanes. But if Spain is neutral or friendly, all these operations, and more, can be better carried out from Spanish bases ... The key phrases therefore were *non-nuclear* and *Spain friendly*. It was not in the power of Britain or Spain to decide whether a war would be nuclear or not; but they could arrange their mutual relationship ... surely? To some extent, yes, but not entirely, because a third element now entered the equation: the people, the rock scorpions, the Gibraltarians. Since they are the core of the British case – and problem – we must have a careful look at them.

They had had a bad war. The summary evacuations had brought home to them what a century of peace had made them forget – that they were chattels of the military, slaves of the fortress. We have seen the growth of the civilian population – first the families of the military and the craftsmen and tradesmen to service their needs; then the growth of other industries and trades; increase in numbers; servicing and trading not only for the military but with each other and outside, until a part of the colony did not economically depend at all upon the fortress.

In accordance with these new circumstances the form of government had changed too, though slowly. In the last resort the Governor retained his autocratic powers to do almost anything he judged necessary for the safety of the fortress. In practice his non-military powers had for years gradually been passing to various forms of council, at first wholly nominated, now wholly elected; and today any Governor who used his full emergency powers, in war or peace, would have to do much explaining to Whitehall.

Demilitarization extends into every area. There are fewer soldiers, and those much less visible. Gun salutes to visiting warships and foreign admirals are no longer fired from King's Bastion, right behind City Hall, but from a battery at a discreet distance. The admiral still lives in a big house with acres of beautiful garden, but more and more War Department land is being given, leased, or sold to the elected government of Gibraltar, which keeps clamouring for still more, and for the cession of still more military facilities ... (while also clamouring for England to defend Gibraltar).

At the last census (1961) the civil population comprised 19,044 Roman Catholics; 1,632 Protestant; 654 Jews; and small numbers of other religions. Most of the Roman Catholics are ultimately of Italian origin, though by now there is a very strong Spanish strain since for generations Gibraltarian males have been marrying Spanish girls. Most of the Protestants are of British origin. The Jews came – or came back – from Barbary, Minorca,

Genoa, and other parts of Italy. The ordinary language is Spanish, strongly Andalusian-accented (indeed there is to the expert a recognizable Gibraltar accent called *llanito*). The language, as actually spoken, might be called Engañol or Esplish, for one hears things like '*Faltan tres* quarts *de* engine oil,' or '*He perdido un* six-inch bastard file *en la casa del* Water Commissioner.' The use of English is increasing greatly, aided by snob-appeal and the current anti-Spanish resentment. Nor is the Gibraltarian 'spirit' truly Spanish. It is considerably more dour, more darkly 'Italian', less *alegre*, than the Spanish.

The people have a very British respect for law, which in Gibraltar is generally sound and well and honestly administered. Judge, counsel, and clerks all look as if they had been borrowed from the Old Bailey and the police not only wear British bobbies' helmets, but they act with the bobby's vaguely bored patience, and go unarmed.

Gibraltarians drink strong tea and heavy beer, enjoy cricket, and worship Manchester United. (This soccer team has become a sort of personification of Britain, as Real Madrid is of Spain. When the two recently played each other, and Manchester won, the score was chalked all over streets and walls in Gibraltar, with disparaging remarks added for the benefit of the Spanish workmen going in and out of the dockyard.)

Whole streets are painted red, white and blue, including the pavements and gutters. The Union Jack is the favourite decorative pattern for window frames, doors, house ends and old jalopies. Everywhere the hand-painted slogans shout *British we are, British remain!: God Save Our Queen!: Born British, we'll die British!: To hell with Franco!*

Towards the royal family – sorry, Royal Family – the people display an enthusiastic subjection which would have done credit to a third footman in the days of *God bless the squire and his relations, and keep us in our proper stations*. Wherever Royalty has stopped, looked, or perhaps visited the bathroom in Gibraltar the fact is recorded in fawning brass and concrete.

Yet several old-time visitors and resident non-Gibraltarians have insisted that until the present Spanish campaign began the general sentiment of the Gibraltarians was anti-British.

They have a considerable political maturity. Not many towns with a ninety-five per cent Roman-Catholic Italian-Spanish majority would elect and re-elect a Jew as Mayor and Chief Minister, as they did for many years to Sir Joshua Hassan. (Incidentally, there are only two Queen's Counsel in Gibraltar: both are Jews.)

What these fascinating people, flotsam from the wreck of an empire, do for a living, apart from taking in each other's washing, is something of a mystery. The official report says 'Gibraltar has no agriculture or other natural resources and apart from small coffee, tobacco-processing and garment-making industries, opportunities for employment continue to be provided mainly by the Official Employers (the Government of Gibraltar, the Ministry of Defence, the Ministry of public Building and Works, and the City Council) and by the wholesale or retail trades, the hotel and catering trades, shipping services, the building industry and private domestic service.'

That 'retail trade' – or perhaps it should come under 'Shipping services' – covers the sale of much goods to ships' crews, particularly Russians, and cruise passengers. Sometimes there are seven or eight Russian freighters and tankers anchored in the bay at one time, and the streets are full of square-faced men carrying huge paper parcels. They buy up vast quantities of one or two items – such as shoes, or blankets, or raincoats – regardless of size, colour, or quality. It seems that when they return to Russia they hold auctions on the quayside.

There is a fair amount of tourism and high hopes are held for more. Gibraltar combines two qualities which many British regard as essential for a foreign holiday resort: (1) it must have sunshine; (2) it must be as un-foreign as possible. In Gibraltar the weather is usually good, the pubs are just like those in a small English town, and the restaurants the same, but even worse. The more sophisticated tourist tends to avoid Gibraltar. Except for gambling at the new casino he can get much more for his money in Spain where the truly 'foreign' atmosphere is, for him, not a drawback but an inducement. When there are currency restrictions in England, Gibraltar also has the attraction that it is within the sterling area and so does not bite into the Briton's tiny foreign exchange allowance.

Some members of the Gibraltar administration want to restore part of the eighteenth-century fortifications – the Galleries – and run *Son-et-lumière* productions there. Others think the money should be put into more and better hotel rooms, marinas, esplanades – anything to mitigate Gibraltar's overpowering claustrophobia. (This claustrophobia is almost tangible, especially in blockade times, such as the present. The civil population is near 25,000; they all seem to have cars; they drive round and round, up and down, in the narrow roads and streets, like animals in a too-small cage.)

The really notable absentee from the list of Gibraltar's principal industries today is smuggling – the export of goods knowing or suspecting that they will evade payment of legal duty in their country of final destination: one can be plain or polite. But before going into that, let us take a look at the other principal actor in the drama – Spain.

As Britain went relatively downhill, Spain went up.
She could hardly go in any other direction. From the start
of her own war in 1936 to the end of the World War in
1945 she had for practical purposes been without external
trade or aid. Her *materiel* was falling to pieces, and her
morale was shattered. Francisco Franco was able to begin
at the bottom, with no opposition. Although antagonism
to his régime gradually strengthened as the years passed,
the Spanish people at first accepted him and his policies
without question. They would have accepted anything
rather than face even the faintest chance of such another
trauma as the Civil War. The U.S.A.'s need for air and
naval bases out of reach of Russia's then rocket capacity,
plus tourism attracted by Spain's starvation level prices,
plus this imposed stability, enabled Spain to climb from a
shattered and bankrupt wreck to a reasonably powerful
and austerely solvent power, of the second class.

In deciding to tackle the Gibraltar problem Franco
may not have been very wise, but he was certainly following a classic line of Spanish policy, which has always
made the recovery of Gibraltar a matter of prime importance. Franco's first measure was to denounce Gibraltar as
a cancer in the Spanish economy – because of the smuggling. This line of attack had many effects, not all of them
beneficial to Spain's case.

There was always a small amount of smuggling *into*
Gibraltar, mainly brandy, wines, and spirits, which are
much cheaper in Spain; but the principal direction, of
course, was into Spain, and by far the most important
item was tobacco. As we have seen, it had been going on
for a long time, and so had Spanish complaints against it
to the Governor, or to London. The British were in general unhelpful. Anthony Eden minuted on one of these

protests that it was not the responsibility of Her Majesty's Government to protect the revenues of foreign states – but there is no doubt that if the French or Dutch had asked for British help in preventing a huge contraband traffic from England into their countries, they would have got it. The Spanish did not get it, and they must take part of the blame. As far as Gibraltar is concerned their attitude has always been non-cooperative or worse, from the punitive quarantines of the 1700s to the affair of the *Olterra*, and they had no right to expect any friendliness from the Gibraltar-British.

The root of the problem, for Spain, was that the organizers and principal beneficiaries of the smuggling were Spanish. The syndicates which bought and operated fast war-surplus Navy patrol launches after 1945 were Spanish. Their bribes and pay-offs penetrated every level of Spanish society and government. And one high-up official publicly stated that the smuggling was necessary because it enabled Spain to provide American cigarettes to tourists without having to buy them in hard currency. The same could be said of streptomycin and penicillin, which were also heavily smuggled in the early post-war years.

In the face of this situation British measures against the trade would have hurt Gibraltarian revenues and made no difference to Spain, for the stuff would have come from Tangier or Italy, as much of it did in any case. Nevertheless, the blatant operations of the smuggling launches based on Gibraltar (to claim British protection and status they had a stooge British subject as nominal owner) began to embarrass the Gibraltar government, and in the mid-1950s they set about harassing the trade in various ways. This caused much of it to leave Gibraltar, to work out of other bases under other flags. Gibraltar also offered the Spanish authorities means of identifying the crewmen of the smuggling boats, all of whom lived in Spain; but the Spanish never took action.

Most telling of all is the fact that Spain and Gibraltar are both members of Interpol. When the Italian government, earlier, mounted a great investigation of the smuggling into their country, they asked for and received information from all other Interpol countries, including Gibraltar. The Gibraltar government later prepared a list of the names, functions and addresses of everyone they had traced in the organization of smuggling in the Western Mediterranean. This list named 4 Latvians, 3 Dutch, 1 Swede, 4 Austrians, 5 Canadians, 4 Cubans, 41 Italians, 195 Portuguese, 4 Albanians, 3 Swiss, 20 West Germans, 12 Danes, 61 French, 9 Belgians, 134 Moroccans, 3 Americans, 158 British (including Gibraltarians), and 1,013 Spaniards. The Spanish Government never asked Gibraltar – or anyone else – for this list of names because every country in Interpol would then have known that the smuggling was connived in and actively supported by the most highly placed in the nation.

In 1964 the position changed. When Franco denounced Gibraltar as a cancer he obviously had to insure that no investigation could implicate the Spanish government or its officials in the spread of the disease. So thousands of officials and Tabacalera employees who had been in the pay-offs were told – fingers out of the pie, *finis*!

The Spanish State Security is extremely tough and efficient, when it wants to be, especially if the Generalissimo himself has given the word. The crackdown began. A few old hands like Juanito el Canario, who hadn't got the message or didn't believe it applied to them because of their previous special connections, found themselves in jail. In a very short time, the smuggling was stopped cold.

To give an idea of what it had been worth, note that in the previous year the Tabacalera had legally imported twelve million packets of U.S. cigarettes for sale in Spain. The year after, they imported ninety-seven million. The difference – eighty-five million packets, at a sale price in Spain of about forty million dollars – was what the smugglers used to supply. With the great flow of tobacco the crackdown also dammed the lesser streams of whisky, luxury cars, refrigerators, carpets, and British wool cloth which also used to pass through Gibraltar. Small amounts of hallucinatory drugs are still occasionally seized, and publicized as being from Gibraltar, but the evidence seems to be that they are not.

So today the contraband business is dead; and with it, one might add, the 'Gibraltar as a cancer in the Spanish economy' argument. General Franco has shown that a strong, tough government which means business can reduce smuggling to negligible proportions. But of course the use of the argument as political ammunition continues, because as long as Gibraltar is not Spanish the smuggling *could* start again . . . if this or a subsequent Spanish government were to permit it.

From the 'cancer' policy, Spain has progressed by gradual stages to the imposition of a blockade against Gibraltar, which can be called the fifteenth siege. Her justification has been a series of motions in the United Nations accepting Spain's position and calling upon Britain to hand the tiny peninsula back to the great peninsula of which it is physically a part. The effects of the blockade are various. Gibraltar imports food from Morocco, and wine from France and Italy, where both would naturally come from Spain. Prices are high and much that ought to be readily available cannot be had at any price. No Spaniards are now allowed to enter Gibraltar to work.

So Moroccans have to be imported – under-scoring still more strongly Gibraltar's historic dependence on a friendly Morocco – but it has also forced Gibraltarians to learn trades and professions they used to consider beneath them.

Spain's most dangerous threats are concerned with air rights and territorial waters. Briefly, she claims that Gibraltar has neither, since they were not mentioned in the Treaty of Utrecht, or any other agreement; but Gibraltar needs territorial waters and air rights if its ships and civil aircraft are to operate. Spain keeps pushing – today anchoring tall-masted ships practically at the end of the airport runway, tomorrow complaining that British aircraft fly over prohibited areas. And day in and day out the grey hull of a Spanish man-of-war slices through the waters of the bay, observing and menacing all maritime activity. This vessel is about forty feet long, has a maximum speed of five knots, and is universally known as *Smoky Joe*.

Stick in one hand, carrot in the other . . . Spain had to persuade the people of Gibraltar that happiness and prosperity awaited them in the arms of the fatherland. This needed major engineering, because for centuries the Campo de Gibraltar – the semi-circle of about twenty miles radius centring on the Rock – had been as poor as any area in Europe. There were, and are, men who work on the estates of great lords for *el cubierto* – fourpence and a bowl of pottage – per day. In all the Campo few but went to bed hungry, and some, starving. Few, that is, except those who worked for the English on the Rock: *they* had a good wage, regularly paid, and the customary right to bring out a little something each day, without paying duty on it.

To remedy this, Spain announced, in 1965, a Plan of Development for the Campo. The plan involves spending

£25 million a year until 1990 to convert the Campo into a highly industrialized zone of great technical efficiency. A huge petro-chemical complex has already been built, factories for plastics, cellulose and the like are going up, modern roads and a huge sports stadium are in construction. All this the Gibraltarians can see over the closed fence on the isthmus. 'Come out,' Spain wheedles, 'you'll never have it so good.'

To put a final dressing on the carrot it has also been announced that a new Spanish province, called Gibraltar, is to be formed. It will consist of the Campo, somewhat enlarged, and the eventual capital, when it returns 'home', will be Gibraltar. There are a lot of jobs and a lot of money, in a capital. People have to go there for all kinds of ceremonies, licences, passes, permits . . .

So far, the Gibraltarians have refused to be cajoled.

At a referendum held in 1967, after Spain took her case to the United Nations, they were asked flatly whether they wanted the British association or an association with Spain. The pro-British response was over 99 per cent. Pro-British, or perhaps, according to the old residents, anti-Spanish: if Spain were as rich as the U.S.A., these say, the Gibraltarians would have clamoured to become Spanish. The sneer has truth in it, but not much. Spain is a dictatorship, and after two centuries of military dictators of their own, the Gibraltarians are enjoying the pains and the pleasures of democracy. Gibraltar Jews, particularly, fear any surrender to Spain's rigid and anti-Semitic Catholicism.

There are, however, at least two sorts of Gibraltarians who would like to see an accommodation with Spain. First are the people Gibraltarians call *palomas* (doves or pigeons of passage). Born Gibraltarian, the typical *paloma* married a Spanish girl from the Campo, but worked in Gibraltar; but first the Spaniards made him apply for Spanish papers, thus forcing him to admit that he was not a Gibraltarian but a Spaniard, from the Spanish city of Gibraltar; and they then closed the frontier altogether, forcing the *paloma* to make a final choice. Thus families have been split, wife and children abandoned – or pride swallowed, and the Rock deserted.

Many of the Indians and Pakistanis, whose shops are so prominent a part of Main Street, also want accommodation with Spain, to the considerable disgust of the true Gibraltarian. Because they come from countries of the British Commonwealth they were admitted without limitation; but none of them *live* in Gibraltar. A family would buy a store and send some member from India to run it. They never hire shop-assistants, but just send over some more young members, to work for nothing. All the money they make gets sent back home. (And they make plenty, for they ally industry and shrewdness: one merchant I know travels always through Russia on his journeys back and forth, so that he can see what consumer goods the Russians lack most severely: it is these goods he stocks, from Japan or Hong Kong, for the benefit of the Russian seamen.)

These factors, plus their aloofness, had already cut the Indian-Pakistan community off from other Gibraltarians before Franco's recent moves. But many Indian families and firms also have branches on the Spanish mainland or in the Canaries. In order to improve their status there, some of the Gibraltar firms cabled the United Nations in support of the Spanish case. This did nothing to increase their popularity on the Rock.

So we come out of history into the continuing 'now'; yet 'now' is always, too, a continuation of history, and cannot be separated or considered apart from it.

The Gibraltarians want to be independent, but protected by Britain; or they want to be welded into the British state. They declare that they cannot be handed, like a chattel, to anyone, least of all to a Spanish dictatorship.

Britain defies the United Nations' mandate to hand Gibraltar back to Spain on the ground that a people's right to self-determination is paramount, taking precedence even over treaty commitments made in the distant past. Whether Britain actually needs, or wants, Gibraltar is highly doubtful: whether she would or could fight for it in the face of a Spanish attack, even more so.

Spain declares that Gibraltar was taken, and has been kept, by naked force: that the Gibraltarians do not have the right of self-determination because they are not a true 'people' but a British importation, a puppet; that Gibraltar cannot be handed over to the Gibraltarians because of Treaty of Utrecht rules that if Britain ever gives it up it must be offered first to Spain *before all others*; that Gibraltar cannot be politically united with Britain because, under the same treaty, Spain retained and retains the Sovereignty.

And behind all this loom huge shapes, giant flares out of the past, nonetheless powerful for being purely spiritual: the Gibraltar Legend, the Sacred Reconquest, the Spanish Inquisition. It is by these lights and shadows, as much as by law and logic, that men will decide the fate of Gibraltar's present human inhabitants.

The Rock itself journeys on, unmoving, through time.

AUTHOR'S NOTE

For those who are interested, the big cave in Book 1 is Gorham's: Eagle's Nest (Book 3) is Martin's: Rachel's Secret and the Hermit's (Book 4) are Genista Two and Glen Rocky Distillery, respectively: Lost Lamb (Book 7) is Pete's Paradise, which must have silted up again before its recent re-discovery.

BIBLIOGRAPHY

The following books and articles have been of value to me in the writing of this book:

Air H.Q., R.A.F., Gibraltar (Intelligence Section). *Flying from the Rock*. Gibraltar, 1945.

Ancell, S. A. *Circumstantial Journal of the Long & Tedious Blockade & Siege of Gibraltar*. Liverpool, 1785.

Anon. *An authentic and accurate Journal of the Late Siege of Gibraltar*. London, 1785.

Anon. *An Enquiry into Pretensions of Spain to Gibraltar, as founded on His Late Majesty's Letter*. London, 1729.

Anon. *Boletin de la Comision Provincial de Monumentos Año IV, No. 15*. Cadiz.

Anon. *Gibraltar Society, Report of Sectional Activities and Papers*. Gibraltar, 1929/30.

Anon. *Jewish Encyclopaedia*. London, 1905.

Anon. *The Medical and Physical Journal*, Vols. 13, 14, 18. London, 1805/1807.

Anon. *Quarterly Publication, Cave Research & Rock Climbing Society*. Gibraltar, 1961.

Arraras, Iribarren, Joaquin. *Historia de la Cruzada Española*. Madrid.

Augusta, Josef. *Prehistoric Man*. London, 1960.

Bögli & Franke. *Radiant Darkness*. London, 1967.

Camon Aznar, José. *Las Artes y Los Pueblos de la España Primitiva*. Madrid, 1954.

Carrington, C. E. *Gibraltar*. Royal Institute International Affairs, 1956.

Castro, Adolfo de. *Historia de Cadiz y su Provincia*. Revista Medica.

Congregation of Spanish and Portuguese Jews. *Ascamot*. London, 1906.

Disney-Roebuck, Wyndham. *The Gateway*. London, 1937.

Dozy, A., *Spanish Islam*. London, 1913.

Drinkwater, Col. J. A. *A History of the Siege of Gibraltar 1779–1783*. London, 1905.

Duckworth, W. L. H. *Cave Exploration at Gibraltar in September 1910*. Typescript.

Eley, D. M. *The Gibraltar Tunnels*. Typescript.

Ellicott, J. T. & D. M. *An ornament to the Almeida*. Portsmouth, 1950.

Ellicott, D. M. *From Rooke to Nelson*. Gibraltar, 1965; *Gibraltar's Royal Governor*. Gibraltar, 1955; *Bastion against Aggression*. Gibraltar, 1968.

Fellows, Sir James, M.D. *Reports of the Pestilential Disorders of Andalusia*. London, 1815.

Frere, Sir B. H. T. *Guide to the Flora of Gibraltar and Neighbourhood*. Gibraltar, 1910.

Gallwey, Lt. Col. H. D. *A hoard of 3rd Century Antoninioni from southern Spain*. Numismatic Chronicle, 1962.

Garratt, G. T. *Gibraltar and the Mediterranean*. London, 1939.

Garrod, D. A. E. *Excavation of a Mousterian Rock Shelter*. Royal Anthropological Institute of Great Britain and Ireland, 1928.

Gibraltar Garrison Library. *The Wild Flowers of Gibraltar and Neighbourhood*. Gibraltar, 1968.

Goodwin, Lieut, E. G. M. *The Galleries, Gibraltar*. Gibraltar, 1927.

Graetz, H. *History of the Jews*. Vols 1–5. London, 1892.

Griffiths, Arthur. *The Question of Gibraltar*. Fortnightly Review, 1902.

Harden, Donald. *The Phoenicians*. London, 1962.

Hennen, John. *Sketches of the Medical Topography of the Mediterranean*. London, 1830.

Homer. *The Odyssey* (tr. S. O. Andrew). London, 1953.

Hort, Major. *The Rock*. London, 1939.

Howes, Dr. H. W. *The Gibraltarian*. Colombo, 1951.

Hudson, Derek, *Gibraltar, July 21–24, 1704*. Cornhill Magazine, 1933.

Irby, Lt. Col. Howard. *Ornithology of the Straits of Gibraltar*. London, 1895.

James, T. *The History of the Herculean Straits*. London, 1771.

Jevenois, Pedro. *El Tunel Submarino del Estrecho de Gibraltar*. Madrid, 1929.

Jones, G. D. T. *An outline of the structure of the Rock of Gibraltar*. Archaeological Society of Gibraltar, 1956–57.

Kamen, Henry. *The Spanish Inquisition*. New York, 1965.

Kelaart, Dr. E. F. *Botany and Topography of Gibraltar*. London, 1846.

Kenyon, Major-General E. R. *Gibraltar under Moor, Spaniard and British*. London, 1938.

Lopez de Ayala, Ignacio. *Historia de Gibraltar*. Madrid, 1782.

Luna, Jose Carlos de. *Historia de Gibraltar*. Madrid, 1944.

McGuffie, T. H. *Siege of Gibraltar*. London, 1965.

Mackenzie, Col. R. H. *The Trafalgar Roll*. London, 1913.

Madrazo, Pedro de. *España, Sus Monumentos y Artes (Sevilla y Cadiz)*. Barcelona, 1884.

Nolan, Comdt. *Une visite aux singes de Gibraltar*. Gibraltar, 1928.

Norris, H. T. *Ib Battutah's Andalusian Journey*. Geographical Journal, 1959; *The Early Islamic Settlements in Gibraltar*. Royal Anthropological Institute, 1960.

Officer then serving with the Allies. *An exact Journal of the taking of Gibraltar by the Prince of Hesse*. London.

An officer who was at the taking . . . *An impartial account of the late famous Siege of Gibraltar*. London, 1728.

Pasley, M. S. *A few of the wild flowers of Gibraltar*. Portsmouth, 1876.

Pla, Jose. *Gibraltar*. London, 1955.

Poley, Antonio. *Cadiz y su Provincia*. Sevilla, 1901.

Pugh, Marshall. *Commander Crabb*. London, 1956.

Quennell, M. & C. H. B. *Everyday Life in Prehistoric Times*. London, 1924.

Quintero, Pelayo. *Cadiz Primitivo*. Cadiz, 1917.

Romero de Torres, Enrique. *Catalogo Monumental de España, Prov. de Cadiz*. Madrid, 1934.

Roth, Cecil. *The Spanish Inquisition*. London, 1937.

Roth, Cecil. *A short history of the Jewish People*. London, 1936.

Russell, Jack. *Gibraltar besieged*. London, 1965.

Sayer, Capt. *History of Gibraltar: and of its political relation to events in Europe*. London, 1862.

Scott. *A History of Tropical Medicine*. London, 1939.

Schulten, Adolf. *Tartessos* (Sp. tr). Madrid, 1945.

Serfaty, A. B. M. *The Jews of Gibraltar*. Gibraltar, 1933.

Servicio Informativo España. *Gibraltar: Historia de una Usurpacion*. Madrid, 1968; *Gibraltar en el Pasado*. Madrid, 1965.

Sordo. *Moorish Spain*. London, 1963.

Spilsbury, Capt. J. *A Journal of the Siege of Gibraltar*. Gibraltar, 1908.

Stewart, J. D. *Gibraltar, the Keystone*. London, 1967.

Waechter, J. A. *Excavations at Gorham's Cave, Gibraltar* (*Proceedings of the Prehistorian Society*). Gibraltar, 1951; *Bulletin of the Institute of Archaeology* (*Excavation of Gorham's Cave*). Gibraltar, 1964.

Warner, Oliver. *Trafalgar*. London, 1959.

White, Anne Terry. *Men before Adam*. London, 1949.

Wiseman, F. J. *Roman Spain*. London, 1956.

A NOVEL PACKED WITH CONTINUOUS EXCITEMENT

THE BREAKING STRAIN
JOHN MASTERS

Two men stumble across an attempt to kidnap a beautiful woman. Through this chance meeting – for they scarcely know each other – they are swept into a sinister plot of world-shaking importance.

Beginning in London, flashing to New Mexico, Scotland, Canada, Iceland, and to the mountains of Spain, this is a novel of high adventure that was described by one critic as 'a man's book ... Robert Ruark with Ian Fleming touches ... has espionage, sex, violence and continuous excitement".

552 08253 8.   25p.

Obtainable from your local bookshop or newsagent, or direct from

 CORGI BOOKS

A SELECTION OF FINE READING AVAILABLE IN CORGI BOOKS

Novels

☐ 552 08651 7   THE HAND-REARED BOY   *Brian W. Aldiss* 25p

☐ 552 07938 3   THE NAKED LUNCH   *William Burroughs* 37½p

☐ 552 08795 5   PLACE CALLED ESTHERVILLE   *Erskine Caldwell* 25p

☐ 552 08835 8   THE BANNERS OF WAR   *Sacha Carnegie* 30p

☐ 552 08821 8   A GRAND MAN   *Catherine Cookson* 25p

☐ 552 08774 2   FANNY McBRIDE   *Catherine Cookson* 30p

☐ 552 08793 9   THE PRETTY BOYS   *Simon Cooper* 35p

☐ 552 08440 9   THE ANDROMEDA STRAIN   *Michael Crichton* 35p

☐ 552 08753 X   THE UNJUST SKIES   *R. F. Delderfield* 35p

☐ 552 08125 6   CATCH-22   *Joseph Heller* 35p

☐ 552 08751 3   THE PLEASURE DOME   *Alec Hilton* 30p

☐ 552 08585 5   THE PHILANDERER   *Stanley Kauffmann* 30p

☐ 552 08652 5   THY DAUGHTER'S NAKEDNESS   *Myron S. Kauffmann* 62½p

☐ 552 08834 X   DINNER AT ANTOINE'S   *Frances Parkinson Keyes* 40p

☐ 552 08797 1   BUT WE DIDN'T GET THE FOX   *Richard Llewellyn* 35p

☐ 552 08833 1   HOW FAR TO BETHLEHEM?   *Norah Lofts* 35p

☐ 552 08832 3   THE ROCK   *John Masters* 50p

☐ 552 08817 X   A FIG FOR VIRTUE   *Nan Maynard* 30p

☐ 552 08701 7   THE SAND PEBBLES   *Richard McKenna* 40p

☐ 552 08791 2   HAWAII   *James A. Michener* 75p

☐ 552 08124 8   LOLITA   *Vladimir Nabokov* 30p

☐ 552 08491 3   PRETTY MAIDS ALL IN A ROW   *Francis Pollini* 35p

☐ 552 07954 5   RUN FOR THE TREES   *James Rand* 35p

Novels – *contd.*

☐ 552 08597 9 **PORTNOY'S COMPLAINT**   *Philip Roth* 40p

☐ 552 08712 2 **UHURU**   *Robert Ruark* 50p

☐ 552 08814 5 **SOMETHING OF VALUE**   *Robert Ruark* 40p

☐ 552 08794 7 **BANEFUL SORCERIES**   *Joan Sanders* 35p

☐ 552 08372 0 **LAST EXIT TO BROOKLYN**   *Hubert Selby Jr* 50p

☐ 552 07807 7 **VALLEY OF THE DOLLS**   *Jacqueline Susann* 40p

☐ 552 08523 5 **THE LOVE MACHINE**   *Jacqueline Susann* 40p

☐ 552 08013 6 **THE EXHIBITIONIST**   *Henry Sutton* 37½p

☐ 552 08217 1 **THE CARETAKERS**   *Dariel Telfer* 35p

☐ 552 08837 4 **THE DETECTIVE**   *Roderick Thorp* 40p

☐ 552 08091 8 **TOPAZ**   *Leon Uris* 40p

☐ 552 08384 4 **EXODUS**   *Leon Uris* 40p

☐ 552 08073 X **THE PRACTICE**   *Stanley Winchester* 40p

☐ 552 08481 6 **FOREVER AMBER Vol. 1**   *Kathleen Winsor* 35p

☐ 552 08482 4 **FOREVER AMBER Vol. 2.**   *Kathleen Winsor* 35p

War

☐ 552 08838 2 **THE PASSWORD IS COURAGE**   *John Castle* 35p

☐ 552 08738 6 **THE BARREN BEACHES OF HELL**   *Boyd Cochrell* 35p

☐ 552 08603 7 **LIQUIDATE PARIS**   *Sven Hassel* 30p

☐ 552 08779 3 **ASSIGNMENT GESTAPO**   *Sven Hassel* 35p

☐ 552 08799 8 **WHITE COOLIE**   *Ronald Hastain* 30p

☐ 552 08621 5 **MEDICAL BLOCK: BUCHENWALD**
      (illustrated)   *Walter Poller* 35p

☐ 552 08536 7 **THE SCOURGE OF THE SWASTIKA**   *Lord Russell* 30p

☐ 552 08537 5 **THE KNIGHTS OF BUSHIDO**   *Lord Russell* 30p

☐ 552 08757 2 **DEFEAT INTO VICTORY**
       Field-Marshal Sir William Slim 40p

☐ 552 08798 X **VIMY! (illustrated)**   *Herbert Fairlie Wood* 30p

Romance

☐ 552 08842 0 **EDINBURGH EXCURSION**   *Lucilla Andrews* 25p

☐ 552 08743 2 **THE PRIVATE WING**   *Sheila Brandon* 25p

☐ 552 08724 6 **ST. LUKE'S LITTLE SUMMER**   *Bess Norton* 25p

☐ 552 08762 9 **RELUCTANT NIGHTINGALE**   *Kate Norway* 25p

☐ 552 08784 X **THE DUTIFUL TRADITION**   *Kate Norway* 25p

Science Fiction

☐ 552 08763 7   **BAREFOOT IN THE HEAD**   *Brian W. Aldiss* 30p

☐ 552 08785 8   **I SING THE BODY ELECTRIC**   *Ray Bradbury* 35p

☐ 552 08843 9   **INSIDE**   *Dan Morgan* 25p

☐ 552 08804 8   **THE AGE OF THE PUSSYFOOT**   *Frederick Pohl* 25p

General

☐ 522 08786 6   **COFFEE TEA OR ME?**   *Trudy Baker & Rachel Jones* 35p

☐ 552 98789 1   **INVESTING IN MAPS** (illustrated)   *Roger Baynton-Williams* 125p

☐ 552 08768 8   **SEX MANNERS FOR OLDER TEENAGERS** (illustrated)
Robert Chartham 30p

☐ 552 07593 0   **UNMARRIED LOVE**   *Dr. Eustace Chesser* 25p

☐ 552 07950 2   **SEXUAL BEHAVIOUR**   *Dr. Eustace Chesser* 25p

☐ 552 08805 6   **WHO DO YOU THINK YOU ARE?**   *Dr. Eustace Chesser* 25p

☐ 552 98572 4   **NEE DE LA VAGUE** (illustrated)   *Lucien Clergue* 105p

☐ 552 98711 5   **INVESTING IN CLOCKS AND WATCHES**   *P. W. Cumhaill* 125p

☐ 552 08745 9   **MAGIC AND MYSTERY IN TIBET**   *Alexandra David-Neel* 35p

☐ 552 08800 5   **CHARIOTS OF THE GODS?** (illustrated)
Erich von Daniken 35p

☐ 552 08677 0   **ON THE EDGE OF THE ETHERIC**   *Arthur Findlay* 30p

☐ 552 07400 4   **MY LIFE AND LOVES**   *Frank Harris* 65p

☐ 552 98748 4   **MAKING LOVE** (Photographs)   *Walter Hartford* 85p

☐ 552 08362 3   **A DOCTOR SPEAKS ON SEXUAL EXPRESSION
IN MARRIAGE** (illustrated)   *Donald W. Hastings M.D.* 50p

☐ 552 98247 4   **THE HISTORY OF THE NUDE IN PHOTOGRAPHY**
(illustrated)   *Peter Lacey and Anthony La Rotonda* 125p

☐ 552 98345 4   **THE ARTIST AND THE NUDE** (illustrated)   105p

☐ 552 08069 1   **THE OTHER VICTORIANS**   *Steven Marcus* 50p

☐ 552 08664 9   **THE HUMAN ZOO**   *Desmond Morris* 35p

☐ 552 08162 0   **THE NAKED APE**   *Desmond Morris* 30p

☐ 552 08611 8   **FEEDING THE FLAME**   *T. Lobsang Rampa* 30p

☐ 552 08765 3   **THE HERMIT**   *T. Lobsang Rampa* 30p

☐ 552 08630 4   **BRUCE TEGNER'S COMPLETE BOOK OF
KARATE** (illustrated)   *Bruce Tegner* 40p

☐ 552 98479 5   **MADEMOISELLE 1+1** (illustrated)
Marcel Veronese and Jean-Claude Peretz 105p

☐ 552 08807 2   **BIRTH CONTROL NOW AND TOMORROW**
Clive Wood 30p

Western

☐ 552 08532 4	BLOOD BROTHER	*Elliott Arnold*	40p
☐ 552 08813 7	SUDDEN AT BAY	*Frederick H. Christian*	25p
☐ 552 08841 2	BAD HOMBRE	*J. T. Edson*	25p
☐ 552 08706 8	SLIP GUN No. 65	*J. T. Edson*	25p
☐ 552 08783 1	HELL IN THE PALO DURO No. 66	*J. T. Edson*	25p
☐ 552 08840 4	UNDER THE SWEETWATER RIM	*Louis L'Amour*	25p
☐ 552 08673 8	NORTH TO THE RAILS	*Louis L'Amour*	25p
☐ 552 08802 1	No. 9 THE DEVIL'S MARSHAL	*Louis Masterson*	20p
☐ 552 08803 X	No. 10 GUNMAN'S INHERITANCE	*Louis Masterson*	20p

Crime

☐ 552 08824 2	A PUZZLE IN PEARLS	*John Creasey*	25p
☐ 552 08809 9	MADRIGAL	*John Gardner*	25p
☐ 552 08739 4	TRAITOR'S EXIT	*John Gardner*	25p
☐ 552 08782 3	THE LITTLE WAX DOLL	*Nora Lofts*	30p
☐ 552 08640 1	RED FILE FOR CALLAN	*James Mitchell*	25p
☐ 552 08839 0	TOUCHFEATHER TOO	*Jimmy Sangster*	25p
☐ 552 08758 0	SURVIVAL . . . ZERO!	*Mickey Spillane*	25p
☐ 552 08801 3	THE SILENT LIARS	*Michael Underwood*	25p

All these books are available at your bookshop or newsagent: or can be ordered direct from the publisher. Just tick the titles you want and fill in the form below.

....

CORGI BOOKS, Cash Sales Department, P.O. Box 11, Falmouth, Cornwall.

Please send cheque or postal order. No currency, and allow 5p per book to cover the cost of postage and packing in the U.K., and overseas.

NAME ....

ADDRESS ....

(Nov. 71) ....